BREAKING OUT

BOB BRINK

iUniverse, Inc.
New York Bloomington

Breaking Out

This is a work of fiction. All of the characters, names, incidents, organizations, and dialogue in this novel are either the products of the author's imagination or are used fictitiously.

iUniverse books may be ordered through booksellers or by contacting:

iUniverse
1663 Liberty Drive
Bloomington, IN 47403
www.iuniverse.com
1-800-Authors (1-800-288-4677)

ISBN: 978-1-4502-2676-9 (pbk)
ISBN: 978-1-4502-2678-3 (cloth)
ISBN: 978-1-4502-2677-6 (ebook)

Library of Congress Control Number: 2010906288

Printed in the United States of America

iUniverse rev. date: 6/17/10

In memory of Daniel V. Bergman,
a great man.

CHAPTER 1

Panic gripped Britt.

He and his two pals, all three juniors at Mayfield High School, had entered the school gymnasium from the north end and strolled to the corner of the bleachers, stopping to survey the rows for an empty space. They arrived just before game time because Britt had worked late at Noll's Drug Store, and the auditorium already was virtually filled. Bobby Jackson pointed at a spot three-quarters of the way to the other end and almost to the top row.

"See it?" he said. "That empty space is big enough for all three of us."

Britt was terrified of walking in front of all those people, completely exposed, with no one or nothing to deflect their attention from himself, Bobby, and Martin Brant. All eyes would fall on them as they walked. He desperately wanted to turn and head the way they'd come.

"Wait a minute," said Britt. "Why don't we go back out to the lobby and head to the other end and use that entrance, since it's a lot closer to our space?"

"What?" Bobby retorted impatiently in his naturally hoarse voice. "Why the heck would we do that? It would just be farther to walk."

"Gee whiz, Bobby," said Britt, "you lug golf bags miles every weekend for those Mayfield big shots. And you're bothered by walking a few extra yards?"

"Not bothered," Bobby said vexedly. "It just doesn't make sense. And the game's about to start. Now come on. Let's go." Martin, a frail fellow with a gentle disposition, was noncommittal.

The gymnasium was packed to its capacity of twenty-one-hundred for a basketball game between two fiercely competitive teams. The host hoopsters and the varsity squad from arch-rival Okeeloosie High were locked in a battle for the Mid-Iowa Conference championship. Fourteen years had passed since Mayfield held the title, and with only one game remaining, a win on this Friday night in February was critical. The atmosphere crackled with excitement as the two teams began warming up.

Students sat on bleachers framing the court and adults occupied fold-down seats above the bleachers. Bobby began the trek in front of them, leaning into each step as though he were bucking a strong gale, with Martin close behind. Britt could only follow. Doggone it, why did they have to move so slowly? He slid his hands into his pant pockets to feign a casual look, then glanced up at the crowd. His eye caught a senior girl student staring at him, then a boy and his date also watching him, and he immediately turned beet red. He knew they could tell just what he was feeling. That made him feel much worse. Now, everybody would see how embarrassed he was.

His agony remained as the three reached the narrow stairs bordering the section with the empty space and they slowly climbed toward the top. Bobby stopped and assessed how big the space was to be sure the three of them could fit, and Britt's pain intensified as he stood, not knowing what to do with his hands or where to look. He saw several persons in the section to the left quickly avert their gazes from him, and he knew why: His acute self-consciousness was apparent and they sympathized with him. Finally, the three were seated. Britt looked into the bleachers on the other side of the court and was sure some people were looking his way.

"These seats aren't the best, but they're not too bad," Martin volunteered.

"Yeah," Britt mumbled, still suffering.

The game began, and in short order the buzz of chatter and laughter in the auditorium metamorphosed into a frenzy of cheering and hollering. Britt realized that everyone was too engrossed in the action to be concerned with him, and he gradually lost consciousness of himself as the game riveted his attention and he, too, began cheering. It was a close contest, the teams frequently exchanging small leads, and the enthusiasm in the audience remained at a fever pitch almost without letup, ebbing only slightly now and then. Whenever a member of the Mayfield five drove for a layup, connected on a long jump shot, or blocked a shot by the opponent, large numbers of people leaped to their feet and roared in approval. Britt had the urge to jump up, but was anxious about being seen by those remaining seated around him. It was only as the half drew to a close, when everybody stood and cheered Mayfield's two-point lead, that Britt felt comfortable doing so.

"Let's go get some popcorn," said Bobby.

"Yeah," Martin agreed. "I need a Coke, too. Let's go."

"Uh … I'm okay," said Britt. "I think I'll just stay here and make sure nobody takes our spot. Bring me a Coke, will ya?" He pulled a nickel out of his pocket and handed it to Martin.

"Huh?" said Bobby, already heading for the stairs. "We can leave our coats. Nobody's gonna grab our space. Come on."

"Actually, I might run into somebody from Noll's and have to have a boring conversation."

"The drug store?" Martin asked.

"Yeah."

"Well, okay, have it your way," said Bobby.

They left, and Britt leaned back, resting his arms on the bleacher a row up. Now it was his turn to watch people as they stood at their seats or milled around the edges of the court, chatting and laughing. They seemed to be so comfortable, so unconscious of anyone watching them, Britt thought. He wondered how they could be so at ease with themselves, and envied them greatly.

Bobby and Martin returned fifteen minutes later and shared a box of popcorn with Britt. The game resumed and progressed in much the way it had in the first half, neither team able to go ahead by more than two or three points. Having risen from his seat only once, Britt's rear end was becoming sore, but he preferred that aggravation to the painful exposure of rising to applaud and shout, even when many others around him were doing so. In the last few minutes of the game, everybody in the auditorium—except for the small contingent that had traveled the sixty-five miles from Okeeloosie—was rising to cheer every basket that Mayfield made. That gave Britt the courage to also rise, and he felt much relief in his buttocks.

The game ended with Mayfield losing by one point, and the dejected fans slowly and quietly filed out the exits, their heads down, as though they had just been engrossed in a sad movie.

"Doggone," said Martin when they reached the parking lot. "That was hard to take."

"Well, I think Mayfield played as good as they could," Bobby said. "Listen, how 'bout we go to Hess's for a sundae?"

They climbed in the 1947 Ford that Britt co-owned with his older brother, Kevin, who was at college, and drove across town to the popular teen hangout on the north edge of the downtown. It was on a corner, next to two seedy bars and the shabby Iowa Theater. As Britt pulled into a parking space, Bobby spotted Rosemary Cramer about to enter Hess's with two other girls.

"See that?" he asked.

"What?" asked Martin.

"What?" Bobby retorted, scornfully incredulous. "That is the best-lookin', sexiest chick in all of Mayfield High."

"You mean Rosie Cramer?" asked Britt.

"I sure as heck don't mean those other two," Bobby declared. "All I have to do is look at Rosemary and I get a hard on."

"Yeah, I agree," said Martin.

"Oh ... yeah, sure. Me too," Britt said hesitantly.

Britt didn't hear "hard on." He heard "heart on." His buddies were using the term a lot lately, and he knew it had something to do with sex but didn't know what. He was afraid to ask because he felt abnormal in his ignorance. It obviously was something other teenage boys were familiar with, because they joked about it all the time. Where did they learn it? Was it something they read about—in dirty books or magazines, maybe? Britt never read that kind of stuff for fear of facing eternal damnation. Hell had been a major theme in the indoctrination that the four Rutgers children had received since birth from their devoutly Calvinist Christian parents, especially their mother. Conversely, heaven had been portrayed as an appealing place populated by pleasant people. Britt's chief concern, however, was avoiding the destination with the awful climate rather than reaching the one with the good company.

Rosie, whose light-brown hair fell like Niagara Falls into a tumult of lush curls at her shoulders, stood at the counter waiting for a cup of hot chocolate she had ordered. She wore a downy, light-blue sweater and a plaid skirt that outlined her luscious figure all the way to mid-calf. Bobby and Martin waited behind her, trying not to stare, while Britt was positioned to their left, his view of Rosie partly obstructed by a teenage fellow. Bobby and Martin ordered sundaes and Britt chose his favorite, a banana split with vanilla, chocolate, and strawberry ice cream, chocolate fudge topping, and nuts. They took their delights to a table.

"I thought I was gonna faint," said Bobby. "I kept lookin' sideways at her butt, and I was gettin' a hard on."

"Yep," said Martin, "she's got it all."

"You're not sayin' nothin', Britt," said Bobby. "Don't tell me she doesn't give you a hard on."

Britt blushed. "Jiminy cricket … I mean, heck … that kid was standing in my way and I couldn't get a good view of her," he stammered.

"Yeah, we know," Bobby snickered. "You're in love with the preacher's daughter, Jane, uh … ."

"Jansen," said Britt, relieved that Bobby hadn't divined the real reason for his consternation. "You gotta admit, she's pretty darned good-lookin'."

"She's all right," said Bobby. "Hey, let's go and drive past her house. We might spot her if she's standing by a window."

"Well … okay," said Britt, "but don't do anything. I've got to go to church Sunday morning."

Britt climbed into the Ford while Bobby and Martin followed, Bobby talking to his companion in a hushed tone. With Martin in the front passenger seat and Bobby in the back seat, the three headed to the other side of the downtown.

"Okay, we're on Third Street. That's where the parsonage is," Britt announced.

"Slow down and point it out," said Bobby.

Britt slowed, and Bobby and Martin rolled down their windows.

"There. The two-story white house."

"Hey Jane, here's Bob," Martin hollered.

"He's got a big hard on for you," Bobby shouted much louder.

Britt jammed his foot on the accelerator and sped away while Bobby and Martin laughed gleefully. "Aw, doggone you guys, now I'm in big trouble," said Britt, mortified to the bone. "Why'd ya hafta go and do that?"

"C'mon," said Bobby. "It's after eleven and the house was dark. They were probably all in bed asleep."

"I saw a light," said Britt. "I'll bet they heard you guys. What am I gonna do now? I'm gonna have to try to hide from Jane in church Sunday."

He drove hurriedly to Bobby's and Martin's houses in Mayfield and dropped them off. Then he headed west of town to U.S. Highway 6 for the fifteen-minute drive to the small farm where the family had moved from Mayfield in the fall of Britt's freshman year. Britt's parents, Milton and Miriam, had gone to bed, as had his younger brother, Dale, and sister, Kyra, the youngest in the family. Britt quickly climbed into his bed, next to Dale's.

A sliver of moonlight leaked between the shade and the window into the dark room. No sooner had Britt's head hit the pillow than the evening's events began flitting through his mind, jabbing his consciousness like darts and keeping him awake. He relived the anguish of walking in front of the crowd at the basketball game, catching the eyes of persons staring at him in his embarrassment, and felt himself reddening. The one person he wanted to notice him, Jane Jansen, acted like he didn't exist, even after the double date they'd had at a football game five months earlier. Well, if she was awake tonight, she knew he existed now. Yeah, and she'd never get near him again. Even if she wanted to, he was sure her dad wouldn't let her after what his pals had done. Hard on: Did everybody except him know what it meant? Did Jane's dad, the pastor, know? Heck, even Jane probably knew. What was the matter with him?

He switched positions a hundred times until the warring within his head subsided and segued into the peace of oblivion.

CHAPTER 2

Britt's interest in girls began early in the eighth grade, when he was thirteen, although his sexual awakening had occurred less than two years earlier when he was in the sixth grade at Washington Elementary School. He had a talent for gymnastics and liked to shinny up the metal pole on the playground during recesses. His legs wrapped around the four-inch-diameter pole, he began to feel a strangely wonderful sensation in his groin.

Life while he attended Mayfield Junior High School was uneventful. He delivered the *Mayfield Daily News* to his fifty-six customers on Route 31 after school, went home for dinner, and spent the evening doing homework or listening to the radio, or both. On the weekends when Mayfield varsity squads played at home, he went to the basketball and football games with a couple of classmates. On Thursdays, after his paper route, he went to the family church, the United Presbyterian Church in Mayfield, for Youth Night, a teen recreation-and-dinner program. The Rutgerses had joined the church because Mayfield had no Reformed Church of America, the church of their Dutch heritage. The "U-P" (as Britt and Dale dubbed it, laughing at the bathroom pun) church was grounded in the same teachings of Reformation theologian John Calvin. Youth Night was the one night Britt thoroughly enjoyed, since he'd become an excellent ping-pong player and had fun with the others. They all sang in the youth choir, and Britt caused the director—an attractive, patient woman in her late forties—some consternation with his constant antics. Youth Night was the provenance of his romantic attraction to the opposite sex.

A pretty blonde named Barbara Conover—she was barely thirteen and Britt almost fourteen—began flirting with him. Britt was in love. Not much later, he fell for Barbara Hutton in *The Greatest Show on Earth*, then Ann Sheridan in *Steel Town,* feeling a warm glow for days each time.

A Junior High mixer at the school gymnasium was set for Saturday night, and Britt asked Barbara for a date. She said she'd meet him there. But when he arrived, he couldn't find her. Then he spotted her across the floor, dancing with another boy. When she finished the dance, he went over to talk to her, but she told him she would see him later. He went to the other side of the floor, where another girl asked him to dance, and showed him how, telling him to relax so his legs wouldn't be so stiff—though Britt couldn't get the hang of it. The dance ended, and Milton picked him up in the family's blue, eleven-year-old 1941 Ford. At home, Miriam teased him.

"So you like Barbara, huh?" she said. "How did it go? When do you expect to become engaged? Can we anticipate a wedding soon?" Kevin was sixteen and had never had a date nor shown an interest in girls, so this was a new experience for Miriam and Milton, though Milton said nothing. But Britt was embarrassed and ashamed by his mother's remarks. After all, he and his brothers had always joked about girls and acted like they weren't interested. When he was ten, he thought Marilyn Murphy was the prettiest girl in school, and showed it by chasing her down in the school playground and razzing her relentlessly, driving her to tears at one point.

(But there was a bit of poetic justice in Miriam's teasing of Britt. On a visit to the northwest Iowa farm of Milton's father a few years earlier, the Rutgerses drove into nearby Millersville to see a cousin who had a thirteen-year-old daughter, Karen. She asked Kevin to show her the Rutgers' car and slid into the front seat next to him while Britt climbed in the back seat. She asked Kevin if he knew how to drive, and he showed her how to work the gear-shift stick while operating the clutch. Moving her body against him, she cooed, "I'll bet you're a really good driver." On the drive back to the farm, Britt said, "Wow, you should have seen Kevin and Karen. 'Oh Kevin, I'll bet you're a good driver.'" He imitated Karen's sensuous voice and laughed derisively. Kevin was deeply embarrassed and said quietly in a helpless, pathetic tone, "Well I couldn't help it. I didn't do anything." Miriam said, "No, of course you didn't. Britt, you cut that out." Now it was Britt's turn to feel ashamed as he realized how he'd hurt his brother.)

Britt silently went to bed. Nonetheless, he still was in a trance over Barbara Conover. Five days later, at Youth Club, she flirted with him again. When the evening was over, she handed him a note and told him to read it at home. Jubilant in the hope she was expressing her fondness for him, he rode his bike furiously through town and one-and-a-half miles down U.S. 6 to the low-income subdivision where the Rutgerses lived. Quietly, he entered the bathroom and took the note out of his pocket. "I don't want to be your girlfriend, and I'm breaking up with you."

Britt felt like he'd been hit by one of those eighteen-wheelers, as the Rutgers kids called the largest of the semi-trailer trucks that roared down the highway only a block from their house. He was stunned. It was as though a knife had been thrust into his heart. He tore up the note and dropped the pieces in the toilet, then emerged from the bathroom and tried to act as though nothing had happened. He went to bed feeling miserable. Three days later, the misery was over. But it was three more years before he was able to again express an interest in girls.

It didn't matter much because he had little time for them. A couple of months after he entered the ninth grade, the Rutgerses moved to a small farm eleven miles west of Mayfield. Britt's dad, Milton, continued working as a bureaucrat for the Iowa State Employment Service in town. Having been reared on a farm in northwest Iowa, he longed for the rural life. With a small inheritance from an uncle, he bought a thirty-acre spread that included a sturdy white house on a knoll and eight other buildings: a small, two-story barn, a large chicken coop, a small chicken coop, two corn cribs, a hog house, a storage shed atop a cave, and an outhouse.

Britt was excited about moving to the farm—as much so as his dad. For the father, it was a diversion from the daily aggravations of his desk job and a return to his boyhood. For the son, it was a new adventure, and he enthusiastically threw himself into the daily duties, or "chores" in farming lingo. Milton purchased one cow from the sellers of the farm, a placid brown shorthorn named Bessie, which they'd had for a decade. Shorthorns had a better reputation as suppliers of beef than of milk, but Bessie was an exception, yielding a full three-gallon pail each morning and evening. Britt didn't know how to milk a cow, of course, but insisted on rising at five a.m. every day to accompany his dad in the performance of this task.

During one night in mid-December, nine weeks after the Rutgerses had arrived at the farm, a heavy snowfall occurred, accompanied by a wave of bitter cold. After his dad had already left for the barn, Britt arose and bundled up, then headed into the darkness. The yard light, a bulb on a twenty-five-foot pole at the end of the sidewalk that led downward at an angle from the house, cast a ghastly, pale-yellow illumination on the snow. Britt gasped as the sub-zero cold shocked his lungs, and in the deathly silence, the fine, dry snow crunched loudly under his rubber boots as he made his way down the slope to the east end of the barn.

While Milton placed ground corn in the stanchion where Bessie's head was locked so she couldn't walk around and trash the barn, Britt scooped up the night's deposits she had made in the gutter and tossed the sloppy, smelly mess onto a pile in the barn lot. It would freeze, then thaw in the spring and be carted to the fields in a manure spreader, which would fling it onto the soil as fertilizer. When Milton was finished with the milking, he went to a little nook to the right of the door and poured a small amount of milk into a little bowl. It was for the tawny cat that the former owner of the farm had left behind, and her four kittens, which were born only a couple of weeks before. Britt protested that the cats needed more than a little milk to survive, but Milton said that too much would make them lazy and they wouldn't go after mice and rats. The cat slowly emerged from behind the adjacent pen, but there were no kittens. Britt walked to the pen, and saw the four kittens lying in a corner. He crawled over the side of the wooden stall, and nudged one of the little balls of fur with his foot. It was stiff.

"Dad, they're dead!" Britt shouted. "They're frozen."

"Let's see," said Milton as he joined his son. "Oh dad-rat-it." He stared at the little felines for a couple of seconds, than announced, "Well, we can't leave them here. They'll attract rats." He grabbed the manure shovel leaning against a far wall, scooped up the kittens, and pushed the shovel through the space between a board and the bottom of the pen. Then he climbed over and flung the animals onto the manure pile.

"Dad, what're you doin'? We've gotta bury 'em."

"We can't. The ground is frozen. We'll just cover them tomorrow morning with the manure the cows leave overnight."

"We should have put down more straw for the kittens to snuggle into, Dad. I told you it wasn't enough. Bessie doesn't have enough to lay on either."

"And I told you we didn't have enough straw to get through the winter," Milton protested impatiently.

But Britt wouldn't relent. "We could buy more straw, Dad. Bessie is gonna freeze, too."

"Now that's enough," Milton rejoined, raising his voice. "We can't afford to buy more straw. Bessie will be just fine."

Britt said nothing as they carried the bucket of milk to the basement of the house, where Milton poured it into the hand-powered separator.

Britt turned the big handle so the nonfat part of the whole milk would break away from the cream through centrifugal force. He and Milton then walked to the pig lot on the north side of the farm yard and poured the warm skim milk into a trough. They retreated as the five pigs that Milton had bought from a neighbor ferociously lapped it up.

At seven-thirty, Britt rode with Milton into Mayfield. Milton parked the car by his office and Britt walked the short distance to the junior high school. After school, he made the rounds of the newspaper route he'd had for five years, then rode home with his dad. They did the chores and had dinner, and Britt did his homework before going to bed.

After a month of rising early for this routine, Britt was tiring. In his late afternoon study period, he was having a hard time keeping awake. The excitement of the new experience was beginning to wear thin, and he decided to forgo the morning chores and sleep in.

"So it's not so much fun anymore, huh? Can't take it when the going gets rough." Milton mocked his son, and a bad memory invaded his mind. He was ten years old and had been spending two or three afternoons a week during the summer after the fourth grade at the swimming pool in Mayfield's Mayflower Park. He'd tried to teach himself to swim, and through mighty flailing of his arms and thrashing of his legs was able to make it from ten feet out to the edge of the pool. One hot evening the family visited the park, and Britt told his dad he'd learned to swim and would show him. "Okay, Dad, watch this," he hollered to Milton, who stood on the lawn outside the fence surrounding the pool. Britt stood in three feet of water, ten feet away from the edge, and began thrashing for all his might, like a fish on a hook desperately trying to shake free. He made it to the edge, stood up, and beamed at his dad.

"Aw, that isn't swimming," Milton retorted contemptuously. "What are you talkin' about—swimming? You can't swim. You just wave your arms around, and you only go a few feet." Britt was crushed. "I swam," he protested feebly, and wanted to cry.

His feeling now matched the humiliation he'd felt five years before. "I can't stay awake in the afternoon," he said helplessly.

"Oh okay, stay in bed tomorrow morning," Milton relented. "But make sure you're ready to go at seven-thirty." Milton was never late for work, and usually was fifteen minutes early. He always feared displeasing his boss.

Britt slipped into the small bathroom shared by all six of the Rutgerses and readied for bed, washing his face, ears, and neck in the small sink.

The water came from a cistern replenished by rain, and in periods of light rainfall, the cistern became low. To conserve water, everybody took one bath per week—on Saturday night. Miriam watched to make sure none of the children put more than four inches of water in the tub.

Britt was still feeling down from his dad's taunt. As he brushed his teeth, he suddenly was in his grandmother's house in Pliny, four years earlier. The Rutgerses were making one of their frequent Sunday afternoon visits to Miriam's mother from their home in Mayfield. Several of Miriam's brothers and sisters still lived in the area and sometimes joined them. Milton enjoyed discussing business, despite his lack of talent for it, and politics with Grant, her oldest brother. Grant, fairly short with gray hair combed straight back, had a girth commensurate with the wealth he had accumulated from the appliance store he founded in Pliny as a young man after his return from combat in World War I. He enjoyed smoking cigars, which cast an aroma Britt always relished. Grant moved and talked slowly, his head usually tilted back and to the side in an attitude of shrewd appraisal. His war experiences had made him hard and wary, deepening his skeptical nature. Milton and Grant sat in the living room, in rocking chairs at a slight angle to each other. Grant puffed a cigar while they chatted, his mouth occasionally opening in a wry, slightly crooked smile as he quietly chuckled in slow motion about something that was said, his big belly bouncing in rhythm.

Britt, always active, entered the room through a doorway from the adjacent dining room. He had only a couple of weeks before bought a seventy-pound York barbell through an ad in *Strength and Health*, a magazine whose covers displayed beach poses of muscular men who lifted weights. He'd had to beg his parents—especially his mother, since his dad was far more lenient—for permission to spend the eleven dollars, which he earned from his newspaper route. A year earlier, less than a half year after he'd started the route, his mother had refused to let him spend six dollars of his own money for a catcher's mitt and baseball. Britt soon realized that if he were to have any of this world's possessions, he would have to take matters into his own hands. On the Saturday in June after school had closed for the summer, he finished making the newspaper route subscription collections and walked to the Montgomery Ward store on the square that constituted downtown Mayfield. He paid five dollars for a thick tan mitt with Bill Dickey's autograph and one dollar for an "Official American League" baseball.

Britt's interest in improving his physique had come about through Rocky Stripling, who worked in the *Mayfield Daily News* press room. The handsome, dark-haired, physically superb man of about forty would stride to his job through the circulation room (accompanied once by his gorgeous, dark-haired wife) where Britt and the other newspaper delivery boys received their routes' papers. A former Air Force paratrooper, Rocky was good at acrobatics, and occasionally would perform a couple of tricks for the boys. On the concrete floor of the second-floor circulation room, he would do handsprings, or on rare occasion walk on his hands down the steep stairs that led there. Britt was full of admiration for Rocky, a friendly, good-natured man, and worked tirelessly at learning to walk on his hands, a feat that he finally mastered. Always looking for attention, he was only too happy to demonstrate his prowess, showing off frequently in the school yard during recesses. Once, at the behest of his physical education teacher, he performed before three-hundred-fifty pupils from two schools.

For about two weeks, Britt had been doing the weight training exercises in the booklet that came with the barbell, and he wanted the world to know about it. He entered the living room during a lull in the conversation between Milton and Grant, and seized the opportunity. "Have you heard about my barbell?" he asked his Uncle Grant. Grant stared at him, mouth slightly open, cigar held upward between the thumb and forefinger of his left hand, and said nothing. "You know—me and my barbell." Silence.

"Aw, he doesn't want to hear about your barbell," Milton scoffed. "Go on and leave us alone so we can talk."

Britt felt only mildly rebuked and left the room to play catch out on the lawn with Kevin, who by now had acquired a first baseman's glove. But on the ride home in their grayish-tan 1936 Ford, Milton turned his head toward Britt in the back seat and said, "What you did today was uncalled for, telling Uncle Grant about your barbell. 'Me and my barbell.'" His tone was ponderously ridiculing. "You don't go around bragging about that to people. Grant looked as if to say, 'What kind of a fool is this kid?' I was so embarrassed." No one said anything, and Britt sat silently, shocked from his upbeat mood into deep shame. For more than a decade, he cringed and turned crimson whenever the memory of that incident popped into his mind. It wasn't until he was a young man and a psychologist said he couldn't see anything wrong with the remark—that there was nothing whatever to be ashamed about—that he felt a sense of relief. But the memory always remained uncomfortable for him.

After a month of barbell exercises four times a week in the living room, Britt was tiring of the routine. Miriam saw the reluctance in the way he began the workout each day, and quietly asked if he didn't want to quit. "Oh no, I like doing it," he lied. But after a few more days, he found excuses to leave the barbell in the bedroom he shared with Dale. Miriam said nothing, even though she'd objected to his spending the eleven dollars to buy the weights. Britt was supposed to be saving his money—for good reason. From age ten, after he'd begun delivering newspapers and mowing lawns, he paid for everything but his board and room—even his clothes and dental care, which was abundant. Dr. Welles wasn't sure he could save a decayed molar on the left side, but said he would try and advised Britt to accept Novocaine.

"What does it cost?" Britt asked.

"One dollar."

"Let's do it without the Novocaine," Britt decided, and managed to endure the pain of the drill. Actually, he almost preferred the pain to the needle, which he feared. The tooth was saved.

Soon after the Rutgerses arrived at the small farm, Cal Binder, the boy who lived on a full-sized farm around the corner of an intersecting road, invited him to attend a 4-H meeting the following Tuesday night at the Binders, and Britt reluctantly accepted. Fourteen teenagers, boys and girls from the surrounding farms, sat in the living room and compared heifers and bull calves and milk cows and hogs while Britt feigned interest. The girls were fat, skinny, short, or tall, except for June, a pretty, soft-spoken redhead whom he immediately liked—alas, in vain. She soon began dating a guy from Colton High, then dropped him and entered a convent, after which she earned a doctorate in Chinese studies and began teaching in a university.

Britt had no desire to join the 4-H Club. He'd been a town boy, and felt ill at ease with these farm kids. After they'd been on the farm for less than a year, however, Britt wanted to buy a cow to earn money from selling the calves it would produce. His parents relented, and he spent one-hundred-sixty-nine dollars of the money he'd saved by mowing lawns for a young Guernsey that they named Fanny. But Milton and Miriam thought he should pay for the hay and grain Fanny would consume—even though Fanny's milk would be used for the cream his parents sold and for feeding the pigs, which they also sold. Britt didn't think this was fair, and argued with them. They finally backed down. Then Fanny had twins, which they named Marilyn and Monroe, but they remained on the farm, producing even more milk, which translated into income for Milton and Miriam. But by that time, Britt was working at Noll's, the same drug store in Mayfield where his brother Kevin worked before going off to college, and he forgot about the cows.

CHAPTER 3

Doing chores and helping with other farm tasks on weekends left Britt with little time for fun. Plus, he had no transportation between Mayfield and the farm, so he couldn't go anywhere evenings unless Kevin, who was now seventeen and had a driver's license, would let him ride along. For Britt, Youth Night at the UP church was over.

But another, more insidious force was affecting him, though he wasn't conscious of it. Since the time Britt was in the seventh grade, Milton and Miriam had begun saying between themselves and to friends that Kevin, now in the eleventh grade, was "college material." It was time, after all, for them to be thinking of his future. But the matter gradually grew in importance, with Kevin taken ultraseriously and held in much esteem. What would he study? As he grew up, his parents had become fond of describing him in solemn tones as "mechanically inclined," so it seemed that engineering would be the proper field for him to pursue. Indeed, he had shown little interest in sports, unlike Britt, who was crazy about baseball and played almost daily in the summer, was good at gymnastics, and variously worked out with a barbell and learned to walk on his hands and stand on his head. Instead, Kevin was making things and fixing his and his brothers' bicycles. He was quiet and serious, and was therefore *taken* seriously. He and Britt fought frequently—verbally and, when they were younger, physically. Britt would always be the peace-maker, unable to stand the silent treatment from Kevin that always followed their fights. It was over, he was in a different mood, and he had no desire to stay mad, so he'd break the silence with some inane remark. But as he grew older, he tired of doing this, and after one big blow-up, resolved that he would not be the first to talk. They lived in the same house, but completely ignored each other—verbally, that is, for each was acutely conscious of the other's presence. They were quiet even on the way to weekend school events in the family's 1941 Ford. Days stretched into weeks, and finally, after five weeks, Kevin, apparently seeing that Britt was not going to give in this time, made the overture.

"Got your activity card?" he asked crisply, referring to the student pass to sports events, as they got into the car to drive into Mayfield for a basketball game.

"Yeah. You got yours?" Britt responded, eager to accommodate but immediately embarrassed by his awkward redundancy.

These high school basketball games were played in the YMCA gymnasium because the school had none until a year later, when a new school was opened. After one game, Britt, who wore his hair in a short crew cut, was heading down the long flight of stairs to the sidewalk below, where he and Kevin had planned to meet. Kevin was exiting with a friend, and Britt heard him say, "Where's that Jap-head brother of mine?" Kevin just then spotted Britt and said, slightly embarrassed, "Oh." Neither uttered a word on the way home.

Whether he was aware of it or not, Milton was replaying his own life in that of his sons, extolling his eldest and paying little heed to the younger one. Milton had grown up with the same scenario: He was the oldest and was studious, a voracious reader, while his younger brother Waymon loved sports. So their father sent Milton to college and pretty much ignored Waymon. Britt did not consciously resent Kevin's favored treatment, but began to look upon him with the same worshipful feelings that his parents held. He did not realize that depression was subtly overtaking him. He became semiconsciously convinced of his lack of worth, to the point that he decided he was not bright enough to take Latin in school, as Kevin had done. Britt had consistently earned top grades in English and was the top speller in his third grade and eighth grade classes, but those facts never occurred to him. And Milton or Miriam, who had virtually no praise for him in anything, never pointed them out.

Britt was unaware of these deeper causes of his unhappiness, and blamed it on his lack of fun at school, where he had no close friends. In fact, his lack of social life, at a time when he was undergoing the process of socialization that gradually transforms maturing teenagers into adults, also contributed to his gloominess. He'd wanted to drop his paper route and go out for football in the seventh grade, but Miriam wouldn't allow such frivolousness. Life was about work—and God.

So he blamed his unhappiness on school. Thinking the grass would be greener on the other side of the farms that lay between Mayfield and Colton, he decided to switch to Colton High School, which was only three-and-a-half miles from home.

The school bus arrived in front of the Rutgers farm at seven a.m., driven by a friendly, kindly man named Harold who had retired after forty years as a railway freight clerk. Britt was a little shy about his new venture; he'd attended several schools, but none with classmates who were rural, and he felt out of place. Britt was one of the first stops on the bus route. Harold, a bespectacled man whose nondescript clerical appearance fit his former occupation, greeted Britt each morning with a smiling "Good morning" and perhaps a few words about the weather, or starting the week over on Monday, or Friday finally having arrived. Despite Harold's attempts to make Britt feel at ease, he kept mostly to himself during the two-hour ride—partly out of choice, but mainly because the other kids all knew each other and had the farm experiences in common. Britt tried to do some of his homework, but the often rutty and bumpy roads made it difficult to read or write, and to concentrate.

On his first day in school, Britt realized he had made a mistake. He departed from the bus and entered an old, two-story, red-brick building. The first thing that caught his eye was a boy a year or two older than he with a wooden leg, climbing the stairs to a large assembly hall. He was proclaiming to no one in particular and everyone in general about what a lousy holiday vacation he'd had, and how life was only going to get worse now that school had resumed. All this kid needed was a black patch over one eye, and one would swear he was Captain Ahab. His name was Johnny Brown, and his blustery, ill-mannered behavior was tolerated by classmates and school officials alike because he'd suffered the loss of a limb. Every Saturday night, farmers flocked to the Colton Sale Barn to buy and sell cattle and hogs, and Johnny had jumped into the arena to try and break up a fight between two boars on a night three years before, when he was thirteen. One of the hogs sank its tusks into his thigh and hurled him into the air. Two men took him home and helped his parents dress the wound. Johnny was in pain, but the next morning, his parents left him lying on a couch while they attended church. Gangrene set in, and the leg had to be amputated.

These kids were unlike those in any of the schools Britt had attended. English class was packed with about thirty kids, and before the teacher arrived that first day, bedlam reigned. These urchins didn't shoot paper wads with their rubber bands—they shot paper clips. "Oowww!" a boy walking in front of the room yelled as he got hit in the thigh with a missile. The victim was Mel Lannix, an olive-complected Italian kid with a glass eye. He'd lost the natural one two years earlier when a bullet from his .22-caliber hunting rifle struck him as he tossed the gun across a creek he was about to fjord. If this mayhem were a daily occurrence, Britt thought, Mel was destined to lose the other eye to a paper clip.

Jimmy Gleason, a short, feisty boy with thick dark hair, was the rubber-band marksman who had fired the paper clip. He and Mel were the chief hell-raisers, though they had minor accomplices. In science class one day, Mr. Stanton, a pleasant fellow who displayed a mild enthusiasm for his subject, was called to the office for a few minutes. Mel rushed to the door and slid the bolt lock into place, then hurried back to his seat and told his pals seated around him not to tell who did it. Mr. Stanton returned and, finding the door locked, was infuriated. "Let me in immediately," he shouted, pounding the door. Mel doubled up with soundless laughter, until his friends became anxious and whispered to him he'd better unlock the door or he'd be in big trouble. Mel tip-toed to the front, ever-so-quietly slid the bolt back, and scurried back to his seat. He barely got there when the teacher came charging through the door and back to Mel. "I saw you through the crack in the door," he shouted, his face red as he hovered over a cowering Mel. He grabbed the desk seat and shook it, but did not strike the boy.

The school's superintendent, Mr. Jenkins, was a roly-poly fellow with thin blond hair and a ruddy complexion. Though pleasantly energetic, he was too gentle to impose the discipline needed to bring order to this dysfunctional school. An increasing number of parents from higher-class homes visited school board meetings and complained about the disorder their children reported. Poor Mr. Jenkins was fired, and Mr. Burton, the deputy superintendent, was given his job. Burton was a quiet, surly man in his upper forties with a thick head of coal-black hair, a sulfuric complexion, and a stern mien with a slightly pinched look. It was rumored that he'd been a boxer in the Air Force, and he was lean and strapping, keeping his six-feet-two-inch frame in optimum shape. Before assuming his new duties, he had taught social studies and presided over study periods in the large assembly hall, sitting at a desk on a stage in front of the room, his chiseled face screwed up in a frown. A new biology teacher was hired to replace him, but he continued monitoring the study periods.

Burton never had tolerated any behavior other than study in the assembly hall, and a malevolent look was enough to persuade an offender to straighten up. But a big, muscular, cocky senior student known by his nickname Jocko, who had pretty much done what he wanted in school, challenging teachers to discipline him, decided to test Burton. Jocko, seated near the rear of the room on the left side, flirted outrageously with the cute girl across the aisle from him, stroking her hair and pestering her to go for a ride in his Ford convertible after school.

Burton looked up at him, leveled a piercing glare and, in his deep baritone voice, slowly and deliberately intoned, "You. Stay in your seat and keep quiet."

Jocko returned the look and said, "You're not big enough to make me."

Burton continued staring at him for several long seconds, then rose slowly and said, "Come on up here." Jocko strode to the stage and, head cocked back with a defiant look on his face, stood facing Burton. The principal said, "Give me your best punch."

Jocko sneered, took two steps forward and delivered a right-handed haymaker. Burton ducked and swung upward with his right fist, catching Jocko squarely in the front of his face. Two teeth flew out and blood spurted from Jocko's nose and mouth as he catapulted backward onto the stage. He lay there, bawling in pain, while Burton ordered, "Get up, get out of here, and don't come back for ten days."

The other students stared in shock. Colton High School had not a single behavior problem for the rest of the term.

Britt went out for the baseball team at Colton that spring, taking the last school bus home after practice or, if the bus had left, walking the three miles home. He then helped his dad with the chores. He had been crazy about baseball since he was ten. It was like everything else in his life: If he liked something, he became enthralled with it. "Why can't you do things in moderation?" Miriam had asked him once in exasperation. He'd determined that he would become a major league baseball pitcher, and worked hard at perfecting his windup, rearing back and circling his left leg outward and forward as his uncoiling body brought his right arm from behind his back in a slingshot motion. He impressed everybody with the professional look of his pitching delivery. All the other players were older, but Britt was allowed to pitch three innings in games against other schools. But he didn't fare too well because, while he threw fast, he lacked control.

After school was out, Britt set about painting the weathered buildings on the farm. He also learned to drive the John Deere model B tractor that Milton had bought, acquiescing to his three sons' insistence on a tractor instead of horses, Milton's preference, to do the field work. Quickly becoming skillful with the chugging green machine, Britt helped plow the previous year's cornfield for sewing a new crop, and mowed the three alfalfa crops that grew about six weeks apart. He also helped the neighbors make hay, using his dad's tractor and making some money in work that he enjoyed.

Arnie Slatkow operated an eighty-acre dairy farm adjacent to the Rutgers'. He was divorced, and his mother and two sisters lived with him. Of Slavic descent, he was a large-boned, strapping man of five-foot-nine, good-looking even though his face was a bit broad under a full head of dark hair. He had a ready, unrestrained laugh that was deep and resonant. For his herd of Holstein dairy cows, he grew alfalfa hay in a field adjacent to the Rutgers' property. When it was time to bale the hay, Arnie needed someone to stack the bales as they ejected from the baler onto a wagon, and Britt was eager to do the work. He quickly got the knack of swinging a hook into the bales, dragging them onto the wagon and, grasping the parallel strands of wire that held the bales together, flipping them into place. Three men unloaded each wagon into the barn.

In mid-afternoon, the crew took a break, lounging on the grass under a tree in the farm yard, the men drinking beer, to which Britt had little exposure. His parents were teetotalers, as were most of his relatives. Miriam's brothers and some of their sisters' husbands would go off from family get-togethers and tipple a few, but Britt wasn't aware of this. But Milton's family never drank, and Britt grew up thinking it was sinful. Each year, the Rutgerses went in late August or early September to the big Iowa State Fair in Des Moines, and Britt thought the people sitting at tables in tents, drinking from those long-necked, dark-brown bottles were wicked. He'd gotten that idea mainly from Milton, who refused to attend parties of the hardware stores where he worked because of the drinking. Britt, who had never been to a party or, like his siblings, never had a birthday party, had come to believe that parties were synonymous with drinking, and hence were evil in themselves. So when his father sounded off about politics to a silently half-listening Miriam, condemning the Republican Party for this or that (he later switched affiliation), Britt figured Republicans were a bunch of boozers. When Britt was seven, the Rutgerses drove to northwest Iowa to visit Milton's father, Gerhardt, who was a Republican. He and Milton loved to discuss politics, and when Gerhardt mentioned the Republican Party, Britt chimed in, "I don't like the Republicans. They drink beer." Gerhardt stared in bewilderment at his grandson for a long moment, then leaned back and laughed uproariously, his mouth open wide and his face aglow with pure joy while his big belly shook. Milton was perplexed and asked his son where he had gotten that notion. Britt told of the soliloquies he'd heard from his dad, and Milton cleared up his confusion. For years afterward, whenever Gerhardt and Milton were together with Britt present, Gerhardt recounted the story, laughing more huskily each time as he grew older, but always with total merriment.

Britt was fifteen now, and found the hay-making crew's drinking only a little unsettling, partly because of his minimal exposure to drinking as he grew up and also because he had become familiar with the others and liked them.

In July of that summer, Dale became a victim of polio at the height of an epidemic that had swept the country. After his release from the hospital, where he endured a spinal tap and painfully hot baths, Dale had to engage in exercises that required assistance. Britt became a strict disciplinarian in administering the regimen. The disease left Dale with a slumped right shoulder and, whereas he had been the fastest runner in his class, he now was slower than his sister, Kyra, who at age eight was three years younger. But he gradually grew stronger and faster. Ambitious to earn money, he worked after school and during the summers for the neighboring farmers. On one hot summer day when he was sixteen, he stood on wagons pulled behind a baler in an alfalfa field and stacked one-thousand-three-hundred bales of hay.

CHAPTER 4

Britt had his fill of Colton High. Regardless of the discontent he'd felt at Mayfield High, his classmates were not so unruly, and he hadn't felt like a foreigner, as he did at Colton. Though Mayfield was only eleven miles from Colton, the kids were as different as filet mignon and hamburger. So back to Mayfield he went. On Friday nights, he attended the high school football games with Bobby Jackson, his pal from elementary school, along with two new friends, Jim Goss and Martin Brant. On Saturday nights he came home and watched TV, which the family had bought only a year earlier.

Britt didn't take Latin because Kevin had talked about how tough it was. Kevin took math courses because he was planning to study mechanical engineering in college, and Britt followed in his path, not quite realizing that he was strongly influenced by the attention their parents focused on Kevin. Britt had taken beginning algebra in his semester at Colton, and enrolled in advanced algebra even though the other students in the class had taken a full year of beginning algebra. The teacher, Miss Dowdep, encouraged him because he had scored an A in the class at Colton.

Miss Dowdep had been named the top geometry teacher in the state of Iowa for several years in a row. Her physical characteristics did not match her math acumen and kindly, clear way of communicating it. She was a rotund five feet seven inches and must have weighed two-hundred fifty pounds. Her close-cropped, grayish hair framed a round face with a bulbous nose, and a few whiskers grew out of her chin. Throughout the year, she wore two frumpy dresses that ended three inches below the knees, meeting baggy beige stockings that reached into a pair of black, old-fashioned, stocky shoes with one-and-a-half-inch heels. Students joked about nearly passing out from the foul body odor upon entering her classroom.

Britt eked out a C in the course, and did about as well in geometry—two classes each day in that smelly room—and managed a B average overall. He rode to town in the morning with his dad and back with him in late afternoon, then helped with the farm chores, which were followed by supper and homework. Kevin had enrolled in Iowa State University in Ames, thirty miles away, and got a ride home every other weekend with a fellow from Colton who was in his second year. On Sunday evenings, the family climbed into the 1950 blue Plymouth sedan they'd bought after the '41 Ford had given out and drove Kevin back to the college. They listened to William Conrad portray a slow-spoken Marshall Matt Dillon on the radio's *Gunsmoke.*

It was a depressing time. Kevin was getting low grades, and complained that he studied constantly and found the mechanical engineering courses awfully difficult. He was unhappy, and a pall of gloom settled over the family. Kevin had worked at Noll's Drug Store during his last two years at Mayfield High School and at first contemplated becoming a pharmacist. A young pharmacist employed at the store, Nathan, had befriended Kevin, who looked up to him as a role model. They talked about mechanics and the pharmacist showed Kevin the dual mufflers he had installed on his car to create a splitting sound that evoked a feeling of power. One afternoon as Kevin reported for work after school, the head pharmacist, Edsel Comte, took him aside and said Nathan had been fired. The management had been keeping tabs on him for weeks, and finally had solid evidence that he was embezzling money. Nathan phoned Kevin that evening and swore it wasn't true, but Kevin knew it was. He was instantly disillusioned, and was no longer attracted to pharmacy as a career.

Britt had begun working at the store after returning to school in Mayfield for his sophomore year, just as Kevin left for college. He rode to Mayfield with Milton and went directly to the store at eight a.m. His job was to spread red sweeping compound on the floors—first on the narrow aisle back of the cosmetics counter, then back of the counter with cameras and medicinals, and lastly on the wider aisle down the center of the store. With a push broom, he swept up the previous day's dirt, then walked three quarters of a mile to the new high school that had been built on the far west side of the town. After school, at three-thirty p.m., he returned to the store. First, he filled the drawers in the pharmacy department with the various sizes of plastic vials, which were stored in the basement, then opened boxes of pharmaceuticals and regular merchandise. Using a crayola, he marked the containers with letter codes that indicated the wholesale prices so Edsel and Arlen, the store manager, would know what retail prices to mark.

Britt also had to fill the shelves with Kleenex and Kotex, and never knew what the Kotex was used for. He had asked Kevin, who answered only that it was for women, and seemed secretive. Britt suspected it had something to do with sex and he should know about it, but never broached the subject again because Kevin had made it sound taboo. Milton never had told his children about the birds and the bees, although he tried once. It was a weekday evening when Britt was eleven and Kevin fourteen. Miriam was ironing the laundry in the living room. Britt was sitting in a chair reading a comic book, and Kevin was in another chair working on his English grammar lesson. Milton put down a magazine he was reading on the couch and walked up to Miriam at the ironing board. With a mischievous smile, he announced, while looking at Miriam, "Boys, I'm going to tell you about the birds and the bees."

"What do you mean—what about the birds and the bees?" Britt asked, bewildered.

"It's about how babies are born," said Milton, casting a wondering, Mona Lisa-style glance at Miriam. "They don't just happen. The husband does something to the wife to make it happen."

"Like what," the always inquisitive Britt wanted to know. Kevin had begun to suspect during the previous year that babies didn't "just happen," and he realized from Milton's tactful manner that this was a delicate subject. He kept his head in his textbook and said nothing.

"Well," Milton began, "you know that you, uh, go Number One through your thing, right?"

Britt laughed. "Yeah, of course I know that."

"Well … ." Milton paused, searching for a way to explain the matter without being too explicit. "A woman doesn't have the thing, but she has something else, and … ."

"Milton, stop," demanded Miriam, her head lowered in embarrassment as she continued ironing.

"What's the matter?" a smiling Milton asked, chuckling softly.

"I don't want you to go any further," she said quietly.

"Why not?" Milton insisted, his expression showing that although he felt a bit awkward, he was getting a mild kick out of this. But he realized Miriam was very uncomfortable, and said, "Oh, all right, we'll just drop it."

So Britt remained in the dark about sexual intercourse and how it sometimes made a woman pregnant, but he certainly knew what sex felt like. Occasionally he was called to the balcony of the drug store to help Cora rummage through boxes of gifts and linens in a large closet. Cora was a handsome woman of forty-six, about five feet three inches, with hair pulled back and attached with a clasp. She had a fairly full figure, but was shapely with a large bosom, which she often displayed with low-cut dresses and blouses. That abundant cleavage, combined with a slow manner and a seductive smile on luscious lips well-layered with red lipstick, aroused Britt enormously. Cora could divine her effect on this innocent, good-looking sixteen-year-old boy, and sought his help when it wasn't really needed, working so close to him in the dimly lit closet that they often touched. Sometimes she asked him to the basement to help sort out boxes of merchandise. There, the two of them alone, she would hike her skirts high on her dark-stockinged, voluptuous thighs while bending over the boxes, filling Britt with intense desire that made him grow hard between the legs.

Loretta Noll, the never-married, forty-eight-year-old daughter of the elderly widow who owned the store, was chief of operations. One afternoon she had Britt accompany her to run an errand in her luxurious Pontiac. As Britt entered the passenger side, he noticed that tall, red-headed Loretta had pulled the skirt of her calf-length dress as high on her long, shapely legs as possible, revealing the garters that held up her stockings. Britt was inflamed with passion and could not avert his eyes from those legs, which Loretta left exposed.

Though his strict Christian upbringing had taught that sexuality of any kind was wrong outside of marriage, he found it increasingly difficult to repress his urges. At night sometimes, he would fantasize about Mrs. Olson, who with her husband were church friends of Milton and Miriam, and whose son was a classmate of Britt's. The Olsons were even more fundamentalist than the Rutgerses, and she was a quite friendly, but also quite proper, person. She also had a voluptuous shape and gorgeous legs, and when she crossed them while sitting at preworship services at the UP church, her skirt rose several inches above her knees, arousing Britt mightily. While he was in the Olsons' living room one evening, waiting to go to a basketball game with their son Stan, Mrs. Olson unconsciously emerged from the bedroom with her dress unbuttoned from top to bottom, her slip fully exposed. It filled Britt with a powerful yearning, and the image appeared in his mind many times for several years afterward. Some nights, before drifting off to sleep, he would fantasize about Mrs. Olson in her lingerie sitting on his lap, or him sitting on her lap.

But he never masturbated. He often wondered about this in later years, and concluded he must have had an unconscious feeling that doing so would be awfully sinful, since the church and his mother had condemned anything sexual and held out the threat of eternal damnation for indulging in it outside of marriage. He remembered his parents having had a brief, off-the-cuff discussion in the living room about dancing when he was perhaps eight years old, and Milton had remarked to Miriam, "Oh, I wouldn't say there's anything wrong with a man dancing with his wife." But he had come close to masturbating a couple of times at the Rutgers home in Mayfield when he lay in the backyard at night and, in the darkness, pulled his pants down.

Though he often fantasized about sex before drifting off to sleep at night, he sometimes lay awake thinking of eternity and burning forever in hell. The idea of no end terrified him. He remembered the few times he'd burned his fingers on a stove, and imagined his whole body burning—not for a day or a year or a hundred years, or even a billion years, but without end. Whenever this thought overcame him, he tried desperately to think of something else. But he became afraid of doing anything proscribed by the Bible, avoiding profanity and determining that he would never allow himself to be tempted by sex. Oh, he definitely noticed the girls, but knew that he never would have intercourse with one before he was married.

Britt's fear of sex kept him from discussing it with his friends. When they got together on weekends, the others sometimes would refer with mischievous delight to a girl's "cunt," as well as joke about getting a "hard on" over some girl. He laughed along with them to cover up his ignorance of what they were talking about, realizing he should know. He didn't ask them what they meant because he knew he would be ridiculed. He felt freakish.

The only time he had shared an interest in sex with friends was in the seventh grade, when he and Stan Olson spent a Sunday afternoon at an acquaintance who had a detective novel in his room. Stan thumbed through it and found a passage that caught his attention. After reading it, he handed it to Britt: "Sam drew a pistol out of the inner pocket of his trench coat and pointed it at Mae. 'This is the end of the road, sister,' he said darkly. Mae looked startled and fearful for a long moment, then recovered her composure and slowly began unbuttoning her dress. Either side fell away from round, firm, melon-like breasts with stiff nipples. Her lovely tan was uninterrupted by any white brazier boundaries, indicating that she had sunbathed in the nude. She continued languorously loosening the buttons, then pulled her gracefully sloping shoulders back and lifted her arms out of the sleeve openings, allowing the dress to drop to the floor. She stood like a sex goddess with a nearly flat abdomen, curvaceous hips, and perfectly sculpted thighs that merged in a V covered with a mound of blond hair. Ever so slowly and sensuously, she stepped toward Sam, reaching out with her arms to embrace him. Bang! The shot reverberated through the room, and Mae grasped her chest between those luscious breasts. She stared at Sam, her eyes big in disbelief as blood flowed over her hand and dripped down her midsection. 'Oh, Sam … .' Then her eyes closed and she collapsed onto the carpet."

Britt was transfixed. Ordinarily, the description of blood oozing from a body would have made him queasy, but he was too riveted by the image of Mae's naked body to be bothered. It was his first experience with worldly sex, and it awakened his primal desires just as surely as sperm fertilizes an egg to create life.

Tenth grade passed, and he and Kevin worked at Noll's during the summer months, when the regular employees were taking vacations and fill-ins were needed. The two bought a 1947 Ford with part of the savings each had accumulated from their newspaper routes and working at Noll's. They rode to work together, working forty-nine-hour weeks. Britt began the day at eight a.m. by washing the big bay windows in front with a bucket and a rubber wiper on a stick. They ate a bag lunch together in the Ford at noon, listening to the Chicago Cubs game on the radio. Kevin barely said anything, maintaining an attitude of near hostility as he responded to anything Britt said with contempt, making him feel as though he were stupid. The two worked until the store's closing at six p.m., then drove home in silence.

Kevin never revealed his private thoughts to anyone in the family, never even mentioning sex to Britt. But one Sunday afternoon, alone with him in the bedroom they and Dale shared, Kevin confided that he didn't want to return to Iowa State. "I can't get the math," he said quietly, almost as an aside. "But dad won't like it if I don't go back. I guess I'll go."

The eleventh grade began for Britt, and he was becoming troubled. He began feeling self-conscious when carrying merchandise from the stock section in the back of Noll's to the front. He felt the eyes of the elderly owner peering down on him from her desk at the edge of the balcony, and was uncomfortable in the open with other employees and numerous customers milling about. At the high school sports events, he felt awkward and excruciatingly embarrassed walking in front of the crowd to his seat in the bleachers.

Kevin never dated or talked about girls, and Britt was reluctant to admit he was attracted to them for fear of ribbing by his parents. If Kevin hadn't set a precedent of dating abstinence and indifference toward girls, it would have been easier for Britt to admit publicly his interest in them and follow the normal path of social intercourse. But he found himself smitten with Jane Jansen, the oldest of two daughters of the UP church minister and his wife. With Kevin away at college, Britt finally found the courage to acknowledge his attraction. She was tall and slender, was quite pretty with a slightly elongated face, and wore her honey-blonde hair parted down the middle so that it fell to below her jaw line and curled outward. She was fairly quiet and beamed a bright but somewhat shy smile that revealed straight, sparkling white teeth. His friend Jim Goss was sweet on Viola Vanderzeen, who also attended the UP church with her family. Britt proposed that they try to arrange a double-date for the high school football game at Grinola, nineteen miles east of Mayfield. The four climbed into the 1947 Ford, which Kevin had left behind when he returned to the university. It was fortunate that the locks on all four of the car's doors worked. Jane hugged the passenger side in the front seat, Jim kept tight against the left side of the rear seat, and Viola seemed to be having an affair with the door on the right side of the rear seat. Bob and Carol and Ted and Alice this was not. The four barely spoke.

"Mayfield oughtta crush Grinola," Britt offered after an initial period of silence that lasted probably three minutes but seemed like thirty.

"You think so?" Jane wondered.

"Oh yeah. Mayfield has a great team this year and Grinola's is lousy again."

"Yep," Jim, who was on the school wrestling team, agreed. "Coach Eldahl has made Mayfield one of the best teams in the state again."

"Well, I sure hope we win," Viola perfunctorily piped in to show she was sociable.

It went like that throughout the evening, the girls maintaining a decorum that made Victorian standards seem loose, and the boys taking their cue and never even entertaining the idea of physical contact.

Britt never had another date in high school. Usually, he got together weekends with Jim, Bobby Jackson and Martin Brant to attend the school sports events or just "cruise the loop" in downtown Mayfield. That's what they did Halloween night, arming themselves with water-filled balloons at the instigation of Bobby. Britt drove the '47 Ford, with Bobby in charge of the ammunition in the back seat and Martin occupying the passenger seat. Bobby announced that he was going to give somebody's car a bath. As they headed east down the main street, a slick-looking 1951 Ford approached from the other direction, and Bobby ordered Britt to slow down. Bobby rolled down the window, reared back his arm with a balloon, and flung it with perfect timing at the car, hitting it partly on the driver's window and partly on the door with a big splash.

"OK, let's get outta here," Bobby shouted. Britt looked in the rear-view mirror and saw the '51 Ford doing a U-turn. He jammed the accelerator and burst through the green traffic light. Bobby looked behind and said, "Uh-oh, they're coming like mad. Get goin', Britt." Britt saw that he couldn't out-race the newer, more powerful Ford, so he decided to try and out-maneuver it. Before the next light was an alley on the left, and he suddenly swung into it. As he did so, Bobby got a perpendicular look at the other car and exclaimed, "Oh my God, it's four sailors. They're gonna kill us. We gotta keep ahead of 'em."

Britt knew what he was doing. He was highly skilled behind the wheel. He'd learned to drive the John Deere quickly at age fifteen, prompting Milton to remark at the dinner table one night, "Britt sure can handle that tractor. Kevin is good with the car, but Britt is really agile with the John Deere." Britt had beamed with pride and glanced at Kevin, catching the smirk on his face. Milton had divined Kevin's jealousy toward his brother, and wanted to needle his older son a bit. It was one of those rare, striking moments that made Britt feel as though his dad were on his side, even though he made the boy feel ashamed and worthless at other times. Despite Milton's high expectations for Kevin, the father never had a good relationship with the son. Once when Kevin was sixteen, Milton became angry at him for something—the only time that had ever happened—and raised his fists as though he were going to strike. Kevin put up his dukes and challenged his dad. Milton was only bluffing, but was astonished at his son's reaction, and the incident widened the emotional distance between them.

At the end of the block-long alley, Britt tore to the right on a side street, the car's tires squealing like a stuck pig, and a block later ripped left. He kept zig-zagging madly through the city streets, shifting the stick on the steering column with clock-like synchronization from one gear to another, keeping ahead of the older sailors in the newer Ford but unable to shake them. Britt headed into downtown again, and Bobby suggested they stop and ask protection from a cop standing on a corner. "No, we can't do that," Britt retorted impatiently. "We threw the balloon."

"But these guys are gonna kill us," Bobby yelled, hunkering down in the back seat.

"All right," Britt decided, "let's try to beat 'em to the farm. If they get out of their car, Sparks will eat 'em alive. Heck, sometimes that dog won't let *me* get out of the car. Here we go. Maybe we can stay ahead of 'em."

"I don't know," Martin said doubtfully. "Their car is faster."

"Not necessarily," said Britt. "Let's try it. It's our only hope."

"Okay," said Bobby.

To avoid getting a ticket for speeding, Britt swung south onto a north-south street, then veered hard to the right and sped west, the sailors in hot pursuit. When they reached the western limits of the central commercial and residential areas of the town of fifteen-thousand population, he made a fast right, then a left onto the main street, which was also U.S. 6. The driver of the '51 Ford may not have been as acquainted with the small city as Britt was—he'd walked its streets as a newspaper carrier for five years—and Britt had gained on the sailors. He raced through the outskirts and into the countryside, and Bobby announced that the sailors were only a hundred yards behind. Britt went seventy-five miles per hour around a sharp curve in the highway, the one where seven drunken people had died in a car that failed to negotiate it at one-hundred-ten miles an hour. He speeded up for a couple of rolling hills. They reached a flat plain, and Britt pressed the accelerator to the floor board. He glanced at the speedometer: ninety-six. But the sailors were going faster, and had almost caught up.

"We're not going to outrun 'em," Britt said, adding half-heartedly, "Maybe we ought to pull over and fight 'em."

That idea held no appeal whatever for Bobby Jackson. "Are you crazy?" he shouted. "They'll massacre us." Britt wasn't sure whether "massacre" was worse than "kill" but didn't want to think about it.

They had come up behind a semitrailer truck and had to slow down, allowing the sailors to come up to their bumper. "See that car coming around the bend way up ahead?" said Bobby. "Move up beside the semi and stay there until that car gets closer, and then swerve over in front of the semi. They'll have to wait until the car passes to go around the semi, and we'll gain on them."

"All right, good idea," said Britt. He pulled parallel with the truck and stayed there as the car approached from the other direction. The sailors, apparently not wanting to play this dangerous game, stayed on the right side of the road behind the truck. Britt waited until he knew it would be too late for the sailors to go around the semi before the car passed, then sped ahead of the truck and over to the right side of the road. He accelerated again to ninety-six mph, the '47 Ford's limit, but the sailors now showed the full power of their newer model. As they went around the bend and headed toward the Scrum River, the sailors pulled up beside. Bobby was down on the floor board when they heard a crash. Britt looked back and saw a shattered side window. The sailors pulled ahead and left. Britt slowed and drove off the road, and the three surveyed the damage. They surmised that the sailors, apparently equipped for more-serious mischief than mere water-ballooning, had chucked what must have been a brick, or maybe just a bottle of beer, at the window. Britt turned back toward Mayfield and dropped Bobby and Martin off at their homes, then headed the eleven miles back to the farm. On the way to church the next morning, he confessed to his parents what had happened. Milton had engaged in his own share of devilment during his college years and wasn't very judgmental. Miriam, likewise, had a rich feel for mischief and didn't condemn her son.

CHAPTER 5

Britt grew increasingly self-conscious as the months passed in his junior year in high school. His ignorance about sex became more and more difficult to hide as his friends' enthusiasm for discussing the subject grew. His feelings of shame and a sense that something was wrong with him—that he was abnormal—deepened. At the same time, his religious consciousness grew, and he wrestled with conflicts that he perceived in the Bible and in the minister's sermons, trying to reconcile them. To admit their existence would be to risk eternal damnation; Miriam had made that abundantly clear throughout his childhood. He kept all this to himself and became increasingly confused and unhappy as time went on. But he did okay in school, getting average or above-average grades in most subjects and an A in American literature, which he loved even though he was a slow reader, making sure he digested every word on the page, a sort of obsessive-compulsiveness.

The school year ended, and he began working full-time at Noll's with Kevin, who had dropped out of Iowa State after the first trimester and transferred to Thessalonika College in Pliny, Iowa, from which Milton had graduated. After work, Britt played with a baseball team sponsored by one of the manufacturers in Mayfield.

The summer passed swiftly, but Britt was becoming more morose as his inner turmoil was exacerbated by a sullen atmosphere at home. Milton was not happy that Kevin had quit Iowa State, and Kevin communicated little with his parents. But parents and son were acutely aware of each other, and there was an unspoken tension. Kyra was only ten, but plans already were under way to groom her, as the only girl and Milton's favorite, for a role as a lady of refinement and culture. Piano lessons were to begin soon. Dale was the favorite of Miriam because he, like she and members of the family she grew up in, had an aptitude for business, and she loved the kidding he gave her. She continually harped at her children to be neat and tidy, and Dale was the most unkempt of them, carelessly leaving his socks and other articles lying around the house. But he shrugged off her nagging and charmed her with his joking,

Britt wasn't much noticed. Miriam suggested once that he might want to go into hospital or hotel management, an idea that Britt found odd. He exhibited no proclivity whatsoever toward business. That was the only time that either she or Milton broached the subject of what he would do after high school, though he would graduate in less than a year. Britt had no conception of where his talent lie, since only one person had ever told him—Rhoda Godwin, who taught eighth-grade English and high-school drama. She shared status with one other teacher, Miss Abbott in kindergarten, as his all-time favorite. Britt earned straight A's in Miss Godwin's class. Though he was quietly studious in that stage of his youth and she was flamboyant, she was quite fond of him and granted him special favors, such as calling on him to run errands. Her remarks in his report card at the end of each semester were identical: "Britt (the other teachers called him by his full first name Brittain, which he detested) is an excellent student of English." In the second report, she added that he'd also excelled in speech and, "I hope he tries out for the debate team. He has the talent." But his parents never mentioned the reports to him, nor ever suggested that he consider becoming a teacher or a journalist.

As far as Britt could tell, the only thing in which he stood out was typing; he was second-best in his class of thirty-odd eleventh-graders. He'd entered the class with an advantage, having been taught the fingering by Kevin on Milton's old Smith & Corona clunker, which Britt used to practice. It seemed only logical that he should become a professional typist, and that's what he decided to do. When he mentioned the idea to his parents, they merely shrugged.

At the beginning of his senior year, he had to choose a category of course work: general, commercial, or college preparatory. He chose commercial in order to get the subjects that would help prepare him for office work, along with social studies and English. On Friday nights, he attended football games with his friends, and occasionally went out with them on a Saturday night. Otherwise, he just stayed home and watched the sugary Lawrence Welk show, featuring "the luffly little Lennon Sisters," with his parents. He didn't know how to dance and was too self-conscious to ever consider going to a high school hop and learning. His self-consciousness became increasingly painful, and when the basketball season began, it was agony for him to walk along the edge of the court in front of the crowd in the bleachers on the way to his seat. It was as though he were hiding something, and if people looked at him, they would discover what it was. Walking out from his seclusion in the back of Noll's to the retail part of the store occupied by customers and the other employees in a group situation likewise required extraordinary effort.

His awareness of people's emotions became tortured. Watching television, he suffered for people on the screen, wondering if they were as self-conscious as he was, and studied their facial expressions so intently that he didn't absorb much of what they were saying. He couldn't understand how they could look each other in the eyes and not become embarrassed. Doing his homework, he found it increasingly difficult to concentrate. His mind flitted about to events of the day and re-enactments of the most casual and perfunctory encounters with students, teachers, and people at Noll's. He felt pain at the perception that he might have hurt someone's feelings, or that some innocent remark made to him had a derogatory meaning. He had great difficulty comprehending what he read because his mind could focus only briefly on the words before an extraneous thought occurred. Any outside noise only made concentration harder, and he repeatedly asked his parents to turn down the television, even though, with the door to his room closed, it was only a dull background sound and he couldn't hear the words spoken. They in turn became annoyed with him, having no inkling of the emotional turmoil he was experiencing. As the weeks went by, the mental agitation intensified, and he became panicky over his schoolwork, fearing his grades would suffer. They did, though he somehow managed to maintain a C average at the end of the first semester.

In early February, Britt posed at a photography studio for his high school graduation pictures. That Saturday he joined Bobby Jackson, Stan Olson, and Martin Brant for a night of bowling at the Lucky Strike Lanes in Mayfield. Britt wasn't much of a bowler but held his own against Martin and Stan; Bobby was the best. They had a good time knocking down the pins, which were reset after each roll by a pin boy who came down from a perch behind and above the alley. At about eleven-thirty p.m., they'd had enough and checked in their bowling shoes and balls. Britt walked in his socks to the spot amidst a row of chairs against a wall where he'd left his street shoes. They weren't there. He walked to the desk and reported them missing. The clerk exchanged a mischievous smile with Bobby, while

Martin kept a straight face. Looking on with a smirk was Stan. It was the same malevolent look Britt remembered from Sunday school class at the UP church eight years earlier when Stan, who was leaning his chair back, came down on Britt's toes with one of the spoked legs and held it there, inflicting intense pain.

"I don't know where your shoes are," the clerk said, glancing at Bobby. "Do you boys know where they are?"

"No, we don't have any idea," said Bobby, grinning broadly. "Stan, Martin—you seen Britt's shoes?"

"No," said Stan. "Are you sure you wore them here?"

The others, except for Martin, burst out laughing.

Now Britt knew he was being played for the fool. He was too naïve—too serious, intense, honest—to be able to laugh it off and make wisecracks back at his compatriots. He couldn't go with the flow, which made him easy game.

"Aw c'mon. You guys took 'em. Give 'em back."

"Now why would we do a thing like that?" Bobby said.

"I don't know, but I can't leave this place until I find them, mister," Britt said to the clerk. He looked around at the now-deserted bowling facility. "I 'magine you want to close, but I'm not goin' anywhere till I get my shoes."

"Nothin' I can do," said the clerk, cooperating with the others in the joke. "Guess you'll have to spend the night locked in here by yourself."

"Yes," chimed in Stan, "guess I won't be seeing you in church tomorrow morning. This place doesn't reopen until noon."

Britt was miserable. What had he done to become the brunt of this cruel joke? Nothing. His hurt and anger were much the same emotions he'd felt over and over for years when he'd argued with Milton and Miriam over something, always losing even though he knew he was right. One time, during his sophomore year, an argument erupted into violence when Milton came down on Britt's back with a flashlight.

All of these incidents had left him crying with hurt and rage from a feeling of impotence at the perceived injustice, and he felt like crying now.

The boys continued their taunting to keep Britt's attention while the clerk left his booth and strolled across the carpet. Britt just stood there helplessly. After twenty minutes of this, Bobby looked to his right and exclaimed, "What's that—over there on the floor? Are those your shoes?"

Britt retrieved his shoes, walked to the row of chairs and put them on.

"How could you not see your shoes when all this time they were sitting right smack in the middle of the floor, all by themselves?" Bobby exclaimed.

Britt said nothing and walked out the door to the 1950 Plymouth. He drove home, wild with grief and rage.

Milton and Miriam were still up when he arrived, Miriam poring over the next morning's Sunday school lesson. Milton was absorbed in *Witness*, the autobiography of Whittaker Chambers, one of two books his children had given him for Christmas only a few weeks earlier. Britt entered the living room and broke down sobbing.

"Oh oh oh, what's the matter?" Milton asked as he rose from his chair and walked up to Britt, his tone full of genuine compassion and concern. Britt was grateful his dad didn't call him "Sweetheart," which he'd done two years earlier, embracing Britt as he got out of the car upon his arrival home and broke down crying. He'd made a bad mistake at Noll's after school, marking the wrong price code on an entire shipment of shampoo and hair dye, and received a strong rebuke from Arlen, the store manager. Milton's awkward spontaneity had erupted from a feeling of overwhelming tenderness, but Britt exclaimed, "Sweetheart?" Completely taken aback by the rebuff to his heartfelt outpouring, Milton asked, "What's wrong?" his face wrought with hurt and confusion. "Well obviously he doesn't want to be called Sweetheart," Miriam admonished.

(Milton had enormous sensitivity toward human suffering when he didn't feel threatened, but could be markedly insensitive toward others' failings if they had a bearing on him. Kevin complained to Britt that Milton, whose job at the Iowa State Employment Service was finding jobs for people, never found him or Britt a job for fear his sons might perform poorly and reflect badly on him. Milton's first boss, a gregarious, heavy-set, beer-bellied, mustachioed man who made Britt think of Throckmorton P. Gildersleeve, the character in the radio show *The Great Gildersleeve*, was a customer on Britt's newspaper route. When the man died of a heart attack, Britt, only eleven, stopped to collect the weekly bill two days later, though he hesitated over whether to do so. The man's daughter, in her early thirties, fetched the thirty cents and handed it to Britt, mumbling something about being left alone. Britt was worried he'd done something wrong and mentioned it to his parents when he got home.

("Oh my gosh, you did what?" Milton shouted. "What in tarnation were you thinking? Oh, Lordie, this is terrible. Oh good heavens, I'm going to lose my job." He wailed, his face red and eyes wild with both fear and anger as he paced the living room. Britt was stunned, thinking he had committed a mortal, unforgivable sin, but not understanding why. To ward off Milton's anger, he cried while walking to his bedroom, where he lay on the bed and continued whimpering. Finally, Miriam came in and told him in a cool tone which bore only a hint of sympathy that he should stop.)

Tears streaming down his face, Britt told his parents what had happened at the bowling alley, then confessed, choking as he talked, that he had been miserable for a long time.

"I can't understand my school books because I can't think about what they're saying because my mind won't concentrate," he blubbered. "I'm constantly thinking of other things. My mind just won't stay on the subject. I'm always thinking people are looking at me. When I have to walk in front of the crowd at a basketball game, I get all red and feel awfully embarrassed because I know everybody is looking at me. At Noll's, I just hate to go to the front of the store where everybody can watch me. When I watch TV, I'm always afraid the people are going to get embarrassed like me, and I don't think about what they're saying. I'm scared that I'm going to go to hell and burn forever." He was too ashamed of his sexual ignorance to tell them it made him feel that something was wrong with him—that he was abnormal because he didn't understand about sex and how women had babies.

"You mustn't feel that way," Miriam said, referring to his fear of hellfire. "Jesus loves you and doesn't want you to go to hell. If you just believe in him, he will save you, as he will all of us."

She paused a moment and resumed. "People aren't looking at you all the time. They're thinking of other things. They're concerned about themselves, not you." Her voice had lost its curtness, and she was softer and imploring.

Britt didn't feel much consoled.

"Do you want to see a psychiatrist?" Milton asked in a tone full of concern. He did not want, or know how, to deal with Britt's fears and anxieties—to talk on such an intimate level with his son. "We can take you to a psychiatrist."

"I don't know," Britt said, and sobbed some more. "I just don't know what to do. My grades are getting worse and I'm afraid I'm going to fail some subjects. I'm just miserable all the time. Sometimes I think about ramming the car into that tree on the way home from Noll's on Saturdays—you know, the one on the gravel road just when you turn off Highway 6."

Milton stared at his son, mouth open, for several seconds, his face registering mild shock.

"Monday morning we're going to call a psychiatrist," he announced.

CHAPTER 6

Milton's mother, Jeanette, died when he was eleven years old during the Great Flu Epidemic that swept the world in 1918. Milton also had contracted the flu, and the doctor expected him to die and his mother to recover. The opposite happened, and Milton's dad, G.W. Rutgers, was left without a wife to care for his two sons, Milton and Waymon. He had no one to do the cooking and washing and ironing and house-cleaning and a million other things that women then, in the rugged farm life of the prairie, were laden with while their husbands plotted with and against nature to raise the crops and animals on which they depended for survival.

Gerhardt Rutgers had a sister, Minerva, who lived alone in nearby Millersville, where she was a clerk at a dime store, as they were then known, selling household odds and ends. Gerhardt asked if she would come to live with him and the two boys, and he would support her in return for serving as their mother. She reluctantly agreed.

But Gerhardt was not an easy man to live with. He'd grown up on a farm in the same region, northwest Iowa, where the summers were so hot and humid that folks often slept outside. Farms were without electricity before the turn of the century, and air-conditioning was nonexistent or consisted of blessed breezes. And the winters were worse, with the frequently sub-zero temperatures exacerbated by howling winds that whipped snow into huge drifts, causing beef cattle to occasionally freeze as they huddled together in the feed lots next to barns made for sheltering milk cows and storing hay. Despite these rigors, Gerhardt had chosen to buy his own farm as a young man, paying the mortgage down payment with money he'd saved by continuing to live for several years into adulthood on the farm of his parents. Both of them had immigrated from Holland and moved west to the prairie. He drew a salary for working long hours helping his father, who, of course, charged him for board and room, as was the custom in the Netherlands. Gerhardt was an independent, strong-willed entrepreneur, a staunch Republican who voted for William McKinley, Theodore Roosevelt, and William Howard Taft. A lover of politics, he might have become one himself except for his stony refusal to compromise on anything and his deficiency and utter lack of charm in the social graces. He stood a trim and solid six feet, and his handsome face, which somewhat resembled a young Franklin Delano Roosevelt, was impassive, a pure reflection of his coldly opinionated character. Arguing politics was his favorite pastime, and he always won the debate, intimidating his opponents with his blustery style, if not his superior knowledge and rhetorical skills.

For Minerva, it was a joyless life with her brother. In Millersville, she was able to stay up until ten p.m. and then rise at six a.m. to prepare for work in the store. Now, she had to turn in soon after finishing with the dinner chores so as to get up in the darkness at four a.m. and make breakfast for Gerhardt, Milton, and Waymon. All gathered in the kitchen and sat silently at a spare, faded, scratched wooden table with matching, unforgiving chairs as Minerva, clad in a drab smock and tattered slippers, poured coffee in their cups. She went to stirring the oatmeal and frying eggs on an iron, kerosene stove that bore the stains of grease spatters and spilled food tidbits, then carried the food across the worn, gray-yellow linoleum floor to the table. The boys helped their father with the farm chores before trudging together three miles to their one-room schoolhouse. After supper, Minerva hunkered wordlessly over the white porcelain sink that was dulled and cracked with age, washing and drying the dishes while Gerhardt repaired to the rocking chair to read the newspaper or a magazine. Afterward, Gerhardt had little to say, and when he spoke, it was speculation on the prices of hogs or eggs or cream, or about news out of Washington. Aunt Minnie, as the boys called her, would listen in silence, except for an occasional "uh-huh" to make Gerhardt think she was listening, though very little of what he said registered because she cared not a whit about any of it. After a half hour, she and the others went to bed.

Her unhappiness grew, and she slipped into ever-deeper depression. After less than two years, she began to behave strangely, muttering to herself and occasionally breaking the supper-table sobriety with loud, insane cackling that frightened Milton and Waymon. They would joke about her as they walked to school, but Gerhardt said nothing to them or to Minnie about her condition. His only response was to talk even less, realizing she was not comprehending. Her condition worsened, and she began to wail, and sometimes scream, in the night, scaring the wits out of the boys. One day, Gerhardt came in for the noon dinner and found her sitting on the floor in a corner of the kitchen, gesturing with her arms and hands while staring into space with glazed eyes. Gerhardt asked what she was doing, and she continued with her bizarre, pantomime-like movements as though she hadn't heard him. This occurred four more times in the next two weeks at dinner and supper time, and Gerhardt and the boys had to make their own meals. Finally, Gerhardt summoned a doctor, who, after questioning her for almost an hour, informed her brother that she was seriously psychotic and was a detriment to the welfare of the boys. Three days later, three men arrived in a Model T Ford and quietly escorted a compliant Minerva into the automobile. They drove thirty-five miles to Cherokee and committed her to the state hospital for the insane.

This was a close-knit community, almost all of whose farmers and townsfolk, or their parents or grandparents, had immigrated from Holland. Everybody—except for a few reclusive and rebellious heathens who had the audacity to renounce religion—attended church in Oatston and Millersville. The two towns were only ten miles apart and had a combined population of about twenty-five-hundred. Each had one place of worship. Oatston had the First Reformed Church (the founders apparently had envisioned a growing town in need of more churches), and its neighbor to the west had the Christian Reformed Church of Millersville. Both were part of the Dutch Reformed Church of America, but the Christian Reformed branch was comprised of folks who had objected to practices they considered too liberal, such as playing cards and allowing young people to express their romantic inclinations by holding hands in public. Of course, neither the main denomination nor its offshoot condoned dancing.

Word of the tragedy that befell Minerva Rutgers had spread very quickly. There were few places to hide in a community where everyone's business was pretty much public. Nonetheless, her quiet, retiring disposition had kept her much in the shadows before she had moved to the Rutgers farm and no one had known her very well. So it was generally assumed that her plight was due to some mental deficiency. If any man or woman held the slightest suspicion that Gerhardt Rutgers might have been at least partly responsible for his sister's extreme unhappiness, he or she never uttered it.

The handsome young widowed farmer again needed a partner to do the woman's work and tend to his two sons while he ran the farm.

He didn't have to wait long to find a replacement. It so happened that a parishioner in the Oatston church had an uncle and aunt in Yountsville, South Dakota, only thirty-odd miles away. Their widowed niece, Deborah, was living with her parents. Her husband had been killed in a threshing machine accident while working with a crew harvesting a neighbor's oats. In Iowa and surrounding states, the wealthiest farmer in the area would own a threshing machine, which was very expensive, and rent it to a group of his nearest neighbors, who would join to help with each other's harvest. It never must have occurred to these staunch Republicans that they were engaging in a socioeconomic practice which more closely resembled the system that had accompanied the recent revolution in Russia than the capitalism they so fervently believed in.

These crews, operating in a loose cooperative, would spend long days in the hot sun, bringing in each farmer's crop over a period of about three weeks. Some heaved the bundles of oat stalks onto a horse-drawn wagon, while others plied the even hotter task of flinging the stalks into the bin of the steam-driven thresher. It would shake the oats from the straw and discard the soft yellow filaments onto a pile for use as barn bedding to warm the cows during the brutally cold winter nights. The threshing process made the men dirtier than coal miners as it produced a swirl of dust and lint that invaded their eyes, turning them red and bleary. The fine pollutants also lined their nostrils, making breathing difficult as they fitfully slept in those hot, torpid nights.

A huge, locomotive-like steam engine powered the threshing apparatus with a belt attached to a flywheel. During one of the threshing operations, a shock flew off a crewman's pitchfork and onto the underside of the belt, wedging between it and the flywheel. The belt came off the wheel and whipped around the neck of the niece's husband, breaking it. The crewmen carried him to one of their cars, but by the time they reached the hospital in Oatston, he had lapsed into a coma. Two days later, he died.

He and his wife had been married four years and, using the rhythm method, had avoided pregnancy, choosing to wait until they could acquire their own farm to have children. The accident had occurred four years previous, and the widow's parents were becoming quite concerned about her diminishing chances of finding a husband. Word had it that the niece, on the other hand, was not the least concerned. Folks said she was shy and diffident and, in fact, preferred remaining securely in the nest with her parents.

One Sunday morning, Casey Van der Voort, the parishioner related to the widow's parents, approached Mr. Rutgers in the vestibule after the worship service. How would Gerhardt like to hop in his Model T and drive over about three p.m. for coffee and some of that delicious Dutch pastry that his wife had baked the previous afternoon? John and Hilda Weirsma, Van der Voort's uncle and aunt, and their daughter Deborah would be there, and they would all have a nice couple of hours before it would be time to do the chores. This would be a casual affair—no suit and tie were necessary.

Gerhardt Rutgers motored the several miles down dirt roads to the Van der Voort farm and, after the greetings, entered the living room where a neatly dressed Deborah Weirsma sat next to her mother on the couch. Gerhardt liked what he saw. Despite her plainness, she was pretty, her hair tied back in a bun. She smiled wanly and weakly extended her hand, which Gerhardt squeezed until she winced in pain. Suddenly realizing his strength, he released his grip and apologized for hurting her. They talked about his farming and her knitting, and the afternoon went fairly well. The Van der Voorts suggested the event should be repeated the following Sunday, except they could all come straight from church and have dinner, as the noon meal was called, the evening meal being supper. Deborah didn't volunteer much in the way of conversation, but she didn't need to, because Gerhardt, once he became comfortable with the situation, was by no means shy and kept up a steady stream of chatter. He asked if she would like to attend church with him the next Sunday—he would pick her up at the Weirsma farm—and she unenthusiastically said it would be okay. After that, he began courting her regularly, usually taking her into Oatston on Saturday evenings for the outdoor band concert in the town square and a cup of coffee and pastry at Vander Ploeg's Café. The next morning, he took her to church and, as time went on, church again Sunday evening.

After six months of this, Gerhardt popped the question. Deborah didn't know. She was attracted to this man, who, though lacking in charm, showed masterful control over every situation. It was a trait that she, utterly lacking in self-confidence, much admired. But she was afraid to break out of the shell of security afforded by living with her parents. With them, as before with her husband, her life had been fairly easy and feminine, with little more required of her than the performance of simple household tasks. She would have to ask her parents.

Of course, the Van der Voorts heartily approved of the idea, and urged their daughter to accept. She was, they pointed out, twenty-eight years old, and it was time to make a life for herself. Not that they didn't like having her at home—she was a joy for them, they assured her—but they were certain that she would be much happier as a complete woman, being a wife and having children.

The following Saturday night, at a social presented by the Ladies Aid Society of the First Reformed Church of Oatston, Deborah Weirsma reluctantly told Gerhardt Rutgers that she would marry him. Three months later, they were man and wife.

For Deborah, the marriage meant moving from one farm to another. It was not quite the culture shock that Minerva, who had lived and worked in town, experienced when she went to live with her brother. But Minerva had at least been on her own, while Deborah had been living a completely sheltered life with her parents. She had shared the woman's role with her mother. Suddenly, she was faced not only with the entire burden of being a farmer's wife, handling by herself the chores that she had shared with her mother, but with caring for two children, as well. The transition was very hard on her, and Gerhardt didn't make it easier. She was now his wife, and that was quite different from being the object of his affections. As he saw it, the fun was over and now it was time to get down to business. Serious business. With the farm work dominating his life from sunup to sundown, and farm prices and politics consuming him at virtually all other moments, there was precious little time for levity. As with all other farmers, he was engaged in a continual struggle with two capricious forces, nature and the American economy, to make a livelihood. But even under less onerous circumstances, Gerhardt Rutgers would have been a relentlessly driven man who found humor mostly in someone else's folly. It was his nature.

He did have his softer, romantic moments. He would grab Deborah's behind in the kitchen when she was preparing supper and the boys were in their room working on school homework. Or he would embrace her while she was washing dishes, which probably meant he would make love to her that night. At first, it was a reprieve from the tedium of the house and farm work, and she welcomed the closeness after a day spent alone, except for dinner, in the house and around the farmyard. But Gerhardt's advances became more and more lascivious, less and less loving, the sex devoid of warmth. Deborah's attitude lapsed into indifference, and soon she began to dread these moments.

But she didn't have to endure them very long. Shortly after announcing to Gerhardt that she was pregnant, his sexual overtures ceased—for her, a blessed relief. The baby was a boy, and they named him Gart. Gerhardt doted on his new son, and his feelings spilled over to his wife, who found joy in mothering. Their passions were revived, and lovemaking resumed. But it didn't last long, for Deborah became pregnant again, and Gerhardt began to withhold his affections. Only one-and-a-half years after the birth of Gart, Frances was born. Gerhardt was delighted to at last have a daughter and spent all of his free time with her, virtually ignoring his wife. For Deborah, the addition to the family was both a blessing and a bane. She now had two babies as outlets for her love, which had atrophied like the milk production of a cow that's not milked, for Gerhardt had grown cold and stony toward her. Caring for two babies gave her life purpose, and she was rejuvenated. But as the infants became toddlers, they grew more independent, and Deborah had to discipline them. She now had four children to care for, and received neither practical nor emotional support from her husband. In fact, he frequently yelled at her for the slightest lapse in performance of household chores—serving the mashed potatoes too cool for Gerhardt, who liked them steaming hot, or forgetting to sew a button on a work shirt. Life became more and more tedious, and the only relief from the routine was a trip to the grocery store Saturday nights and church on Sunday morning, and sometimes Sunday evening, when the sermon was delivered in Dutch. She and Gerhardt hardly talked at meals. Gerhardt, realizing that his wife didn't love him, stopped making even his infrequent amorous overtures at bedtime and on Sunday afternoons, when he rested from the farm work in observance of the Lord's Day.

Deborah became increasingly morose, and spoke less and less to the children, even her own. Milton and Waymon, who were now fifteen and thirteen, noticed her condition deteriorate and said nothing to her or their father. Once, when school let out early because of an impending blizzard, they walked into the kitchen and found her sitting at the dinner table, her head cradled in her arms, weeping. They quickly went to their room, knowing that something was very wrong. While doing chores together the next morning, they talked about her, wondering if she would end up like Minerva. As time went on, Deborah began muttering to herself and quietly giggling at nothing. At dinner one evening, she suddenly picked up her dinner knife and stabbed a piece of roast pork so hard the plate cracked. Then she looked toward the ceiling with glazed eyes and clasped her hands together as though praying. Even Gerhardt was shocked as a forkful of food intended for his mouth spilled back on the plate and his mouth fell open. The boys looked at her wide-eyed, then at their dad, frightened. Just as suddenly, Deborah emerged from her trance, glancing warily at Gerhardt and lowering her gaze to her plate as she resumed eating. No one said anything.

Incidents like this became more frequent, and Gerhardt could not ignore the situation any longer. A quiet, withdrawn woman even before she began behaving abnormally, she didn't seem any different to the church parishioners for a long time. But she occasionally would say something that made no sense when they made small talk with her as she entered church with Gerhardt and the children, and they began to whisper about her. Months later, he decided to leave her at home Sunday mornings. He told Milton and Waymon of his decision while they were in the barn that first Sunday, finally acknowledging that she was sick and saying there was nothing he could do about it. To people at church who asked, he explained that she was not feeling well and wished to stay home and rest. No, nothing was wrong with her physically, he assured them; she was just going through a phase of mild depression that he was sure would pass.

But it didn't pass. At lunch one autumn afternoon, after Gerhardt had loudly and vehemently chastised Deborah for spilling a glass of milk on the table, she leaped from her chair and flew out the door. She was lean and strong, and, despite wearing a long frock, was able to run fast. Streaking down the long driveway, she headed west up the dirt road, in the direction of South Dakota, presumably hoping to reach her parents. But Gerhardt also was lean and strong, and he ran in pursuit, catching up to her on the road only a few hundred feet from the driveway. He grabbed her, and she fought, but in vain. Milton and Waymon watched from the front yard as their father approached—dragging a screaming Deborah by the hair.

Such incidents began to occur regularly. Deborah would flee the house, hoping for some escape from her intolerable existence. Milton would chase her down, then drag her back by the hair, her bare heels dragging on the long driveway to the house and farmyard. If she had walked with him instead of resisting, she could have avoided the intense pain to her bleeding feet and her scalp, but the physical torture was a diversion from the continual suffering of her soul.

For months after the dinner-table episode, the boys were afraid and stayed away from her as much as possible. It wasn't difficult, because after dinner she would repair silently to the bedroom, where Gerhardt had furnished her with a separate bed. Gradually, the boys' fear subsided as they grew accustomed to Deborah's occasional violent outbursts, which never were directed at them. She somehow managed to perform all the household chores, preparing meals, washing everyone's clothes, ironing, and keeping the house clean—though she neglected her own appearance and was generally unkempt. But at least she did what was required of a mother and a wife—except for engaging in sex, of course, which Gerhardt did not seek. So he tolerated her condition and kept her on the farm rather than have her committed. Then too, unlike Minerva, she was his wife.

For the boys, it was a grim and dismal existence. They received no mothering, and their father was a tough, brusque man who offered little warmth. After the eighth grade, Milton had left the country school a few miles away and entered the Reformed Church Academy in Oatston, the area's high school for boys. He studied Latin and Greek, Chaucer and Shakespeare, algebra and geometry, American history and the history of western civilization. Waymon joined him there two years later.

One Saturday morning in spring, after Milton and Waymon had finished the farm chores and were washing up for breakfast, Gerhardt entered the house.

"Boys," he yelled, "come along." His usually stony face registered concern, even alarm. He turned the crank on the Model T, and it coughed and shook and settled into a rough tappa-tappa-tappa-tappa idle. They drove off down the dirt road, Gerhardt wrestling with the steering wheel as he negotiated the deep, muddy ruts produced by rains that fell frequently this time of year. In late fall, the ruts would freeze and glisten with frost in the early mornings, resembling silvery railroad tracks mangled after a train wreck.

Gerhardt told them something bad had happened at the Bernie Waubemas. Waubema, who operated an eighty-acre farm four miles to the southwest, was a squat man of forty-one years whose gentle, easy-going manner belied a shrewd business sense. He owned the threshing machine that eight of the farmers in the area rented each summer to harvest their oat crops. Another neighbor had driven by the Rutgers farm and told Gerhardt he'd heard the sheriff was at the Waubemas' place, and there was a big commotion. He thought it involved Mrs. Waubema, but wasn't sure.

As Gerhardt and the boys pulled up at the long driveway leading back to the Waubema farm, they saw several of the black Model T's, just like their own because that was the car common folks owned, if they owned one at all. One of the cars had "Sioux County Sheriff" in big red letters emblazoned on the driver's side and the rear. Gerhardt pulled his car up behind the others, and they all got out. After stopping to look for a moment, they advancing slowly and warily to where several area farmers and the sheriff were gathered in a circle. The group surrounded an open, narrow well, peering over the edge. Three of them—hefty men—held a thick rope in large, gnarled hands.

"I've got 'er!" came a hollow, urgently strained voice from below. "Pull me up!"

The three men bent down, their broad backs arched, gripped the rope lower, and gave a mighty upward thrust. The two in the rear held the rope stationary while the one in front reached down for another grip, which the other two duplicated, one after the other. They repeated the maneuver about a dozen times until a man's rubber-encased feet came into view, then the man, wearing a rubber suit. The diver's hands grasped the ankles of a woman, and the others in the circle grasped him and the woman, laying her limp body on the ground. Her dress and matted hair were soaked and her face was ashen, the mouth agape and the open eyes staring crazily at nothing. Gerhardt and the boys saw that it was Emma Waubema.

Waymon spun around and covered his face. Gerhardt's jaw dropped, and Milton stumbled backward. Someone fifteen feet to their left moved, and they turned to see Gordie Waubema—at age sixteen, a year ahead of Milton at the academy—begin to collapse, his face frozen in shock. His father, Bernie, caught him and led him staggering half-consciously into the house. The men stood silently for a few moments, staring at the body. Then the sheriff's deputy asked them to carry the body into the house, saying he would summon a hearse.

Gerhardt told the boys to go and wait in the car. He approached the young, slim deputy and asked if he knew how Emma Waubema could have removed the thick oak well cover, which had been bolted at angles into the concrete sides of the unused well. A strong, voluptuously shaped woman of five feet seven inches, she nonetheless would not have had the strength to accomplish the feat, even with tools, and none was found. The deputy said Bernie had reported finding the well open after he woke at five a.m. He'd seen that Emma was not in the house and gone outside to check, almost stumbling into the well himself because of the kerosene lantern's limited illumination. He'd roused Gordie and, telling him only that his mother was missing, had driven with him to the sheriff's sub-office in Millersville. The deputy said he would have to investigate.

Two weeks later, the banner headline in the weekly *Millersville Bulletin* read, "Well Victim Mystery Solved." A young, muscular, handsome blacksmith in Millersville, one of three in the town, had admitted having sexual intercourse with Emma Waubema after he had finished shoeing Bernie's team of horses, while Bernie and Gordie were away helping a neighbor harvest the first cutting of alfalfa hay. He had come to the house to be paid, and Mrs. Waubema had greeted him wearing only a corset and brassiere. After they had made love, she'd asked him to break open the well cover, telling him her husband was going to have the well filled with dirt. The deputy surmised that she replaced the cover before her husband and son returned so they wouldn't notice it was unbolted. She arose during the night, removed it, and plunged headfirst down the well.

For months after the Waubema incident, Milton had a frequent nightmare. He would be waiting beside the well, and when the diver emerged with the woman, his mother's face would appear, smiling wanly. He would waken and sob silently until sleep overcame him.

CHAPTER 7

In the fall, classes resumed at the academy. Milton excelled in most of his courses, but was only average in geometry. Waymon was a whiz at geometry and okay in other subjects, but was chiefly interested in sports. He successfully begged Gerhardt to let him play on the academy football squad and, when spring arrived, to try out for shortstop on the baseball team. It was a perfect position considering his short stature and quick feet. Milton enjoyed playing catch with Waymon on summer evenings, but was too immersed in his studies and extra-curricular reading to join the team. For that reason, his father regarded him more seriously and decided to send him to college to become a minister, ignoring Waymon's future.

Gerhardt determined that Milton would attend tiny Thessalonika College, two-hundred-fifty miles away in the Dutch town of Pliny in central Iowa. Thessalonika was affiliated with the Dutch Reformed Church and maintained high scholastic standards as a liberal arts school with about two-hundred-fifty students. Most of them were from Pliny, Oatston, and other little Dutch communities in Wisconsin, Michigan, and New York.

Despite its Calvinistic theological orientation, Thessalonika did not restrict its curriculum to courses that were in line with a strictly literal interpretation of the Bible. If Gerhardt had known this, he might not have been so willing to have his son enrolled there. Sure, studies in the Old Testament and the New Testament were required, along with Latin and Greek. But Milton also studied Nietzsche, Schopenhauer, Spinoza, and Darwin—thinkers whose views were much out of synch with Christian dogma. He had never encountered such ideas nor had the opportunity to question the beliefs that the church had fed him from his birth. Now Milton's eyes were opening. Was this whole matter of creation nonsense?

Did those biblical miracles really happen? Was Christ really born of a virgin? Was he really divine—did he really rise from the dead and ascend into heaven? Had he, Milton, been brain-washed all his life?

Miriam worked in a women's clothing store that Milton passed on the way from his room in town to the campus. In the middle of his freshman year, after trading smiles and hand-waves for several months, he finally approached her, then began seeing her regularly. Like virtually everyone else in Pliny, she was Dutch, and was a member of the Christian Reformed Church.

After a while, he began voicing his doubts about biblical teachings to her.

"I just can't accept these ideas in the Bible anymore, Miriam," he told her fervently. "That story about Adam and Eve—it's baloney. An English scientist named Charles Darwin showed that humans weren't created just like that. They evolved from lower forms of life over millions of years. And some of the most brilliant minds in history make strong arguments against the existence of God, not to mention the virgin birth of Christ and his resurrection from the dead."

Miriam was taken aback by what he said, but at first she just listened without commenting. By the time Milton was nearing the end of his junior year, his convictions had been seriously eroded, and he was beginning to wonder whether he could enroll in the seminary after his senior year, as his father had planned. Miriam was becoming alarmed. There was no way she could marry anyone but a Christian—a Protestant one. She began to remonstrate him, insisting that the Bible was right and that it was a sin to question its authority. Did he not want to be saved? Did he want to suffer eternal damnation along with all the other unbelievers?

Milton knew that his relationship with Miriam depended on his faith. At this point, he could do without the latter, but not the former. Miriam was a rock that would never change. She was, as Shakespeare put it, the star to his wandering bark, a steady compass that he longed for after a childhood filled with vicissitude. He loved the weekend visits to her house on Main Street, where Miriam's older sisters would flirt with him. At the end of the Saturday night meal, her father, a carpenter who had immigrated from Holland at age twenty, would deliver an eloquent, prolonged prayer, perversely delaying the two lovebirds' plans to get away and be alone together. But Milton so admired him that he didn't mind.

So Milton decided to refrain from raising the subject with Miriam, and just keep the faith. Reluctantly, he told Tris Vanderwerf, his best friend and a brilliant student, of his decision. Tris was a lean fellow of less than average height, with shallow cheeks, a thin, somewhat long nose, large eyes, and a big curl of hair just above his forehead. A lover of history and literature, with a huge vocabulary, he had nothing but disdain for all religion and especially Christianity, which he'd been force-fed since birth. In his early teens, he confided to Milton, his mother had gone off the deep end. She constantly washed herself, spouted Bible verses, stayed up all night reading the Bible, and hardly ate, losing weight almost to the point of starvation. After she was committed to an institution, Tris had stopped going to church with his dad and siblings. He refused to close his eyes when grace was said at the dinner table, mocking the ritual as "talking to the plates." At Thessalonika, he was fond of quoting Mark Twain's sardonic condemnation of piety, "Give me heaven for climate and hell for company." It was a flouting of the faith that made Milton both admire his friend for his daring honesty and wince at its brazenness.

Tris was disappointed that Milton had let romance dictate his direction in religion, leaving himself as the only heretic on campus, but only kidded him with predictions of a henpecked future. Their friendship remained strong, but they avoided religious discussion. Milton knew, however, that he could not enter the ministry, and decided to become a history teacher. Just before graduation, he applied for an opening at a tiny nearby town, only to discover that more than nine-hundred others had applied. It was 1932, and the Depression was in full swing. Milton and Miriam had planned to marry once he landed a teaching job, but that seemed out of the question. Milton said he would have to return to his father's farm. Miriam wanted to get married, anyway. Milton protested that farming was no life for someone who was unaccustomed to it, and doubly difficult under these circumstances, with a deranged woman occupying the household. But Miriam was not about to let her intelligent, handsome beau get away, and insisted on moving to the farm with him. Immediately after graduation, they packed Milton's clothes and Miriam's few belongings into the old Model A Ford that his father had bought him at the start of his sophomore year and drove to Oatston. Three days later, they were married in a ceremony attended only by Milton's family, the trip being too far for Miriam's parents or siblings to undertake on their meager incomes.

CHAPTER 8

Had Miriam visited her husband's home before they were married, she might not have been so bent on marrying him, since it meant living there. Milton had told her about his stepmother, of course, but even Milton didn't know how Deborah would react to a strange woman in her house. Miriam was frightened by the woman's baleful looks when they were alone. Deborah would never speak directly to Miriam, looking away as she muttered responses to Miriam's attempts at conversation while they worked together in the kitchen. Some days were okay, but on other days, Deborah would cackle nonsensically, and Miriam would get the shivers. Gradually, however, Miriam had become more comfortable around her.

Four years later, late on a weekday afternoon, she erupted in anger when she cut her finger while the two peeled potatoes for the evening meal. They stood side by side at the square, rough-hewn, wooden preparation table in the center of the large kitchen, their backs to a table against the wall a few feet away that was used for breakfast and, usually, lunch. Deborah threw the paring knife on the table, sprang back several feet to the paint-chipped, off-white cabinet adjoining the sink, and grabbed a butcher knife from a drawer soiled with fingerprints. She raised it threateningly and laughed hideously at Miriam, who was standing nearest the door to the combined dining room and living room, into which she fled. The spartan living room, with its worn lavender couch, rocking chair, and wing chair resting on a frayed blue-gray carpet, offered little protection for Miriam. Just around the corner from the kitchen, however, was the dining room table, a sturdy mahogany rectangle with a tarnished finish partly hidden by a rust-colored center cloth. Six hard-backed chairs were positioned on the ends and either side. Miriam ran to the far end and grabbed the posts of the chair as Deborah entered and stood momentarily at the other end, her face witchlike, eyes blazing crazily.

Suddenly Deborah sprang, knife raised, running around the table in pursuit, a terrified Miriam managing to stay ahead of her. Deborah switched directions repeatedly, but the younger Miriam was able to out-maneuver her. The cat-and-mouse chase continued for several minutes until the sound of the screen door opening came from the entryway outside the kitchen. Deborah quickly returned to the kitchen and resumed peeling potatoes. Gerhardt had come in from the barn to deposit his straw hat. It got in the way when he sat down to milk the cows toward day's end, and was no longer needed as a shield from the blistering sun. He walked through the kitchen door and, sensing something was amiss, stood momentarily. Speaking in Dutch, he asked Deborah if anything were wrong. She muttered that she had cut her finger, but it was okay. Gerhardt got a glimpse of Miriam in the dining room and figured she was setting the table. Without saying anything to her he left the house. Miriam remained in the dining room, too afraid to get near Deborah, until the men came in from their chores.

She said nothing about the incident until she and Milton were alone that evening.

"That's it," he said. "We've got to get out of here. This can't continue. I'm not going to have you living like this anymore. Before it was just hard work, but now it's gotten dangerous." Miriam didn't protest. She, too, had had it.

The two began talking in the evenings, as they lay in bed before going to sleep, about what kind of job Milton might be able to land, given his education. On weekends, they bought the *Sioux City Journal* and the *Des Moines Register*, and scoured the classifieds for jobs. But the Depression was still in full sway, and what few jobs were available offered such low wages that the two would scarcely have been able to survive.

Two months later, as the two were readying for bed one night, Miriam told Milton there was something important she had to tell him.

"Uh-oh," said Milton, guessing what it was.

Miriam smiled and said, "That's right." Her smile metamorphosed quickly into a frown, and she said, "But Milton, I can't have the baby here. I wouldn't feel safe leaving the baby alone for even a few minutes."

"I know," said Milton. "We have to do something." But they were at a loss what to do. Milton discussed the matter with his father, telling him about the incident with the knife and insisting that Miriam could not be left alone with Deborah for more than short periods. Gerhardt agreed, and he and Milton arranged to have Gart or Frances, Milton's much younger step-siblings, in the house when no one but Deborah and Miriam was around. Of course, when the two children were in school, either Gerhardt or Milton would have to stay close by.

Miriam gave birth to Kevin, and two months later Gerhardt announced that a visitor was coming to the farm. Milton's Aunt Georgianna, sister of Jeanette (Milton's mother), was driving from Lorraine, Ohio, to stay for a few days. Georgianna was something of an outcast in the family. She was a medical doctor who had gone to Kentucky as a missionary, full of zeal for ministering physically and spiritually to impoverished heathens in the Appalachian region. She returned seven years later, a disillusioned woman who had abandoned the faith. She had come to realize that most of these poor, plain folks embraced the true spirit of Christianity more than did the Christians in the community where she had grown up. There was greater interdependence among them, with less stress on material gain. Theirs was a socialistic society whose philosophy of sharing and mutual nurturing was foreign to her background. She had been indoctrinated in the aggressive independence of capitalism espoused by the Protestant Calvinism of a God-fearing community and by the Dutch seminary where she had studied for a divinity degree before entering medical school.

On the recommendation of a friend from her seminary days who likewise had renounced Christianity, Georgianna had left the church and married a German immigrant. Fritz Scharf was an intellectual who was employed as a mechanical engineer. He also operated a small farm that resembled a commune, practicing European agricultural methods. During an extended coffee break on that Saturday afternoon, Miriam confided to Georgianna the dilemma she and Milton faced. Georgianna said Mr. Scharf was looking for a good hired hand to help with the farm work, and suggested he and Milton would have much in common. Miriam asked Georgianna to talk to Milton, and that night the three stayed up late discussing the possibility of a new life for Milton and Miriam. All agreed the environment would be far more favorable for raising a child.

Georgianna returned by train two days later to Ohio. Two days after that, the phone on the kitchen wall rang—Gerhardt's party-line code was two longs and a short. It was Georgianna, who said Fritz Sharf wanted to talk to Milton.

"Ya, Mil-tun, gut eefning," Scharf said in his guttural German accent. "I vould luf to haf you und your vunderful vife moof to Lorraine und haf you manach za farm. Vee haf a larch room vare za sree uf you can stay." The next day, Milton called back and said they could be there in a week.

European farms were considerably smaller than those in the United States, and the farming methods were antiquated. The crops were raised in a sort of large-scale gardening fashion. Scharf's farm consisted of only fifteen acres. The principal difference in modus operandi involved fertilization. In this country, manure spreaders were used to cover large tracts with the dung of livestock. Scharf taught Milton how to make compost, a mixture of dung and dead plant material left from harvests. This was placed in holes at intervals in the fields where the crops were planted.

It was hard work, and life for Miriam was no easier. She was given the responsibility for maintaining the Scharf household, which included Fritz, Georgianna, and Carly, their somewhat retarded, nine-year-old son, who was placed under Miriam's care. She was charged with all the laundry, cleaning the large house, and cooking for the Scharfs and her own family, which included the baby Kevin.

In the evenings, after Miriam had cleaned up following supper—which she, of course, had prepared—she and Milton were required to join Fritz, Georgianna, and invited guests in the library for intellectual discussions. Miriam comprehended not a whit of what was said and had to force herself to keep from nodding off. Milton, though comprehending and eminently capable of contributing to the conversations, found them stilted and stuffy, and became involved only when called upon.

Milton had kept up a correspondence with a college friend, Chad Wissink, who had entered the seminary and been ordained a minister in the Dutch Reformed Church. His first appointment was at a church in Muskego, Michigan, a small-to-medium-sized industrial city on the shores of Lake Michigan with a population consisting mainly of the Dutch. Milton told his friend about the adverse conditions at the Scharf farm, and the Rev. Wissink suggested he move the family to Muskego. Jobs were not as scarce as elsewhere and they likely would find support among folks who shared their ethnic background. Wissink would check into the job situation and report back.

Ten days later, he wrote Milton that a local hardware store was looking for someone who had worked with his hands and was familiar with tools. Milton's predilection was academia, but he certainly had plenty of experience getting his hands dirty, and he called the owner. They chatted for ten minutes, and Milton was hired.

CHAPTER 9

Milton and Miriam found an apartment above a barber shop, and Milton learned the hardware business quickly, diving into his new job with enthusiasm. On Saturdays, he worked from eight a.m. to nine p.m., constantly tending to customers, walking throughout the store the entire day to retrieve wares from shelves or the rear storage area. Life on a northwest Iowa farm had been anything but soft, and Milton could take a lot of physical punishment, but those Saturdays so exhausted him that he collapsed onto the bed without even taking his clothes off. By Sunday morning, he had recovered after an extra-long night of sleep, and he, Miriam, and Kevin were off to church. Before attending worship services at the Unity Reformed Church less than a mile from their home, they motored to a little white schoolhouse near a lake outside Muskego, where Unity members converged to hold Sunday school classes for the poor rural folks.

Milton and Miriam were warmly welcomed into the church, and they soon developed a cadre of friends. Their social life blossomed, reaching a crescendo when they spent most evenings in the company of their friends, either at their homes or at church events.

It was the best of times for them, but it also was the worst. They began to argue, and the family atmosphere was full of strife. Bickering graduated into shouting matches and, finally, threats of violence. While never complaining about his job status, Milton was frustrated. He possessed a high degree of intelligence and a natural curiosity about every aspect of life, from baseball to botany. His passion was the world of knowledge and ideas. Hardware was hardly a challenge for his probing mind, though he worked to learn the details of the business. When he came home from work, he wanted to retreat into the newspaper, magazines, and books. Miriam had been tending all day to the loneliness and drudgery of household work, which was exacerbated by the fractious duties of minding three small children: Britt, a roiling cauldron of energy who was born a year after their arrival in Muskego; Dale, born less than four years after Britt; and Kevin. She longed for companionship and attention, and had a streak of stubborn determination that refused to let Milton disengage himself from her and escape into the private world of thought. Her persistence turned into nagging, and tempers flared.

The worst incident occurred late on a Sunday afternoon. Britt, Kevin, and one-year-old Dale were in the combination living and dining room, playing together, when their parents began arguing in the kitchen over the family's finances. The disagreement escalated into an imbroglio, with Milton and Miriam throwing all kinds of accusations at each other in awfully loud and angry tones. Finally, Milton pulled a butcher knife from the utensil drawer and, bending toward Miriam, pointed it at her.

"I'll do it," he yelled at her. "I'll do it." His face was red, the expression revealing deep, intense hurt more than anger, and his eyes bulged crazily.

"Go ahead," said Miriam, crying but unflinching. "Let's get it over with. My life is miserable anyway." Later, Britt realized what a bluff his dad was—he never had as much as shoved or slapped his wife—and understood that he never would have stabbed her. But at the time, the threats seemed authentic, and he was terrorized. He and his brothers had stopped playing and sat side-by-side at the mahogany dining room table, facing toward the kitchen, where only a half wall allowed them a direct view of the action. They began crying, and Britt and Kevin begged their parents to kiss and make up. They'd seen it happen all too often, and knew the routine, though it had never reached this point—the point of a knife. "Come on, kiss and make up," a sobbing Britt implored.

"See what you've done," Miriam said.

Chastened, Milton lay the knife on the counter and turned toward his children, his face transformed to near-shock, mirroring his realization of the enormity of his deed. "What do you want me to do?" he asked in an innocent tone. He knew what they wanted, and now he had the same desire—not just to placate his children, but because he was feeling remorse. But his pride prevented him from voluntarily showing it, and the kids' supplication enabled him to express his feelings without seeming to admit to them. "Kiss and make up," the three boys pleaded, almost in canonical fashion.

Milton reached out to his wife and kissed her quickly on the lips. "Come on," Britt insisted. "That's not enough."

"Well what do you want?" It was Miriam's turn to play innocent. "Kiss Dad," said Britt. Milton embraced his wife and they lingered in a hug, then began kissing each other tenderly, and the fight was over.

Britt was greatly relieved, but knew the peace was only temporary, for something else would set them off sooner or later.

Milton wasn't the only one who felt the brunt of Miriam's insistent ways. Britt chafed under her domineering style of parenting, which she had unwittingly assumed from her father—in the same way, but not nearly so severe, that children whose parents have physically abused them tend to be physically abusive as adults. Garrett Vanderborg had come to America and made his way to Thessalonika, where about two thousand other immigrants from Holland had formed a community in the midst of the rich Iowa farm country. He was a hard-working, no-nonsense man who had never strayed from his strict upbringing. Yet he had his hands full in Mildred, whom he met at the same church they attended, the Third Christian Reformed Church. She was a mischievous young lass, with a devilish twinkle in her eye and an almost omnipresent sly grin playing on her lips. He could not resist her wiles, and after six months of dating her, succumbed to his overwhelming physical temptations and impregnated her. They quickly married, and the child was stillborn. Devastated, they determined to have another, and a succession of eight children followed, close upon the heels of each other.

Miriam was the second to the youngest, Donnie. One summer day when she was thirteen and Donnie was eleven, she heard him screaming outside while helping her mother clean the house. It had rained the night before and Garrett was at home, waiting for the sun to dry the wood at a house he was building. He and Mildred hurried to the front door and saw Donnie lying in the street, blood running from his mouth down his chin. An unoccupied car was stopped a few yards ahead of him. "Go get a doctor!" shouted a man, presumably the driver of the car, as he leaned over Donnie.

The front right wheel of the car had run over the boy's midsection when he slipped and fell, trying to stop after chasing a ball into the street, and the rear wheel ran over him at the pelvis. He had been critically injured internally.

Garrett, his face ashen, walked swiftly and resolutely—he didn't run—to his son. Cradling him gently in his arms, he carried the groaning boy into the house and lay him on the couch.

Donnie began to cry and begged, "Am I going to die? Please don't let me die." "Hush!" his father commanded. "Of course you're not going to die, and I won't put up with any more of this whimpering." His voice was hard and tough, but inside, he was hurting more than his son, in a different way. Garrett Vanderborg was a strict disciplinarian who had a thick shell around a soft heart. He rarely used corporal punishment on his children, even the five boys. But he was a serious man with little disposition for humor. Mildred was the opposite, full of impish fun, and the two were a good balance for each other. All eight of the children had inherited their mother's slyly comic nature, and Miriam loved to laugh and have fun as much as any of them.

Today, Garrett was the one whom the children leaned on. In the midst of his misery, he was rock solid with nary a crack in his composure. All wondered if Donnie were going to die, but Garrett's mien filled them with confidence. He had to be this way—like Canio in *I Pagliacci*, who entertained though his heart was breaking. To let his grief show, to lose control of his emotions, would leave his family without a leader, he felt, though he did not understand this consciously. For Donnie, especially, he had to conceal his fear and anguish, or the boy would believe he'd been mortally injured. Which he had. After a little more than four hours, the doctor whispered in Garrett's ear that it was almost over. Only then did Garrett grip his son's hand and squeeze while the boy began convulsing, then went limp and stopped breathing.

Garrett, stone-faced, walked heavily to the back porch. He stared hard toward the bright northern sky as if incredulous at the God to whom he had always paid devout homage, and quietly succumbed to his grief as tears slid slowly down his cheeks. He sat on the hard, spindle-backed wood chair positioned against the stucco wall and breathed hard. Then he leaned his elbows on his thighs, buried his head in his hands and sobbed almost soundlessly, his torso heaving in spasms.

But Miriam was inside the house and didn't see this. She only knew the stern, rock-hard man who showed no emotion, and hardly ever showed his love for his children. In this aspect of his personality, he and Mildred were like two strands of the same chromosome. While she was whimsical and mischievous, she was never soft and emotional. Miriam longed for the soft touch, the caress, the kind word—but never got it. Never having received it, she never learned how to give it.

Britt was a live wire at birth. As a baby, he would grasp the spindles of the headboard and shake the bed. While sitting in his high chair, he often rocked so hard that the chair would teeter on two legs, and his parents continually feared that he would tip it over and crack his head open on the floor.

For Christmas, five weeks before his fourth birthday, Milton and Miriam bought him a basketball. Two days later, Britt sat in the doorway between the kitchen and living room with the ball between his legs and poked the air pump needle through the air hole to deflate it. He then took the misshapen piece of rubber to the outhouse in the backyard and dropped it down one of the three holes. He'd felt out of sorts when Miriam ordered him to stop taking books out of the bookcase. It was one of numerous incidents during those formative years in which he experienced frustration and anger. Usually it involved his mother, who frequently barked at him for this or that offense, although he seldom felt his actions warranted her sniping.

The Rutgers' rented house was a small but attractive white frame building, with several concrete steps leading to the front door. Railroad tracks ran a half-block behind it.

It was a neighborhood with families of modest means. The street was unpaved, and an oil truck occasionally would spread the black goo to contain the dust. Miriam ranted against the city for this because the oil stuck to her children's shoes and they tracked it into the house. A vacant, sandy field with sandspurs was at one end. A boy named Davey, about Britt's age, lived with his mother in the fourth house from the end. It was rumored that whenever he uttered a swear word, she would force him to hold a small bar of soap in his mouth until it had melted. One summer afternoon, Britt encountered Davey on the sidewalk leading to his beige, wood frame house with a wide porch. His cheeks were bulging as viscous, milky liquid dripped out the sides, and his face was pinched with anguish at the torture, which brought tears streaming from his eyes. Davey's mother sat rocking on a chair on the porch, watching her son to make sure he didn't spit the soap out, one corner of her mouth twisted in a demented smile.

The other end of the block was more inviting, with oaks and elms shading pretty bungalows with manicured lawns. In one of these houses lived the Young family, which included two teenage boys. Mr. and Mrs. Young were devout evangelical Christians. Mr. Young was a short, nice-looking man with neatly parted, dark hair and a ready smile that reflected a genuinely kind and friendly disposition. He drove a city bus.

The Young youths gained a reputation for rowdiness. Late afternoon on a summer day, Britt was pulling his little red wagon up the sidewalk near the Youngs' home when he came upon a police car parked in front. Mrs. Young, a slender, pretty brunette with hair that cascaded past her neck and part-way down her back, had both hands around the right wrist of one of her teenage sons. She was trying to pull him away from the police car, while the officer, seated in the car, pulled on the other arm, attempting to get him through the open door. The boy in the middle was a human rope in a tug-of-war contest. Mrs. Young pleaded with the policeman to let her son go—to no avail. The lawman threatened to call for backups and have her, too, arrested and taken to jail. She finally relented, weeping softly as the police car drove away with her handcuffed son inside.

Civility took a back seat in this neighborhood as emotions were vented with little restraint and primal instincts occasionally surfaced. Toward dusk one spring day, Britt walked aimlessly back toward the house from the seedy end of the block and came upon a small group of persons in their teens and early twenties gathered in a semicircle in the street. A fellow raised a two-by-four above his head and came crashing down with it. Arriving at the edge of the circle in front of his house, Britt saw the victim—a large turtle, blood seeping through cracks in its crushed shell. The young man lifted the thick board again and smashed the helpless reptile, while the others watched, transfixed, as the gentle, helpless reptile lay dying. Savagery, a composite of hatred and fear, was etched on the stony faces of these witnesses to the execution of a foreign creature that had dared invade their neighborhood.

Years later, when Britt was eleven, he bought a BB gun with money saved from his newspaper route and shot, at close range, sparrows that roosted in a row of pine trees on the edge of the family's property in Mayfield, Iowa. He felt nothing as blood leaked out of the birds and they dropped to the ground, mortally wounded. As he grew older, the remembrance, which filled him with remorse, was always paired with the spectacle of the turtle killing and the sadistic enjoyment of the onlookers.

On the west side of the Rutgers lived Heinie and Hilda Vanderstelt and their five-year-old son Gary. Heinie was a small, unobtrusive, middle-aged man with a full head of dark hair and a mustache. He operated an automobile service station. Hilda was taller and of considerable girth. Nonetheless, Hilda would complain to Miriam during occasional daytime visits that Heinie abused her, verbally and physically. One evening she came and asked Milton to intervene. He persuaded Heinie to lay down his baseball bat and stop drinking for the night.

To the east of the Rutgerses was a large, two-story house coated with light-brown shingles, owned by the Schaeffers. Mr. Schaeffer was a mild-spoken, friendly man in his early forties. In the left rear corner of the Schaeffer property was a square, shack-like cottage that Schaeffer rented to a man in his early thirties with sandy hair and sharp facial features. Britt walked outside to the yard on the Shaeffer side one crisp day in autumn and stopped a dozen feet from Mr. Schaeffer standing outside the screen door of the shack. Inside the door was the renter, clad in a pants and white undershirt, holding a shotgun pointed at Mr. Schaeffer, who leaned forward fearlessly, his light-brown hair slicked back.

"Get away from me or I'll blow your head off," the renter yelled at Mr. Schaeffer. He was a man of soft facial contours and average height and build.

"I'm not goin' anywhere until you hand me at least one month's rent," Mr. Schaeffer retorted. "And I'll give you two weeks to get the other two months you owe. You needta stop drinkin' and get a job, 'cause if you don't, I'm gonna throw you outta here."

The man said he didn't have any money but would have enough for one month's rent in three days.

"Okay, but if you don't, I'm gonna throw you out on the street," Mr. Schaeffer warned, and walked away.

The Rutgers' refuge from the despair they witnessed all around them—and experienced in their own lives—was the church and their friends, which were intertwined. Every Sunday morning, without exception, they attended the Unity Reformed Church, which had a Dutch congregation and Calvinist theology that they felt comfortable with. The vast majority of people don't choose a particular religion, or to be religious in any way, Britt would later come to understand. They don't evaluate the validity or worthiness of any persuasion, but simply continue, as adults, in the same religion in which they were reared. The security of familiarity rules.

With World War II in progress, school teachers were having their charges make little model Jeeps and Red Cross ambulances, and paint them in the Army khaki. In his kindergarten class, Britt had finished putting a Jeep together and was painting it, dipping a small brush into a half-pint can. Holding the brush, he turned momentarily to look at what another pupil was doing, then returned to his task, swinging his right arm with the brush into the can and knocking it over, the paint spilling onto the table. Immediately, Miss Abbott—a plain-looking woman in her late thirties who always wore a gray dress—was by his side. He instinctively shrank, fearing a tongue-lashing. Instead, she looked down with a soft smile and gently reassured him that it was all right, that everybody made mistakes and they would just clean it up. It was a reaction he'd never experienced before, and he loved her forever after.

CHAPTER 10

Milton Rutgers was wearying of the social whirl with church friends. Whenever he and Miriam visited, Milton was gregarious and ebullient. He was a hypnotizing, dramatic raconteur as he narrated humorous incidents that occurred at the hardware store. Discussing politics was his favorite pastime, and his pervasive knowledge of issues and events left him with little competition as the other participants were rendered mostly mute while he held sway with exuberant polemics.

Nonetheless, he increasingly resisted Miriam's attempts at socializing. He longed for a more sedentary life in which he could read and wax introspective. And after seven years, he was homesick for the verdant pastures of Iowa, for its rolling hills and flat fields laden with geometrical rows of cornstalks bedecked with drooping, deep-green leaves.

Miriam, however, had no hankering to depart from their friends, who provided her with the communication that she lacked with the cerebral Milton. One thing she absolutely would not do was go back to living on a farm. Finally, she agreed that it would be nice to live in central Iowa and see her mother and siblings on a regular basis. However, she most certainly would not spend much time with Milton's clan in northwest Iowa. They would have to live somewhere around her family.

That was no problem, Milton said, and he placed a call to the Iowa State Employment Service in Mayfield, a central Iowa city that was small but had a lot of manufacturing. It was only fourteen miles from Pliny. Soon, he received a letter notifying him of a job with a company that made farm implements. Miriam suggested that they live temporarily with her mother Mildred in her three-story home, which had spare bedrooms.

Miriam's father, Garrett, had died a few years earlier, and Mildred would love the company.

In August 1944, the Rutgerses boarded a Greyhound bus that would take them the five-hundred-odd miles to Pliny.

The stucco-covered house was accessible via several wide, deep concrete steps that led from a sidewalk paralleling the main street into town. It was much larger than the one in Michigan because of its height and depth. A living room with an old Oriental rug, a sofa, and two rocking chairs looked out onto the street through three large windows. Back of it was a bedroom, and back of that the dining room. Farthest back was the kitchen, which had a hand-powered water pump attached to the sink. A roofed porch ran the width of the house in the rear. A narrow staircase led at an ultrasteep, sixty-degree angle to the second floor, which had three more bedrooms. An even steeper, winding staircase reached to the attic.

Three weeks after the Rutgerses had arrived, Britt was entering the first grade at Thessalonica Elementary School. On the first day, his cousin Gail, two years older, greeted him with a big smile on the school yard. In the two months that he spent there, that was his only pleasant experience. His worst was the time when he had climbed the stairs to the top of the slide and was about to sit for the ride down. Out of nowhere, he felt a shove and saw the slide's supporting iron pole go by in a blur, then was lying on the ground, gasping to recover the wind that was knocked out of him. In class, he sat in a semicircle with the other pupils and read aloud about Jack and Jill and their dog Spot.

Each weekday morning, Milton was picked up in front of Mildred's house by a car with two other passengers for a fourteen-mile ride into Mayfield, where they all worked in the small factories.

Britt, who was easily bored, found this new living situation mildly exhilarating. His grandmother Mildred often wore a perplexing smile, much like the Mona Lisa's except that it suggested she was on the verge of doing something mischievous, and Britt continually wondered what she was thinking. Just before her daughter Miriam married Milton and moved away from Pliny, Mildred confessed that she and Garrett had gotten married shortly after their first child, Frederick, was conceived. Garrett and Mildred were on a date one balmy summer evening, riding in a horse-drawn buggy on a dirt road outside Pliny, when Garrett pulled to the side of the dirt road. Their passion grew stronger than their fear of hell and damnation, and they had intercourse. Mildred was midway between her last and upcoming menstrual periods, and they knew of the danger that she would become pregnant. So they shrewdly made plans for a quick wedding in case her next period was not forthcoming. After waiting ten days beyond the normal time, they announced to their parents that they were in love. Fearing they no longer could contain their passion for each other, they drove secretly to Okoosa, sixteen miles to the southeast, and had a justice of the peace marry them. Miriam, Mildred's youngest child, was the only person she revealed her secret to.

Milton had been scanning the jobs section of the *Des Moines Tribune.* He figured work would be more plentiful in the Iowa capitol, only fifty miles to the west, than in a small town. The two months living with Mildred had worked all right so far, but tensions were beginning to emerge. She wanted her house perfectly neat, and Milton, while personally clean, was anything but tidy. Mildred had a catty way of disapproving of his less than fastidious habits.

"Oh, so you like to leave the newspaper lying around on the floor," she said of his penchant for dropping the paper in disarray beside the chair where he'd read it. Her voice was edgy and a little raspy, and she talked through tight, thin lips. After dinner, Milton would dry the dishes that Miriam washed, and Mildred scolded him once: "If you don't wipe them till all the water is gone, they will hold dust."

Milton wanted independence, and Miriam agreed it was time to move. His experience working at a hardware store in Michigan landed him a job at one in downtown Des Moines. Now the question was where to live. He'd had enough of living inside the city, with neighbors causing problems. A real estate agent found them a two-bedroom, two-story house off U.S. Highway 6, a mile outside of Urbanside, a tiny suburb of Des Moines. The neat white house was on a large lot with a garage in back. The nearest neighbors were a similar house a little to the east that was owned by the same landlord and was unoccupied, a farm on the other side of that, and a farm across the road from that farm. For Milton, it was the perfect location—in the country, but close enough to an urban area with its conveniences.

Britt and Kevin attended Urbanside Community School in the small town a mile east of where the Rutgerses lived. Britt finished first and second grades, and did fine in his classes, excelling at reading and writing. He was well-behaved in school, partly because he, like all the pupils, feared Superintendent Rosenberg. The towering, stern-looking man was known for brooking no unruliness. Britt had become quite affected by his parents' religious piety and loved the melodious hymns they sang in church. On a Sunday afternoon, he took the hymnbook from the piano that came with the house and, lying on his parents' bed, softly and earnestly sang to himself *The Old Rugged Cross*. Its sadly beautiful melody and message of hope amid a world of woe tugged at his heartstrings. It was during this time that he decided he wanted to become a missionary when he grew up—a short-lived ambition.

Most often, though, he was a bundle of energy and curiosity, always running about and chattering, and getting in Miriam's hair. But on two occasions over those two years at Urbanside, when he was seven and eight, Britt felt, for no apparent reason, despondent as he lay awake for a short time after going to bed. His mood had metamorphosed, like that of an exuberant drunk who quickly becomes quiet and morose. His ebullience had created an image of independence, and his parents heeded him only when he misbehaved, a child to be tolerated but not taken seriously—unlike the comparatively sedentary, reticent Kevin. But on these random nights, the need for affection came from nowhere and hit him hard, and sucking his thumb did not put him to sleep as usual. His pride would not allow him, however, to ask for attention, so he softly whimpered, just loud enough for his mother to hear him but not loud enough to make her think he wanted to be heard. It worked, and she came to his bedside.

"What's the matter? Why are you crying," she asked quietly, the harshness absent from her voice.

"I don't know, I just feel sad," Britt said softly through his tears.

"Well, there's no need to feel that way." Miriam hesitated, then added huskily, "We love you, so everything is going to be all right." She continued consoling him for a couple of minutes, then brushed his hair back and placed her hand on his cheek in an exceptionally rare expression of physical affection. "Go to sleep now."

Soon Britt was in dreamland.

The Rutgers' dog, Roxie, birthed a litter of pups, which, against Britt's protestations, his parents put up for adoption. One Saturday afternoon, while Milton was working on the tan 1936 Ford, a source of much consternation and an object of considerable cursing, Britt let the pups out of the box on the porch. One was an especially cute specimen that had been promised to a young woman. It managed to crawl into the driveway beside the porch at the moment that Milton had finished the repair work and was driving the car forward in the gravel driveway. Standing at the head of the driveway, near the garage, Britt saw the tragedy about to happen and started to wave his arms at his dad, feeling helpless as if in a dream in which one tries to run or move but can't. Only after the left front wheel of the car had caught the side of the pup's face and Milton heard the tiny yelps did he know what was happening and stop the car. Britt and Milton knelt over the pitifully whining pup, whose little jaw was bloody and obliquely deformed. Milton angrily chastised his son for letting the brood out of the box and said he would have to destroy the pup. He went to the house, emerged with a hammer and took the pathetic, whimpering little animal back of the garage. Britt followed and watched as his dad held the pup with one hand and gave it two heavy thumps on the head with the hammer. The pup went limp and its eyes closed. Milton told Britt to get a shovel from the house, and they buried it.

U.S. Highway 6, a two-lane road, separated the Rutgerses from a one-hundred-sixty-acre farm operated by a childless couple in their middle ages. Roy and Hazel Strain were quiet, gentle, hard-working folks who befriended the Rutgers family and indulged their children. Roy was a somewhat stocky man of a little less than medium height. He had rosy cheeks, sparkling eyes, and a ready smile. He spoke in slow, soft tones and moved at an unhurried pace.

Hazel was of similar disposition, though her eyes, in contrast to the twinkle in Roy's, had a wise and resigned look that stared from beneath drooping eyelids. She was a slender, wiry woman, as tall as Roy with straight, medium-length, graying hair framing a smallish, leathery-skinned face. The Strains sold plucked chickens and fresh eggs to townsfolk who would drive to their farm. Hazel handled this part of their farm business—feeding the chickens, gathering and cleaning the eggs, killing and preparing the chickens. Britt and Dale often accompanied her through the chicken yard in search of a correct-sized bird to fill an order. She had an exceedingly efficient, no-nonsense executional modus operandi, wasting no time with the traditional method of chopping the chicken's head off with a hatchet. Hazel would stalk her prey, then finish it off in one continuous motion, lashing out with a long arm, squeezing her strong, bony fingers around its head and neck, and wringing it in a few ferocious twirls.

Tough as she was, Hazel had a soft heart and was protective of the Rutgers boys. On one of Britt's visits, Roy had hired a man to come with a rifle and shoot a steer and a hog for butchering. Hazel reluctantly allowed

Britt into the graveled farmyard to watch the execution of the steer. The rifleman stood near the fence that corralled the animal, which stood perpendicular to the aimed gun, perhaps one-hundred-fifty feet away. Britt stood fascinated as the rifle cracked and the steer simultaneously slammed to the ground on its side. Moving in an arc through the farmyard, the rifleman positioned himself outside the pig lot, aimed again and fired at a large white hog. The bullet only wounded and enraged the pig, which began running in crazy twists and turns, bawling and snorting with its head lowered, blood streaming down its side. Hazel came running toward Britt, snatching him in her arms. But Britt, oblivious to the danger, was spellbound and kept his gaze on the desperate animal, which by now was charging toward the rifleman. Unflinching, the man steadied the gun and fired, the bullet striking the hog between the eyes as it hurtled to the ground.

The Rutgerses attended a tiny Reformed Church in a low-economic community called Merritt, a few miles east of Urbanside. The small development was named for the Merritt Publishing Company of Des Moines, which operated a dairy farm adjacent to the group of small, prosaic homes connected by gravel roads. The parsonage for the church minister, a two-story white house at the edge of the farm pasture, was a mansion compared to those bungalows. Milton, by virtue of his grounding in Greek and Latin and his one-time plan to enter the ministry, had a rapport with the Rev. Hubrecht. In a conversation after church one Sunday, Milton mentioned that the family might be leaving that area because the landlord of their house was raising the rent. The following Sunday, Rev. Hubrecht made a proposal to Milton: Convert the unused garage back of the parsonage into living quarters and they could stay there for a small rental fee.

A week later, Milton and a handyman he hired were installing studs and plasterboard to form a tiny kitchen, two tiny bedrooms, a small all-purpose room, and a bathroom without a tub or shower. Milton and Miriam painted the walls the next weekend, and installed a thin, cheap, pale-green carpet that Milton had bought at a big discount from the hardware store. The handyman installed the plumbing, a sink, and a wood stove, and Milton had an ice box delivered. The Rutgerses moved in that summer.

Britt was eight-and-a-half years old and Kevin was eleven. In the fall, they rode the school bus four miles to Jansen's Station, a town even smaller than Urbanside. It was time to adjust again, this being Britt's fourth school from kindergarten to third grade. Each new school meant dealing with certain mean kids who didn't cotton to newcomers. His nemesis at Jansen's Station was Meryl, a slow-witted, slow-moving kid with brown eyes, a mop of dark-brown hair, and an olive complexion. Meryl stared at others with a slight smirk and his otherwise expressionless face reflected a paucity of emotion. When he called Britt an egghead, Britt countered that the description fit his brother Dale, whose head was shaped just like an egg, but not him. He felt guilty for cowardly using his younger brother to deflect animosity, but had no hankering to fight Meryl.

Kevin wasn't having any better luck with adjusting to his new classmates. Britt watched helplessly one afternoon as a boy much bigger and older than Kevin bullied him in the school yard. The bully had found a rope lying next to the fire escape and tied Kevin's hands behind him, then shoved him around the yard before wrapping his jacket over his head and pushing him to the ground. This went on for several minutes before the school bus arrived and the bully left. Britt felt badly for his brother and told his parents what had happened, even though Kevin kept silent.

Britt's teacher, Gladys Knight, looked like a Hollywood starlet, beautiful with dark-brown hair that spilled in waves over her shoulders. He was in love with her, and scored big with her in a spelling bee she held one afternoon. All the pupils had missed words and sat down, leaving only Susan, the "brain" in the class, and Britt standing. Miss Knight had gone through all the words in the lesson book and got out the dictionary. Susan missed "despair," spelling it "despare," but the teacher allowed her to continue standing. Britt correctly spelled "cradle" and wondered why Miss Knight had picked such an easy word. Both correctly spelled two more words each—Britt's were "parallel" and "fantasize"—and Miss Knight declared the match a tie. As Britt sauntered out of the classroom at the end of the day, she partly turned toward him from the blackboard that she was cleaning with an eraser and said, "I think I should take you to the national spelling bee in Chicago." Britt glowed all over and told Miriam when he got home. "That's nice," she said. Miss Knight never broached the subject again—and neither did Miriam.

Christmas was the warmest it had been in many years—sixty-eight degrees by two p.m. Kevin was eleven, Britt was almost nine, and Dale was a few days from five. They formed a line and paraded down the gravel road.

Kevin led with the brand-new, shiny, red-and-white Schwinn bicycle that Santa Claus had left him. Britt, who had received a sled, rolled an old car tire. Dale brought up the rear, joyfully beating a drum attached to a strap around his neck in celebration of Santa's largesse toward him.

Summer arrived, and the boys had little to keep them occupied. Now and then they played in the creek that ran under a bridge just up the road. Bored with no outlet for their energies, Britt and Kevin took to feuding with each other and getting in Miriam's way as she struggled to prepare meals, sew clothes for four children, do the six-member family's laundry in a small washing machine, iron the clothes, and mend socks. She lamented her plight to Milton. The two decided to send Kevin and Britt to their Grandpa Gerhardt's farm in the northwestern part of Iowa for the two-and-a-half months remaining in their summer vacation from school.

At seven on a Saturday morning, the family crammed into the 1936 Ford and started on the forty-mile drive to the town of Indium, where Kevin and Britt would board a train bound for Haywaller. Milton shook hands with his sons at the station and Miriam told them to be good. No hugging, no kissing, no touching from her. Two-thirds of the way, in an isolated rural stretch, the train slowed to a crawl as it passed over a spot where the right side of the tracks sagged due to a settling of the limestone bed. Britt thought the train was going to tip over and was scared until the black steward's smile reassured him everything was going to be okay.

At the train station in Haywaller, Kevin and Britt were greeted by their grandfather, Gerhardt Rutgers, and their Uncle Gart, one of the two children Gerhardt bore with Deborah. They drove in Uncle Gart's 1942 blue Chevrolet fifty-odd miles down highways and gravel roads, then turned into a long driveway. At the end of it loomed a big red barn with large white letters that read, G.H. RUTGERS.

The boys were excited by this new venture and eagerly accompanied their granddad and uncle into the fields on the John Deere tractor to check on the clover that had been cut in preparation for baling. With Kevin sitting on the front of the seat between Gart's legs, his uncle taught him how to drive the tractor.

Next morning, a neighbor brought his baler to the farm, and another neighbor came along to help, along with his hired hand. The men baled hay and let the bales drop on the ground. In the afternoon, they went out to pick up the bales in a truck and a wagon pulled by a tractor. Kevin worked on the wagon. Gart asked Britt to drive the twenty-four-foot truck, showing him how to release the clutch to make the vehicle move forward and depress the clutch while pushing the brake pedal with the other foot to stop. After Britt had made a couple of jerky tries, Gart figured he was ready. He let the clutch out and held onto the steering wheel as the truck moved slowly to where two bales lay opposite each other. He stopped to let Gart and another man on the ground heave the bales into the back of the truck.

"Okay, Britt, move ahead," Gart yelled to his nephew. Britt was less successful this time, letting the clutch out too fast so that the truck lurched forward. "God-damn mother-fuckin' shit, what the hell is goin' on here?" yelled the hired hand in the back of the truck, a Sioux Indian. The sudden start had jerked him backward and he cracked his head on the truck's metal wall. Gart ran to Britt and admonished him to let the clutch out gradually.

But most of the time, Kevin and Britt had nothing to do. Gerhardt handed Britt a juvenile book about a cowboy who'd gone to New York City. Britt, who usually was too energized to do anything as sedentary as read, rapidly became deeply absorbed in the tale and finished it in a few days.

Life at their granddad's farm was dismal, for the most part. In the evening, Deborah would go to bed after washing the supper dishes. Gerhardt would sit in the dimly lit, spartan living room, barely furnished with a well-worn gray carpet, a tattered couch, a stuffed chair, and a rocking chair, and read the newspaper or *Collier's* magazine. Gart, who was twenty-five, would go to his room and read books that he never allowed Britt or Kevin to see, always insisting that they were too young and wouldn't be interested. But Britt was never satisfied. He demonstrated his insatiable curiosity two years later when, at a confirmation session for Kevin and Britt at the Rutgers' church in Mayfield, the minister lectured them about the requirement that they have faith in the existence of God. Britt asked what faith meant, and Dr. Davis explained by pointing out that he sat on a chair out of faith it would hold him. (Not satisfied, Britt puzzled over the explanation for a decade until it suddenly hit him that the principle involved wasn't faith, but solid evidence: He'd never seen a chair collapse under someone.) Gart would merely laugh at Britt's inquisitiveness and tell him he'd understand when he grew up.

Kevin and Britt would rise at eight a.m., after Gerhardt and Gart had finished chores, eaten their breakfast, and left to do other farm work. At first, the boys tried to eat the runny eggs and lumpy oatmeal served by Deborah, but gave up after gagging over every breakfast for several days.

Britt kept remembering his dad's story of having dinner as a teenager at the home of a neighbor whose wife served him five runny eggs in a row, each one rotten. It didn't help that Deborah, who had a chronic cold, continually coughed up phlegm, which she didn't bother to deposit in a handkerchief, instead using the sleeves on her long, matronly dress. Kevin managed better than Britt, who ate a bowl of Cheerios. He had two more bowls of Cheerios for dinner and repeated the meal for supper—five bowls of Cheerios each day—cheerily insisting that he loved Cheerios and never revealing the real reason.

During the first ten days or so of their visit, Deborah was virtually mute. Then, during breakfast with Kevin and Britt the only ones present, she began muttering occasionally, always unintelligibly. The boys stopped their conversation—Britt did most of the talking—and looked at each other inquisitively across the kitchen table, but said nothing. "That woman is really strange," Britt told Kevin in the farmyard afterward. Kevin reminded his brother that they'd been apprised of her condition before they came, and they should just ignore her. The muttering increased, and she began making shy, sideways glances at the boys and letting out little giggles, her face brightening. This was something entirely new, and Britt and Kevin were mystified. The giggling increased every day, and Britt just looked at Kevin and shrugged, having no idea what was amusing her. Whenever Gerhardt walked in to check on things, the giggling stopped abruptly and Deborah's face froze into its permanent expression of despair.

Britt became homesick. One evening he told Kevin that he wanted to go home. Kevin said he wasn't happy, either, but would stick it out for the rest of the summer. He declined Britt's request to join him in asking Gerhardt to convey their mutual desire to Milton and Miriam.

"Then I'm going to ask him by myself," Britt said, to which Kevin muttered that he didn't care what his brother did. The next night, Britt went up to his grandfather, who was in his rocking chair reading the newspaper, and said, "Grandpa, I want to go home."

"Ach, what's the matter?" Gerhardt said with uncharacteristic gentleness. "Don't you like it here?"

"There's nothing to do," Britt answered plaintively.

"But we took you out to the fields to cut the hay and pick up the bales. Didn't you like that?"

"That was only two days," Britt protested. "Most of the time we don't have anything to do."

"Does Kevin feel the same way?"

"He said he's bored, too, but he doesn't want to complain."

Gerhardt was silent for a few seconds, then took a deep breath, his big belly bulging further, and said quietly, "All right, I'll call your ma and pa."

At seven a.m. Saturday, three days later, the boys carried their suitcases through the kitchen to the door leading to the utility room and the outside. Deborah was in the kitchen, and mumbled something to Gerhardt, who said, "Ya, they're leaving."

"Oh," she said, her face darkening. Looking pathetically forlorn, she nodded to Britt and said, barely audibly, "Bye."

"G'bye, Grandma," Britt answered, realizing she was awfully sad.

Gart drove the boys to the station at Haywaller, and now it was Gerhardt's turn to look dismal. "You come back again, boys," he said huskily.

But Britt felt no sadness. The three-and-a-half-hour trip didn't seem long to him, and he and Kevin walked off the train at Indium and down the boarding platform toward the station. Milton and Miriam were waiting on the platform, Milton beaming and Miriam wearing a disciplinary look, as if to warn everybody not to be too happy. Milton reached out his hand to shake Kevin's, then Britt's. Miriam stood rigidly and impassively, never touching the sons she had not seen or talked to for six weeks.

(Miriam could show her love for her children only when they were in pain. When Kyra was five, she farted during a Sunday evening service at the UP church in Mayfield, and was embarrassed almost to tears. Miriam wrapped her arms around her daughter and snuggled her lovingly.)

Back home, Milton announced to the boys that he had applied just the day before for a job with the Iowa State Employment Service in Mayfield. At the dinner table that night, he talked about the written test he'd taken. It was awfully difficult, with questions such as who the seventh president of the United States was, and he was sure he had flunked. On the following Monday, Miriam received a phone call from the manager at the Mayfield office, who said Milton had passed with flying colors and they would like him to start in two weeks. Milton had scouted for houses in Mayfield in anticipation of getting the job, and told Miriam he'd found one in a little enclave called Country Club Community, on the outskirts of town. Miriam thought it sounded wonderful. Milton thought the price was reasonable—he had no negotiating skills—and told the owners he'd take it if the job came through. They signed a contingency agreement that would allow the Rutgerses to rent the house until the closing, and Milton obtained a bank-loan guarantee. The family climbed into the Ford after Milton came home from his job at the hardware store the next day, and they drove forty miles to Mayfield.

Country Club Community consisted mostly of shabby, neglected homes lining two sides of a gravel road that led from U.S. Highway 6 and stretched back and around in horseshoe fashion for three-quarters of a mile. The road ended back at the highway a block to the west. Dogs roamed freely and snotty-nosed kids played in unkempt yards. The house Milton had picked was the fifth from the highway on the east side. He pulled the car into the driveway.

"This is not what I expected," Miriam declared, her tone full of contempt. "Country Club Community sounded fancy, but *this* … ." Her face was scrunched in disdain.

"Well, it'll take a little work," said Milton. "I figured we could have dirt hauled to the front yard and build it up so it wouldn't slope, and sow grass. It could look pretty good." Miriam just stared, saying nothing.

"It's all we can afford," Milton protested. "What did you expect, a castle?"

"Of course not, but I had hoped it would be in a better neighborhood."

"Those two houses on both sides aren't bad at all," said Milton. He pointed right to a modest but well-kept house and a yard with a lovely shade tree. On the left, atop a small incline, a comparatively large, fairly attractive two-story white house stood on property that included a spacious backyard with a green lawn. A row of bushes and three trees separated the two properties. At the rear of the proposed Rutgers property, an outhouse belonging to the house on the right stood on a narrow strip of land, just across a wire fence.

"Well, I guess this is the best we can do," Miriam sighed. "But we're really going to have to do some sprucing up."

Two weeks remained before the moving date. The prospect of better times suddenly loomed, with Milton about to take a better-paying job that was, though still far beneath his intellectual capacity, less pedestrian. Indeed, Milton felt it was a big step up, and spoke of it with pride, as if it were a position that held some prestige.

Though she was not pleased with the new house, Miriam saw the move as the beginning of stability in the family's life. They would be living only a mile from a downtown that had a J.C. Penney, a Montgomery Ward, a Thriftway grocery store, and two drugstores. Everything she needed. Britt and Kevin could get newspaper routes to earn money for their needs and contribute to the increasing financial needs of a family whose children were growing older.

It occurred to Miriam that if Britt were going to have a job, he should discard a blatantly childish habit—thumb-sucking. He was nine-and-a-half years old, way beyond the age when it should have stopped. Dale also sucked his thumb at night before going to sleep, but he was five-and-a-half and the abnormality not as pronounced. She mentioned the problem to a friend from church, who said she'd cured her daughter with a nasty-tasting liquid that she found at a drugstore. The woman let Miriam have the partly used bottle and instructed her to apply it to Britt's thumb with the applicator brush.

Miriam told Britt the purpose of the liquid was to kill germs, and he shouldn't taste it until he went to bed. But Britt's curiosity got the better of him, and he inserted his painted left thumb in his mouth that afternoon.

"Aw, that's awful," he yelled, and ran to the bathroom, where he washed the thumb with soap and water. "You tricked me," he said to his mother, feeling hurt. Miriam said nothing, and never painted his thumb again.

CHAPTER 11

At home, Britt's exuberant and willful behavior vexed his parents, with whom he continually fought, to the point where they labeled him "the black sheep" of the family. In school, though, he'd been a well-behaved pupil through the third grade. Britt had never caused any trouble, doing the work required of him and getting decent, sometimes excellent, grades, depending on how he felt about his teacher. His parents never commented to him about his school work.

Four months after he entered the fourth grade at Washington Elementary in Mayfield, the classroom phone rang late one morning while Britt was quietly doing his work at his desk. Miss Rippel answered. She was a good-hearted, middle-aged woman, about five-feet-four, a little chunky, bespectacled. But she was slow in getting her points across and seemed perpetually nonplussed. She spoke a few words on the phone, hung up, and turned to Britt. "You're wanted in the principal's office," she said. Uh-oh, what's this all about? Britt wondered. The principal's office always meant trouble, and he was scared. Miss Verritt, the venerable, slow-moving principal with a permanently reassuring smile, greeted him from behind the office counter. Her salt-and-pepper hair always was tied in a bun and she seemed like a female pope in a long, dowdy dress with purple and brown designs. She looked grave this time as she instructed Britt to come back into her private room. There stood Schools Superintendent B.C. Berg—Ivan the Terrible to children in the Mayfield Public Schools system. His ruddy face, snow-white hair, and royal-blue suit contrasted keenly, making his six-foot-two-inch presence even more imposing. He didn't come around often, but whenever he did, he never smiled. Now his face was even more solemn as he told Britt to sit down. Terror struck Britt's heart.

"Britt, it has come to my attention that you have been unruly in Miss Rippel's class during almost the entire semester," Berg began. "Your behavior is disrupting the class, and we cannot tolerate any more of it." Britt tried to swallow and choked, fully aware that he had continually talked and bothered others in class, and had become nearly uncontrollable. Berg's face softened a bit and he continued, "If you do not become more cooperative, we are going to have to place you in Second Class." Referred to by pupils as "The Twos," it was the class for underperforming pupils. "We don't want to do this," Berg said, "because we feel that you have the potential to do much better if you will apply yourself conscientiously and desist from any further obstreperous activity."

Desist? I can spell that, Britt thought. Have to look it up. What was that other one? He sounded it out in his head: ob-strep-er-ous. Yeah, I think that's it.

"Do you understand?" Berg asked ominously. Not entirely, Britt said in his mind, but he got the message.

"Yes," he answered quietly, his eyes bulging.

He returned to the classroom, and for the rest of that year and the next, the fifth grade under the stern Miss Granit, was a model student, his grades soaring. That school year was notable for another reason: Early in the second half, Britt turned eleven and began feeling shame over his thumb-sucking. He decided on his own, with no urging from his parents or anyone else, to stop the habit. It was as difficult for him to do as it must be for smokers to stop smoking, considering that he was so young. On the first night, the urge to plant the left thumb in the mouth was overpowering as he laid his head on the pillow. Sleep would not come for about two hours, and after it did, he awoke several times before it was time to rise and get ready for school. But he never once put that thumb in his mouth. The next night also was difficult, as he lay tossing and turning before sleep overcame him. But he awoke only twice, and drifted quickly back to sleep. On the third night, he lay only a short while before going to sleep, and awoke only once. After that, he had no problem. Like a reformed heroin user, he'd kicked the habit—cold turkey.

Dale, only seven at the time, was aware of the event. Three-and-a-half years later, at almost the same age that Britt had overcome the baby habit with sheer willpower, Dale did the same. For him, the accomplishment was especially significant, since he had for years needed the feeling of security even more so than did Britt. Dale suffered horrible nightmares, occasionally running screaming from the bedroom, his face a sheet of terror, and into the lap of Miriam as she sat in a living room chair knitting.

One Sunday morning, Dale announced to his parents that he wasn't feeling well and didn't want to go to church. It was decided that Kevin and Britt would remain at home with him while Milton, Miriam, and Kyra attended the UP church. That morning, fire broke out in a small, square house across the street and two doors down, the blaze engulfing the frame building. Kevin, Britt, and Dale watched from the side windows of the Rutgers house, Dale's eyes growing wide as he stared transfixed. A half-hour later, red welts formed on his face, and when Milton and Miriam arrived home, they found more red splotches on his torso. Miriam had seen this in her siblings growing up, and knew that it was hives.

In time, Britt faced up to a painful memory that had popped into his mind occasionally over the years. While at Urbanside, Dale, when he was about three-and-a-half years old, had fallen into the bathtub just after Miriam had turned on the faucets to fill it, intending to check it later for temperature. The water apparently was quite hot, because Dale screamed as he writhed on his back. It was all Britt remembered. But he finally looked at the question of how Dale had fallen into the tub. He wouldn't have fallen by himself, short as he was at that age. How did it happen? Eureka! Did Britt, about seven-and-a-half then, push him? Britt wrestled with the idea and decided that if he had done the deed, it must have been as a joke. He hadn't known the water was so hot, or the memory of Dale screaming and writhing would not have haunted him. Also, he would remember how Dale fell in. He must have involuntarily suppressed that part of the incident from his consciousness because it was too painful to remember. But he wondered if Dale's hives when he saw the fire were a result of the burning pain he'd suffered only a few years earlier from the hot water in the tub. Or was it because he had been traumatized by all the warnings about hellfire that he'd heard from his parents and the church? Kyra once revealed that he had occasionally mentioned to her his fear of going to hell for some misdeed while they were children.

Britt had shot sparrows at close range with the BB gun he'd bought against the wishes of his mother, and his insensitivity metastasized from animal to human. He began harrassing Galen Epscott, a cheerful boy who also lived in Country Club Community, the next stop away on the route of the school bus. Britt rode the bus on rainy days or when his bicycle was broken. On the bus and the school playground during recesses, Britt, usually goaded by Bobby Jackson, rode Galen mercilessly, poking fun of the way the cheerful blond boy looked, which was in no way homely. Galen's parents were Seventh Day Adventists. His mother was a soft-spoken woman who wore no makeup on her lovely face and had reddish-brown hair that fell to her shoulders. Her gentle, kindly nature had gravitated to her only child. But one afternoon at recess, after several weeks of Britt's taunts, Galen began crying and, shouting that he wasn't going to take it anymore, started swinging his fists. Britt, utterly surprised, swung back, and the two locked for about twenty seconds in a wild flurry of unaimed blows, none of which made much impact. Neither boy sustained a bloody nose or black eye, and the fight ended as suddenly as it had begun. Several days later, Miriam mildly chastised Britt, saying she had been told of the incident by Mrs. Epscott at a school meeting for parents. Galen had followed her urging that he stand up to Britt. Britt's brief infection with the virus of meanness had been rendered impotent.

After the spartan fifth grade under the severe Miss Granit, Britt was only too ready for fun. The sixth-grade teacher, Miss Skittle, was a lot like his teacher two years earlier, Miss Rippel, except prettier and slimmer with a hint of sexiness. She had a pert smile, her slight overbite exposing glistening teeth. She also was more forceful. But she didn't have the control that Miss Granit wielded, and Britt took advantage of an air of distraction in her governing to talk with other pupils while he was supposed to be studying. But he was two years older, and had lost some of the rambunctiousness that he exhibited under Miss Rippel.

The sixth grade under Miss Skittle over, Britt entered Mayfield Junior High School, where there was no "home room," each class lasting fifty minutes. He wasn't required to be quiet for a span of several hours, and was better-behaved. Although he had loved baseball since he was ten and planned to become a Major League pitcher, he had taken a casual interest in football. In the fall, he had joined a group of boys who gathered to play tackle football in a vacant little valley, bordered by a narrow creek, between two hills on his paper route. He was a good zigzaggy runner, always winning at dodge ball and pom pom pull-away in grade school. Now, in the seventh grade, he wanted to try out for the junior high football team, and told Miriam that he would have to drop his paper route in order to join the team in practices after school.

"Oh no you're not," was her reply.

"Aw, c'mon," Britt pleaded. "I wanna do what the other kids are doin'. I've had that route for three years and I'm tired of it."

"That's just too bad," Miriam said sternly. "You don't need to be doing anything so useless. You get enough chance to play during the summer when school is out. There are plenty of other boys with paper routes. You need to earn money and save it."

"But hardly any of 'em started when I did," Britt whined. "Besides, they don't care about sports or they'd be going out for the team too. I bet their moms would let 'em if they wanted to." Miriam would not be swayed. "I said you're going to keep your paper route, and that's that. I don't want to hear any more about it."

"You never let me do anything," Britt rejoined, verging on tears. Mumbling about "that stupid paper route," he grabbed his baseball glove and ball from his room and pestered Kevin to go outside with him and play catch.

CHAPTER 12

For the first Sunday morning in many years, the Rutgers family stayed home from church. Milton and Miriam had gotten little sleep after Britt had come home from bowling with his buddies the night before and confessed that he was miserable. It was like an alarm clock jolting them into a consciousness of their son, who had just turned eighteen and was a senior at Mayfield High School. Oh, they knew he was there, but they had no idea of what was going on inside his mind, no clue of the emotional turmoil he was suffering. Britt had finally fallen asleep after sobbing into his pillow. He dreamed that all the employees and customers at Noll's Drug Store, where he worked before and after school, joined Bobby Jackson in laughing and pointing at him as he walked in his stocking feet through the store, hunting everywhere for his shoes. He slept late, and in the afternoon talked to his parents about the self-consciousness that made it excruciatingly painful for him to walk in front of the crowd to reach a seat in the bleachers at high school basketball games. It even was difficult for him to leave his work place in the back of Noll's and enter the front, where customers might look at him. He would blush, he said, and that made him feel even worse. Milton and Miriam told him he shouldn't feel that way—that people were too wrapped up in their own lives to be so aware of him. It made sense to Britt, but didn't make him feel much better. He even was uncomfortable watching many of the television programs because of the empathy he felt toward the persons whom the cameras were trained on, feeling that they must be awfully embarrassed.

At eight a.m. Monday, Milton called the state employment office in Mayfield and told Jim Randall, the office manager, "I'll be a little late today, Jim. I've got a family emergency. What? No, nobody's hurt or sick. It's my son Britt. I think he's having a nervous breakdown. I'll tell you about it later. I have to call Dr. Sanger and see if he can refer me to a psychiatrist."

Britt stayed home from school. On Wednesday morning he climbed in the back seat of the family's sky-blue Plymouth while Milton and Miriam got in the front, and they traveled to Des Moines. The two consulted each other about directions and finally drove into a hilly section northwest of downtown, then up a long driveway that wound briefly through a woods up to a plateau where two large houses stood. The property had been converted into the Woodside Sanitarium.

An attendant escorted them to an office in the main building. A lean, bespectacled, straight-haired Dr. Millard Sanders, a late-middle-aged man of medium height, extended his hand in welcome. They all sat down and Dr. Sanders said, "Now what seems to be the problem?" Britt looked at his parents, and the doctor looked at Britt. "Would you like to tell me, Britt?" So Britt narrated the Saturday night bowling episode and told how he couldn't concentrate on his studies and felt awfully self-conscious and embarrassed when he was in a crowd or a group of people.

"Do you ever hear voices?" Dr. Sanders wanted to know.

"Huh? Yeah, all the time. I just heard you."

The doctor broke into a big smile that hinted of condescension, and Milton and Miriam laughed politely.

"No, I meant, do you ever hear voices from people who aren't present with you?"

"Gosh," Britt said. He thought a moment and answered, "No, not that I can think of."

"Okay, that's fine," responded Dr. Sanders. "Tell me this: Do you ever have delusions of grandeur?"

"Huh? What's that?"

"Pardon me. Do you ever feel that you are someone famous or that you have accomplished something amazing—something that people will marvel at?"

Britt stared at the doctor's large, heavy oak desk for a few moments. "Well, the only thing I can think of is when I was thirteen and Dad took me and Kevin—that's my older brother—to a Des Moines Bruins baseball game, and I daydreamed—actually, it was a night game—I imagined that a foul ball was hit to me, and I caught it and hurled it back to the pitcher's mound with such speed that the team manager came up after the game and told me I had a lot of potential."

Milton and Miriam stared at Britt, a bemused look on Milton's face and a blank expression on Miriam's. Dr. Sanders smiled paternally—or was it patronizingly—Britt wasn't sure.

"Uh-huh," the doctor mused, his head bent forward, hand holding his chin. After a few seconds, he said, "Britt, you've not been very happy lately, have you? Can you tell me how you've been feeling?"

"Well, I keep feeling that people are looking at me. Mom calls it self-consciousness. She says there's nothing wrong with that, but I feel really awfully embarrassed. And I can't concentrate on my homework at night. My mind keeps jumping all over the place when I try to read, and then I get panicky because I know I'll do lousy on the tests and my grades will go down. And they have gone down. I just got a C average last semester."

"Good. Britt, could you step into the vestibule outside my office for a moment?"

Britt complied, and the doctor spent about ten minutes with Milton and Miriam. They then shook hands with the doctor, left the office, and told Britt they were going home. But they asked if he would be amenable to coming to Woodside for a short stay. Britt said if that's what they thought he needed, it was okay with him.

Two days later, Friday, Britt ate a breakfast of corn flakes and two hard-fried eggs that Miriam prepared, the edges brown and brittle as usual because she skimped on the lard in the pan. Then he loaded a suitcase containing clothes and toiletries into the car and climbed aboard with his parents. They drove to Des Moines and onto the sanitarium grounds.

A male orderly emerged from the house Milton had driven up to and helped him and Britt carry luggage inside. Britt was led to a room where he was to stay, and his parents told him goodbye and said they would see him in a couple of weeks or so. The orderly showed him the closet and chest where he could keep his clothes, and told him the times for breakfast, lunch, and dinner. He then led Britt to the "dining room." It was a long, narrow porch on the second floor, with chairs lining one side, facing the wall. The attendant then escorted Britt outside and down a sidewalk that led to the other building through a wide, neatly trimmed lawn graced with towering oaks and elms. This was the women's quarters, the orderly said, and the men would join them three mornings a week for social sessions.

It was time for lunch, and the other men—seventeen besides himself—gathered in the dining porch. A board running the length of the room was hinged to the wall and hung almost flat against it. At mealtimes, it was lifted perpendicularly to the wall and supported by steel braces that hugged the wall while not in use and were rotated outward on pins for mealtimes. Britt took a seat and looked to the left. The fellow next to him was probably about fifty, gaunt with hollow cheeks, and had disheveled grayish hair. He looked straight ahead, ignoring Britt's stare. Suddenly Britt became conscious that he was staring. He remembered the photo from about 1943, when he was five, taken at the country schoolhouse in Michigan where the family attended Sunday school with their childless friends, the Eglands. Ralph Egland was a quiet man who wrote a gardening column for the *Muskego Crier* and painted landscapes for recreation. His tall, slender, always pleasantly energetic wife, Helen, kept active doing church and community work. The group of about seventy-five people stood outside the white building for the photo, the children sitting on benches in front. Britt, wearing the white knickerbockers that he hated—he wanted to wear long pants like most of the other kids—was staring with a scowl at the girl next to him. She looked different, and was, in fact, retarded. Here at Woodside, his muddled frame of mind did not register the irony of his situation: He was again staring at someone with mental problems, but this time he was in the same predicament. He didn't see it that way, however. This fellow looked to be in a lot worse shape than Britt.

Britt slid his chair back from the "dining table" to get a look at the others down the row on either side of him. It was a motley group of men whose ages, he surmised, ranged upward to the early fifties. There were two youths in their late teens—himself and a blond-haired, good-looking fellow. Most of the men looked somewhat slovenly and, as Britt described them later to his parents, "out of it." One was impeccably dressed in a suit, white shirt, and tie. He was a tall, lean man with a thin mustache, forty-five-ish, whom Britt had noticed walking ramrod straight to the dining room. He held his hirsute head raised slightly and wore an expression of haughty disdain on his chiseled face. The others were for the most part nondescript. Britt decided he would talk to the other teen when lunch was finished.

After a few minutes, a late-middle-aged, frumpy woman with her hair in a bun and garbed in a well-worn white waitress dress entered the room bearing a tray with plates of food. She placed them in front of the men and returned twice more to finish dispensing dinner. The meal consisted of a cold plate—slices of spam, modest portions of potato salad and baked beans, and a dinner roll—with red Jello for dessert. Beverage was a choice of water, tea, or coffee, and Britt chose water, since he'd drunk coffee only a few times, with pastry. The men ate in silence. The guy to Britt's right—hefty, overweight, about thirty-five—caught his attention for the man's rapacious way with the food, shoveling it in as though more were forthcoming. He was too busy to talk, so Britt said nothing. But it occurred to him that the guy probably was going to lose weight here and was not going to be a happy camper.

The orderly standing by announced that the men were free to return to their rooms when they were finished. Britt and the other young fellow, nearly six feet tall like himself and dressed neatly in a medium-blue sweater and tan corduroy pants, encountered each other walking out. Britt said, "Hi. Looks like we're the youngest ones here."

"Yeah," the youth answered, wearing a smile that was friendly but somewhat vacant.

"I'm Britt Rutgers. I'm from Mayfield."

"My name's Johnny Kanton. I'm from Okeeloosie."

"You're Johnny *Kanton*?" Britt exclaimed. "The all-star basketball player from Okeeloosie High? The one who won the state championship game last year against Keokuk—made the winning basket with three seconds left?"

"Yeah," the youth said, grinning from ear to ear.

"What the heck are you in here for?" Britt blurted, genuinely puzzled. How could a guy known all over Iowa have emotional or mental problems?

"Aw, I don't know. Hey, bein' a big wheel doesn't mean nothin', ya know? Before, my pop used to whup me a lot—when he wasn't fightin' with Mom. Then I got to be a big hero athlete, and suddenly he's braggin' about me to everybody. Plus, I'd gotten bigger and stronger, and he was scared to pick on me. I just went kinda crazy one Friday night after a game when I saw him actin' like a big shot with some Okeeloosie bigwigs. Grabbed a hammer from the garage and busted a bunch of windshields at the Ford dealership where he's a salesman. So they sent me here."

"Wow!" was all Britt could say as he stared, open-mouthed.

"So why are you here?"

"Oh, I just wasn't feelin' happy and couldn't concentrate in school anymore. My grades were gettin' worse, and I got kinda panicky."

The orderly walked up and said, "Boys, I'm going to have to ask you to leave the room so the maid can clean up. There's a pool table in the basement. If you want, you can go down and shoot some balls."

"That's okay," said Johnny. "I'm just gonna go to my room and put my clothes away."

"Okay, see ya later," said Britt, then to the orderly, "Think I'm gonna do the same and after that go down and play some pool."

He took his time with his clothes—nothing to hurry for—and headed for the basement a couple of hours later. The orderly was shooting balls into the pockets by himself. He was about six-foot-one, well-built and somewhat handsome with blond hair combed straight back. Despite his physical condition, he didn't strike Britt as the kind of guy who would throw his weight around.

"Have you played before?" he queried.

"Yeah, but it's been a while," said Britt. "I used to play a lot at the YMCA in Mayfield."

"Good. Why don't you grab a stick and we'll play a game of eight-ball? By the way, I'm Jim." He didn't offer his hand, probably so as not to give the impression that they were equals and Britt could get by with ignoring the rules of the place. But Britt found him in no way threatening, even detecting a hint of effeminacy.

At first, Britt's judgment was off on slices, and then he cut two balls that were straight shots to the pocket but had a lot of green between them and the cue ball. But he gradually regained his finesse and had only two balls left on the table when Jim won. Britt won the next game by a ball, scratched on the last shot for the eight-ball in the next game, then took the last game, leaving Jim with three balls on the table.

"Oh goodness, I've had enough," said Jim. "You're too good for me. Actually, I've got some duties to attend to. We'll play again—if you promise not to trounce me too badly."

Britt smiled, slightly embarrassed, and insisted that Jim was a worthy competitor. Jim climbed the stairs and disappeared, and Britt followed. On the second floor, he passed the Community Room. Six or seven patients sat in lounge chairs, a couple of them thumbing through magazines and others staring at the walls or the floor. Two fastened their eyes on the two guys immersed in the magazines but looked up when Britt arrived at the entrance, which accommodated French doors that were swung open. Britt returned their looks in his direction and they averted his gaze. He decided these gents were not in a communicative mood, and they didn't look very interesting anyway, so he ambled off to his room to use the restroom and await dinner.

At five-fifteen p.m., a different orderly walked up to the open door of Britt's room and advised him that dinner would be at five-thirty. The man looked like a Marine sergeant—short and stocky, with a crew cut—but seemed agreeable to Britt, not at all authoritative.

Britt said hi to Johnny Kanton as the two walked to their places in front of the board that served as a table, Britt near one end and Johnny the other. The waitress with her hair in a bun carried in a large tray with plates of food, set it on a small table in a corner, distributed the plates to the men, and went back to the kitchen for another tray. The meal consisted of chunks of roast beef, mashed potatoes with brown gravy, cut green beans, and a roll with a pad of margarine. Britt thought it tasted pretty good. It was much like Sunday dinner at home after church, but the beef didn't have that viscous fat and the gravy was free of the grainy texture and lumps that usually defined his mother's gravy. Britt glanced at the men up and down the "table" as they ate in silence and decided he liked it that way. Most of them wore old-looking clothes—pants that were baggy with the belt pulling the waist together in folds, or pants that were too short, faded corduroy shirts. Virtually all had disheveled hair, some in various stages of baldness on top but with the hair in back tickling their shirt collars. Their faces were either puffy or gaunt, and they either looked down or stared, seemingly without comprehension.

Though Britt was somewhat repulsed by the scene, it also held some fascination for him, and he wasn't bored—at least not yet. The waitress silently and efficiently gathered the empty or partly empty dishes and returned with little plates of chocolate-frosted white cake. Britt watched as she doled out the cake and was transported to the scene of his birthday only about three weeks before. His mother had cut a chocolate cake and served dishes of vanilla ice cream, the favorite of him and his dad. That was it—after the initial birthday song and candle blowing. No present, not even a card. But that hadn't bothered Britt, because he didn't expect any. None of the Rutgers children had ever received a present for their birthday. There just wasn't enough money. That was partly because their dad spent so much on insurance. He always feared some catastrophe that would leave the family bankrupt and force them to accept welfare, which he and Miriam regarded as a taboo that seemed to rank just below incest.

Johnny Kanton's room was just down the hall from Britt's, and the two began chatting as they walked there after dinner. Britt stood in Johnny's doorway and joked about how upset he'd been at the game between Mayfield and Okeeloosie in the year before. The basketball star made twenty-four points to lead the Bearcats to a 65-64 victory over the Tigers.

"Every time we'd get ahead, you'd make a couple more baskets and we'd lose our lead again," said Britt.

A big, beaming smile broke over Johnny's handsome face and he laughed. "Yeah, I remember that game. But my high this year was thirty-six points against Grinola. That guard for Mayfield held me down. What was his name … ?"

"Ron Akers?" Britt offered.

"Yeah, that's him. Little guy, but he was really pesky—hung onto me like a piece of chewing gum to your shoe. I had a tough time getting my shots off."

"He's really quick," said Britt. "A bunch of us kids used to play baseball in the summers at our grade school diamond, and Ron usually played shortstop. He covered a lot of ground."

After a pause, Britt said, "I suppose you're goin' back to school in the second semester next year and finish school, aren'tcha? Will you join the team again?"

"Nah. Everybody'd be talkin' about my nervous breakdown and me goin' to the nuthouse. I just wanna get high school over with and go on to college where nobody'll know me. I'll probably go to a small college so I can play basketball."

"Heck, you could play on a Big Ten team," Britt rejoined.

"Huh-uh, I don't think so. You've really gotta be good to play at that level. And big. Those guys are mostly over six feet and I'm just five-ten."

"Well, I don't think you oughtta sell yourself short." Britt chuckled and added, "No pun intended."

"Ha! That's good," said Johnny.

"Think I'll go to my room now, then maybe watch a little television in the community room," Britt said.

"See ya," Johnny said cheerily.

Britt used the rest room, then ambled to the Community Room. A commercial was running on the black-and-white television as Britt found a vacant chair. The announcer boomed, "The Gillette Cavalcade of Sports is *on* the air." The rousing Gillette song played, and then the announcer proclaimed dramatically, "Gillette presents the *Gillette Friday Night Fights.* Tonight, here at Madison Sqwaah Gahden in New Yawk, Joisey Joe Walcott will face the up-and-coming young Floyd Patahson in a fifteen-round heavyweight bout." The announcer's New York accent fascinated Britt every time he heard it. He had often imitated the voice to his brothers.

The two boxers slugged it out, but it was a pretty even match with neither scoring a knock-down. By the tenth round Britt was getting bored and headed to his room. At breakfast the next morning, Jim instructed the men to gather afterward in the living room with their winter coats. He was going to escort them down the winding sidewalk of the sanitarium grounds to the women's building for the period of socializing that was held Tuesdays, Thursdays, and Saturdays.

The women—twenty-three compared to the eighteen men—were about the same age range as the men, except the youngest looked a little older than he and Johnny Kanton. None stood out to Britt as attractive. They were just a blur of eminently forgettable females: depressed-looking, sexless, dowdy with no makeup, stringy hair, loose-fitting dresses or skirts that hung to mid-calf, never a hint of cleavage in the bodice, flat-heeled shoes. He had no desire to mix with them; on the contrary, he wanted to avoid them. But he couldn't because Miss Dalwood, the social facilitator, had other ideas. She was a cheerful blonde in her upper thirties whose somewhat pretty face was mildly marred by acne pockmarks. She instructed all of them to sit in chairs arranged in a circle at one end of this spacious basement. The cellar had been converted into a large room with walls of light wood paneling, a false beige ceiling, and a gray linoleum floor. The men began to congregate, but Miss Dalwood stepped in and playfully said, "Now come on, gentlemen, let's not all stick together. I want you to mix with the ladies so you're not all sitting together. That would be pretty boring, now wouldn't it?" It was going to be either way, Britt figured, and he sought out the best-looking young woman there, who was maybe twenty-one or twenty-two, and sat next to her.

"Now everybody get to know each other," Miss Dalwood encouraged. The young woman looked furtively at Britt, who said, "Hi."

"Hi. I'm Lynn. Where are you from?" Plain-looking with long, straight, dark-brown hair and bangs in front that accentuated a round, almost pretty face, she had an intelligent look enhanced by thin-rimmed glasses. Her expression was strained, however, as though she were a little frightened. She held her right hand on her lap with the fingers crossed like a bird's claw and the wrist bent as if broken.

"Oh, I'm Britt. From Mayfield. How 'bout you?"

"Earltown. It only has a-thousand-five-hundred people. Mayfield is a lot bigger, isn't it?"

"Yeah, it's about fifteen thousand. My high school class is a hundred ninety."

"It *is*?"

"Yeah."

"No, I mean, are you still in school?"

"Oh … yes, I haven't finished my senior year. I had to drop out. Couldn't concentrate. What do you do in Earltown?"

"I'm an assistant in the town library. My dad owns a Phillips 66 gas station."

Miss Dalwood entered the circle and announced: "You all may help yourselves to refreshments on the table over there by the wall."

"I think I'll get some cake and coffee," said Lynn.

"Yeah, that's a good idea," said Britt. Johnny was already at the table, and said, "Hey Britt, wanna play some ping pong? Jim said there's a table behind that curtain over there." He pointed to the other end of the room.

"Great," said Britt, his spirits immediately buoyed. "I love ping pong. Played a lot at the Mayfield YMCA."

"Uh-oh," Johnny said with a big smile. "You'll probably whup me. I haven't played a lot. Been playing basketball since I was a kid."

"Nah. Let's go."

Lynn was left to her own desserts, literally and figuratively, as Britt joined Johnny, both carrying a paper plate with a small piece of white cake and a glass of milk. Jim walked up and said, "Here, I'll pull the curtain aside so you can play."

Britt and Johnny placed their refreshments on the floor next to the wall and took to either end of the table. "Uh-oh, I hate sandpaper paddles," said Britt.

"Mine's rubber. I like sandpaper. I'll trade you. You'll beat me anyway."

Britt laughed and they began warming up.

"Ready for a game?" Britt asked?

"As ready as ever."

They vollied for the serve and Britt won. He soon was way ahead, using his forehand to repeatedly slam Johnny's arching shots.

"Whoa!" Johnny said loudly, laughing at his inability to compete with Britt. "You're a ringer."

"What's that?" said Britt.

"Come on. You're putting me on."

"No. I never heard of that."

"It's a guy who's an expert but doesn't tell anybody and places a bet. You're a pro!"

"Nah," Britt said shyly. "I've just played a lot."

They finished the game, and Miss Dalwood announced that the session was over and she hoped everyone had a good time.

The day passed quickly and uneventfully. Britt was settling into the routine.

The next morning, Sunday, a different orderly was on duty. He told the men at breakfast time that if they chose, they could go to the women's building for a service that would include hymn-singing, reading of Bible passages, and prayer, with a local clergyman officiating. Britt didn't want to be with the group. Besides, Lynn might be there and he felt a little guilty about having left her in the lurch to play ping pong. So he walked to the Community Room and browsed through *Life* magazine, then to the basement to play some pool by himself, and finally repaired to his room. It was a humdrum day, much like those Sundays at home, when nobody said much to each other and nothing happened. Soon it was time for bed.

Jim the orderly woke Britt at seven a.m. The nurse wanted to see him at eight, before breakfast, in the examination room at the end of the hallway past the dining room. He didn't need to take a shower, Jim said. So Britt took his time brushing his teeth, going to the bathroom, and dressing in a shirt and pants. At seven-fifty he sauntered to the room, where the nurse already was at a desk doing paper work. In one corner was a green, cylindrical tank supported by an apparatus on two wheels.

"Good morning, Britt," the nurse said quietly, wearing a hesitant smile. She was probably in her mid-fifties, was a bit more than plump, and had white hair that matched her uniform. "I'm nurse Gloria. We're going to start you on a series of treatments that will relieve the anxiety and stress you've been feeling lately. They're called ECTs, and are harmless and painless. Now I want you to remove your shirt and pants and put this gown on. You tie it in back."

"What does ECT stand for?" Britt asked.

"Oh, that's an acronym for technical language that you wouldn't understand," Gloria said with a smile that was at once reassuring and a bit patronizing.

Britt removed his shirt and pants, and, wearing only his J.C. Penney white underpants, draped the gown over himself and lay on his back on a wide couch. Gloria sat on the couch beside him and said, "Okay, now I want you to hold this little wooden piece between your teeth. That's it. All right, I'm going to give you an injection. This is going to pinch just a little, less than a bee sting. Then you're going to go to sleep, and thirty or forty minutes later you'll wake up feeling wonderful." She told him to squeeze his fist, felt for a vein in his right forearm, near the elbow, and expertly slipped the needle in. Britt felt only a twinge of pain, and Gloria said, "In just a few seconds you'll be in dreamland. I'm going to count backward, and I want you to nod your head after each count. Okay?"

Britt nodded, and then began nodding some more as Gloria counted: "Ten, nine, eight, seven, six ..."

Jim was sitting on a chair next to Britt when he awoke.

"What happened?" Britt asked.

"You just had your first treatment," said Jim, smiling. "Why don't you take a shower and get dressed, and come to the dining room, where you can have breakfast all by yourself? Connie the waitress will bring you whatever you want. Well, at least she'll bring you *as much* as you want." He chuckled softly.

The rest of that day was uneventful. Britt followed the routine and whiled away the time playing pool and watching television.

On Tuesday morning, he was somewhat looking forward to seeing Lynn again during the social period in the women's building. They sat together and chatted about what each had done since Saturday. Finally, Britt asked her why she was there. Lynn looked down shyly, hesitated, then confessed that she'd dropped out of Northern Iowa State College midway through her sophomore year, thoroughly lonely. She returned home to work at the library, where she'd worked part-time while in high school. But she still was terribly sad—so much so that she one day refused to get out of bed in the morning and go to work. That's when her parents consulted a therapist, and she ended up at Woodside. Britt was telling her he was sorry to hear that when Johnny came bounding up, a big grin on his face, and interrupted.

"Okay, you ready to pound me again at the ping pong table?" he joshed. "Bet you don't beat me as bad this time. Come on, let's go."

"Oh, Johnny, this is Lynn."

"Hi," said Johnny—and Britt detected a smirk as his friend grabbed his arm and pulled him away.

"See ya, Lynn," Britt said over his shoulder. Lynn looked crestfallen as she gave a delicate little wave, and he couldn't concentrate very well on the ping pong.

"Hey, come on, let's get with it," Johnny chided Britt, who kept glancing across the room at Lynn. "Geez, you're not falling in love, are you? Not with *her*."

Johnny's playing already was improved, and they went through three games, all a lot closer than the previous time, before it was time to head back to the men's side. Britt wanted to leave and walked quickly to the front of the group of men gathered at the door behind Jim, waiting for him to escort them. He didn't wait for Johnny, and reached his room before any of the others had gone to theirs.

The next morning, Wednesday, Jim again told Britt to skip breakfast and be in the examining room at eight. Britt knew it was coming but hadn't worried about it. He had only a mild case of the butterflies as he entered the room and was greeted by Gloria with a "Good morning" and a nod. "I think you know what to do," she said, and he answered, "Yep." Removing his shirt and trousers, he donned the gown, lay on the couch, and accepted the piece of wood that she placed in his mouth. She began to count backward slowly, and he nodded after each count: "Ten ... nine ... eight ... seven ... six ... five ... four ...."

Jim was there again when he awoke. This time, Britt was confused. "Where am I?" he asked.

"You're in Woodside Sanitarium and just had another ECT," Jim said. "Are you feeling okay?"

"Yeah. Now I remember. This was the second one, wasn't it?" Britt said it more as a statement than a question.

"You're doing this very well," said Jim. "These treatments don't seem to worry you at all."

"No. What's to worry about?" Britt shrugged. After lunch, of which he ate only a little since it was so close to his delayed breakfast, he went to his room and sat at his desk to write a letter to his parents.

> Dear Folks,
>
> Everything is going well here. Most of the patients are quiet and uninteresting, and their appearances leave a lot to be desired, as do their table manners. But I've gotten used to that and don't mind much anymore. Of course, I'm the youngest male, except for Johnny Kanton, who is my age. You probably don't know him, but he was on Okeeloosie's state championship basketball team last year and was chosen as an all-state player. He and I have had some fun playing ping pong when we mix with the women at their building a little ways from the men's. We go there three times a week.

> They've started giving me these treatments that they call ECTs. I'm not sure what they are. All I know is that this nurse puts me to sleep, and 30 or 40 minutes later I wake up and feel the same as I did before. They don't amount to a hill of beans. I had my second one this morning, and the next one is Friday morning.
>
> The food here is okay, and I'm okay, and I suppose you're okay. I think I'll go to the basement now and shoot a little pool.
>
> Bye for now,
> Bob

He sealed the letter in an envelope from the desk drawer, addressed it to "Milton Rutgers, Rural Route 1, Colton, Iowa," and walked to the office at the opposite end of the hall from the examination room. Jim sat at a desk doing paper work. He told Britt the letter would go out the next morning and arrive Saturday.

After dinner that night, *The June Allyson Show* was under way on the TV in the Community Room. It was only a half-hour drama, but Britt was quickly riveted by the story of a young woman who becomes ill and is treated by a young doctor, who falls in love with her. The analysis by him and other doctors at the hospital determines that she has leukemia. The young doctor quietly informs her of the diagnosis and that she has only a few months to live. He tells her that medication will keep her strong enough to travel for a few weeks, and he wants to take her to Europe to see the great historical landmarks. She protests that he cannot abandon his responsibilities as a physician. Sitting on the edge of her bed, he draws her to him. Looking ardently in her face, he says softly: "Gather ye rosebuds while ye may, old time is still a flying. And that same flower which blooms today, tomorrow may be dying."

"William Ernest Henley," she says, smiling through tears.

The doctor nods, and says, "My hospital duties will have to wait. You are my most important patient. I've already made travel arrangements and let the chief of staff know we'll be leaving in four days." He holds her face in his hands and gently kisses her as the program ends.

Britt wanted to cry but wasn't about to in front of the other patients. He stared while Rod Serling's *The Twilight Zone* came on, watching disinterestedly. Soon, however, he was caught up in the drama of a habitual criminal who has been arrested and is offered a deal by a mysterious prosecutor. If the man will confess to his crimes, which include murder, the prosecutor, who wields supernatural powers, will see to it that after his execution, he will go to heaven. There, a palace occupied by beautiful, sexy women awaits him. Gustatory delights will be served at every meal, and bikini-clad lovelies will fan him and serve Tom Collinses while he lolls at a beach. He will have the freedom to indulge in any pleasure that he chooses. The man confesses, goes happily to the gallows, and in the next scene is in heaven. He's having a great time—at first. But after a while he becomes bored, and gradually abandons all the pleasures, finally reaching a point where he is becoming unglued. "I can't stand this life anymore," he screams. "Please, somebody give me some rules. I'm going crazy." And he sobs uncontrollably as the program ends.

At the social session Thursday, Britt couldn't find either Johnny or Lynn. He figured they must not have been feeling well, or maybe had to see their doctor, or whatever. Disappointed, he sat around munching on the refreshments and watching the others until the period was over.

Friday morning rolled around, and ECT number three was scheduled. Britt had begun musing about the treatments and he wondered what was done to him when he was unconscious. He didn't say anything to Gloria, but was somewhat nervous. Everything went fine. But when he awoke, Gloria was in the room making some adjustment to the oxygen tank.

"How do you feel?" she asked.

"Okay. I've been wondering … . What does ECT stand for?"

Gloria frowned, waited, then said, "It's short for electroconvulsive therapy."

"What does that mean?"

"I'll sit down with you in a few days and explain the whole process. I can't now because I have to attend to other patients. Okay?"

"Yeah," said Britt, thinking that she was being evasive. She'd looked taut.

At the social session the next morning, Saturday, Britt looked around for Lynn but again didn't see her. Johnny wasn't there, either, but Britt figured he probably was a little late and would be allowed to come over unaccompanied. After all, he seemed to be a trustworthy patient and his problems seemed mild. But after ten minutes, neither Lynn nor Johnny appeared. Britt approached Jim, who was chatting with Miss Dalwood, and said, "Isn't Johnny coming today?"

Jim and Miss Dalwood looked at each other concernedly, and Jim said, "Uh, no, Britt. Johnny has left Woodside."

"Huh?" Britt said with surprise. "How come?"

"Well … I really can't say."

"Why not? And where is Lynn?"

Miss Dalwood looked down and said, "I'd better be tending to the refreshments, Jim." She walked away.

"Come on, Jim. What's going on? How come Miss Dalwood had that serious look on her face?"

"Britt, I suppose I shouldn't tell you this, but you're going to wonder, so I will. After the social session on Tuesday, Johnny did something that we can't tolerate here. So his parents were called and they came yesterday and took him home."

"What did he do?" Britt demanded. "I need to know. He and I had become friends."

"He has a very bad temper," Jim began slowly. He was silent for a few seconds, then said, "After you two played ping pong, just before we all went back to our building, Johnny walked up to Lynn and said, 'I know you quiet types. You're really clever.' Then he said something like, 'Think you're gonna put the make on Britt, huh?' and called her a slut. When she stared at him, he gave her the finger, and she called him a bastard. He walked up and pushed her real hard, and she fell backward. Fortunately, a chair was behind her and broke her fall, but she was bruised. She was quite upset over the incident and didn't feel like socializing quite yet. Miss Dalwood said she probably would return Tuesday."

Britt just stood with his mouth open, looking at Jim as if not comprehending, saying nothing.

Finally, he said, "Who saw all this?"

"Miss Dalwood saw the shoving part, and two of the women patients saw and heard the whole thing and filled her in on the rest. I'm sorry, Britt. He apparently wasn't a very nice guy."

Britt was dumbfounded, and was in a funk the rest of the morning. The only male patient he could communicate with was gone. This place was going to be pretty desolate. In the afternoon, as he lay on his bed thinking of Johnny, his mind drifted to the ECTs. Finally, he decided to play some pool, and went to the basement, where Jim was clearing the last ball from the table.

"Want to play a game?" Jim asked.

"Yeah, let's play. Hey Jim, what exactly happens with this electroconvulsive therapy?"

"Who told you that's what ECT is?

"Gloria. She was in the room when I woke up and I asked her. I wanted to know more but she had to see some patients."

"Oh," said Jim. "Well, okay. After you've been put to sleep, Gloria rubs some lubricating jelly on your temples, and then she places these things—like earmuffs, only smaller—on the temples. She places this apparatus beside the bed, and when she turns it on, a low-power current of electricity passes through the earmuffs and into your brain. This lasts for about a minute, and it causes you to have convulsions."

"You mean like when somebody has epilepsy?" Britt asked, his eyes wide.

Jim saw his concern and quickly added, "But it's not dangerous or anything. Nothing can happen to you. What it does is cause you to forget a lot of things that have happened recently in your life, so you won't be bothered so much. But later it all comes back, when you can deal with it better."

Jim had decided it might be too unnerving for Britt to know that a second shot was administered after he was asleep to relax his muscles to reduce the chance that bones would fracture.

The two played three games of eight-ball. Britt said little, and then told Jim, "Think I'll go to the community room and get a magazine to take to my room and read."

"Okay, Britt. Listen, you're not worried about the ECTs, are you? There's nothing to be afraid of."

"Oh, no. I was just feeling a little sad that Johnny's not going to be around anymore. That's all. I'll get over it."

Britt was lethargic the next day, Sunday. After dinner, he ambled into the Community Room, where a troupe of acrobats was performing on the *The Ed Sullivan Show.* "Let's give them a big hand," said Sullivan, his neck buried between his shoulders, his hand extended toward the bowing acrobats wearing tights. "And now, I want you to give a big hand to one of the biggest stars from our neighbor to the North, Canada's own Giselle McKenzie." Britt had seen her on the show before, and was filled with lust for that hourglass-shaped body with the long, voluptuous legs revealed through a wide slit in a tight gown that barely concealed her form. He stared at her, transfixed, and, making his way to an empty chair, stumbled on the foot of a dour-looking fellow, who looked up and glared, saying nothing. *What's My Line* followed, and this time it was Arlene Francis who made Britt desirous. As she often did, she was wearing a gown with the straps falling off the shoulders, sexily baring those beautifully sloping parts of her anatomy along with an alluring cleavage in front.

At ten p.m., the short, stocky orderly, whose name Britt had learned was Amos, entered the room and announced in his husky voice, "Afraid I'm going to have to ask you all to return to your rooms now. Lights-out is in fifteen minutes. Thank you."

Slowly the men rose and shuffled off to their rooms. Britt likewise complied, changed into his pajamas, and crawled into bed. But for the first time in the ten days he'd been at Woodside, he couldn't get to sleep. He imagined what he looked like during the ECTs as the electricity made him shake uncontrollably and bite hard on the piece of wood. He was frightened. Gloria had been doing something with the oxygen tank when he woke up the last time. Did they have to use it on him? And what if they had to and it didn't work? Could a person get epilepsy from the treatments? Was this good for his brains? Didn't people who got hit by lightning sometimes have brain damage? Yes, but lightning was a lot more powerful than these ECTs. Still, why wouldn't they at least cause a little damage? And it would add up with each one. What if something went wrong with the machine and too much electricity went into his brain and it killed him? Holy Moses! Yeah, what if something went wrong? Or what if all that convulsing caused him to have a heart attack? Had it ever happened? Had anybody ever been killed?

Britt was becoming panicky. He had to know the answers to these questions. He got up and switched on the light. His bedside Westclox showed ten-forty. He had to see the doctor. In his yellow pajamas dotted with a baseball-and-bat design, which his parents had gotten him for his stay at Woodside, he strode quickly into the hallway. At ten o'clock it had been dimmed, with a single, low-wattage bulb on a ceiling light casting a pale orange glow. No one was in sight. He walked briskly down the hall, past the room patients called "the cage." It had a heavy iron door, three-foot-high wood paneling and, above that, steel mesh so an imprisoned patient would be visible. It was empty except for a narrow, low-lying bed covered only with a white sheet. Reaching the end of the hall, Britt saw Amos sitting at the desk, catching up on his regular paper work by filling in a day log on each patient. The ceiling light here was brighter. Jim sat on a lounge chair in the corner, reading a book.

"Jim, I've got to see the doctor," Britt demanded. Jim looked up quickly, saw the fear in Britt's eyes, and rose.

"What's wrong, what's happened?" said the orderly. "Aren't you feeling well?"

"I'm feeling okay. I just have to see the doctor about something."

"Wait a minute. Just calm down, Britt. Tell us what the problem is."

"I have to ask the doctor about the ECTs."

"What about them? Amos and I can answer anything you want to know. We've probably seen several hundred shock treatments."

"Shock treatments?" Britt said, his eyes growing larger.

"I mean ECTs," said Jim.

"Why did you call them shock treatments?" Britt demanded. Now he was downright scared. "Do I get shocked? People die of electrical shocks. You read about it all the time in the papers. Sometimes they're not even high-voltage. Shocks are dangerous."

"Now take it easy, Britt. You don't get a high-voltage shock. You just . . . ."

"Then why did you call it a shock treatment?" Britt interrupted.

"That's just the common term for it. ECT is the technical term."

"So how many volts do I get hit with?" Britt was too frightened to relent, and probably wouldn't have, anyway. He'd always been persistent, often driving his father to remark, "You've got to learn the hard way, don't you?"

"I don't know exactly," said Jim. "It's not much."

"But it goes through my brain," Britt insisted.

"Look, Britt, there's nothing to worry about," Jim said, his tone now hinting of impatience. "Just go back to bed and get a good night's sleep, and in the morning you'll have your treatment, and it'll be over real fast, and then we'll play some pool."

But Britt wasn't about to go to bed. His fear had grown, not diminished, and he needed answers to the questions that were darting around in his mind.

"I want to see the doctor. Doctor Sanders. He hasn't seen me since I've been here. How come?"

"I'm sure he plans to see you after you've had a few more shock tr... —I mean, ECTs. He wants you feeling better before he talks with you about your problems."

"I thought he was supposed to *help* me feel better. He told my parents he was going to help me. But I haven't even seen him. I need to talk to him now, before I have another shock treatment."

"Let's not call them shock treatments," said Amos, who had stopped his paper work and been watching the exchange between Britt and Jim.

"That's what Jim called them," Britt shot back, "because that's what they are. I get shocked."

"Britt, we just use that term casually when we're talking among ourselves," said Jim.

"Yeah, and I'll bet there's a lot of things you talk about that you wouldn't want me to know. That's why you won't get the doctor. You don't want me to find out what happens with these shock treatments. I need to know whether they cause brain damage."

"They don't cause brain damage, Britt," said Jim, sounding more impatient now.

"And I want to know how many people have been killed with these things."

"Nobody has been killed, Britt. Now you need to go to your room and go to bed."

"I'm not going anywhere until I see the doctor."

"It's too late. It's eleven o'clock. Doctor Sanders is probably in bed, like you should be. Now let's go." There was urgency in Jim's voice, and he nodded to Amos, who opened the desk drawer and put something that tinkled in his pocket, then rose from behind the desk. Jim put his left arm around Britt's shoulders and nudged him gently.

"How come Gloria was working on the oxygen tank when I woke up last time?" Britt was shouting now.

"She was just dusting it and making sure it would work okay because it hadn't been used in a long time," Jim answered.

"In a long time? So it was used before. Just what I thought. See? You guys are hiding things from me. These shock treatments are dangerous. I need to see the doctor."

"Britt, you're going to wake up all the other patients," said Jim. "Now let's get to bed." He nodded again to Amos, who approached and, shorter than Jim, extended his right arm around the patient's back, below Jim's arm.

"No!" Britt yelled. "I'm not going to bed. I need to see Doctor Sanders."

"Come on now, Britt, let's go," Jim said as he and Amos tightened their grip and pushed forward on his body.

"Get your hands off me!" Britt shouted as he shook himself free of the two men's grip.

"Britt, if you won't go to your room and get in bed, we're going to have to lock you in the cage," Jim said ominously. Some of the patients knew about the cage and feared it. In the Community Room just the day before, Britt had overheard an older patient, who was bruited to have been at the sanitarium the longest at several months, tell a naïve-looking thirty-ish patient of having seen an unruly patient strapped to the bed in the cage. The patient wriggled and screamed as Gloria injected him in the arm with a needle. It had happened when everyone except the older patient, who hadn't felt well that morning, was attending the social session in the women's building.

"Now don't fight us," said Amos as he and Jim grabbed Britt's arms.

"Where are you trying to take me?" Britt hollered. "To the cage? Yeah, you're going to put me in the cage, aren't you? Like that other guy I heard about."

The two orderlies didn't answer and tried to pull Britt down the hall.

"Get your hands off me!" Britt yelled. He tried to jerk himself free, but the two strong men held him like a vise. It was about twenty-five feet to the cage, and they pushed and shoved and dragged a writhing, jerking, kicking Britt. Finally, they were in front of the cage, and Jim and Amos stopped pulling. Amos kicked open the door, which was held shut by a spring device that snapped against the inside when it was closed.

"I'm not going in there!" Britt screamed, his face wild with panic. He was six feet tall, but weighed only one-hundred-sixty pounds. Jim was about one-hundred-ninety and the muscular Amos two-hundred-ten. They got behind and to the side of him and pushed him up to the doorway. Britt grasped the doorposts and locked his arms. Amos grabbed his right arm and dislodged it, but Britt kicked him hard in the back of the knee, causing him to buckle in front of Britt, in the doorway. Britt put his open right hand on Amos' face to keep him away. Jim was trying to grab Britt around the neck, and he swung his left arm back as hard as he could, his elbow catching Jim squarely in the abdomen, the "breadbasket." Jim doubled up momentarily, gasping for air, then straightened and got behind Britt and began reaching around his neck again. Britt simultaneously thrust his buttocks out and bent forward, at the same time swinging at the shorter Amos to keep him from getting a hold. Now they were on either side of Britt, and all three were flailing and wrestling wildly. The mighty struggle had been going for several minutes, and Britt was gasping for air. His strength was ebbing, and his will was waning.

But Jim and Amos were spent, too. Just as Britt was about to drop his arms and surrender, Jim dropped his, and then Amos did likewise. Amazed, Britt leaped away from them and ran for the stairway, heading toward his room and then taking a right turn. He sped the ten feet to the stairs. Hurtling down three, five, six steps at a time, he reached the first floor and spun to the right, bounding across the living room toward a window at the end of a couch. He plunged his right fist through the lower of the wood-framed, three-by-three-foot double windows. But a heavy screen was attached to the outside. Fully expecting to see Jim and Amos scrambling down the stairs after him, he turned to look, prepared to resume fighting. Complete surprise—no one there. The two orderlies had given up and remained upstairs. Britt grabbed the thirty-inch-high metal base of an ash tray next to the couch and plunged it through the screen. He grabbed the window frame with his right hand for support, coming down on a shard of glass remaining in the window but feeling no pain. Then he vaulted through the window, the back of his head catching another shard at the top of the frame.

A thirty-foot span of grass lay on the back side of the sanitarium, and he sprinted across it into the woods that separated the psychiatric hospital from the surrounding residential neighborhood. Terror-struck, he ran wildly into the darkness, never conscious of the winter cold or feeling pain from his bare feet ripping into brush and dead branches. Ahead, he saw a light, and as he got closer, realized it was a porch light. He needed to get to the police so they could call his parents, who would take him home, away from this house of horrors.

His right hand and feet bleeding badly, the hair on the back of his head matted with sticky blood, his pajamas torn, Britt ran up the several stairs and onto the wide porch of the neat, middle-class residence. He pushed a white, round doorbell to the left of the screen door, then opened it and pounded on the heavy mahogany door. A man's face appeared through separated vertical blinds in a window fronting the porch, then disappeared as the blinds closed. In a second, the man swung open the door, then the screen door. He was tall, probably in his mid-to-late thirties, handsome with thick brown hair combed straight back. His face registered mild alarm, but no fear.

"They're after me," Britt blurted. "Please call the police."

Now a likewise tall, attractive, kindly looking woman, perhaps a little younger, appeared behind the man, obviously his wife.

"Now don't be afraid," the man said calmly. "You're going to be all right. You're safe here. Why don't you just come in, and we'll call the police for you."

"Oh my goodness, you're bleeding," his wife said, her voice full of concern. "Let me get a towel so you can wipe off the blood and we can see how badly you're hurt." She left and returned a few seconds later with a warmly wet, yellow towel. "Let's see your hand. Oh, you've punctured your finger awfully and sliced flesh off the side of your hand. That's nasty. And what about the back of your head?" She placed her hands on Britt's shoulders and gently turned him. "Ah, that's not so bad. You're going to be okay. Those feet are badly cut up, though." She went to a bedroom and returned with a card-table chair—"Here, sit down"—and carefully pressed the towel against the gashes.

The man, who had gone to another part of the house, strode easily up to Britt and announced, "I've called the police and they'll be here in a minute." Britt had calmed down somewhat, and he thanked the two.

"I'm Steve and my wife is Jill," the man said. "What's your name?"

"Britt. Britt Rutgers."

"Would you care to tell us what happened?" Jill asked, while bandaging his feet. "Only if you want to, of course."

"They were trying to put me in the cage," Britt said, not yet relaxed. "At Woodside. I'm supposed to have another shock treatment in the morning, and I wanted to see the doctor 'cause I'm scared something might go wrong or the electricity might make me brain-damaged. They wouldn't let me see him."

"I'm so sorry," Jill said. "Where are you from?"

"A little farm outside of Colton. My dad works for the Iowa State Employment Service in Mayfield."

"Well, I'm sure your parents will see that you're taken care of and you'll be all right."

"It looks like a squad car just pulled up," Steve announced in an upbeat tone. "The police will do what's good for you. Don't worry." He opened the door as two officers approached.

"Hello gentlemen," he said in a reassuring voice. "We have a young man here who's just had a bad experience. He's a patient at Woodside, and apparently was going to have an electroshock treatment in the morning and became frightened—and then things got a little out of hand. But I think he's feeling much better now. Aren't you, Britt?" The question was sincere, not rhetorical.

"Yeah, I guess so," Britt said.

"Fine. These gentlemen are here to protect us, so you're in good hands."

The older of the two officers smiled knowingly at Steve and winked. The policemen gently took each of Britt's arms and escorted him to the squad car, motioning for him to get in the front.

The squad car drove away, and Britt asked, "Are you taking me to the police station?"

"'Fraid we have to take you back to Woodside, son," said the older cop, who sat on the passenger side while his partner drove. "But you're going to be okay. I'm sure the doctor will call your parents and they'll come so you can tell them what happened. Woodside is a good sanitarium."

Amos was waiting at the front door.

"Where's Jim?" Britt asked.

"He went to the hospital," said Amos.

The two cops escorted Britt into the vestibule, where Dr. Sanders waited.

"Hi Britt. I understand you became upset about the ECTs," he said paternally. "You don't have to worry. We're not going to give you any more of those. Let's go into the living room and sit down." The officers took Britt to an armchair.

"I'm going to give you something that will make you feel much better," Dr. Sanders said. He raised his right hand from his side and revealed a hypodermic needle. "You've had injections before and know they don't hurt, and this won't either. Can you pull your sleeve up for me?"

Britt complied, and the doctor injected him in the upper left arm. Britt immediately began to feel hazy.

"Can you walk okay?" Dr. Sanders asked, and Britt rose unsteadily and took a couple of steps.

"Good. We'll help you up the stairs." An officer on each arm, they propped up the wobbly Britt as they climbed to the second floor and over to the cage. Britt felt too groggy to care much.

"Lie on the bed on your back," Amos instructed. He did, and the orderly drew three straps attached to the metal frame on the bed's underside and pulled them over Britt's body. His arms were at his sides where he couldn't move them. Britt was now almost unaware of what was happening, and was too weak to resist, anyway. So he just lay there, the faces around him growing dimmer as he lost consciousness.

CHAPTER 13

Before lunch on Monday, Amos released the straps, took Britt to the bathroom, placed him in the water-filled tub, and asked him to bathe, making sure to get the matted blood out of his hair. Amos waited, then fetched clean clothes from Britt's room. Back in the cage, nurse Gloria applied gauze and tape to the fourth finger of his right hand, and put fresh bandages on the cuts on his feet. She gave him another shot to make him groggy and reattached the straps. The next few days were a fog of sleeping, going to the bathroom under Amos' escort, and eating on a TV tray placed at the edge of the bed in the cage. Each time Britt finished eating, Gloria administered a shot in the arm, and he again was in a haze as she reattached the straps.

After lunch on Thursday, Gloria came to the cage empty-handed. No hypodermic needle.

"Your parents will be here this evening to take you home," she said. Britt was still feeling groggy, but not so much that he didn't understand.

"Wonderful," he mumbled.

Gloria left without strapping him to the bed, and Britt gradually became more aware of his surroundings as the memory of what happened returned.

Amos came at seven-fifteen p.m. and told him his parents would arrive shortly and he wouldn't be having dinner at the hospital.

Fifteen minutes later, Amos appeared at the door, carrying Britt's suitcase, Milton behind him.

"Thank you, sir," Milton said politely but coldly to Amos, then gazed for a moment at Britt.

"Come on, let's go home," he said quietly.

They drove away, and after a couple minutes of silence, Miriam said, "We're very unhappy that we weren't told what had happened until this afternoon when Dr. Sanders called Dad at the office. We would have been there right away."

"We talked to him," Milton said, "and he advised us to take you to the psychiatric hospital at the University of Iowa in Iowa City. He said they had an advanced program there, and they could help you."

"When am I going there?" Britt wanted to know.

"I'm going to call first thing tomorrow morning," said Milton. "Dr. Sanders thought we could get you commit ... admitted on Sunday."

Britt said nothing.

"Is that all right?" Milton asked, turning his head sideways and glancing at Britt sitting in the right corner of the back seat.

"Yeah, I guess so," Britt said noncommittally.

"Dr. Sanders said it was a modern place, and much larger than Woodside. He said you would have a lot more to do. Lots of recreation."

The next day, Friday, Milton went to work at the employment office. Britt slept late, then spent the rest of the day telling Miriam about the hospital, Johnny Kanton, and the breakout, and watching television. At four o'clock, he began doing the farm chores so his dad wouldn't have to do them. He put ground corn in the cow stanchions, then herded in the five cows, which had been milling around the barnyard on this mildly cold winter day. He went about it at a leisurely pace, because the cows couldn't be milked too much before their usual time of five-forty-five or it would disrupt their digestive pattern. By the time Milton arrived home, Britt was almost finished with the milking. Milton stayed inside while his son put the cows' output through the separator and returned to the barn to mix the warm skim milk with ground oats in five-gallon paint buckets. Britt carried the heavy pails to the hog lot, where the seven hogs rushed to the wooden trough and voraciously lapped up the mixture that he poured.

That evening, Britt watched TV with his parents. Milton, smiling approvingly, said, "They told me at Woodside that you got that attendant in the stomach so hard he spent two days in the hospital." Britt grunted, not sure whether to be pleased.

On Saturday, he helped his dad grind more corn and oats in the grinder that he set up outside the corn crib, on the bottom of the hill that fell away from the driveway, which formed a crescent around the house and yard. A six-inch-wide belt ran from the cylindrical pulley on the side of the tractor to its equivalent on the grinder. As the tractor turned the belt,

Britt shoveled cobs of corn into the mouth of the grinder, which churned them up, creating a deafening din. The ground corn passed through a chute and into a wagon parked beside it. After an hour of this, Britt began shoveling the ground corn from the wagon into a wheelbarrow, which he then dumped into a separate part of the corn crib. Meanwhile, Milton shoveled oats from another part of the wagon into the grinder, which gave rise to a white dust that engulfed him, covering his cap and denim coat and pants, and turning his eyebrows white. Now and then he removed his gloves and, holding his thumb against either side of his nose, blew out the dust, wiping the mucous that stuck to his hand on his pants.

The Rutgerses skipped church the next morning. They ate at noon, and at one-thirty the five of them climbed into the Plymouth—Milton and Miriam, Dale, Kyra, and Britt—and set out on the ninety-minute trip to Iowa City. They crossed the bridge over the Iowa River to the University Hospitals, a complex of modern buildings affiliated with the expanding medical school. They found a sprawling, one-story building with a sign in front that read, Psychiatric Clinic. A grassy spread fronted the building, and on one side were tennis and volleyball courts partly covered in snow. The ambience was cheerier and less foreboding than that at Woodside.

A nondescript nurse at the front desk smiled and handed a clipboard with several forms attached to Milton, who thanked her. They sat on chairs in the waiting room while Milton filled out the forms and handed them back. In five minutes, a trim, bespectacled orderly who looked to be in his upper twenties—"probably a graduate student," Milton muttered—entered the room and spoke briefly with the nurse. The fellow turned and said, smiling, "You must be Mr. Rutgers."

"How do you do?" Milton responded.

"I'll take Britt to his room and get him oriented to the routine here at the clinic," the orderly said in a relaxed and casual manner. "Life here is quite pleasant, and I'm sure he'll quickly feel right at home. Why don't you all hug and say goodbye, and I'll show Britt around?"

"Okay, Britt," said Milton, extending his hand for his son to shake. "We'll be here to see you next Sunday," Miriam said, standing stiffly beside Milton, showing no inclination to approach Britt.

"Bye," said Britt.

The orderly stood staring for a moment, a strained smile on his face. "I'm in no hurry," he said

"It's okay, we're through," Miriam replied.

"Uh ... oh. Well then, let's go, shall we, Britt?"

Britt lifted his suitcase and the orderly placed his hand on the new patient's shoulder before leading him out of the office. They walked down a wide hallway with polished gray tile to a dead end with a glassed-in office to the left of double doors. The orderly opened one and they entered a large rectangular room with single beds lining the walls on the long sides.

"This is what we call the Sleep Room in the Men's Ward—because, believe it or not, it's where you sleep," the orderly said with mock amazement, extending his arm in a sweeping gesture. Britt chuckled. "That will be your bed," the orderly added, pointing to the third one from the end on the far wall. Britt took a quick count and came up with ten beds on each side. Off the front end of the room was a small covey with a wide, open entrance. Inside were a round coffee table containing an assortment of magazines and newspapers, and several cushiony chairs. "That's the reading room and you can use it whenever you want to. Now I'll take you to the locker room." Deep, two-foot-wide metal lockers lined one side of the room, which had parallel wooden benches in the middle and a row of porcelain sinks with mirrors directly across. A door in the back of the room led to an identically sized room that had six toilet stalls on one side facing a curtain-enclosed shower stall with six showers. "Why don't you put your suitcase down next to your locker here, number one-eleven, and I'll finish showing you around?"

They walked back out the double doors to where another, narrower hall turned to the right, then a short distance to another set of double doors that fed into the dining room, a bright room with sixteen tables for seating eight. On the opposite side was a wide hallway, and on the other side of it a large, airy room with a lot of natural light coming from windows that were ten feet off the floor. Several patients sat in soft lounge chairs, reading magazines and books from shelves against the walls. In a far corner, more patients were lounging on couches and cushioned chairs positioned in an arc in front of a television.

"Okay, Britt, you're on your own," the orderly said. "Feel free to walk around and explore the place. If you need any help, just ask the fellow in the office by the Sleeping Room. Let's see, what time is it? Going on four. In about an hour-and-a-half, you need to be back at the Sleeping Room, where the guy in charge for the night will give you instructions on dinner and bedtime and so forth."

"Thanks," said Britt. He walked through the dining room to the leisure room. Perhaps a dozen patients of both sexes and ages ranging from probably sixteen to the fifties sat around. The youngest was a very cute girl who caught his eye immediately. She spotted him right away, too, and flashed a big beautiful smile that revealed pearly white teeth. Britt wanted to smile back, but his pulse rate had jumped and his facial muscles were frozen, so he could only stare at her. "Oh darn," he thought, "she probably will think I don't think she's good-lookin'." Sitting on the couch directly in front of the TV was a red-haired, fairly rotund man who held a smoking cigarette between two trembling fingers of his cocked right arm, which was covered with freckles.

Britt took a chair to the left of the couch and could feel the gaze of the girl, who sat in a chair on the other side of the couch and ahead some. He glanced at her, and she smiled again, then gave a little wave. Britt gave a little wave back, then saw her rise from her chair and head toward him. She was about five-feet-two, he figured, and a fetching figure showed through her slacks and buttoned blouse.

"Hi," she said in an electric tone, again breaking into a broad smile. "I'm Susan. I guess you're new here, huh?"

"Oh, hi," Britt said, a little flustered. "I'm Britt. Yeah, I just got here today."

"So what's your problem?" she said, emphasizing "your," then added with a seductive look, "I'll tell you mine if you tell me yours." She giggled and said, "I'm just teasing. I've been here a couple of weeks, and I don't much mind it. Except that I don't get to do all the things I want to do."

"What do you want to do?" Britt asked innocently.

"Oh, that'd be telling," Susan answered coquettishly. Then she began pouting. "I don't like school—so boring—and you have to sit in one place so long. I can't stand it. I wanted to drop out this year—I'm a sophomore—but my dad and mom wouldn't let me. I like having fun."

"What do you like to do?" Britt asked again.

"Ride around in souped-up convertibles, go to the drive-in and get in the back seat with a guy. Heck with the movie. Most of them aren't exciting enough. I'd rather have fun with the guy—if you know what I mean." She smiled oh so seductively, and Britt felt himself getting hard between the legs.

An attractive woman in her upper thirties with shoulder-length brown hair, wearing a knee-length blue denim skirt and a matching sweater, came into the room and walked their way. "Come on, Susan," she said in a sexy, contralto voice that had a hint of admonishment. "It's time to get back to the ward."

"Oh, Barbara, I'm having such a good time with Britt. He's awfully cute, don't you think?" Susan had that coquettish grin again, and Barbara took her by the hand. "Come on, let's go."

"What for?"

"I think you need to be alone in your room for a little while before dinner."

"I hate being alone," said Susan.

"I know you do," Barbara answered. "But you need to learn how to be alone."

"It was nice talking to you, Britt. I hope to see you again," she said, flashing that big smile as she was led away.

Britt checked his watch. Five-fifteen. He rose and headed out of the leisure room, through the dining room, and down the hall to the Men's Ward. Some of the patients were sitting or lying on their beds, and others stood or wandered about the room, chatting with each other or deep in thought. Two middle-aged men on opposite ends of the room were muttering, one with his head down and the other looking straight ahead, obviously oblivious of his surroundings. A corpulent, bald man, about fifty, sat on his bed and stared blankly at the wall. Britt walked to his bed, propped the pillow up against the wall and lay on his back. He closed his eyes, and was drifting off to sleep when a young, tall, rotund, bespectacled fellow with curly hair, wearing a white jacket, announced from the doorway of the office that it was dinner time, and they should all follow him to the dining room.

The food, served in a cafeteria line, was good—lettuce-and-tomato salad with blue cheese dressing, pork chop with gravy, green beans, mashed potatoes, and chocolate cake. Men sat on one side of the room and women on the other. Susan already was seated when Britt arrived, and she sat facing away from him, so they didn't exchange looks. Afterward, the patients were free to spend time in the leisure room or return to the ward and look at magazines off the Sleeping Room or simply lie on their beds. Britt went to the leisure room and watched the Ed Sullivan show, then went to the locker room to prepare for bed. Lights went out at ten, except for the light in the office, where the rotund attendant sat and pored over a book at the desk. The attendants apparently were students at the university, probably graduate students, since they appeared to be in their upper twenties. Britt lay awake, wondering what awaited him in the morning, until sleep overtook him.

For breakfast, at eight, there was a choice of cereals with cream—not milk, but pure, thick cream that was delicious with his corn flakes. He also had two eggs and a piece of toast. Back at the ward, a new attendant was on duty.

"Hi Britt. I'm Don. Don Billings," he said, extending his hand. Billings was a short fellow with a nose that curved a little, forming a slight beak, and a receded chin. He had a crew cut, wore loafers and a V-neck yellow sweater, and had a sprightly, athletic step that complemented his ready smile and upbeat air.

"Patients make their own beds, and I'm going to show you how to make a hospital bed," he told Britt. He pulled the sheet and blanket off the bed, then replaced them, checking to see that each hung over both sides equally. With his fingers, he grasped the covers in a corner at the bottom, lifted them level with the bed, and tucked the part that hung down at an angle under the mattress, leaving a forty-five-degree angle. He repeated the process on the other side, then had Britt try it, which he did with ease.

Billings told Britt that the psychiatrist who'd been assigned to him, Dr. Reginald Campanella, wanted to meet with him in his office after breakfast, at nine-thirty. Britt ate his breakfast in leisurely fashion, downing corn flakes with more of that decadent cream, along with French toast with butter and syrup. Billings then led him down a labyrinth of hallways to the doctor's office. Dr. Campanella rose from his chair behind a big wooden desk, extended a hand, and greeted Britt with a hint of a smile, loudly introducing himself. He was of dark complexion and had a mop of dark hair—Britt guessed he was Italian or Indian. He was a little under six feet and was fairly thickset. Speaking with a New York accent, his mouth opening wide, he said, "I'm going to be your doctor, and I think we're going to get along just great."

Britt always felt almost instant vibrations in meeting strangers, even though he couldn't always intellectualize his feelings. He understood what resonated from Dr. Campanella: The man seemed more like a car salesman than a psychiatrist.

"Now Britt, we're just going to sit here and have a little chat," he said in a loud, condescending tone. Britt was glad Billings had closed the door as he left, because otherwise half the hospital would have heard this conversation. "Tell me how you have felt recently. Obviously, you must not have been feeling very happy or you wouldn't be here."

Britt recounted his feelings of extreme self-consciousness and his inability to concentrate on his textbooks in school. He told of the incident at the bowling alley which seemed to be the straw that broke the camel's back. And he mentioned his fear of the shock treatments at the Des Moines hospital and his breakout.

"Didn't you have any fun in high school?" the psychiatrist wanted to know. "Did you have any friends who you did things with, and date girls?"

"Well, I had a crush on a girl when I was in the eighth grade and met her at a junior high mixer, but my parents kind of teased me about it, and I didn't have another date until my junior year—with the preacher's daughter, who I also had a crush on."

"Did you have her alone and neck with her?"

"Nah. It was just a double-date to a football game. These two girls didn't act very interested. They kept their distance from us."

"What else did your social life consist of? Did you belong to any clubs or groups in high school, or participate in extracurricular activities?"

"I guess not. I wanted to go out for football in the seventh grade, but my mom wouldn't let me. She said I had to keep doing my paper route so I could earn money. Then in high school I worked at a drug store before and after school. Mainly I just ran around on weekend nights with a few pals."

"Did you have a college in mind that you were going to attend after you graduated?"

"No."

"Didn't your parents talk to you about it?"

"No. They just talked about college for my older brother Kevin. They always said he was college material. He took mechanical engineering at Iowa State, but wasn't getting good enough grades so he dropped out in his second year and switched to Thessalonika in Pliny."

"What did you want to do with your life? Weren't you thinking of an occupation?"

"Yeah. I was the second-fastest typist in my class in eleventh grade, so I figured I'd become a typist."

Dr. Campanella went silent. He stared a few seconds at Britt, his mouth open, then said, "Don't you think you're a little too intelligent for that? What subjects were you best at in school?"

"I was always real good in English—always the top speller in the class, got A's. That was in the language part of it. I wasn't as good with the literature, although I wasn't bad. I've never been a very fast reader because I've always wanted to read every word. I was like that in other things, too. My parents called me a perfectionist. But also, my mind always strayed from what I was reading. Except when I really was interested in something—then I read fast. Like I remember I was reading this Western story in the *Saturday Evening Post* when I was about eleven, and I was going through it real fast because it was so exciting. The family was visiting friends of my parents at their farm, and it was time to leave but I didn't want to put the magazine down."

"Well, maybe you should study a language in college. Did your parents ever suggest that to you."

"No."

"Did they praise you for your good grades in English and being the top speller in your class?"

"No. Not that I can remember."

"I see." Dr. Campanella frowned and lowered his head for a moment, then raised it and gazed at the ceiling. "Okay, let's talk about something else. Britt, have you been hearing voices when the persons talking aren't present?"

"Hearing voices?" asked Britt, puzzled. "What kind of voices? The doctor at the sanitarium in Des Moines asked the same question. I don't understand."

"Voices that scare you, or tell you to do something naughty or violent—just something that you wouldn't ordinarily do."

"Where would these voices be coming from?" Britt asked, not knowing where the doctor was going with this.

"Well, they would be in your head."

"You mean voices that I would imagine? Yeah, I love baseball and wanted really badly to be a major league player when I grew up, and my dad took me and my brothers to a minor league game in Des Moines a couple of times. Once I imagined that a foul ball was hit at us, and I caught it and threw it back to the pitcher, and the manager of the team came into the stands at the end of the game and told me I was going to be a great pitcher some day with an arm like that."

"And when was that, Britt?"

"Oh, that was way back when I was thirteen years old."

"Have you heard any other voices since then?"

"No—but I didn't hear any voices back then either. I just imagined it."

"Hmmm. Are you sure you haven't been hearing any other voices lately? It's okay to be honest about it, you know, Britt. I'm your doctor, and I'm here to help you."

Britt just stared at Dr. Campanella for a moment. The guy acted so patronizing, and it seemed like he wanted Britt to admit something that wasn't true. "No, I haven't been hearing any voices. Never have. Like I said, I didn't hear that voice at the ballpark—I just imagined it. You mean people actually *hear* voices? I never heard of that—no pun intended." Britt smiled at his little joke, but the doctor didn't respond. "That's kinda strange, isn't it?"

"Okay, that'll be all," Dr. Campanella said brusquely. "You can go back to your ward." He rose quickly, strode to the door and opened it. Britt walked out and hesitated, then headed down the hallway.

"Oh—do you know your way back?" the doctor called.

"Yeah, I can figure it out," Britt answered, just wanting to get away from him.

He made a couple of wrong turns on the way, but soon was back at the ward, where Billings was in the office doing paper work. "What do I do now?" Britt asked the attendant.

"It's a couple hours yet till lunch," said Billings. "Why don't you just go to the reading room over there, or the leisure room past the dining room? This afternoon, we're going out for a long walk to get some exercise."

Lunch was pleasant—tasty vegetable soup, a Reuben sandwich, cole slaw, and Jello. Billings walked up to most of the men patients and told them to gather in the ward at two p.m. with their coats because they were going outside.

It was mid-March and the air was a crisp forty-five degrees as the troupe of thirteen men and eleven women headed out to the sidewalk in front of the hospital and turned east toward the university campus. Barbara, gorgeous in her fur-collared coat, Britt thought, marched in front and to the side of the group, and Billings took up the rear—like sheep dogs keeping their flock together. Snow made a patchwork quilt of yellowed lawns, and snow on the curbs had turned to slush. The motley group passed the other medical buildings, then the sports complex with the big gymnasium and football field. They arrived at the bridge over the Iowa River, which led to the main part of the campus. Through the streets they trudged, some silently and some chatting with each other. Susan looked back, saw Britt and waved, flashing her big smile, the white teeth contrasting sharply with her red lipstick. They walked up the tiers of wide steps to the majestic edifice that had been the capitol building many decades before, until the capitol was transferred to Des Moines. After following the sidewalks along this part of the city, which rose above the river banks, the entourage returned to the bridge and crossed it on their way back to the psychiatric clinic.

Next morning, after the seven o'clock wake-up, the orderly announced, "The following people must remain here while everyone else goes to breakfast: Alvin Bottoms, Donald Stroh, James Whitman, Britt Rutgers, Harold McElveney. Please stay in your pajamas. You will be allowed to shower and have breakfast later."

Uh-oh, Britt thought. This sounds familiar. Shock treatments. Fear struck and his heart began to pound. He rose from the edge of his bed and walked over to the couch to wait. Ten minutes later, Dr. Campanella strode into the room, his untied white doctor's gown parting at each side as he walked with long, flowing steps. His commanding countenance made Britt think of the biblical story of the Red Sea opening to allow the Israelites to cross over. The doctor had followed the path from his office in Egypt and came sweeping through the sea of patients. On the other side were double doors that he swung open, entering the hallway leading to the ECT room. There, he would administer shock treatments to select patients, wandering through a wilderness of uncertainty as to how the ECTs worked and what damage they might cause to the brain. He knew only that they temporarily erased from memory the recent experiences and thoughts which were so painful for the patient that he or she slipped into a world of fantasy as an escape from reality. Some of these persons imagined that people were against them, maybe even out to do them harm. They heard voices telling them unpleasant things, sometimes directing them to commit deeds that might include acts of violence.

But Britt, while being extremely, painfully self-conscious, never had thought anyone planned to harm him, and he'd never heard such voices or engaged in fantasy that he couldn't identify as such. He just had a misconception about what kind of person he was, in both temperament and aptitude. He was ignorant of Socrates' admonition, "Know thyself," but no matter—he would have utterly failed to heed it. At age ten, when he'd been named an Outstanding Newspaper Carrier by the *Mayfield Daily News*, the caption accompanying his photo in the paper referred to him as a "happy go lucky boy." In fact, he'd denied who he was and tried to emulate his older brother because Kevin was the object of adoration from his parents and Britt was an object that was pretty much ignored by them.

Kevin was in the high school Glee Club, but it had never occurred to Britt to join, because no one had ever told him he had a good voice, though he did, or even suggested that he might want to get involved. He didn't take Latin as his brother did, because he thought he wasn't smart enough—even though his eighth-grade English teacher had described him as "an excellent student." His parents never acknowledged that assessment to him. Failing to realize who he was, Britt did not participate in these courses and extracurricular activities. Instead, he took math courses—advanced algebra, college algebra, geometry, trigonometry—because those were the subjects pursued by Kevin in his aim to become a mechanical engineer.

"Alvin Bottoms, please come to the therapy room," the orderly called out.

Therapy room? What did that mean? It couldn't be group therapy because he'd have called out more names. Besides, why would group therapy be held before breakfast? Some kind of physical therapy? You wouldn't do that in your pajamas. This had to mean electroconvulsive therapy.

Britt's heart began racing again. Fifteen minutes later, the orderly emerged from the double doors and announced, "Donald Stroh." Alvin Bottoms hadn't emerged, so he was still in there—unconscious—Britt realized. Yup, these were ECTs.

Another quarter-hour passed. "James Whitman." And then Britt heard what he dreaded hearing—his own name. He rose from the couch and strode to the orderly, who led him through the double doors into a hallway, and down a short distance to a room on the right. A black examining table was to the right of center, and in the left rear corner was an oxygen tank. Dr. Campanella and two nurses, one a man in his thirties and the other a very young, trim blonde, stood waiting.

"Hello, Britt," the doctor said slowly, sounding cautious. "Just climb up onto the table, if you will, and lie on your back with your head on the pillow. We're going to administer a treatment that will help clear up your mind and make you feel happier. You won't feel a thing, and you have nothing to fear."

Britt's heart pounded, but he complied. The nurse raised a strap attached to the underside of the table and drew it across his pelvis, attaching it to the other side. The female nurse began to massage Britt's temples with the cool gell that he remembered from the sanitarium in Des Moines. The male nurse, who turned out to be an anesthesiologist, wrapped a rubber tube tightly around his right bicep. He then inserted a needle into Britt's right forearm.

"Now I want you to slowly count backward from ten," the doctor instructed Britt.

"Ten … nine … eight … seven … six … five … ."

He woke up on a recuperation table in a room across from the ECT room. The young nurse was standing next to him. "Where am I?" he asked

"You just had an ECT," the nurse said. Her face, somewhat pretty in a hard, pinched way, bore the hint of a smile, and her speech was somewhat crisp.

"Oh, yeah, I remember now," said Britt. He gazed at her. "You look really young to be a nurse."

"I'm a student in the university nursing program," she answered in a noncommittal tone. "You can get up now. Your clothes are hanging up in the shower room, the next room over. You need to shower, and then I'll walk with you to the dining room."

"Great. I'm really hungry."

Only a few patients were scattered about the room having breakfast, and Britt and the nurse took a table by themselves after passing through the cafeteria line.

"What's your name?" Britt asked.

"Sandy."

"Like your hair," said Britt. She smiled slightly.

"Where are you from?" she asked.

"Mayfield. They sent me here after I broke out of a hospital in Des Moines."

Sandy stopped eating and stared at Britt, obviously taken aback.

Hey, I'm not in here for chewing gum in class, Britt thought, but kept silent.

"Why did you break out?" she finally asked, speaking more deliberately, her voice lower.

"I was scared of the shock treatments and wanted to know more about them the night before I was gonna have my fourth one. The two orderlies didn't know the answers to my questions so I wanted to see the doctor, and they wouldn't get him, but I wouldn't let up so they tried to put me in the isolation room. I fought them and won, and ran down the stairs and rammed my fist through a window and jumped through."

Sandy resumed chewing, more slowly, and stared at her plate, then said, "Have you finished high school?"

"No, I have a semester to go."

"Are you going to college?"

"I don't think so. I don't know what I would study. I don't think I'm very good at anything—except English and typing. I thought I'd become a typist."

Sandy tried to repress an amused smile. "You seem pretty bright to me. Why don't you study English?"

"I don't know what kind of job I could get."

"You could teach."

"I s'pose so. But I don't like to get up in front of people."

"Oh, you'd get used to that."

"I don't know."

"Are you finished? Can you make it back to the ward okay? I need to be in class in fifteen minutes."

"Sure. I'll see you later."

Britt walked slowly back to the ward. The guy who'd been sitting on his bed staring straight ahead was now pacing in the open area of the sleeping room. He was quite tall and lean, had light-brown hair combed straight back, and wore wire-rimmed glassed atop a narrow face. He smoked a cigarette and was deep in thought, seeing no one.

"Hi," said Britt, walking up to him. "I just came back from breakfast. Great pancakes. The food here is good, don't you think?"

The man stopped pacing, slowly turned his head toward Britt and stared expressionless for several seconds. "Yes, it's fine," he finally said.

"My name's Britt. What's yours?"

The man stared silently again, then said, his face still blank, "Everett."

"What do you do for a living?" Britt asked, trying to get a conversation going.

Another stare. "Aeronautical engineer."

"Oh, wow. That takes a lot of brains. My older brother just dropped out of engineering school at Iowa State. He was studying mechanical engineering. It was too tough."

The stare again, and finally, "Yes." He resumed pacing, and Britt realized he didn't want to talk.

That night, the same tall, hefty, curly-haired orderly was in charge. At ten o'clock, after everyone had gone to bed and the lights were turned off,

Britt lay on his back, watching the orderly in the corner office at the front of the room, poring over a book. He most likely was married, which was why he had to work while attending college, Britt surmised. He pondered these possibilities for a few minutes, then turned on his side and fell asleep.

Upon rising the next day, he saw the overnight orderly holding the arm of the corpulent man who'd been staring at the wall a couple of days before. The man was wearing his pajama bottom and was naked from the waist up. His pajama and body were heavily smeared in excrement, the most disgusting sight Britt had ever witnessed. "Come on," the orderly said with gentle insistence. "Let's get you in the shower and cleaned up." Britt marveled at the orderly's attitude, wondering how he could even stand to touch the man. Two patients told Britt that when the man underwent shock treatments, he declined anesthesia.

Patients considered functional were given a lot of freedom to do as they pleased in the hours between and after meals, except for those times when activities were scheduled, which were fairly frequently. But the only treatment Britt received was the shock treatments; he received no individual counseling, or even group therapy. The chief benefit he received from his hospitalization was the complete removal from the environment that caused him so much stress and unhappiness. At a time when his confusion and inner turmoil rendered him incapable of filling the roles that his family and society expected of him, he was relieved of those burdens and pressures. Nothing was demanded of him but to follow the rules of the hospital. It was a time-out from responsibility, like coming home from work at the end of the day and relaxing with a cocktail. He wondered later if the same result might have been achieved without the shock treatments.

On this day, a small group of the younger patients were escorted to the campus sports facility for swimming in the indoor pool. Britt had never learned to swim properly, and was to receive an individual lesson from Burt Johnson, a candidate for the United States Olympic team. He was a fairly muscular fellow, maybe five-feet-nine, with prematurely thinning blond hair. He appeared not entirely comfortable with the idea of dealing with a mental patient. But Britt was so eager and normal-acting that the athlete, who was only a few years older, soon was devoting all his attention to the task at hand. He positioned Britt in water reaching to just below his chest. Demonstrating how to breathe, Johnson bent his head sideways and out of the water as he stroked with his left arm and turned his head into the water as he came around with his right arm. When Britt seemed to have gotten the knack of that, Johnson had him hold onto the side of the pool and paddle his legs. Then Johnson synchronized the two techniques, swimming easily through the water. Britt tried to emulate him, but had difficulty coordinating the two motions, which seemed much like patting one's head and stroking one's tummy simultaneously. But he kept at it, Johnson patiently correcting him, and had made considerable progress after a half hour. The lesson was over, and Johnson gave Britt a cordial handshake.

Two days later, Don Billings and the comely Barbara, the two daytime aids in charge of social activities, walked up to the tables of several patients, including Britt and the flirtatious Susan. They were to go and get a sweater or jacket and gather in the hall outside the dining room. The group was going to take a ride in two cars to the varsity baseball field, where the university team was just beginning spring training, even though temperatures were in the mid-fifties. Britt and Susan sat in the back seat of the car driven by Barbara, Britt next to the right door and Susan next to him in the middle. As the car pulled away from the hospital lot into the road, Susan snuggled close to Britt and flashed her radiant, white-toothed, red-lipped smile. Britt felt a surge of desire and wanted desperately to throw his arm around her and kiss those luscious, sensuous lips. Just then, Susan, who had been spying in the rear-view mirror, intervened. "Hey there, young lady, behave yourself," she admonished in her low, sexy voice. Britt wasn't sure which of the two females excited him more. Susan giggled and drew slightly away from Britt.

At the ball field, Britt was transfixed as he watched the college players shag balls that one batter after another sent sailing deep into the outfield. On an adjacent diamond, infielders practiced handling sharply hit ground balls that reverberated from the bat of a coach standing at home plate. Three pitchers on the sidelines wound up and fired rockets into the waiting gloves of catchers. Britt marveled at the skills these young men possessed. Their caliber of play so far out-shone that of the high school teams he'd played with and against that it would be insulting to the college players to compare them, he decided. Suddenly he realized that his dream of becoming a major league pitcher was over. Now he knew that he simply didn't have the talent. And it was okay. The dream gradually had been fading for the previous couple of years as he never was able to achieve consistent control. He had an impressive windup, which he'd practiced since he was ten or eleven, and threw pretty fast. The speed and lack of control scared the dickens out of many batters, causing them to swing wildly at pitches far out of the strike zone, which gave Britt a lot of strikeouts. But he gave up so many walks that the other team often scored a lot of unearned runs. He finally figured out why he had so much difficulty putting the ball where he wanted: His hands were too small.

Evenings were lackluster, usually devoted to watching television. On Sunday nights, however, the men and women patients were paired in a large room to play cards and board games, with refreshments served. A few coeds from the university majoring in psychology or sociology assisted the attendants. On this Sunday, Britt spotted a girl he'd known casually in high school. He remembered her name—Linda Gandon, about five-feet-four, somewhat pretty in a soft way, with dark-brown hair gathered back of her ears and falling to her nape. He watched as she instructed a table of six women how to play a board game that Britt was unfamiliar with. After they got the hang of it, she looked around and saw Britt looking her way. He walked hesitantly toward her, feeling uneasy, but she handled the situation well.

"Hi, you're Britt Rutgers," she said cheerfully. "Sorry to see you in here. I mean, it's good to see you, but I wish it were elsewhere. How are you doing?"

"Okay," Britt answered, feeling relieved, but still a little embarrassed. "I was just feeling rotten in school. But I thought you were still a senior, like me. What are you doing here?"

"I took classes in summer school for two summers, and was able to graduate a semester early."

"So are you doing this to make a little extra money?"

"Actually, I get course credits for doing this. I want to be a social worker in a psychiatric hospital—like this." She glanced over her shoulder at the table of women she'd been supervising, where a woman in her thirties was looking angry and beginning to talk loudly. "I'd better get back there," she said. "I'm sure I'll see you again, Britt. Bye."

Britt felt a little ashamed. Here he was, in the same place with a high school classmate, but in opposite roles—hers noble, and his … . Well, he felt weak, and a bit freakish.

Linda had managed to pacify the woman who was upset, and Britt wandered slowly around the room. Two middle-aged women drinking sodas sauntered up to him and started a conversation with small talk about the hospital living conditions. One made a motion toward a stockily built man in his late twenties and asked Britt if he knew anything about the fellow. Britt didn't, and wondered why they were curious.

"His name's Louis. He played football for the university and was in medical school here, and he had a bad car accident," said the one, a scrawny woman with pointed features and dark hair that gathered mostly at the back of her head. She seemed jumpy, and lighted a cigarette. "The psychiatrists are letting him do physical examinations on us women, and he's a little scary. He doesn't seem all there."

Britt was amused. Hmmm, he thought, I guess that's why he's here—because he isn't all there. In fact, that, presumably, is why we're *all* here.

"He's got this weird look in his eyes," she continued. "And he's built like a bull."

Britt peered again at the man, who was looking off into space, wearing a wacky smile on a round face topped by a closely cropped crew cut. Apparently sensing that he was being watched, he turned his head toward Britt and the two women, and his smile metamorphosed suddenly into a baleful look.

Just then, an attendant announced that the party would adjourn, and everyone was to return to his or her ward. "See ya," Britt said to the women. Back at the ward, he readied for bed, then lay there, anxious about the shock treatment scheduled for the next morning. After a half hour or so, he drifted off to sleep.

"Britt Rutgers." Even though this was his seventh treatment—he'd had three per week—he hadn't grown accustomed to them. Hearing his name called filled him with the same dread he'd felt in the fourth grade when the teacher told him to go to the principal's office. He marched into the therapy room and lay on the operating table.

"Okay Britt, now count backward slowly, starting with ten," Dr. Campanella said in a tone that was meant to be soothing. Britt's heart pounded, nevertheless. "Ten ... nine ... seven ... six ..." Suddenly he felt as though he were in another world that was spinning fearfully.

"Ahhhhhhh!!!" he yelled, simultaneously bolting upright on the table.

Campanella and the nurse reached out to grab him. "It's all right, Britt," Campanella said. "Everything's going to be all right." Britt sat for a moment, then lay back on the table. He awoke in the recovery room, student nurse Sandy sitting beside him.

Nothing was scheduled that afternoon, and he listlessly thumbed through a magazine in the little reading room at the end of the ward near the entrance. He looked up as several white-coated psychiatrists entered the ward and pulled up chairs from the office and the patients' bedsides, forming a circle in the center of the room. They wandered in over the course of a few minutes. Then Louis, the football player/med student, entered, escorted by one of the doctors. The doctor asked him to take a chair separated in the circle a little from the others.

"We want you to just relax, Louis, while I ask you a few questions," said a psychiatrist whom Britt had never seen before, presumably the one assigned to Louis. "The other doctors are here to help assess your, uh, situation, and may take a few notes and cut in now and then with a question of their own.

"I'll tell you anything you want to know," Louis replied with a big, cocky smile. "I'm here to please," he added, chortling.

Britt kept his head lowered in the magazine but turned his eyes upward to watch the proceedings. The doctors hadn't seemed to notice him sitting there.

"How have you been getting along, Louis?"

Before he said anything, Louis leaned sideways and farted loudly. A few of the eight doctors glanced solemnly at each other while the others lowered their heads in embarrassment.

"Oh hell, I've been getting along great," Louis retorted. "Just great." He leaned forward and farted again, even louder. His doctor looked dismayed, but two others smiled slightly.

"I'm having a ball," he went on. "I think I'll just stay here—the hell with getting my degree. You guys give me all this attention—hey, what more could I want?" And he erupted in a big horse laugh.

"Uh, Louis, the reason you're here is to . . . ." Whatever Louis had for lunch was really going to work now, and he let go a real boomer. Now all but two of the doctors were looking down, obviously trying to suppress their impulses to laugh out loud. This in turn prompted Louis' doctor to abandon his façade of decorum and smile in amusement. "As I was saying, Louis, we want you to recover so that you can use your abundant intelligence and contribute to society."

This time Louis let loose a mighty explosion that reverberated through the room. These serious, dignified, erudite men could restrain themselves no longer and broke out in big grins and muffled laughter. Louis' own doctor laughed haltingly while admonishing his patient, "This is a serious matter, Louis, and I hope you regard it as such."

"Sorry, gentlemen," said Louis, grinning broadly. "I seem to have a little problem." And he ripped off another thundering stink bomb.

Now the doctors, no doubt divining the hilarious irony of the situation, made no effort to contain themselves. Eight psychiatrists, shaking with mirth, looking at one another and laughing loudly like a bunch of guys at a beer party, their pretenses of professionalism blown away, literally, by this recalcitrant patient.

"Well, we don't seem to be getting very far," Louis' doctor finally announced. "I guess we'll just adjourn this meeting and get together again at another time. Meanwhile, I think I'll have a talk with the food-and-beverage management about their menus." Shaking their heads and smiling amusedly, the doctors rose and filed out.

Britt wondered who had gotten the most therapy out of that session—the patient or the doctors.

The shock treatments continued. After the eleventh, Britt asked Dr. Campanella how many he was scheduled to have, and was told one more. They were given Monday, Wednesday, and Friday mornings, and the twelfth was on a Wednesday. Britt was fearful that morning, but anxious to get it done and over with. He was happy when he awoke afterward.

When Friday morning arrived, he got out of bed and headed for the locker room to dress. The attendant called, "Hey, Britt, where are you going?"

"I'm getting dressed," he said. "The treatments are finished."

"That's not what our instructions are," he said. "You're on the list for a treatment this morning."

"But Dr. Campanella told me I was only supposed to have twelve, and the twelfth was Wednesday," Britt protested.

"Just a minute," the attendant said. "Let me go back into the therapy room and ask Dr. Cardenas. He's doing them today."

The attendant returned and said, "'Fraid you have one more," Britt. "They decided to finish out the week."

"Aw, no. They told me I was finished. Oh, doggone it." He went to the plastic couch at the end of the room and waited, thinking that fate might cause something to go wrong this time. His name was called, and his heart beat more furiously than ever as he walked to the therapy room. But he managed to control his fear and lay quietly as the needle was injected into his arm.

He woke up with Sandy standing beside him. "Are we ready to begin?" he asked.

"It's over," said Sandy.

"What? It's over? I already had the treatment?"

"Yes," Sandy said, wearing that Harriet Nelson smile. Like the wife in the popular television show *The Adventures of Ozzie and Harriet*, her smile was always restrained, even a little pinched, never radiant. "You're through."

Now he was even happier than after the previous treatment, knowing that he no longer would have to dread the next morning when he went to bed three nights a week.

On Sunday, at two p.m., Milton and Miriam arrived, as they had each Sunday afternoon in the ten weeks Britt had been at the hospital. They would pack a lunch to eat in the car during the eighty-mile drive after leaving church at noon. They spent two hours with him, filling him in on the week's happenings and listening as Britt described events and people in the hospital. A patient walked by in the hallway beside the reception room where they visited. He was in his early forties, about five-foot-nine, portly, red hair and a ruddy complexion. A half-smoked cigarette hung loosely between the fingers of his left hand. He gazed straight ahead through wire-rimmed glasses, apparently lost in thought.

"That's Bielefeld," Britt said. "He's kind of a cantankerous character. Always smoking. He's so red, and his hands tremble—looks like he's about to have a heart attack. I think he drinks coffee like crazy. He's always got an opinion on something, and likes to argue with the attendants, sometimes getting a little loud. But he's never gotten really mad or anything. Doesn't seem like too bad a guy."

Milton and Miriam told Britt about the farm and Dale deciding that he wanted to play football the next school year, when he would be a freshman at Colton High School. Kyra had begun taking piano lessons from Mrs. Fraley, who lived with her husband and their two boys on a nearby farm. She told Miriam that her daughter was making rapid progress on the instrument. Kevin, who had dropped out of Iowa State University at the end of the first quarter and transferred to Thessalonika College in Pliny, was much happier. He had decided to major in biology.

"Kevin left Iowa State and is at Thessalonika?" Britt asked.

"Huh?" Milton asked, looking quizzically at his son. "Yes. You knew that. He left in December, before you went to the hospital in Des Moines."

"Oh," Britt said. "I don't remember anything about that."

"Sure you do," Milton insisted. "Don't you remember—he was having a hard time with his mechanical engineering courses?"

"Yeah, I knew he was taking mechanical engineering, but I didn't know he'd quit and gone to Thessalonika."

"He did construction work for Bill Miller for a few weeks before the semester started at Thessalonika," Miriam joined in.

"Bill Miller? Who's that?"

"He's the contractor in Mayfield who builds houses," said Miriam.

"His son is on the Mayfield High track team," said Milton. "You talked about how fast he was at running the mile."

"Gosh, I don't remember him at all."

Milton and Miriam looked at each other, their faces registering concern.

"Do you remember that Kevin went to see Bobby Jackson and Stan Olson, and told them off for teasing you so badly that night at the bowling alley? We told you about that a couple days after we took you to the Woodside hospital in Des Moines."

"What night at the bowling alley?"

Milton and Miriam stared at each other again, their mouths agape.

"You don't remember that night?" Miriam asked, incredulity in her voice.

"'Fraid not," said Britt.

"Well, I guess the shock … ." Milton cut himself off, and Miriam fumbled with her purse, then checked her watch.

"Oh, my goodness," she said. "It's four-fifteen. Come on, Milton. We've got to get home."

"Yes, the cows will be waiting to be fed and milked," Milton agreed. "Well, we'll see you next Sunday."

They rose, said goodbyes, and walked down the corridor to the entrance.

On Wednesday, the attendant told Britt after breakfast that Dr. Campanella wanted to meet with him and Bielefeld at ten a.m. in the psychiatrist's counseling room adjacent to his office. Bielefeld was there when Britt arrived, staring ahead as usual, and jammed his smoldering cigarette butt in a glass ashtray on the wooden side table next to the steel-and-vinyl couch.

"I wonder what this is all about," he wondered, slowly turning his head toward Britt and making expressionless eye contact. Before Britt could reply, Campanella swooped in, his open white doctor's gown resembling two sails billowing in the wind.

"Good morning Larry and Britt," he said loudly and expansively, as always his tone tinged with condescension. He pulled an armchair from a corner closer to the couch where the two patients were sitting, and sat. "Well, I'm sure you're wondering why I called you to meet with me. Britt, you've been here almost three months and are finished with the ECTs. And you've been with us more than four months, Larry. I have observed a marked improvement in the well-being of both of you, and want to prepare you for an imminent return to life in the outside world."

"How imminent?" Bielefeld piped up. Britt had noticed him frequently immersed in magazines and newspapers, and the ten-dollar word didn't faze him.

"Well, that depends a lot on how comfortable you feel about returning to society and accepting responsibility for your life," Campanella replied, his voice returning to a near-normal level. "I don't think you're a danger to yourself anymore, do you? You don't seem depressed anymore."

"No, I think I'll be fine," said Bielefeld. "Everything got to be just a little too much for me to handle, you know? When you lose your wife and your job, one right after the other, and then when she took the house, after all those years I'd spent fixing it up—the state-of-the-art kitchen cabinetry, the sunroof. But that's all past now. I'm glad to be alive. I'm just so glad that cop talked me off that ledge."

"The important thing," Campanella said, "is that you made the right decision. You decided to come down. And that step off the ledge was your first step toward recovery."

"But how the hell am I gonna get another job in accounting after employers find out I've been in the nuthouse?" He stared straight ahead, and his face brightened. "And then if they find out I was trying suicide from the fifth floor, they'll think I can't even count. Hell, I might not even have killed myself and been a cripple for the rest of my life." He broke into a big, wide grin as he pulled out another cigarette and lighted it with shaking hands.

"It's great that your sense of humor has returned," Campanella said. "Do you think it will be necessary to volunteer that you spent time here at the institute? Don't you think that it would suffice for you to answer any questions by briefly stating that you needed a breather after undergoing a wrenching divorce, and took time to assess your life and decide what direction you wanted to go in? After all, you were laid off only because of down-sizing. Your previous employer surely will give you a good recommendation if called upon for one, don't you think?"

"Yeah, I suppose so," said Bielefeld. "Yes, I think I can handle it."

A moment of silence. Then, "And what about you, Britt?"

"What do you mean?"

"Do you think you will be able to readjust to living outside the hospital?"

"I'm still not sure what you mean by that?"

"I'll try to be more specific," Campanella said. "How are you going to feel about people knowing you were in a psychiatric institution? You know, having mental and emotional problems is no different than having physical breakdowns—such as diabetes, or a weak heart, or cancer. These have to be treated, just as mental difficulties have to be treated."

"Oh, I won't have any problem with that," Britt replied, sincerely. "My parents told me the same thing you did—that mental illness is like any other disease. So that doesn't bother me."

But what Britt felt was unrealistic. The shock treatments had rendered him less sensitive—toward himself and toward others. While mental health professionals were insisting that mental illness was indeed like any other disease, the general population did not feel that way. Mental illness carried a stigma, regardless of the preaching of experts. Society was not convinced, as witness the case of Sen. Thomas Eagleton of Missouri, whose vice-presidential candidacy in 1972 was doomed after the media revealed he'd undergone three shock treatments. The vast majority of people viewed persons with psychological illnesses as unstable, weak, even dangerous to themselves and others—and sometimes for good reason. The psychological demons that tortured the soul were conceived and nurtured during childhood, and they became firmly ensconced in the human psyche. Battling these demons continued throughout one's life, and often the best that could be hoped for was to keep them from getting out of control. One might overpower them, but they were never completely subjugated and, when their owner was especially vulnerable, would lurch forth and try to break their bonds.

But he didn't feel that way now. He wasn't worried about what people might think of him.

"Will you be able to do your school work and relate to other people comfortably?" Campanella continued.

"What do you mean—relate? Do you mean, will I be able to get along with people, and not feel uptight around people who aren't members of my family?"

"Uh ... yes, I guess that's what I mean."

"I'm not sure. I feel pretty good about everything right now. Actually, I've never had much trouble getting along with people. I've just gotten embarrassed easily with people I don't know well."

"Well, Britt, hiding from people isn't going to help you conquer this problem. You're going to have to face people and try to deal with the pain. You know, people aren't thinking about you all the time. They have their own problems that they're much more concerned with. You are exaggerating their interest in you."

"You think so?"

"I know so."

"I suppose you're right," Britt shrugged, unconvinced.

"Now—what do you intend to do when you leave this institution? Have you thought about the future?"

"Not a lot. I've just wanted to get well enough to get out of here. But I have to finish the last semester of high school."

"And what will you do after that?"

"Well, I'm a real good typist. I was the second-fastest in my class in eleventh grade. And it was a big class. So I was thinking I'd become a typist."

Campanella stared at Britt, and finally said, "Britt, that's what you told me in the interview when you arrived. But I think you are intelligent enough to do something a little more challenging. It's good that you can type fast, but what else have you excelled at in your school studies? You told me you were good at English, is that right?"

"Well, I was the best speller in the third grade. And I've always gotten good grades in everything about English. Except literature—I don't read very well. I'm slow, and can't concentrate—unless I'm reading something that I'm really interested in."

"I think you told me you hadn't studied a foreign language," Campanella said. "Why not?"

"No. My older brother Kevin took Latin, but I didn't think I was smart enough for that."

"But you were always good in English. Didn't you know that if you're good in one language, you're likely to be good in others, too?"

"Huh-uh. I never thought about it that way."

"Well, maybe you ought to think about taking courses in another language. Or perhaps you could take more English courses and aim toward becoming a teacher. I'm sure that once you are able to relax, you'll be a better reader."

"I hope so."

"Okay, Britt … and Larry. I think both of you are ready to go back out into the world and lead happy, normal lives. Not that you won't have times when things seem difficult. But I think you've reached the stage where you can handle these low periods. So I've scheduled your release for four days from now. I'll notify your parents, Britt, and they can come and get you. Larry, as you know, your sister has arranged to have you live with her until you can get a job and get back on your feet. Good luck, gentlemen."

Campanella rose, and Britt and Larry followed suit. The doctor extended his hand to each of them, and then they returned to the ward.

On Sunday, Britt packed his belongings in his suitcase, and was ready when Milton and Miriam arrived at noon. They'd skipped church that day. As Britt walked with his parents down the hall toward the exit, a wave of regret and shame swept through him. What had been lying dormant in his subconscious suddenly rose to a semiconscious level. Now that he was leaving this place, he knew that it wasn't necessary for him to have been there. He couldn't fully comprehend the emotion that he was experiencing, but what it meant was that breaking down was the only way he had of getting attention—and love.

CHAPTER 14

It was late May, and Britt's class at Mayfield High School was about to graduate and face the world or college. Britt had a reprieve from both. He had to finish high school first. But the second semester didn't begin until January, so he needed to find a job. Milton had bought an old, beat-up pickup to haul grain and tools around the farm, and painted it silver. Its springs were shot, and driving the thing—dubbed the Silver Streak by Dale—over the bumpy fields was like riding a bucking bull. Britt drove it a few miles to the construction site of Interstate 80, the new highway that would replace U.S. 6 as part of President Eisenhower's nationwide interstate program. He asked the crew foreman if he could use a laborer.

"You going to college?" asked the foreman, a stocky man in his forties, less than average height. He wore a neatly trimmed mustache, and in a suit and tie he could have passed for an insurance salesman.

"I have to finish high school next year, and if I can make enough money, I'll go to college that fall."

"Okay, I'll put you to work," the foreman said gruffly. "You can start now. Go help that guy unloading those sacks of cement off that truck. They weigh a hundred pounds. Think you're strong enough? You're kinda skinny."

"Oh yeah, no problem," said Britt.

"Okay, go to it."

The young man by the truck jumped into the back and dragged the sacks to the edge, where Britt took over and carried them a dozen feet to a culvert that other workers were building. The bags were heavy, but Britt was stronger than he looked—he'd fended off two burly sanitarium guards, hadn't he?—and had little trouble handling them.

The work on the culvert continued for three days, and then the foreman looked around for something else that Britt could do.

"That pile of lumber over there," he said, pointing to a large, scattered assortment of boards that had been used in making frames and borders, two hundred feet away up a mild incline in the bare earth. "Sort 'em out and arrange 'em in neat stacks."

As the temperature rose to the high eighties, the sun beat down relentlessly in a nearly cloudless sky, with no breeze offering relief. After several hours of rummaging through the wood pile, Britt was soaked in sweat and bored in the extreme, with no one to talk to as he worked. He became listless and glanced frequently down the incline to where the other workers were now laying concrete drainage pipes that led away from the culvert. He was hoping the foreman would summon him to help the men. Finally, the foreman called for him.

"I've been watching you, and you're shirking," he said vexedly.

"It's awful hot up there," Britt whined.

"Well, if you can't take it, then you can go home. I didn't really have a job for you, but I wanted to help you out since you were planning on college. Go on home."

Britt said nothing and walked with his head down to the Silver Streak. He was ashamed, and knew his parents would be angry. Their staunch, Dutch work ethic did not countenance slacking, and getting fired from a job was a disgrace. During the Depression, Milton had worked himself nearly to the point of exhaustion to avoid such embarrassment.

They were indeed upset, and would have reacted more strongly if Britt hadn't just re-entered society after months of facing no responsibilities and recovering from an emotional breakdown.

"What? You got fired?" Milton said, his face registering mild shock. Then he fell silent and hustled out the door to do the evening chores.

"You obviously weren't doing your job if you got fired," Miriam said angrily. "You need to get the lead out of your pants and be responsible. We're not going to take care of you for the rest of your life."

Britt didn't respond and was despondent the rest of the evening, watching television in silence. The next day, he rose to help Milton with the chores, then decided to placate his parents by tending to the manure pile in the barnyard. He spun the big flywheel on the John Deere B until the motor caught and it went into a tut-tut-tut-tutting idle, then hooked the manure spreader's tongue to the back of the tractor and drove to the edge of the pile. The winter cold had ended a few months before, and by now the pile had thawed so Britt could shove the pitchfork into it and fling green gobs into the spreader. In April, Milton had run the tandem discs over the cornfield from the previous year to cut up the stalks before plowing up the field for replanting. He planted corn in mid-May, later than usual because of cold weather and snow that fell in early April. The corn hadn't sprouted through the soil yet, so it was not too late to spread manure. By day's end, Britt had obliterated the manure pile in four loads that he spread throughout the eleven-acre field. Then he milked the five cows, ran the milk through the cream separator, and fed the skim milk with a mixture of ground oats to the hogs.

Milton was delighted with the large amount of work his son had accomplished. After dinner, while Dale was doing school homework and Kyra was practicing her piano lesson, Britt remained at the dinner table and discussed his immediate future with his parents. They'd decided he needed a little time before returning to a full-time job, and it would be best for him to work on the farm and earn money by hiring himself out to the neighboring farmers. In January, he would return to high school to finish his last semester.

Dale's best friend at Colton High School, Fuzzy Tomovic, lived on the farm adjoining the back side of the Rutgers' farm. Dale told him that Britt was looking for work while waiting to finish high school. Fuzzy told his dad, and soon Britt was asked to help ring some hogs. Britt walked with Fuzzy's dad, Vance, and his brother from up the road, Jan, to a low-lying shed. They entered, Vance carrying a rope with a noose. The long, narrow shed was filled with white Yorkshire hogs—large, elongated animals whose bristly backs reached to only eight inches below Britt's waist. There were about sixty packed together so tightly they couldn't turn around, and their grunting and squealing made a cacophonous din. Britt was terrified.

"Okay, let's go," said Vance, a short, lean, curly haired man. Though of Slavic background, his twinkling eyes, impish grin, and high energy gave him the look and manner of an Irish sprite. He and Jan squeezed themselves through the congregated swine, with Britt following. "This is the biggest one," Vance said, pointing to a specimen straight ahead. "Let's get that sucker out of the way first." He dangled the noose above and behind the animal's head until it opened its snout and raised its head in curiosity, whereupon he snagged its jaw. Jan was a tall, slightly bent fellow who wore a hook on the stump of his left forearm to replace the hand amputated in an accident with a corn-picking machine. He straddled the bellowing hog to hold it in place. Vance handed the noose to Britt, who was petrified with fear. What, he wondered, would prevent these hogs from sinking their tusks into him and the two men and devouring them?

"Hold it tight," Vance said, his voice as taut as the rope. Vance pulled the pliers-like ringer from his pocket and inserted an oval ring. "Pull his head back," he yelled to Britt, then reached down to the hog's gaping, tusk-filled jaw and, the animal screaming hideously, clamped the ring into its nostrils. "Let up on the rope," Vance ordered, and slipped the noose out of the fearsome jaw.

"My gosh, do we have to do all of these hogs?" Britt asked.

"Whatsa matter, you tired of it already?" Vance mocked, grinning mischievously as he winked at Jan. "Let's see," he said, looking at his watch, "it's one o'clock. I figure we'll be through by midnight."

"Oh, it'll probably go way past that," Jan added in a semi-drawl.

"Don't you see the rings in most of their noses?" Vance said. "We only have eleven to do—ten left."

"So why are the ones that already have rings in the pen?" Britt wondered.

"You want to run around the pen chasing these guys?" Vance answered. "When they're so packed in like this, they can hardly move, and that makes our job easier."

"But what if they get scared or angry and attack us?" said Britt.

"They know that if they did that, they wouldn't get fed tonight," Jan kidded, sounding almost like a Southerner with his slow-paced delivery. "Come to think of it, they wouldn't need to be fed. We'd be their dinner." His triangular face opened into a wide grin and his eyes brightened through thick-lensed glasses. He and Vance chortled.

"Hogs don't attack humans unless they have pigs and you get too near," said Vance. "And unless you fall. Then you're in trouble. They'll pounce on you like a tiger. So don't slip—'cause we won't be able to save you."

Britt's fear gradually subsided as the other hogs were ringed and it became obvious to him that they were harmless as long as he remained upright. The whole job took less than three hours.

"There," Vance declared as he pulled on the rope that raised a hatch at the far corner of the shed, allowing the hogs to exit. "We won't have any more problems with those bastards rooting under the fences." He led Britt back to the house and made out a check for six dollars—better than the pay of between a-dollar-fifty and one-seventy-five an hour that he usually received for farm work.

Britt was scheduled to return to the Tomovic farm the next day to help with hay baling. A little rain had fallen during the night, and he knew the baling wouldn't begin until after the sun had dried the hay, so he arrived after lunch. Vance and one of Jan's teenage sons were in an outdoor pen, castrating pigs. Britt had helped his uncle Don castrate a few pigs on the Rutgers farm the year before. He'd held the pig's head in the dirt with his knee while his uncle sliced the sack holding the testicles of the hellaciously screaming animal with a razor blade, then slit the inner membrane, and cut the connecting cord. Finished, he tossed the testicles aside. Britt would release the pig, which would scamper off, grunting as though it were no big deal.

Britt was squeamish about any bloody procedure on man or animal. He was apprehensive about having a needle stuck in his arm for drawing blood. But he had endured this gruesome episode without becoming nauseated. However, the pigs that the Tomovics were castrating were much larger. Britt hated his unmanly queasiness in such situations, and was determined to watch the castrations. Soon, however, nausea overcame him, and he had to avert his eyes lest he throw up before the hay-baling had even begun. That afternoon, he rode in a wagon behind the tractor-drawn baler and stacked four loads of bales, a task he'd performed several times in his first year on the farm.

The word spread through the area that Britt was available, and he was called upon increasingly. In late June, it was time to cultivate the corn. One evening he and Milton mounted the antique piece of equipment on the John Deere A, a larger tractor than the B, which Milton had purchased to speed up the field work. Britt spent two days in the field, guiding the tractor up and down the gently rolling hills of sprouting corn. He steered precisely in the middle of the even rows so that the V-shaped shovels dug up the weeds on either side and didn't hit the corn. Strips of grass were allowed to grow at the bottoms of the hills to absorb runoff from rains and prevent ditches from forming. Approaching them, he stood on the tractor platform and, with his right hand, pushed hard on the long lever that raised the mechanism holding the shovels. As the tractor crossed the grass, he pulled the lever back to lower the shovels.

After Britt finished the Rutgers field, he was hired by Howard Watson, a short, good-humored World War I veteran, to hoe a twenty-acre field on his nearby farm. The Watson farm was one-hundred-twenty acres, and he owned a Farmall tractor that was much newer and larger than the Rutgers' John Deeres. The cultivator was hydraulically operated by way of a small lever that required little effort to manipulate, and Britt swept through the field in two days, earning twenty-eight dollars.

Milton had bought a Guernsey bull to sire Fanny, which gave birth to twins. The herd now comprised five cows, and the barn wouldn't hold more, so he decided to have the bull castrated. His friend and neighbor Carl Klatsch came over one day in late summer, and he summoned Britt to the barn, where the bull was held in a stanchion. Britt told the short, powerfully built, ruddy-complectioned man that he probably would get sick watching the cutting. Klatsch assured him no cutting would occur. It was an easy, bloodless process of using a clamp to sever the internal cords through which the semen passed.

Relieved, but still anxious, Britt stood back of the bull while Klatsch positioned the large steel clamp above one of the testicles and pushed the two handles together. Strong as he was, however, he couldn't get the clamp to close.

"Help me," he gasped, the veins protruding in his thick neck. Britt moved in to his right side, placed both hands on Klatsch's, and pushed inward with all his strength. The clamp closed, and the two stepped back. The bull, not feeling too feisty, emitted a slow groan and lowered itself to a lying position. After about fifteen seconds, it scrambled to its legs. Klatsch repeated the procedure above the other testicle, and Britt again helped force the clamp to close. The bull again went down, then rose, and Klatsch released it to the barnyard.

Kevin had asked Milton to use his resources at the Employment Service to find him a job for the summer. After all, finding jobs for people was Milton's responsibility, so he surely could find one for his own son. But Milton resisted, saying very few jobs were available and Kevin should go out and look for work himself.

That night in the bedroom Kevin and Britt shared, Kevin groused about their dad. "Everybody thinks we have it made finding jobs because Dad works with the Employment Service. But he's afraid that if he finds us a job and we screw up, it'll make him look bad."

Two days later, however, Milton said the Mayberry Company, maker of farm wagons, needed a man to prepare the roof underside of its large warehouse for painting. Kevin went to the site and was joined by another young fellow looking for work. The supervisor pointed to a platform atop a scaffold from which two twelve-inch-wide, parallel planks extended to another scaffold on the other side of the open warehouse. Awaiting them atop the scaffold, he said, were two gas-powered air-blowing contraptions.

These they would carry onto the planks to blow the dust off the aluminum underside of the roof, fifty feet above the concrete floor. He cautioned them to be careful and go slowly at first, because if they tripped or lost their balance as they held the blowing machines above them, it was curtains.

"The other guy looked up and said, 'I'm not going up there,'" Kevin told Britt that night. "So I walked out on those planks, and they weren't even connected to each other, so each one bent a little with each step I took. I was terrified. But by the afternoon, I was okay; I wasn't scared anymore."

"But if you'd fallen, you'd have been killed," said Britt.

"Yeah, that's why I was so scared."

"Boy, I never would have gone up there," said Britt, adding, "Didn't Dad know how dangerous that job was?"

"The company guy who placed the job opening with the employment office must have described the job," Kevin said.

"And Dad is scared to death of heights," Britt said, shaking his head. "He won't even fly in an airplane."

"Yep," said Kevin. "I know."

Kevin returned to Mayberry the next day and finished the job. Then he decided to call Bill Miller of Miller Construction, whom he'd worked for before, in case he needed someone again. Kevin worked for him the rest of the summer.

From late October to mid-November, Britt was busy helping with the corn harvest. In the several weeks after that, he did odds and ends around the Rutgers farm and the neighbors'. During the eight months after his release from the hospital, he did little other than work during the day and watch television at night. His friends had graduated from high school and enrolled in college in the fall, so Britt stayed at home with his parents and siblings. But Bobby Jackson, home from nearby Drake University on a weekend in late September, called and asked if he wanted to join a group of guys for football that Sunday afternoon in Mayfield. Britt met the gang of a dozen or so high school students and recent graduates for a game of tackle football on the large grassy spread atop the water reservoir. Britt loved the rough play and the chance to mingle with peers, and the Sunday sessions continued until the end of November, when it became too cold to continue. Although no one wore any protective gear, the only injury in those ten weeks was a broken finger sustained by Sammy McCaffrey, a sophomore who became a star halfback for the Mayfield varsity team. Sammy suffered more-serious injuries a year later when a car occupied by him and three other teenagers collided head-on with another car at the crest of a hill on a rural gravel road. All four were killed.

About the only other time Britt left the farm was Sunday mornings to attend church. He sat in the balcony, in the back row. The church deacons gave him the responsibility of passing the collection plate on one end of the half-dozen rows of pews. He had to accept it from a parishioner at the end of a row and make sure that he handed it two rows up instead of to the next row. Another plate was headed down that row, and a collision of collection plates would have resulted along with mass (in a Protestant church, no less) confusion. He tried to seem nonchalant but felt a little stiff and self-conscious. But it was a good exercise in preparation for his return to society, which kicked into high gear in mid-January with his resumption of school classes.

CHAPTER 15

Britt took a class in chemistry, mainly out of curiosity. He did okay in the course, but didn't excel. He was beginning to loosen up and have fun—too much fun, in fact. The teacher, Mr. Chisolm, was a quiet, tall, good-looking, middle-aged man who possessed a lean, muscular body that gave him an athletic appearance. In fact, he doubled as wrestling coach. He had a pensive, bespectacled face that conveyed an academic bent. His slow, deliberate method of instruction rendered him boring, and Britt began to lean forward frequently to get the attention of the girl in the seat ahead of him. Finally, Mr. Chisolm tactfully warned, without looking at Britt, "Will the person who is incessantly chattering please be quiet and pay attention?"

Early in the term, Rhoda Godwin, Britt's English and speech teacher from the eighth grade, spotted him at the end of a school day and asked if he would help her unload some materials from her car. She was one of Britt's two all-time favorite teachers, and he was glad she'd asked him, just as she'd chosen him to run errands five years earlier.

"Britt, how would you like to try out for the next school play?" she piped up as he lifted a box out of the trunk.

Britt hesitated, then said, "Naw, I couldn't. I wouldn't be able to perform in front of an audience. I mean, I can act pretty good when I'm messing around with my brothers. I do a pretty good Ed Sullivan imitation, and I got everybody laughing with my imitations of preachers in the churches we've gone to. But that's just doing it without thinking, and not before a lot of people."

"You didn't have any trouble in my speech class, remember? You were very good. I gave you an A." Miss Godwin spoke quietly and smiled softly, almost shyly, showing a different side from the one that appeared in front of a class. In fact, it struck Britt just then that this was the real Miss Godwin, and her carefree, flamboyant classroom image was something of an act.

"Yeah, I know," he said. "But I'm different now. I'm just awfully uncomfortable if a lot of people are watching me."

"Really? There's no reason for you to be that way. Well, how would you like to work behind the scenes—putting up the sets, helping with the costumes, that sort of thing?"

Britt wanted to please Miss Godwin, but felt so self-conscious and awkward in mixed groups. And she, an astute reader of personalities, saw clearly what had happened to her star pupil, and wanted to help him find the self-confidence that he sorely lacked. Alas, it was hopeless.

"Thanks an awful lot," said Britt. "But I don't think so."

"Well, okay Britt," Miss Godwin said, shrugging. "I'm sorry you don't feel up to it. But if you change your mind, be sure to let me know anytime. Okay?"

"Sure, Miss Godwin. Thanks again."

If Britt found Mr. Chisholm's chemistry class tedious, he didn't get much chance to be bored in the English class of Miss Spahn, a late-middle-aged woman, slightly plump, who kept her gray hair tightly braided and wore long dresses and wire-rimmed glasses. Her aim was to prepare the students for college, whether they were headed there or not, and she wasted no time, lecturing without pauses. One day, she announced that the students must take notes of her lecture, because that's what they would have to do in college. Britt wrote madly, but was much frustrated that he couldn't get it all down, and was angry with her for speaking so rapidly. He handed in his notes as required, thinking he had done poorly. Two days later, after class, Miss Spahn stopped him as he was leaving and told him he had done quite well. She was similarly impressed with a short "theme paper" he had written about a baseball game that he had pitched at Colton High School. He'd described the sunlit, well-manicured field and the ball smacking into his glove, concluding with the observation, "Everything was happy." She said that she loved baseball, too. She asked Britt what else made him happy.

"Well … hmmm." Britt rested his chin on his hand, his elbow on the desk, and thought for a few seconds. "I guess that's it."

"What else do you do well?" Miss Spahn asked.

Another pause. "Not much of anything, I guess."

"You write well," the teacher said.

"I do?"

"Yes. Didn't you know that?"

"Well, I guess I never gave it much thought."

"Are you going on to college?"

"I'm not sure yet. I think so."

"I think you should, and you should consider majoring in English."

"Somebody else told me that," Britt said.

"Okay, Britt, I'll see you in class tomorrow," said Miss Spahn.

Britt was still having trouble concentrating in the afternoon study hall sessions. "Pop" Lenahan, the amiable and popular high school principal, stopped him in a hallway one day and asked how he was doing. Lenahan, an average-sized man in his mid-fifties, balding with wisps of white hair, had a ready, sincere smile for everyone. He knew, and was concerned about, all the young people under his jurisdiction. Britt said he was having difficulty coping with the distractions of a lot of kids around. Lenahan authorized him to study in the usually empty student lounge, where he could get comfortable on one of the plastic-covered couches.

Britt soon became too comfortable, chatting with an occasional student who for some reason or other was free for the period and stopped to talk. One afternoon, Pop Lenahan strolled through the lounge while Britt was talking and laughing with a fellow student. This time Lenahan didn't smile as he slowed to stare at Britt. The principal didn't say anything and kept going, but Britt got the message. If he were to continue receiving this special privilege, he'd better buckle down and study like the other students were doing in study hall.

In early April, Britt decided he'd like to try out for the track team. He never had been particularly fast, but was able to run long distances without tiring. On a Sunday evening when Kevin was home from college on spring break, Britt mentioned his plan to join the track team and run distance events. Kevin, a fast, sprint-styled runner, challenged Britt to see how fast he could run a mile. He would run down the gravel road leading from the farm to U.S. Highway 6, with Kevin following in his car to measure a mile. They'd finished dinner an hour before, and Britt, wearing his street shoes and long pants, set out running. He felt strong and stretched out at a brisk pace. But a half mile into the run, he began to flag.

"You're slowing," Kevin yelled out the window of his car.

"I'm getting winded," Britt panted.

A quarter mile later, he was gasping, but Kevin drove the car close behind him so he could not slacken.

"You don't have much farther to go," Kevin shouted, leaning out the window. "Don't stop. Keep up the pace."

Finally, almost ready to collapse, Britt heard Kevin shout, "That's it. That's a mile." Britt immediately stopped, but Kevin told him to walk it off, saying it was bad for his heart to stop abruptly. Britt stumbled a few yards, gasping all the while, until his wind returned, and he turned to Kevin, who kept following.

"Five minutes and thirty-five seconds," said Kevin. "Not bad for the first time."

Britt got in the car and, as they drove back, Britt said he wasn't so sure he wanted to go out for the team.

"Oh, it'll be a lot easier once you get in shape," Kevin assured him.

On the Monday a week later, Britt told the track coach, Ken Tennet, that he wanted to go out for the team. Tennet, a tall, lanky, but slightly bent man who wore glasses on a narrow face, told him to bring shorts and tennis shoes and be ready to run the next day. It was a mild, sunny day, and Tennet had Britt join three veterans of the two-mile relay in a half-mile jaunt. The four, with Britt bringing up the rear, took off on the grass of the practice football field and circled beyond it to the outside of the field used for varsity games. It was a fast pace, but Britt kept up until the last fifty yards, when he fell a few yards behind and was gasping in misery when he finished. He fell to the grass, but Tennet ordered him up. "Walk it off," he insisted. "That's bad for you. You have to gradually reduce your heart beat."

Britt had managed to almost keep up with the team members, though they were not nearly as winded. Tennet looked at him approvingly and said, "You'll do all right. Come on back tomorrow. We'll get you some track shoes, and you'll be able to run better."

"Yeah, but I couldn't keep up with these guys," Britt said.

"You did fine—a lot better than I expected," said Tennet. "They've already done this for two or three years. And they're in better condition. You'll get in better condition too. You might be the slowest of the four, but not by much. We probably can use you for the two-mile relay."

After two weeks of daily running, Britt's speed and conditioning had improved, and he was ready for the first track meet, against Myrtleton, at Mayfield. He ran in the slowest spot, number two, in the four-man, two-mile relay, and the Mayfield team won. Britt ran his segment in two minutes thirteen seconds.

The season progressed. Meets were on Friday afternoon, and Britt's last class of the day was Social Studies. He became excited and nervous as the class wore on, and hoped some of his classmates would be aware that he was facing something very demanding and important.

On the last meet of the season, Mayfield faced Nathan High School of Des Moines, the big city thirty-five miles away. Nathan had the best two-mile relay team in the Central Iowa Conference, with the speedy, six-foot-five-inch Stan Dorsey running anchor. Dorsey was the guy who made the team what it was. He would receive the baton with his team behind, and invariably would catch up and pass the other team's anchor for the victory. The first Mayfield runner handed off the baton to Britt ahead of the Nathan runner, and Britt managed to hold the lead, losing no ground but gaining none, either. Mayfield's third runner widened the gap, passing the baton to the anchor, Karl Bradley, giving him a substantial lead.

Bradley, a sophomore, was a newcomer to the team. He was a sandy-haired, ruddy-cheeked farm boy whose dad had died the year before. Karl, the oldest child in the family, was left to manage the farm while attending school full-time. It was a huge responsibility for a boy of sixteen, and now he was faced with another big challenge—holding the lead against Stan Dorsey. Karl sprinted with the baton and swept around the cinder track, completing the first quarter-mile in an amazing fifty-two seconds, a fast time just for the quarter-mile. Tennet and Karl's teammates were awestruck, and stared silently with mouths agape. Karl actually had gained ground on Dorsey. But coming around the first turn in the second lap, he began showing the effects of the blistering pace, gradually slowing. Dorsey was gradually narrowing the distance between them, but Karl kept running at what actually was a normal pace. He made it around the second turn and headed into the final stretch. Dorsey was gaining, but he had a lot of distance to erase. As Karl came closer, Tennet and the other Mayfield runners realized that he was going to win by about a dozen yards. But they also were alarmed at what they saw. Karl's lips were blue and his eyes bulged from their sockets. He crossed the finish line and collapsed into the arms of Tennet and two of the other runners, who mostly carried him forward on the track as his legs repeatedly buckled.

"Try to walk," Tennet shouted, looking very worried. Karl's face was the mirror of agony, much like that of Christ on the cross in the ubiquitous painting. He continued gasping for several minutes as he staggered, until he finally was able to walk unsupported. Dorsey, feeling much less spent, walked up to Karl, put his arm around his shoulder, and said something congratulatory. Karl in turn put his arm around the middle part of the back of the youth who was seven inches taller. Mayfield had tied Nathan for the conference championship.

The school year came to a close, and Britt joined his two-hundred or so classmates in parading across the gymnasium stage to receive his diploma. But they were not the classmates he'd been with until that semester, and he knew them only as acquaintances, not as friends. It was not a joyful occasion for him.

CHAPTER 16

Kevin had transferred from Iowa State to Thessalonika two-and-a-half years before and was home again for the summer. He went back to doing carpentry for Miller Construction. Miller needed a laborer, Kevin said, and asked if Britt wanted the job. Britt jumped at the opportunity to have steadier work than the neighboring farms offered, and hopped in the car with Kevin at six-forty-five the next morning to begin the new job in Mayfield. Except for operating a typewriter, Britt had no talent with his hands, and he drove nails into boards at about half Kevin's pace. Miller had him help Kevin with the carpentry only when there were no other tasks, such as mixing concrete and hauling it in a wheelbarrow. Britt carried boards from the pile of lumber to the house under construction and held pieces of wood in place while his brother and the boss wielded the buzz saw in cutting them to size.

Britt knew his job would terminate at summer's end, when Kevin returned to college. It was time for him to decide what to do with his life. Going back to doing farm work for any length of time would make for a bleak future, he realized. Besides, he had felt increasingly comfortable with himself as the school term had wound down. Dr. Campanella, Miss Spahn, and Miss Godwin had all told him directly, or inferred, that he had talent and brains, and he should make use of them. At last he understood that he was smart enough for college.

Milton and Miriam had not broached the subject, but after a month or so, Britt brought it up.

"I think I'll go to Thessalonika," he announced one night after dinner while Miriam washed, and Milton wiped, the dishes. Ordinarily, washing dishes goes faster than wiping them, but the meticulous Miriam was the opposite of the slipshod Milton, and the dishes went back into the kitchen cabinets only half-dried.

"Go to college?" Milton said, surprise in his voice. He held the plate he'd begun working on motionless in his hand a few seconds, then gave it a swipe and deposited it on the shelf. "When?"

"This year. I think they start in September, don't they?"

Miriam stood still with her hands in the water while she and Milton looked at each other.

"What made you decide you want to go to college?" asked Miriam.

"Well, you know, I don't want to do this for the rest of my life. Get up in the morning and do the chores, putter around the farm, help the neighbors, do chores again, eat, watch television, go to bed. Watch Lawrence Welk with you two on Saturday night and go to church Sunday with you and Dale and Kyra. That's not doing much with my life. Besides, my teachers think I'm talented and smart."

"Don't you like being with us?" asked Milton.

"No, it's not that at all," Britt countered, a bit peevishly. "But what other kids do this? They either get a job or go to college, and then get a job. And I might want to get married some day. I don't want to sit around at home and depend on you two all my life. I want to lead a normal life."

A long pause ensued, and then Miriam said, "Well, why don't you think it over a little while longer? You don't have to decide right away."

"I don't have much time," said Britt. "I have to apply for admission, just like Kevin did, and can't do that at the last minute."

"Okay," said Miriam. "But consider it for a couple of days, and then we'll talk about it again. All right?"

Milton customarily went to bed at nine o'clock, with Miriam retiring later, but on this night she went to the bedroom with Milton.

"What do you think?" Milton asked.

"I don't think it's a good idea," Miriam replied. "Look how depressed Kevin got at Iowa State when he studied all the time but still couldn't get good grades in those engineering subjects. Britt would have even more trouble."

"Well, there's a lot of pressure in college, that's true," said Milton. "But Britt's not dumb, and if he applies himself, maybe he'll do all right. On the other hand, he might have difficulty mixing with the other students. It's a whole different environment."

"Living away from home is what has me worried," said Miriam. "I don't know if he can handle it."

"Well, if he decides to go and gets homesick, he can always drop out," said Milton. "Maybe he'll think it over and change his mind. Let's let him bring it up again. He might just forget the whole thing."

"Yes, I think we should do that," Miriam agreed.

Two days later, Britt announced after dinner that he'd made up his mind for sure. He was going to Thessalonika.

"But do you think you'll be okay?" Milton asked, his tone soft and searching.

"What's the matter? Don't you think I can handle it?" Britt demanded.

"Oh, no," Milton protested. "But … you know, you've had some problems, and we don't want you to be unhappy."

"I think I'll be all right," said Britt. "Do you think I'm not smart enough—not as smart as Kevin?" Kevin was in the living room, and the television muffled the kitchen conversation.

"Oh, of course not," Milton replied, his face twisted in pained concern. "No, no, not at all," Miriam concurred.

"Well, okay. So I'm going."

That week, Britt telephoned the college, and three days later an application form arrived in the mail. He sent it back, and in three weeks received notice he'd been accepted.

The day after Labor Day, Britt loaded his clothes into Kevin's 1950 Ford. Kevin had applied a chrome strip along the doors and fenders, then painted the part below the strip white and green above it. Britt and Kevin would room together for the first semester, after which Kevin would graduate. At the registration tables in the college gymnasium, Britt discovered that he'd have to take two years of a foreign language because he'd had none in high school. Which should it be: French, German or Spanish? Other students were faced with the same decision, and they chatted with each other about the pros and cons of each. Several upperclassmen who were milling around overheard the chit-chat and offered their knowledge. Opinions varied little: German was the hardest, Spanish the easiest, and French the most practical. They agreed that German was the closest to Dutch, which Britt's parents had spoken in the house frequently during his childhood. One student offered that both were Teutonic languages. Britt decided he'd study German the following year, after he'd gotten other required courses out of the way.

Those courses were freshman English; botany, which he chose over biology because he didn't like the idea of cutting animals open; physics;

Western civilization; an introduction to philosophy; and Old Testament to partly fill a requirement of six hours of Bible. All but the Bible, philosophy, and physics courses were two-semester classes. In the first semester, he did best in English. The female instructor petulantly drilled her students about using the dictionary to look up the meanings of words they didn't know, and Britt followed that advice, building his vocabulary. In the second semester of the course, he didn't do as well. A big reason was that, instead of heeding the professor's lectures, he continually gazed around the room. His repressed desire for human interaction came to the fore in the quiet environment. The professor administered a reading comprehension test, and Britt did badly. He was placed in a remedial section. His low comprehension, however, had nothing to do with his speed of thinking and absorbing, which were fast. Rather, it resulted from an inability to maintain concentration on a topic for all but brief time segments—unless the material engrossed him, and none of the texts for the courses did. He had too much emotional upheaval stirring within. So the brief remedial work did little to help him.

His problem with "Western civ" was the same as with other courses: He was not relaxed enough to concentrate on the textbook. He scored an A on a paper describing the Parthenon, but received a C for the course. Botany was a four-hour course, half of it laboratory work that involved a project of partnering with another student to collect and identify forty plants. Britt's reticence in forming friendships left him doing the work himself because he couldn't find a partner. Kevin, who was majoring in biology with the goal of becoming a medical technologist, took the same course and partnered with a friend. Britt found it very difficult to identify the plants under a microscope. However, the task became quite enjoyable—even exciting—one afternoon when Agnes Verblum, a senior, noticed him muttering in consternation at the microscope and came over to help.

"Having trouble?" she asked. Agnes was a blonde, not particularly pretty but in no way homely, slightly plump, and very well-endowed. She was friendly in a coy way, as if unaware of her physical attribute—or attributes, both of them. But the tight sweaters she wore belied her naïve demeanor. She dated a nerdy music student named Arnold, an unlikely companion for such a sexy gal, Britt thought.

"Yeah," said Britt. "I can't for the life of me find the filament in this flower's stamen."

"Let's see if I can help," said Agnes. Standing back of Britt, she leaned forward to peer into the microscope. Her breasts touched his back, and he felt a surge of indescribable pleasure, quickly becoming hard between the legs. "There it is," she breathed. "That long, stiff stalk with the bulbous end, which is the anther." She pulled her head back from the microscope but remained bent over Britt, her soft breasts pressed against his back, while Britt looked into the magnifier.

"Oh, yeah, I see it now," he said, gulping. Looking sideways at her face, which was very close to his, he emitted a feeble, "Thanks."

"Anytime," Agnes said as she walked away, looking back with a deliberately innocent smile that failed to completely disguise the coquette in her.

After a week of school, Britt tried out for the football team, which Miriam had forbidden him from doing in the seventh grade. In his college physical education class, he won a race through a course of metal folding chairs positioned in a zig zag pattern down the gym floor. Afterward, instructor Peter Dykstra, who also was the football coach, explained to the class that someone with the ability to negotiate that course speedily would make a good broken-field runner in football. He glanced at Britt. Hint, hint. In class two days later, Britt told the coach that he'd like to try out for the team. Britt said he hadn't played in high school, and the coach told him he'd be at a disadvantage but could have a go at it if he wished. Practices began the following week, mostly with calisthenics and sprints, and Britt fared well, though he wasn't especially fast. Saturday would be the first major scrimmage, lasting from nine a.m. to one p.m. Although he weighed only one-hundred-sixty pounds, Britt was placed on the defensive line. Despite being lighter than the opponents on the offensive squad, he didn't mind, and even enjoyed, the rough contact in blocking the offensive line. But it was an unseasonably warm day in the second week in September, and as the practice wore on, he grew increasingly uncomfortable wearing the bulky pads, which restricted his movement. Players were not allowed to drink water, and Britt became powerfully thirsty. He was miserable. Finally, coach Dykstra and his assistant, Martin Kregel, the college basketball coach, called an end to the scrimmage and announced that they would spend twenty minutes on the passing game. Britt was sent running for a long pass, but he felt like a clown in the heavy outfit he was wearing, and clumsily threw out his arms for the ball, which sailed through his fingers, though it should have been an easy catch. The practice ended, and Britt, who had never been so thirsty, gulped down glass after glass of cold water in the locker room.

Before practice began the following Monday, Britt told Dykstra that he didn't think he was cut out for football. The coach asked if he'd like to try out for the track team in the spring, and Britt told him he'd run in the half-mile relay his last semester in high school. Dykstra said the team needed a distance runner. Britt said he had good endurance but not a lot of speed, and he'd maybe give it a try.

Every morning, from eight to eight-fifteen, the students were required to attend "chapel," held in the stately building called "Old Manse." An opening hymn would waken the bleary-eyed matriculants. They were motivated to make a joyful noise unto the Lord by a pipe organ pouring out dramatic peals of gorgeous music. Not long after Britt's encounter with the sexy Agnes, he discovered that the person playing it was Arnold—and understood what she saw in the guy. The hymn would be followed by a motivational speech of sorts by a different professor each morning. The message was based on some Christian, or at least spiritual, slant, depending on the speaker's religious persuasion. However, all were required to profess a belief in the basic tenets of Christianity when they were hired.

That requirement probably was not as strict as some of the students' parents, most of them members of the Dutch Reformed Church, assumed it would be. All students were required to take six hours of Bible, and Britt chose the Old Testament in the second semester. He heard things from Professor Kryjnberg that he'd never heard before, and wondered how his parents would feel about the suggestion that those supposed miracles probably had natural explanations. Britt himself was dumbfounded at the proposal that the parting of the Red Sea to allow the Israelites to flee from the Egyptian army occurred in a shallow part of the sea on a night when strong winds affected the tide.

Britt was becoming confused. Who was right about the Bible? And all those admonitions about what was right by the professors in their daily chapel perorations: One advocated living this way and another, another way. On Tuesday, the idea was to be humble for the meek "shall inherit the earth." On Wednesday, the head of the Business Department preached that "God helps those who help themselves," and one had to be aggressive to "get ahead in the world." Most of the students half-slept through these sessions and, if they listened at all, paid no heed to the messages. That was especially true of the upperclassmen, who had heard hundreds of these words of supposed wisdom and learned to tune them out. But Britt took them seriously, and struggled with the conflicting concepts.

He never discussed the chapel sessions with Kevin, who spent little time in the room with Britt, studying mostly in the library and consorting with classmates. Growing up, Kevin had been regarded as the serious, thoughtful Rutgers boy, mainly because he was quiet and not much interested in sports. Not so with Britt. His ebullient, active temperament led people, especially his parents, to take him for granted. As they reached adolescence, however, it was Britt who wrestled with the teachings of the Bible and the church. Kevin, on the other hand, never indicated that he questioned anything, and the chapel sermons didn't seem to faze him. He'd never dated in high school and still didn't, but had a coterie of male friends at Thessalonika and seemed to be enjoying his time there.

Britt had a couple of friends, too: Jamie Dustin, a laid-back, good-looking sophomore and neighbor in their dormitory; and Jerry Thornton, a freshman from Chicago who, like Britt, was an excellent ping-pong player. Jamie was better than both of them, and the three played in the Student Union every evening for an hour after studying. Jamie played a defensive game, standing close to the table and using only his backhand. Britt was an offensive player, dropping back several feet and slamming frequently, always with his forehand. Britt's prowess grew, and no one in the student body of some four-hundred-fifty could compete with the three closely matched players. Each time Britt missed a point, he would slap the paddle, either sandpaper or rubber, on his right thigh. By the end of the semester, he had worn a hole in three pairs of corduroy pants.

On Halloween night, Britt joined a group of male students intent on deviltry by scrawling messages with soap on windows of campus buildings. They smashed watermelons on entrances so classes would be delayed a little the next morning while janitors cleaned up the mess. A Pliny police car cruised slowly past the students gathered on the sidewalk in front of the gymnasium. Britt, wanting to show that he was one of the guys, did something that could have landed him in jail: He threw a large chunk of watermelon at the car, hitting it broadside. The car stopped, but the two officers inside didn't get out.

Henry von Stade was a nebbishy junior who roomed by himself next to Jamie Dustin, two doors from Britt. Henry knew a freshman coed from his hometown in Wisconsin and offered to introduce Britt to her. Their chance came in the cafeteria lunch line, when the three happened to be near each other. Her name was Candace Ten Horst and she was quiet and not too bad to look at, although Britt was a bit bothered by her proboscis. He asked if she'd like to have a Coke in the Student Union after classes the next day, and she accepted. They chatted about the courses they were taking, their hometowns, their families—but Britt felt no sparks. Nonetheless, he took her to the only movie theater in Thessalonika to see Alfred Hitchcock's *North by Northwest*. They didn't happen to be there on the same night that zoology Professor Marjorie Carlson attended, a Thursday, or they'd have experienced even more excitement than the film generated. It happened during the memorable scene where Cary Grant is standing by the roadside in a flat, desolate area of the West. A small airplane swoops down on him from nowhere and fires a round of bullets as the actor runs ahead of it and then dives to one side before the plane circles around and returns for another attempt to kill him. Professor Carlson, whose only life as a single, fiftyish woman in Thessalonika was anything but exciting, became so absorbed in the scene that she lost consciousness of where she was. Leaping to her feet, she screamed, "Run for those boulders!" That, at least, was the story that circulated through the small campus after she canceled her classes the next day, reportedly suffering from acute embarrassment.

Kevin graduated at the end of the semester, and Britt was assigned a new roommate, Wayne Scrit, whose roommate had left school. Wayne was a lean, blond farm boy with a ruddy complexion and a good-humored, energetic temperament. He planned to become a minister and studied diligently, though with less than remarkable success. Demonstrating self-confidence despite his ordinary intellect, he had launched a relationship with Martha, a bespectacled fellow freshman who was quietly bright and had a pensive mien. Wayne reveled in socializing, and when Friday rolled around, he was chomping at the bit to see Martha and their friends. As he happily readied to leave the room, Britt often was lying on his bed, staring at the ceiling in a melancholy mood. He was unhappy with his grades and felt quite apart from the small coterie of male classmates in his dormitory, most of whom had grown up on farms or in tiny towns. They doubtless were among the top students in their high schools and had received a lot of adulation, and Britt figured that was because they hadn't had much competition. The good natured Wayne was bothered by Britt's unhappiness and would urge him to get up off the bed and go out for some fun.

"That's okay," Britt would say. "I'm all right."

Late in the semester, the daily chapel admonitions on conducting oneself in ways that would meet the Lord's approval combined with Britt's feelings of alienation to make him even more introspective than he already was. What he needed was freedom to be who he was without oppressive pangs of guilt. He began to worry about where he would end up when he died, and became obsessive-compulsive, whispering prayers for several minutes as he lay in bed each night before going to sleep.

"What are you doing?" Wayne asked one night from his bed on the other side of the room.

"I'm praying," Britt answered.

Wayne also prayed before going to sleep—he was headed for the ministry, after all—but made a quick ritual out of it, and did it silently. He didn't respond to Britt.

Britt continued seeing Candace Ten Horst about every other weekend for the rest of the school year. They usually watched television in the large upstairs room of the Student Union and occasionally went to a movie. Neither had a car, and women's dorm mother Harriet Prims watched from the lobby to see that her charges met the midnight curfew. So Britt was never able to plant a kiss on Candace. That was okay with him, because he wasn't much attracted to her sexually. Her pretty, flirtatious little blond friend, Cece Jones, was a different matter. He desired her, and willingly allowed her to kiss him under the mistletoe at the top of the stairs in the Student Union at Christmas time. But she was dating another student, and Britt stayed with Candace, mainly out of habit and a sense of obligation.

In mid-March, Britt joined the track team as it began drills for the upcoming schedule of competition. He was already in pretty good shape, and after running daily for two weeks felt ready to go. Coach Kregel slated him for the mile run early in the meets and the two-mile run near the end. The first was at Thessalonika, against Samson College only fifteen miles away. In the mile, Britt placed third out of five runners, finishing in a slow five minutes fifteen seconds. But he'd run as fast as his relatively short legs would allow him and had nothing left at the end. He didn't fare any better in the two-mile: eleven minutes thirty seconds. But Coach Dykstra, who assisted Kregel, told Britt he hadn't done badly for the first time. Britt got the mile down to five minutes five seconds in the next meet, at Provident College sixty-five miles to the east, and did the two-mile in eleven minutes twelve seconds. In the following few meets, his mile times ranged from five minutes three seconds to four minutes fifty-eight seconds and he once got the two-mile down to eleven minutes three seconds.

The last meet was the Mid-Iowa Conference Invitational, which drew five teams to Thessalonika. It was a beautiful day, seventy degrees, with a slight breeze and a bright, azure sky softened by the lazy motion of a smattering of white clouds that looked like giant tufts of cotton. Five runners participated in the mile, one from each school. As Britt made his second lap past the grandstand, his mouth was filled with saliva, which he unthinkingly let loose in the direction of the seventy-five or so applauding students. Making matters worse, his winded condition rendered him too weak to put much force behind the ejection, and the mess blew back in his face, which he hastily wiped with the back of his left hand. The grandstand grew hushed. Britt was holding the number three spot heading around the first turn on the fourth and last lap. As he reached mid-point in the straightaway, he realized that he had strength left and poured it on. Just before the last turn, he passed the number two runner. The audience—either having divined that he'd meant no contempt by his crude act a couple of minutes before, or feeling that he was exonerating himself—cheered loudly. Britt knew that he couldn't catch the runner from Warbury College, the fastest in the conference, but gave it his all as the students yelled madly for him, and finished only four yards behind. His time was by far his best of the season: four minutes fifty-and-a-half seconds. The two-mile was not as popular a race, but Britt tied his personal best: eleven minutes three seconds. It was a happy ending to the season.

Days later, the school year was over. Despite his inability to concentrate on his studies, Britt had managed a C-plus average.

He was home less than a week and trying to figure out a way to earn money for the next year's college costs. He had enough left from his savings to buy a car, which he would need in order to work because Kevin had moved to Cedar Rapids. He was training in a hospital to become certified as a medical technologist. In church that Sunday morning, Britt chatted before the service began with Ronnie Gurney, who'd been a year ahead of Britt in school. Ronnie mentioned that he wanted to sell his 1954 Ford, and Britt asked him how much he had to have for it. He said three-hundred-fifty dollars, and the next evening drove to the Rutgers farm so Britt could give it a test run. The 1954 Ford had a good reputation, and Britt bought it.

The construction of Interstate 80 had advanced westward several miles over the preceding year to just north and east of Colton, a few miles from the Rutgers farm. Britt decided to see about getting a job on that project again. He drove to the site and asked the foreman—a nondescript man, different from the one before—if he needed laborers for the summer. Britt was hired and began the next day. The hours were long—seven a.m. to five-thirty p.m.—and the work back-breaking, but he was strong after his conditioning on the track team. He unloaded trucks carrying sand, steel rods, and lumber, and helped build the wood molds for the cement. After a stretch of the highway was completed and the cement allowed to cure, he helped remove the plastic covering and joined other young men in sweeping the sand and dirt onto the shoulder.

Evenings were short, because he had to go to bed early. Kyra was taking clarinet and piano lessons, and Britt began playing the piano exercises from her lesson book. He didn't set a schedule for himself, but played frequently during that summer. He also undertook the reading of *The Americanization of Edward Bok*, a 1921 Pulitzer Prize-winning autobiography of a Dutch publisher and editor. Milton kept it in a small, vertical bookcase, along with a world atlas and *For Better or for Worse*, a marriage self-help book. Britt figured his parents must have bought it back in Michigan fifteen years before when their marriage had become especially turbulent, with arguments erupting continually. The rest of the time he watched television, and the summer passed quickly. For the first few weeks, Britt wrote about once a week to Candace Ten Horst in Wisconsin and she wrote back. Finally, in a letter telling about how much fun she was having at evening beach parties on the shore of Lake Michigan, she informed Britt that she didn't think their relationship was going anywhere and they should break it off. Britt was a bit taken aback and hurt, but fretted little because he never had felt any stirring when he was with her. Besides, he'd felt from the outset that the size of her nose detracted from her looks. By the time the fall term of his sophomore year began, he had all but forgotten her.

CHAPTER 17

Over the summer, Britt had begun to think of what kind of career he would embark on after college, because that would determine his major field of study. Miriam had suggested he might like to become a salesman. He had been a loquacious child from about age ten to thirteen, and occasionally entertained his siblings with mimicry. Ministers were his favorite targets. His expression smug and deeply serious, he would intone slowly and pompously, "We will read from the Scriptures, the first Book of Corinthians, chapter twelve, verses nine through eleven." A long pause, then, "Verily, verily, I say unto you, he who faileth to brush his teeth shall have bad breath, and shall be banished from the congregation, especially during Communion, when every worshipper in his midst will gag and be unable to eat Christ's flesh as it is passed down the pew in the silver tray." In card games and board games with family members and relatives, he would pay little attention to the playing, continually joking instead. His witty remarks and comic behavior often evoked amused head-shaking from the other players, who were failing in their attempts to be serious. His parents regarded Britt as a fun-loving, extroverted kid. In fact, they boasted to relatives that their second son had "the gift of gab." There was some truth in that; an English teacher had urged him to try out for the debate team. Miriam concluded that this aptness at verbal expression and conviviality would serve him quite well as a salesman.

But selling required manipulation, and Britt was far too innocent for that. Besides, he wasn't the least interested in business. He also had shown little aptitude for science, and an ability in only some aspects of mathematics, which ruled out accounting. His natural inclination was linguistic. But what to do with it? Britt figured that teaching was about the only outlet for someone with such a bent, and decided to pursue courses in English and education. And, he thought, it would be interesting to see how he fared in German, which he'd decided on as his foreign language requirement.

As it turned out, he felt an immediate affinity for the language, and studying it was no chore. It was the one course he really enjoyed.

"Herr Rutgers was the only one to score a hundred on this test," Professor Fowler announced to the class of thirty-two students one day. Britt glowed with pride, considering that the class included some especially bright kids, such as the brilliant Vernon den Adel, a straight-A student who commuted from his parents' farm.

Once when Dr. Fowler called on him to translate aloud a passage in a short story by Thomas Mann, Britt stumbled on an idiom and said in a frustrated tone, "I really have trouble with the idioms. They're awfully hard to figure out."

The professor was a lean six-feet-two, and his straight, neatly trimmed salt-and-pepper hair framed an elongated face that wore wire-rimmed glasses propped over half-closed eyelids. He was a gentle, kindly man. "Uh, ja, Herr Rutgers," he said with deliberate hesitation, breaking into a slightly amused smile, "we'll be studying idioms in later lessons. You don't need to be too concerned about that yet. Rome wasn't built in a day either." The class laughed, and Britt smiled sheepishly, realizing he had become a bit overwrought.

Britt had no affinity for physics, and eked out only a C-minus even though the professor was entertaining. An ebullient, roly-poly man who wore thick-lensed glasses and stuttered, he taught with such demonstrations as marching in circles in front of the class to convey the principle of the Earth revolving around the Sun. The two-hour Appreciation of Music course was enjoyable, with one hour devoted to book work and the other spent listening to recordings of the most revered pieces of classical music. Students were expected to recognize forty master works. Britt did well with these, though not as well in the history and elements of music, which interested him little. But he likely impressed the corpulent, convivial Professor Edith Lamb (who probably had sung opera and would have made a great Brunhilde) on one wrong answer. The question asked who the conductor of the New York Philharmonic was, and Britt wrote "Jascha Heifetz," even spelling it correctly. Leonard Bernstein was a more popular figure, but Britt remembered hearing Heifetz's name in a concert that Milton had listened to on NBC radio's *The Bell Telephone Hour.*

A new professor of psychology, Daniel V. Bregman, had joined the faculty of Thessalonika, and Britt enrolled in his General Psychology course. He learned, among other things, that a monkey was smart enough to grab a stick left in its cage, reach outside to a banana lying on the ground, and drag it toward the cage. Bregman was born to Scandinavian parents in a university town in the Northwest. He told the class that, while studying at the University of Chicago, he had been a protégé of Carl Rogers, the developer of client-centered, or non-directive, therapy. After leaving the university, he'd embarked on a decade-long career as a clinical psychologist. One day he told the class about the power of that form of therapy. Its guiding principle held that the therapist spoke only occasionally to the "client," whom he encouraged to talk freely about his feelings and experiences.

"A man came to me seeking help because his doctor had told him his bleeding ulcers were killing him," Bregman narrated. His soft but slightly gritty voice and measured way of speaking cast him as a man of gravitas, of deep seriousness. "We engaged in two one-hour sessions a week, and after three months, the tensions that he had been feeling subsided and his ulcers were in remission. Such is the curative capacity of the Rogers approach, if used skillfully." Bregman then invited students who were experiencing personal problems, or who merely sought career counseling, to meet with him alone after classes.

Britt had only a D-plus in Bregman's course by midterm. On the final exam, however, he scored an A on the essay part and a B on the multiple choice part. Though he liked the professor, the final grade was a C, and Britt thought he deserved a B-minus.

In the second semester, New Testament Survey was his favorite subject. It was taught by Dr. John W. Bardley III, a man who looked as professorial as his name sounded. When he walked, his short, scrawny frame pitched forward with each step, as though he were heading into a gale, while his arms swung wildly. His hair was thin and white, and his face was as gaunt as his body. He peered through wire-rimmed glasses with such a piercing stare that he seemed to see right through objects. Rumor around the campus had it that his IQ was one-hundred-eighty-five and that he was only thirty-eight years old. Students guessed him to be about sixty. Another story was: At a meeting of the Bible Club, he slowly read aloud a passage from the holy book. After the session, a student asked why he'd taken so much time with the reading. The professor replied that he was reading in Hebrew. In fact, Bardley read and wrote Latin, Hebrew, and

Greek. A few years later, he left Thessalonika for the more liberal New Brunswick Theological Seminary, also affiliated with the Dutch Reformed Church, in New Jersey. While there, he won acclaim for his work in translating the Dead Sea Scrolls.

The New Testament class was at one p.m., and Bardley invariably came dragging in at the last minute—or a couple of minutes late. He always had difficulty breaking away from the lunch period. One beautiful spring day, he came bounding into the classroom and slammed his roll-call pad on the desk. Throwing his arms in the air, he shouted, "Let's go out and get up a band!" Britt found his style much more interesting than that of Old Testament Professor Krjynberg, whose loud, declamatory lecturing annoyed him and distracted from the subject matter. That made a big difference for Britt, who scored a B under Bardley.

In the large Economic Geography class, Britt sat at the center of the front row. He was so self-conscious that he couldn't concentrate on Professor Priscilla Turnby's lectures, in which she spit out streams of facts in machine-gun fashion. Finally, he mentioned his problem to her after class one day, and she quietly indicated that he could take an empty seat in the back, adding, "We won't say anything more about it." But Britt, while feeling more comfortable, didn't do any better from that vantage point as he yielded to the temptation to look around the room. He wanted to look at the other students, but he didn't want them looking at him.

The track season arrived, and Britt debated whether to participate again. Running a mile and two miles as fast as his body would allow was torture for him, because he wasn't a natural runner. He decided to ask if he could run the quarter mile, instead. Not wanting to lose a team member, the coach relented, and Britt ran in the one-mile relay. In one meet, he got his time down to a respectable fifty-six-and-four-tenths seconds. The shorter distance was not nearly so grueling.

The year was over, and Britt needed a job again. His Uncle Don and Aunt Josie, operators of a farm a few miles away, knew of one. They mentioned to Milton and Miriam that a contractor in nearby Prairieville had begun a summer-long project of installing sewers in Colton and needed a worker. Britt called, and the contractor told him to report the next morning.

"You the college kid sent to work for me?" the foreman demanded. He wore bib overalls that followed his ample girth in an arc from his chest down to his groin. His face was hostile and his voice confrontational.

"Yep," Britt answered.

"You got a name?"

"Britt."

"Here," he said, without introducing himself, and handed the newcomer an implement that looked something like a pogo stick, with a round, flat disc on the end. "This here's called a tamper. Squeeze that lever and the rod pumps up and down real fast so you can pack the loose dirt around that manhole we just finished."

Britt found the tamper easy to operate and began tamping the dirt, moving the device randomly over the newly dug area. Suddenly the beefy hand of the foreman closed around the handle of the tamper and jerked it away.

"You don't know what the hell you're doin'," the hefty fellow yelled. Britt wanted to counter, "No kidding," but instinctively realized that this guy would not brook dissent. The man took the tamper and began methodically tamping in a line to where the loose dirt ended, then moving the other direction in a parallel line. He thrust it back to Britt and said, "Now do it right. You have to pack every bit of dirt, not just jump around helter-skelter." Britt had no problem completing the job once he knew what was expected.

"Is that okay?" he asked a short construction worker in his fifties. Britt had heard the foreman call him Bill.

"Yeah, that's good," Bill said in a gruff voice. The foreman had gone to get something from his truck, and Bill said to Britt, "So now you know what Jack Simpson is like. Ain't he a sweetheart? We call him the Bull Moose. That's 'cause he's always chargin' around like he wants ta knock somethin' over. Real friendly fella." Britt chuckled.

"Okay, here's what we're gonna do," said Bill. "See that trench starting from where we just put that manhole in? We gotta lay pipe all the way down that trench for eight blocks and then around the corner and up the next street. There's four parts of the town where we're gonna work this summer. Me and Clem over here will be in the ditch layin' the pipe, and you can lower the pipes down to us. Them babies are four feet long and weigh one-hundred-thirty-five pounds apiece. Ya roll the pipe to the edge of the ditch. Don't try ta carry them sons-a-bitches. Toss this here rope with the hook through to the other end and hook it on the lip, and then lower it over the edge. Think ya can handle it?"

"Yeah, no problem." And it wasn't. Bill and Clem grabbed either end of the pipes that Britt lowered to them, and laid them in place. Inside the wide lip where the next pipe would be inserted, Clem already had smeared tar from a bucket and then wrapped insulating material around it. After each pipe was laid, Clem rested a level on top, in the center, to determine whether either end should be elevated with dirt underneath. If the level showed the pipe was close to straight, Bill would invariably make a profound pronouncement: "Ya gotta 'low for the windage." And he'd call to Britt for the next pipe.

When two buckets of tar were used up, Britt had to trudge to the end of the block, where a machine kept the tar hot. He loaded the buckets and carried them, each weighing fifty pounds, back to the trench. Up the street, a truck loaded with more of the orange tile pipes arrived. While Bill and Clem took a break, Britt unloaded the truck as it rolled slowly alongside the trench. The June sun poured down, and Britt doffed his sweat-soaked tee-shirt. The Bull Moose inspected each pipe for straightness and possible cracks at the male end, painting a big black X on the few that he rejected.

The work day ran from seven a.m. to five-thirty p.m.—ten-and-a-half hours—and Britt was too tired to go anywhere in the evening. Besides, he had to get up early. So he immersed himself in a ragged copy of *David Copperfield* that Milton kept in the tiny, vertical bookcase. The story of a boy's hard, lonely life, complete with such colorful characters as Uriah Heep, resonated with Britt even more, he decided, than *A Tale of Two Cities,* which had been required reading in high school.

The crew worked until one p.m. on Saturdays. On one such day, Jack drove Bill and Britt to the site of a three-foot-diameter concrete drainage tunnel that had been installed under a rural road. The foreman had been dispatched by the company owner to determine why debris was clogging up one end, causing the water to back up and form a large puddle on the adjacent land. Each six-foot section of pipe had been lowered into place by a crane dangling a cable that held a "pin," a three-foot-long iron bar that looked like a giant hairpin, which in turn held the pipe. The pin was still in place in the pipe at one end, its top and bottom halves forming a wedge parallel with the top of the pipe.

"I'm going in there with my flashlight," Jack announced to Bill and Britt, who stood at opposite ends of the tunnel. Simpson always wore a steel construction helmet, which was about to prove its worth. He crouched and began crawling through the thirty-foot-long tunnel. But he apparently had forgotten about the thick bar along the roof of the last pipe. Suddenly, a yell emerged from within the tunnel, followed by a string of expletives that no sailor could have competed with. Bill, on the end of the tunnel farthest from Simpson, bent and peered inside. Holding his tummy, he began rocking up and down, laughing in silent glee, while pointing inside and motioning for Britt on the other end to take a look. Britt bent forward, and there sat the Bull Moose, helmet in hand, rubbing his head. For the moment, the Bull seemed more like a steer—castrated.

CHAPTER 18

The summer ended soon, and it was back to Thessalonika for Britt's junior year. He was getting short on cash, and decided to take a job waiting tables in the student dining hall. Students dined together for the evening meal, sitting at tables of six. A different student was assigned each night to read a passage from the Bible and deliver a prayer. When he or she was finished, the waiters emerged in unison from the kitchen carrying large trays above their heads. All the waiters were men students, probably because the trays, loaded with bowls of food, were heavy. Each waiter was assigned three tables, or eighteen students. He had to check each table periodically throughout the meal to see if any of the diners wanted more food, and to replenish the glasses of water or ice tea, or cups of coffee. Before the dining hour, he set up the tables with tablecloths and dinnerware. At the close, he cleared the tables. Finally, the waiters sat together and ate what was left, which always was more than they could finish.

Britt was an energetic waiter—too much so. He became almost obsessive about checking with the diners for anything they might want. His attentiveness became a nuisance as he interrupted conversation, and they began to dismiss him with a wave of the hand. Finally, a kindly student named Beth told him that he didn't need to check so frequently. What she was too polite to say was: "Lighten up, guy. You're a pain in the ass."

Britt's roommate this year was a fellow from Wisconsin who had just served two years in the Army after graduating from high school. Gene stood six feet, had a medium build and wore a crew cut. He talked unhurriedly and seemed unflappable. Britt and Gene spoke to each other only occasionally, partly because Gene did all of his studying in the library and was seldom in the room. Their different personalities did not connect, which probably was why Gene kept away. Britt also divined that his roommate had a mischievous nature. Indeed, school officials discovered that he was the one who had been spotted occasionally late at night over a period of several weeks, riding on a horse on the outskirts of the campus while clad in a black cape and mask. The next morning, students would find the words *Zorro was here* spray-painted on the stadium grass, a couple of trees, and other spots. None damaged any property, and Gene was merely placed on probation for the remainder of the term.

But Britt's confused emotional and mental state prevented him from having such fun.

Three hours of political science were required for graduation. Britt found a vacancy in his schedule that would allow him to take Dr. Mao Wu's course in American National Government before he would become entrenched in the courses of his majors—German, English, and education. The professor, about forty-five, had come to the United States from China to study at the University of Chicago, where he earned a doctorate. His wife taught college in Chicago. On some weekends they took turns traveling by train and bus the three-hundred miles between the major metropolis and the tiny town to visit each other. Professor Wu was a lean six-feet-two and wore glasses that enhanced his always smiling face, which complemented a soft voice and a kindly, gentle demeanor. A few years later, Dale later took the same course. He remarked once that if the class had been asked to name the president of the United States and a student answered Winston Churchill, Wu likely would have replied, "Not exactly." At a junior-sophomore baseball game late one afternoon, Britt was bursting with eagerness to show off what he erroneously assumed was a superior talent for the great American pastime. Batting in the second inning, he drew a walk, and began dancing off first base like a jackrabbit on methamphetamine. Then he caught sight of Wu standing along the sideline, casting him an ever-so-fatherly smile that was at once approving and calming, carrying the message, "Just relax a little, Britt." Britt relaxed a little too much in Wu's class, earning a C in a course that held small fascination for him.

Britt had begun taking education courses the previous year, and enrolled in two more. One was Adolescent Psychology, taught by Professor Dan Newell, an imperturbable man with gray-tinged white hair who wore the same brown suit every day. He stood erect at six feet and was bulky, with some extra weight, but was by no means corpulent. Standing with his hands behind his back, he spoke slowly and determinedly, always wearing a Mona Lisa smile—slight and mysterious. He had to know that few in the class were listening to his monumentally boring lectures, especially since some seemed to write feverishly, which wasn't required by his snail's-pace delivery. They were, in fact, writing personal letters. Newell was so disarming and quiet-spoken that Britt's dormitory neighbor, Jamie Dustin, labeled him Dangerous Dan. In one lecture, however, he revealed a side of himself that surprised the students and grabbed their attention. Speaking on the subject of disciplinary problems, he told the story of a teacher in a tough high school who had under his charge two recalcitrant, bullying pupils. On one occasion, they decided to challenge the teacher's order for them to discontinue talking to each other, and strode together toward him at the front of the class. In his mild, understated way, Newell slowly demonstrated with outstretched arms how the teacher had simply placed a hand on the side of each of the ruffians' heads and slammed them together, knocking them out cold. Later, when that moment popped into his head for whatever reason, Britt realized the teacher probably was Newell.

Another required education course was titled Tests and Measurements, a statistics-oriented subject that awaited Britt like spinach on a child's plate. Now was as good a time as any to be done with it, he figured. It turned out not terribly distasteful, mainly because the professor was eccentric and easy-going. In his unvarying attire—an oversized brown suit of the same dark shade as Professor Newell's and a bland tie with the knot always loose—Dr. Jonas Hacken could have been the archetype for a homeless person. That image was enhanced by a drooping jaw and lower teeth that seemed to be in the way when he talked, like moguls impeding a skier on a mountain slope. He appeared soporific, as though under the influence of a mind-altering drug. Lecturing one afternoon about the value of testing students, he outlined three points, first writing the point on the blackboard and then reciting it: (a) motivates them to study, (b) is the most practical method of evaluation for the teacher, and (3) makes for objectivity in evaluation. In other words, the ab3's of testing. A few muffled chuckles alerted Hacken to his little miscue, and he walked back to the blackboard, grinning sheepishly as he changed (3) to (c). The stereotypical absent-minded professor, Britt thought.

But Britt wasn't sure if teaching should be his career. He didn't have any inclination to teach, and had chosen that route only because he didn't know of anything else to do with a major in German and English. He remembered that Professor Bregman, the psychology professor, had invited students to counsel with him. Britt knocked on his office door after classes one day and asked about a counseling session.

"Sure, Britt," Bregman responded quietly and pleasantly. "Is there a particular subject you want to discuss?"

"Well ... yeah," Britt said hesitantly, feeling awkward. Bregman waited, saying nothing. "Uh ... I don't know if I'm taking the right courses, and ... and ... ." He stopped, stuck on how to tell the professor his stronger reason for seeking help. "I've had some problems in the past," he finally blurted.

"I quite understand, Britt," Bregman said, to Britt's huge relief. "I'll tell you what. Let's set up a series of meetings, and we'll see if we can't deal with what's bothering you. Would you want to do that?"

"Oh, for sure. Yes, that would be great."

"Okay then." Bregman pulled a schedule book out of a desk drawer, scanned it a few seconds, and said, "Would Wednesdays at four p.m. work for you?"

"Yes, my last class is over at three."

"Okay, I'll see you a week from today." He extended a hand to Britt, who noticed how small and delicately artistic it looked.

The week passed swiftly. Bregman greeted Britt pleasantly and gently in his tiny office on the third, or top, floor of Old Manse, the small college's principal building. It was a majestic brown-brick edifice that dated to the turn of the century. Bregman opened by asking what Britt was majoring in and why he had chosen that major.

"German," said Britt. "I chose it because I'm getting A's in it, better than any of my other courses. But about the only thing I can do with it, I suppose, is teach, and I'm not sure I'm cut out to be a teacher."

"Well, you may or may not be," Bregman responded. "But it makes sense to pursue what you do best. Did you ever consider becoming a translator?"

"No, I hadn't thought of that."

Both paused for a few seconds, then Bregman said, "Perhaps the best thing for you to do at the moment is continue with the education courses. You've finished most of your junior year, but you'll have the summer to think about it and then another year of school. I don't see it as a critical issue at this time. Lots of young people take several post-education years searching for what they should make of their lives."

"Okay, that sounds good."

"You mentioned earlier that you had some problems in the past. I suspect that these are still of some concern to you."

"Yes." Britt hesitated, reluctant to tell of his breakdown. "About four years ago, when I was a senior in high school … when I was eighteen … ."

"Britt, I want you to know that I was a clinical psychologist for a number of years, and have listened to hundreds of persons tell me every kind of story that you can imagine. So you don't need to feel embarrassed. What you tell me will not leave this room."

"Yes, I remember from your class the story about the man with the bleeding ulcers who you treated."

"Well, I'm delighted that you remember something from that course," Bregman said, smiling wryly. "I hope you remember more than that."

"Yeah, I got an A and a B on the two parts of the final."

"I seem to recall that you did well on the final, and that I liked your writing on the essay part. Now, why don't you try to relax and tell me what's on your mind?"

"I had a nervous breakdown," Britt blurted, hating to say the word "nervous," which he somehow equated with weakness.

As if reading his thoughts, Bregman calmly replied, "Well, that's not so unusual. But I don't like to use the word 'nervous,' because the nerves don't break down. The term refers to a person's inability to cope with life's everyday situations because of emotional pain he or she is experiencing."

"Good, because I don't like the word either," said Britt. He hesitated, then said, "I had to be taken to a mental institution." It was out, and he could talk more freely now. He told about the bowling evening that culminated in his collapse and admission to a sanitarium, about his breakout, and his placement in the state hospital in Iowa City.

"Would you like to tell me about the feelings you were having before that night at the bowling alley?" Bregman asked quietly. He was about five feet eight inches tall and had a paunch. His left elbow rested on the arm of the chair. His head, thickly covered with wavy, deep-brown hair, tilted to that side, supported by his hand, the forefinger extended alongside his face and the thumb resting under the chin, with the other fingers curled in front of his mouth. His left leg was crossed perpendicularly over his right leg with the ankle resting on the thigh just above the knee. Britt liked that position and often took it himself. It bothered him to see men with their legs crossed thigh over thigh, because it seemed effeminate.

"Okay. Well, I was just awfully self-conscious—still am—and when I did my homework, I couldn't concentrate. I'd start reading the assignment in the book, and thoughts of what had occurred that day would pop into my head and then I wasn't thinking of what I was reading anymore. My mind was flitting all over the place."

"These things that happened during the day—were they things that made you anxious?"

"Yeah. You know, maybe something somebody said, and I'm wondering how he or she meant it. And whether the person was hurt by what I said back. That kind of thing."

"Were your parents aware of the difficulties you were having?"

"Oh no, I never revealed these thoughts. I would just tell them to turn the television lower when I was doing my homework so I could concentrate. Because I would read the same sentence over and over without having my mind on it. The bedroom I shared with my older brother Kevin was pretty far from the TV set, which was at the far end of the living room. And I would close the door. But any slight sound seeping through would distract me."

"How did they react when you told them to lower the volume?"

"Well, it was okay the first time, but when I got after them the second and third times, they got annoyed and told me it was so low they could hardly hear it."

"When did this inability to focus begin, Britt?"

"It started sometime in the second semester of my junior year, but then it got bad in my senior year, and kept getting worse. Plus, I didn't understand about sex and felt guilty about the bad thoughts and feelings I had about a couple of women in the church we went to and in the drug store where I worked. And sometimes before I went to sleep, I'd think about hell and eternity, and I would be terrorized. Because the idea of suffering that horrible pain of fire and it never ending made me panicky. Even if there wasn't any fire, the idea of eternity just made me terrified. I'd try to think of something else, and finally I would go to sleep."

"You don't seem to have had many pleasant thoughts, have you, Britt?"

"No. I wasn't happy. I was miserable."

"How did all this play out?"

Britt went into more detail about the night at the bowling alley, his subsequent hospitalization, the breakout when he panicked over the prospect of more shock treatments, and the resumption of those violent sessions interchangeably labeled "shock therapy" or, at once technically and euphemistically, "electroconvulsive therapy."

"Would you care to tell me about what college has been like for you?"

Britt paused, not quite sure how to begin.

"Tell you what, Britt. Why don't we break here? We've been at it for about forty minutes. Let's get together next week, if you'd like, and we can resume where we left off."

"Yes, please. I'd like to."

Bregman extended his hand, and Britt reciprocated.

"Have a good week, Britt."

"Thanks."

The week passed unremarkably, and on Wednesday, Britt returned to Bregman's office.

"So how has life treated you the last few days?" Bregman asked cheerfully.

"Oh … so-so," I guess. "But … ."

"What's on your mind, Britt?"

"I was kind of bothered by what Dr. Kirkland, the sociology professor, said in chapel Monday about how we should live our lives unselfishly, always thinking about how we can help our fellow man. He mentioned the Golden Rule—"Do unto others as you would have them do unto you"—and he also brought up that beatitude, "Blessed be the meek, for they shall inherit the earth."

"And why did that bother you, Britt?"

"Well … it wouldn't have. But in chapel just last week, I think it was Tuesday, Professor Miersma—you know, the one who teaches business—said "blessed be the meek" didn't mean we're supposed to let people run over us. He made the point that Christ got angry at the money changers in the temple and drove them out, and he said that showed Jesus could be aggressive, and we should be, too, in certain circumstances. But what circumstances is he talking about? See, I just get all confused when one professor says you're supposed to be one way and another turns around and says almost the opposite."

"Hmmm." Bregman was quiet for several seconds. Then, "You really take what you hear in chapel very seriously, don't you, Britt?"

"Well, yeah. Aren't I supposed to? What are we going to chapel for if we just let all that stuff go in one ear and out the other?"

Another pause.

"Britt, I think the idea is that we absorb a plethora of ideas … ."

"What's plethora mean?"

"It means a lot, many. We need to take these ideas and ponder them, but not obsess over them. They are useful as food for thought. One lecture might have meaning for one student, whereas another student might just pass it off as having little relevance in his or her life. Perhaps in the future, something will trigger in you the remembrance of what was said, and it will have significance."

"But I'm all mixed up," Britt said in an almost desperate tone. "Not just because of these lectures, but from what the Bible says and how preachers say we're supposed to live, because nobody does what the Bible says. How can we go to church and pray and read the Bible and don't live the way it says? I mean, somewhere in there it says you're supposed to give everything you have to the poor and follow the Lord. So why doesn't anybody do it? Oh yeah, and when somebody hits you in the face, you're supposed to turn your other cheek so he can hit you again. Nobody does that."

Britt paused, and Bregman said nothing.

Another thing," Britt resumed. "When I was ten, I got really excited about baseball. I even tried to get my older brother Kevin to go outside and play catch in the winter if there wasn't any snow on the ground. He thought I was crazy. So anyway, I became a big fan of the New York Yankees because they had these great players—Whitey Ford, Yogi Berra, Joe DiMaggio, Phil Rizzuto … ." Bregman nodded that he understood, and said, "Okay Britt, you can continue."

"Yeah, and my dad really liked baseball, too. He would talk about these great players in history, like Ty Cobb and Honus Wagner and Tris Speaker and Walter Johnson and Grover Cleveland Alexander and Christy Mathewson and Babe Ruth and Lou Gehrig and … ."

"Why did you become so fascinated with baseball, Britt?" Bregman interrupted.

"Gee, I don't know. I don't remember. I guess just because I heard my dad talk about it and read about it in the papers. I remember the first time I saw pictures of Big League Baseball. I was nine and was standing beside my dad while he was looking at the Sunday *Des Moines Register*, which had these photographs of this great double-play by the Yankees against the Brooklyn Dodgers."

"Do you think you might have become interested in baseball because your dad was interested in it?"

"Naw. I mean, I don't think so. Gee, I don't know. I never thought about it."

"Did he show more interest in you after you took up baseball?"

"Oh yeah. He seemed to like the idea. He even went with me once on a Saturday to the school playground and pitched to me and a couple of my baseball friends. He told us how to choke up on the bat so we could swing it around easier."

Bregman stared meaningfully at Britt, who didn't understand.

"Well, anyway, I was going to tell you that when I was ten, in 1948, my dad and I sat on the floor in front of the radio for a little while one Sunday when the Cleveland Indians played the Boston Braves in the World Series. Bob Feller was the famous pitcher for Cleveland, and he was from a farm in Iowa, so my dad really liked him. But we only listened for maybe ten minutes and my dad turned it off. He said it wasn't right that they played on Sunday, because it was work for them and all the people who sold hot dogs and popcorn and so forth. I begged him to keep the radio on, but he wouldn't."

"How did that make you feel, Britt?"

"Well, I was really disappointed, of course. But that's not what I'm talking about. When I was fifteen, we'd just gotten a television set and my dad watched the Sunday games of the World Series on TV. I couldn't figure it out. All this time we hadn't been listening to the World Series on Sunday on the radio, and all of a sudden my dad was watching it on television."

"Were you glad that you could now watch, too?"

"No. I was really confused."

"Did you say anything?"

"I think I said something like, 'Dad, I thought it wasn't right to watch the game on Sunday.' And he just mumbled that it wouldn't hurt. I didn't say anything more. But I actually didn't want to watch it, because I thought it was wrong."

Britt stopped and breathed deeply.

"So I just don't get it when I go to church and hear the preacher talk about the Bible and we read it at home after supper, and Dad says the prayer, and it seems like most people say they're Christians but don't really follow the Bible."

Bregman dropped his hand from his chin and cocked his head to one side while looking at Britt with a furrowed brow. He said nothing for a couple of seconds, then: "It's not my purpose to defend or criticize the Bible, Britt, but it seems to me that it might help if you could regard the teachings in the Bible as ideals that we can strive to live up to, but know that we will fall short.

"You know, the commandment to refrain from working on the Sabbath is in the Old Testament, and there are many strictures in the Old Testament that no one in civilized society would consider following. For example, the Book of Exodus demands that anyone caught working on the Sabbath shall be put to death."

Britt's jaw dropped open.

"Really?"

"Yes. I don't remember the chapter and verse, but you could look it up. Maybe your dad began thinking about that and wondered if the rule perhaps shouldn't be observed quite so strictly."

"Hmmm," Britt murmured, his face a mixture of confusion and understanding.

"We departed from the subject of the chapel lectures and I'd like to return to that," Bregman said after allowing Britt to reflect for a few seconds. "I gather that what these daily lectures are doing, Britt, is exacerbating your feelings of aimlessness, your sense of having no direction. And I wonder if this isn't a result of your uncertainty as to who you are. I'm going to throw another lesson at you, Britt: Know thyself."

Bregman's tone and deliberate manner of speaking took on the redolence of profundity. "It's an admonition from a man named Socrates. And although he harks back eons, to the early stages of man's modern development, the wisdom that he imparted has been an infallible guidepost for mankind down through the ages, all the way to the present.

"Now, of course, knowing who you are isn't as easy as it sounds. It requires a lot of self-examination, a lot of reflection. There have been times in my life when I've had to engage in introspection of my own. In World War II, I was drafted into the Army and realized I might one day be faced with a situation in which I either had to kill someone or be killed. I decided that I would have to take a bullet rather than take another life. Fortunately, I was sent to Australia and never had to make that choice."

He paused, hand on chin again, deep in thought. Then: "Britt, we didn't get into the idea of the self-concept in the course that you took with me. But let me explain what it means. Put simply, it's how you see yourself—what kind of person you think you are. Do you think you're an extroverted person—an outgoing person who is the life of the party and never has taken life very seriously, and doesn't feel things very deeply? Or do you see yourself as an introspective, sensitive person whose feelings are easily triggered?"

"Oh, that's easy," Britt said, almost jocularly. "I'm extroverted. Always was. When I was a kid, I didn't sit around reading or fixing bikes like my older brother Kevin. While he was doing that stuff, I was out playing baseball or working out with my barbell or learning to walk on my hands or how to box or do jujitsu. Kevin was always quiet and I was always noisy. When I was ten years old, I had a paper route and won an outstanding newspaper carrier award. The *Mayfield Daily News* ran a photo of me and the caption said I was a happy-go-lucky kid. That's always how I've thought about myself."

Bregman lowered his hand from his chin to the arm of his chair and said nothing for a pregnant few seconds.

"Britt," he began slowly, "I have to tell you that I don't really think you have a very good picture of yourself."

"I don't?"

"No Britt, I think not. Don't misunderstand me. I don't mean to indicate that's a failure on your part. It's simply a result of the totality of your experiences. From what I've heard you talk about—your acutely painful self-consciousness, the anxiety you felt over the possibility you might have hurt someone's feelings with a remark, the embarrassment you feel for others, your tortured religious concerns—it's become apparent to me that you are the opposite of your self-image."

Britt stared open-mouthed at Bregman, then grunted with a tone of amazement, "Huh!"

"I think you have a vivid imagination and are extremely sensitive," Bregman said gently.

Britt didn't quite know what to make of this, and then a light bulb popped on in his head.

"Come to think of it, my grade school art teacher always said my pictures showed good imagination. I never could quite figure that out, because I usually was trying to draw a horse but I was terrible at drawing. The horses looked so unreal that I finally began to wonder if she thought I was making them look that way on purpose."

Bregman broke into a grin and chuckled softly.

"Yeah, you know, I *was* really hurt when Barbara Conover, a girl I had a crush on in the eighth grade, gave me a note at the church Youth Night saying she didn't want to be my girlfriend. She'd been flirting with me before, and I was stunned. I guess I should have expected it, because I was supposed to meet her at this Junior High mixer, but she never even looked at me the whole night."

"Did you get interested in other girls after that?" Bregman asked.

"Well, yeah, but I didn't ask anybody out till the eleventh grade. My parents teased me about Barbara Conover, and I was really embarrassed. And Kevin, who was two-and-a-half years older than me, never went out with any girls. He just ran around with a couple of guys. So that's what I did."

"Why did you want to do what your brother did?"

"I don't know. I didn't really want to. I just . . . ."

Britt shifted in his chair and looked down. Bregman waited without moving, gazing softly at Britt.

"He just seemed to do everything right," Britt finally said. "I mean, my parents always talked about him being mechanically inclined, and he decided he wanted to be a mechanical engineer. So he took a lot of math subjects in high school. Well, when I got there, I did too."

"Did you like math?"

"Just algebra. I was good at beginning algebra. But when I switched schools in mid-year, I'd missed the first semester of advanced algebra and had to try to learn it all in the second semester. I managed to get a C. Then I took geometry, trigonometry and college algebra and got a couple C's and a D. Kevin was at Iowa State by this time, and he couldn't get good enough grades. So he switched to Thessalonika. He graduated before you came here."

"What were your best subjects, Britt?"

"English, for sure. Not so much the literature, because my mind always wandered when I read, but I always got really good grades in the language part, and also whenever we had to write a theme. Oh yeah, and typing. I was the second best typist in my big class in eleventh grade. That's why I thought I was going to become a typist. Oh, and I just thought of something else. Miss Godwin, my eighth-grade English and speech teacher, said I was really good at speech and should try out for the debate team when I got to high school. She put it on my report card."

"And?"

"I just forgot about it."

"Didn't your parents suggest that you should go out for the team?"

"Not that I remember."

"Well, they must have been proud of you."

Britt paused, then: "Miss Godwin—I was her pet. When I went back to high school to finish the last semester—this was four years after I had her as a teacher—I was riding with her in her car one day to help her deliver a heavy package, and she asked me to join her drama class so I could be in the plays. But I said I just didn't feel like I could. So she asked if I would work backstage. And I said no."

"Do you think she was trying to help you, Britt?"

"I guess she must have been."

"Yes, Britt, I'm sure she was. Why didn't you let her?"

"I just didn't feel up to it. I was too scared."

"Of what?"

"Mixing with the other kids. And I sure as heck was too scared to get up on stage in front of a bunch of people."

Bregman sat with his hand covering his mouth, a slight frown wrinkling his forehead as he stared silently at his patient. Finally: "I don't normally use the direct approach in counseling, but I think it may be warranted in this instance. Britt, you seem to be really lacking in self-confidence."

He paused to let that sink in.

"I don't see any reason for you to feel inadequate, Britt. You are a bright, talented, good-looking young man, and you measure up well with any of your peers. I know you don't feel it, and I can't make you start feeling it. But remember what I said."

Bregman placed his hands on the arms of his chair. "We've had a long session and need to end it. I have a full load in the next few weeks, and I expect that you will want to begin working on the final exams, so we won't be able to meet for awhile. Let's play it by ear, so that if you need to see me before the term ends, you can let me know."

"Yes, that would be good. Thanks."

CHAPTER 19

"Hi, I'm Bud," the sewer-construction foreman said in a gravelly voice, smiling faintly as he reached out with his hand. He was about five-foot-nine and ruggedly good-looking with a rakish mop of yellowish hair. He held a smoking cigarette between two fingers that matched his hair color.

Britt landed a summer job with the same company that he worked for the previous summer, and was assigned to a crew installing sewer tile for several blocks in a residential site in Colton. He was greatly relieved to find a different crew foreman than the Bull Moose. Bud, around forty, chain-smoked and moved about with agitated energy, frequently cursing quietly but always amiable, in an impersonal way.

Bud was under pressure from the company owner to complete the job as cheaply as possible, and the strain on him was evident, though he never took out his frustrations on the men who worked under him. His nemesis was Jerry, the county inspector. Although Jerry was a good-humored man, with an ample girth that didn't prevent him from moving around agilely, he insisted that work was done properly, according to code.

Jerry would check the pipes strung alongside the ditch, ready to be laid, and paint slightly bent ones or those with minor surface cracks with a black X, which meant they were not to be used. But Bud figured most of these would not cause any slowing in the flow of sewage or be prone to deterioration. He'd have his men lay all but the most flawed ones on random days in late afternoon, because Jerry usually came before noon. Jerry would arrive and ask what was done with the marked pipes. Bud would tell him they had been loaded onto the same truck that brought new pipes, and carted away for disposal. One day, Jerry dropped by near the end of the day and caught the men laying a marked pipe.

"Aha, I thought you might be doing this," he said, his good-natured attitude markedly changed.

"Look," said Bud, "we were running out of pipes and that one barely has a bend. Look at it for yourself."

"I'm not interested in your explanation," Jerry countered, his face reddening with anger. "When I determine that a pipe isn't to be used, it doesn't get used, or I'm slapping this company with a big fine. Is that clear?"

"All right, Jerry, all right. It won't happen again." Then, to Britt, "Lower the hook." The men in the ditch slipped the hook, attached to a rope, into the pipe, and Britt pulled it out. Jerry stalked off in a huff.

"God-damn motherfuckin' diddly dipshit cocksuckin' son-of-a-bitch," Bud softly cursed, the colorful obscenities tripping so dexterously off his tongue that he could have been speaking Spanish.

In most places, the ditch was only six or seven feet deep. At an intersection, however, a large, deep hole was dug to make room for a circular concrete emplacement that merged sewage coming from opposite directions and routed it in a perpendicular direction. Bud moved close to the edge to check on the progress, then moved back.

"Christ, I jumped out of airplanes as a paratrooper and here I am scared to look down ten feet," he muttered in his grainy voice, chuckling slightly at himself.

Bud was nonplussed one hot afternoon when Hubie, a crew member hired a couple of weeks before, suddenly toppled onto the ground, his eyes rolled back in his head and his mouth frothing.

"Holy shit," Bud said, obviously alarmed. "What the hell is wrong with him? Is he havin' a heart attack?"

"He's having an epileptic attack," said Britt as he hurriedly scanned the ground around him. He dashed a few feet to pick up a wooden lathe, ran over to Hubie and inserted it in his mouth.

"Oh fuck," Bud said.

"Beer—car," Hubie gasped, barely intelligibly.

Britt ran to Hubie's old Chevy, found a can of beer on the floor in the back seat, and hurried back to Hubie. Prying it open, Britt put it to the lips of the convulsing young man, who slugged it down in what had to be record time. The convulsions stopped, and Hubie got up. Blood smeared the side of his mouth where the lathe had scraped him.

"You okay?" Bud asked.

"Yeah," said Hubie, an affable, heavyset fellow who made Britt think of Lennie Small in Steinbeck's *Of Mice and Men.* He'd read the work in the months between his release from the hospital in Iowa City and his enrollment in college.

"I think you'd better go home and take it easy, don't you?" Bud said.

"I guess so," said Hubie, looking embarrassed.

"Can you drive?"

"Yeah, I'll be all right." Hubie shuffled off to his car, his head down, and drove away.

"Well I'll be dipped in shit," said Elmer, a short, skinny, young crew member who had watched the entire incident as though dumbstruck. The indecorous remark usually was prompted by an event of far less dramatic nature. In fact, Elmer uttered this expression of amazement an average of perhaps fifteen times a day. He interspersed it with, "I told him to take a flying fuck at the moon." It was the denouement of every story—a half dozen or so a day—in which someone allegedly had tried to cheat or otherwise take advantage of the young construction worker. The exclamation pertaining to excrement probably was not without substance: He previously had worked for his father, who operated a business emptying septic tanks.

Hubie did not come to work the next day, nor the day after. Britt asked Bud if he were okay, and Bud replied, "I had to call him and tell him it was too dangerous for him to be doing this kind of work with that condition. I hated like hell to do it. He could fall in a ditch and kill himself, and Hank would be all over my ass. Anyway, I don't like people dying in front of me. I had my fill of that in the war in Germany."

Britt liked Hubie, and realized the days would drag on a little longer without him around, for he had his own mantra for dealing with the world. It rivaled Elmer's proclamations in frequency if not necessarily in profundity: "That's what *she* said." Hubie disclosed this pithy piece of information during the course of virtually every conversation, always with an air of utmost authority. Britt decided Hubie either had known a lot of females or a few who were inordinately loquacious.

Hank Osmer was the owner of the construction firm, and he worried Bud almost as much as Jerry did. The worry turned to dread one Saturday afternoon in mid-summer. The crew usually didn't work Saturday afternoons, but the project was running slightly behind schedule, so Hank had ordered the overtime. It was an oppressively hot, humid day, and at three-thirty p.m. Bud told everybody to lay off. He went to his car and brought a cooler with three six-packs of beer, and the men lounged on a shaded, grassy slope beside the ditch and began to guzzle. Bud was chatting and laughing lightly with his men when something caught the corner of his eye and he stopped abruptly. Britt turned to look, and there was Hank's new, shiny black Cadillac rolling to a stop on the street perpendicular to the sewer installation site.

"Oh, son-of-a-bitch," said Bud. "Don't panic. Just act casual."

Hank was a short man, about sixty, with a full head of dark hair combed straight back. He wore tinted glasses and fine apparel, and could easily have been taken for a Mafia don, sauntering forth casually, a slight sardonic smile crimping his thin lips. The only thing he lacked was a cigar.

"Hello, gentlemen," he said, his head tilted back a bit.

"Hi Hank," Bud answered. "The guys have been going at a fast clip all day in this awful heat, and we've gotten a lot done. So I told them to take a break so they don't get heat stroke or something. We've still got a couple hours of work left." Actually, he'd told the men they were finished for the day.

"Okay," said Hank. "Do you think you can get to the end of the block today? You're pretty close."

"Oh, yeah," Bud said. "That's what we had planned. The job is coming along good."

"Uh, do you think it's a good idea to be drinking on the job?"

"Yeah, I know, Hank. The guys have a couple of beers when they finish work, but today is so miserably hot. I let 'em break open a can early. It's not going to affect their work, believe me."

"Well, I just wanted to see how you were doing," said Hank. He and Bud talked about supplies and upcoming projects for a few minutes, and then Hank walked to his car and drove away.

"Whew," Bud said to no one in particular. "That was hairy. I guess we better get back to work. Hank might just remember something and come back. But if we crank it up, we can finish this block in an hour and go home."

Only a Saturday later, near the end of the next block on the downward sloping road, Bill and Elmer were in the ditch, laying a pipe in place, when a loud clatter erupted. They looked behind. The backhoe, which had been filling in the ditch where they had laid pipe, was plummeting toward them, its metal tracks creating a warning racket. Bill, who was in front of the pipe they had laid, scrambled forward, with Elmer following so fast he almost ran over his partner. Harry, the backhoe operator, released the boom, which plunged into the ditch, the bucket smashing several pipes before the machine came to a stop.

The portly Harry, looking as though he'd seen a ghost, climbed out of the cabin and announced, "The goddamned brakes failed."

Elmer and Bill scrambled out of the ditch, wide-eyed.

"Holy shit!" Elmer shouted.

For once, he wasn't dipped in it.

CHAPTER 20

The work days were long, and Britt was too tired to go out evenings. But he stayed home weekend nights, as well, because his friends from high school days were married or dating girls or living elsewhere, and he knew no one to pal around with. It was a spartan existence in a household with parents whose lives defined the phrase. This life ill-suited him, for, unlike his older brother Kevin, he had a social temperament and a ready wit. He had thoroughly enjoyed "Youth Night" at the church Thursdays when he was in junior high school, laughing and joking and playing games. But those two years were the last time that he had real fun with both boys and girls. Living on the farm in high school, he was geographically separated from the activities of his classmates. Besides, he had to work and had little time for socializing. Then, too, his parents subtly, if not overtly, discouraged involvement with girls. After all, Kevin didn't socialize with girls. Britt had one date—in his junior year. So on the weekends when he went out, it was with pals who felt awkward around girls.

Thus, he returned to Thessalonika College to begin his senior year feeling morose. He had done almost nothing but backbreaking work five-and-a-half to six long days a week, eat, watch a little television and go to bed. On Sundays, he'd accompanied his parents and younger siblings, Dale and Kyra, to church. He heard sermons that triggered conflicting thoughts on the Bible and Christianity, making him even more confused and troubled.

The college, which was gradually growing, had insufficient space in the men's dormitory and acquired a two-story house off-campus for renting to six students. Britt decided to be a part of the innovation and moved in, sharing a room with a student upstairs, where another student took a separate room. All of them joined in painting and sprucing up the well-worn wood-frame house on the first few Saturdays as part of their rental agreement. While working in the sunny, crisp autumn air, Britt suggested the house needed a name, and proposed "Alpha House," because it was the first venture in living off-campus. The six occupants, he reasoned, could form their own little fraternity, which also would be a first for the college. The others bandied the idea about and finally settled on it. One of the students, an art major, devised stencils and the name was painted in black on the front of the house.

On weekend nights, most of the other guys recruited dates and went to Pliny's only movie theater or sat in the upper level of the student lounge and watched television while eating popcorn. During the previous two years, Britt had become much attracted to Deena DeBarr, a pretty, mildly pert girl who was in his German and geography classes. But she had her sights on another guy and never noticed Britt. His ping-pong partner from the previous three years had graduated, and he was left alone while the others went out on these evenings. The weekday chapel lectures were torturing him, and he rapidly descended into the misery that he had felt in his last year in high school.

He had to get away, and drove home on a Saturday, collapsing into his mother's arms and sobbing. She took him into the living room and, sitting with him on the couch, read the 23rd Psalm: "The Lord is my shepherd … He restoreth my soul." Then she prayed aloud that her son would "be made whole."

Just what Britt needed: more religion. No, what he needed was a long, long talk about his lack of participation in school activities in junior high school and high school because of discouragement from his parents. He needed to talk about how they had held him back while promoting his older brother Kevin, to the point where Britt had begun emulating Kevin, even though his sullen, pessimistic personality was in marked contrast to Britt's ebullient, bright-spirited nature.

But he was temporarily calmed, and drove the twenty miles back to the college after church and afternoon dinner the next day. The inner torment soon returned, and he knocked on Professor Bregman's office door a few days later and made an appointment.

Britt told the professor of his visit home a few days before, and his mother's intercession with the Almighty in his behalf. Bregman's brow furrowed and one eye closed half-way as he attempted to conceal his disdain, which nonetheless broke through in a slightly twisted smile.

"I don't quite think that sitting down with your mother to read the Bible and pray is going to relieve the torment that you're feeling, Britt," he said in a tone that exuded irony. "I can't stress enough that you need to summon the courage to mingle with the other students, male and female, and become a part of the life on campus. You have the characteristics that should make it easy. All you lack is self-confidence."

But that self-confidence had been deeply undermined, and Britt was too ridden with feelings of rejection to venture forth and risk embarrassment. The possibilities were simply too painful to contemplate.

"I just feel like I'm different from everybody else," he said. "I think I was always that way." He handed Bregman an envelope and said, "Look at this photograph." It was the same one he'd remembered while looking at the other male patients during dinner at the sanitarium in Des Moines. During his visit home, he'd found it in a family photo album buried in an unused chest of drawers. The photo was of a group of adults and children posing outside a rural school in Muskego, Michigan, where they attended Sunday school classes. Britt was sitting on a bench in the front, next to a girl his own age, four or five, and was staring at her because she looked different. She happened to be retarded.

"See how I'm looking?" he asked Bregman. "See how mad I look? I don't look normal."

Bregman shrugged and said, "I don't see anything unusual. You merely appear to be curious about this little girl who apparently has Down's syndrome." Then, "You're not different, Britt. You just have a bad feeling about yourself."

Eleven days later, he attended the Sunday evening service at Second Reformed Church with three of his housemates. The pastor there, the Rev. Rodney Hamerkamp, was considered a highly learned, intellectual man. On this night, however, his sermon was unusually mundane as he spoke of the travails that may befall good, God-fearing people.

"Recently, three persons from our congregation have fallen victim to the dreadful vicissitudes of life," the tall, trim, bespectacled minister with a shock of medium-brown hair announced. "Randall Burgermeister returned home from a day of work last week and was walking up the concrete steps in front of the sidewalk to his house when he tripped and fell face-down, knocking out two of his front teeth."

Britt and his companions, sitting in the front pew of the balcony, separated by several feet from the nearest members of the congregation, did not find this particularly tragic, and repressed smiles of amusement that began to cross their faces.

"This week," the preacher continued in utter seriousness, "Mrs. Emma Vanderkrijn was walking her precious little dachshund Minnie past the site of an office building under construction in the south end of our town. Dear Mrs. Vanderkrijn's curiosity got the better of her, and she walked up to inspect the building. Peering into an elevator shaft, she slipped and fell eight feet to the bottom, breaking her right leg."

Now the college students in the balcony had everything they could do to keep from laughing. Britt stole a sideways glance and saw that a few people were looking their way.

"And only yesterday," said Pastor Hamerkamp, "my own Aunt Esther Vermaaden accidentally poked a stick down her throat while she was tending her garden and had to be treated for bruised tonsils."

That was too much. Britt and his cohorts wrapped their arms tightly over their chests and shook with laughter that they could not entirely muffle. Hamerkamp seemed oblivious to the commotion and droned on. The young fellows regained their composure and the sermon mercifully came to an end a few minutes later. Britt was embarrassed and kept his head down so he didn't have to look at the other congregants as they filed out of the church. He deftly sidestepped the minister so he wouldn't have to shake his hand. The foursome walked the few blocks back to the house, and all but Britt seemed to have forgotten the incident already and were chatting about classes and their girlfriends. But Britt's embarrassment lingered. He felt he'd made a spectacle of himself.

That night, he reached a breaking point. He attempted to study in his room on the second floor of Alpha House after church, but a hodgepodge of thoughts about death and hell and the purpose of his existence raced through his mind. He could not concentrate on his books. So at eleven p.m., he climbed into his single-width bed and fell into a troubled sleep.

He awoke after three a.m., lying on his back, his whole body shaking uncontrollably. Frightened, he jumped out of bed and rushed noisily to the restroom, where he turned on the light and looked in the mirror. Who was he looking at? Jesus Christ? He was different from everybody else. Maybe he *was* Jesus Christ. Maybe God had sent him to Earth to interact with people and affect them with his upright living. After all, his mother had repeatedly insisted that Christians such as her family were "in the world, but not of the world," an oral manifesto of moral superiority.

Then he remembered his sexual fantasies and the BB gun and baseball and catcher's mitt he'd bought against his parents orders, and the many arguments he'd had with them, and the time he and his cohorts had stolen the Mayfield High School mascot. Suddenly, while still looking in the mirror, he did an about-face, so to speak, and decided he must be the devil. Napoleon had no monopoly on narcissism over Britt. His mother had always admonished him for going to extremes—though never to the downside. This time he'd reached not just the zenith, but the nadir.

Britt's two upstairs roommates were out of bed now, and asked him what the matter was.

"I think I'm dying," said Britt, explaining that he had been shaking like a leaf. "I have to call Professor Bregman." He found Bregman's number in the phone book and dialed.

"Hello," Bregman answered.

"Dr. Bregman, I don't know what's happening to me. I woke up shaking like crazy and went to the bathroom and thought I saw Jesus Christ in the mirror, and then the devil."

"All right, Britt. Now just try to calm down. You're not Jesus Christ and you're not the devil. You're just feeling very, very stressed, and your emotions are playing tricks with your mind. Your body reacted to your stress, but you'll be okay. Just go back to bed, and try to let your muscles relax. In the morning, I want you to go to your classes. You need to keep up your routine. I'll see you in my office at four p.m."

"Well … okay," Britt said, somewhat calmed. He returned to bed, thought about his tense muscles, and forced them to relax. Soon he drifted off to sleep, and was startled from deep slumber three hours later by his alarm clock. The thoughts of the night before entered his mind immediately, and he couldn't go to breakfast at the cafeteria or classes, despite Bregman's admonishment.

He was thoroughly confused and in a desperate state of mind. He had to talk to a minister about his nocturnal thoughts. Getting out the phone book, he called the office of the Third Reformed Church, which he sometimes attended on Sunday mornings. He asked the secretary if he could meet right away with the Rev. Kolenbrander. She supposed he could if it were urgent, and he assured her it was.

Kolenbrander was a fairly stocky man of less than medium height with a thick blond mane that framed a cherubic, though intense, face. He was a tireless worker who preached three long sermons every Sunday, two in the morning and one in the evening. His large, beautiful church was supported by four-hundred-twenty-five members. They lived humbly and modestly though many had built up sizable bank accounts by heeding the same work ethic of their pastor and living frugally. Almost every one of them attended at least one of the three sermons. Kolenbrander delivered his Calvinist-based messages with an intensity that bordered on anguish. He admonished his flock to lead upright lives by unerringly following the teachings of Christ so they would escape the pangs of hell wrought by Satan and reap, instead, the rewards of heaven, living in eternal bliss with their Creator. Britt absorbed these unsettling sermons, which only made him more conscious of his behavior and deepened his fears.

Kolenbrander greeted Britt with a quizzical smile and asked him to sit down.

"What's on your mind, son?" the preacher asked, underguessing Britt's age of twenty-two.

Son? The preacher had no idea what a loaded question that was.

"You didn't mean Son of God, did you?" asked Britt.

Kolenbrander was speechless. He stared at Britt with mouth agape, wondering if this were a deadpan joke, and a sacrilegious one at that. When Britt's expression didn't change, the minister realized he was serious.

"You said your name was Britt, didn't you?"

"Yes."

"Well, uh, Britt, why did you wonder if I meant Son of God?"

Britt related the thoughts that had occurred to him the preceding night, mentioned that he'd had a breakdown in high school, and said he felt he was different from other people. He asked if Kolenbrander thought there was any possibility he, Britt, were Jesus Christ or Satan.

The minister listened intently to this exposition, which Britt delivered logically, coherently, and without undue passion. He straightened in his chair, took a deep breath, and said, "Britt, I don't see this as a religious matter, but rather a psychological issue. Where do your parents live?"

"On a small farm about twenty-five miles away."

"Good. Britt, can you step into the secretary's office for a moment?"

Britt complied, and Kolenbrander emerged a few minutes later.

"I've spoken with Dr. Haversham, the dean of students, and he wants to see you. Can you promise me that you will go to his office?"

"Sure."

Britt walked briskly to Old Manse, which held the administrative offices, and knocked on the door of the dean, who had been a commander in the Navy.

"The Rev. Kolenbrander has informed me that you are not feeling very well," Haversham said in a patronizing tone. Britt always felt a lack of sincerity in Haversham, as though his smile hid an autocratic nature. "Is that true, Britt."

"I've been having problems."

"I've called your parents, and they've asked that you pack your belongings into your car and drive home. They didn't think you would have any problem doing that. Do you think you can make it home all right? You appear to be functioning well, despite what I understand was a highly unusual episode you experienced last night."

"Yes, I can get home with no problem," Britt assured the dean.

"Well then, best of luck to you, Britt. We'll notify your professors that you won't be taking their classes anymore."

Britt's roommates were in their classes as he carried his clothes and miscellaneous belongings to his car. He drove away without saying goodbye to anyone. On the way home, after he'd turned off the highway onto a country road where there was no traffic, he began sobbing at the wheel. His tears almost blinded him to a rabbit that darted in front of the car. He jammed on the brakes, and thus regained his composure.

"What's the matter, son?" Miriam Rutgers beseeched when he arrived home. She was clearly upset. Tears streamed down Britt's face as he squeaked, "I don't know. I just can't go on."

The next day, Milton Rutgers called Dr. Sanger in Mayfield, who got in touch with University Hospitals in Iowa City.

"They looked up your records, and they were surprised you lasted this long, Britt," Milton said. "They asked us to bring you there the day after tomorrow."

CHAPTER 21

The premises of the psychiatric center at University Hospitals in Iowa City were the same as when Britt had left the place four years earlier. The personnel had changed, however. The overpowering Dr. Reginald Campanella was no longer there. Britt was assigned to Dr. Jonas Brower. He was in his early forties, stood about six-feet-two, slender-to-average build, an oval face, black hair but balding in spots, bespectacled. In personality, he was the opposite of Campanella—soft-spoken, gentle. Britt felt an immediate rapport.

Of course, the patients were not the same, either. The colorful characters from his previous stay were unique. Troubled though he was, Britt could see the humor in the situation. He'd returned to the neighborhood, only to find that the old gang was gone. No grumpy, chain-smoking, coffee-guzzling, ruddy-faced Bielefeld; no Louis, the intimidating, flatulent ex-football player; no Susan, the coquettish teenager; no Everett, the taciturn aeronautical engineer.

Equally compelling patients took their places. Hank was one of the most interesting to Britt. He was maybe forty, about five-feet-eight, fairly stout with a little paunch, slicked-back hair that was prematurely graying, somewhat handsome in a rugged way. Hank walked the halls with a limp, glumly stone-faced, staring away from most persons he encountered. But as time went on, he finally began acknowledging Britt's casual "Hiya" or "How's it goin'?" with a grunt. One afternoon, Britt watched him shoot pool by himself on the pool table that had been added to the recreation room since Britt's previous stay. He wasn't a bad player, and Britt asked if he wanted to play a game of eight-ball. Hank's face lighted up, and he asked if Britt wanted to break. Britt told Hank to go ahead, and the five-ball sailed into a side pocket. Hank then cut the one-ball into a corner pocket, but missed the same corner on a bank shot of the nine-ball. "I didn't cut it enough," he said in slurring speech, smiling faintly. The game ended with Britt winning as Hank left two balls on the table.

"Good game," he mumbled, his smile widening now.

"The guy is shell-shocked," a male patient who had no noticeable abnormalities told Britt at lunch the next day. Britt had gestured to a nearby table where Hank was sitting and remarked that he was a decent pool player. "Battle of the Bulge. I found out one night before you got here. He started screaming in the middle of the night and dove under his bed. Woke everybody up and scared the hell out of us. I asked the attendant what the hell was going on and he told me what had happened to the guy. Since then they give him a pill before he goes to bed."

Two days later, Britt sat with Hank at a table for dinner. Leaning into Britt's ear, he mumbled, "The bowl of peas is poisoned." Britt dropped his spoon of peas onto his plate and said, "What are you talking about?"

"I know," Hank slurred. "I saw the attendant take the bowl into the kitchen and come back out with it. Know why he did that? He secretly doctored it."

"Maybe he was just filling it up," said Britt.

"Huh-uh. They can't fool me. I know what's going on. They want to kill all of us. Why do you think they brought us here? We're prisoners. Be very careful what you eat."

Britt stared at Hank for a few seconds, not knowing what to say. Finally: "Okay, Hank. I'll be careful. But I've already eaten quite a few peas and feel just fine, so I think everything will be all right."

"Well, I'm not taking any chances," said Hank. "I'm going back to the rec room to watch television."

Not quite so colorful was Brent, a fellow about ten years younger than Hank, though he looked even younger from a distance. But he had an air of mystery that held a certain fascination for Britt. This cryptic countenance was evinced by a perpetually blank look on his face and enhanced by an omnipresent chessboard that he carried, along with the requisite pieces, in a green leather case. Brent always ate alone, hunkered over his chessboard, positioned directly in front of him with his plate of food relegated to his left side. He occasionally moved a king or a queen with his left hand while wielding a fork in his right hand. The same nondescript fellow who had passed the lowdown about Hank told Britt that Brent was prone to delusions of grandeur. Britt asked about the source of the information, but the fellow only nodded knowingly. Britt was tempted to ask him what his own problem was, but sensed that the guy would take umbrage.

But not everyone was new to Britt. Two days after he arrived, Don Billings, the attendant who wore loafers, walked into the ward, looking as upbeat as Britt had remembered him. Spotting Britt, he broke into a warm grin and said, "Hi Britt. Welcome back—though you probably aren't glad to *be* back."

"Gee whiz, you remember me," Britt said, beaming.

"Oh yeah, I never forget a patient. Besides, you were one of the more likable ones." He was about five inches shorter than Britt, but managed to playfully wrestle him into a headlock, saying, "I learned that in the Marine Corps." Britt felt a twinge of discomfort at Don's physical familiarity, sensing something slightly untoward.

"Do you remember how to make a hospital bed—with the sheets forming an angle at the corners?" Don asked.

"Oh sure," Britt said. "I've been making my bed that way ever since you taught me the last time I was here."

"Atta boy," said Don, throwing his left arm around Britt's shoulders. "Well, time for lunch. See you later."

After lunch, the ward supervisor told Britt that Dr. Brower wanted to see him in his office. Britt was pleased because he liked the psychiatrist, and walked briskly down the hall to his office.

"Hi Britt," he said quietly, smiling slightly. "Take a seat."

"How have you been feeling?" he asked of his patient.

"Oh, not too bad," Britt shrugged.

"Britt … ." He hesitated, then continued gently, "I think we need to do a series of ECTs. I hope that doesn't bother you too much."

Britt's heart simultaneously sank and began beating fast.

"You mean shock treatments?"

"Yes. I'd like to begin them Wednesday, day after tomorrow, and do fourteen total."

Britt had a fleeting impulse to run away, but simply slumped in the chair and said nothing.

Dr. Brower looked at Britt for several long seconds, then: "I'm sorry, Britt, but I think it's the best thing for you. You'll be okay."

Britt looked down and away, feeling a little bit queasy and saying nothing. Finally, "Well, if that's the way it has to be." He rose to leave, and Dr. Brower placed his hand on Britt's shoulder.

"You'll be fine, Britt."

The next night, the night before the first treatment, Britt lay awake, envisioning the treatment room with the table in the center and the green oxygen tank in a corner. He could feel the nurse applying gell to his temples, her fingers working in a circular motion. They're going to shock my brain—shoot an electric current into it for about a minute, he thought. What if they get the setting on the equipment wrong, or it malfunctions, and the current I get is too strong? What if I bite my tongue off? What if I die from the convulsions? What if I can't breathe and the oxygen tank doesn't work. He didn't fall asleep for several hours. In the morning, it was the same routine he remembered from four years before.

"Attention everybody," the ward attendant announced to the sixteen men just after he'd turned the lights on at seven a.m. "The following people will not go to the dining room for breakfast." He slowly read four names, and Britt hoped a mistake had occurred and his name had been missed. Then, "Britt Rutgers."

Patients were summoned at fifteen-minute intervals, and Britt was third. Heart pumping, he walked the short distance to the room, where Dr. Brower and two nurses stood waiting. "Hi Britt. Just remove your pajama top, if you will, and lie on your back on the table. This will be completely painless." The doctor had a reassuring smile and talked softly. A nurse began massaging his temples with the gell, and the other one inserted a needle into his right arm.

"Now, Britt, please count backward, starting with ten," Dr. Brower said. Britt reached five. He awoke forty minutes later on a table in the recovery room, the nurse who had administered the gell by his side. "Take a shower and get dressed, Britt, and then you may go to the dining room for breakfast," she said briskly, smiling brightly.

The routine continued every Monday, Wednesday, and Friday. On the tenth treatment, one of Britt's fears was realized. He partly awoke, apparently just after the treatment had ended, and couldn't breathe. His eyes didn't open, and he was in a hazy, dreamlike state but could hear Dr. Brower say he was going to be okay. Just then he felt something against his face and began breathing again before losing consciousness.

A week later, the psychiatrist summoned Britt to his office and asked him to sit at a table and take a few short tests. Britt had no trouble with them, and then Dr. Brower said, "I want you to illustrate this concept: Two heads are better than one." But he gave it away, saying, "You can use stick figures." Britt was going to do that anyway: He drew stick figures of two persons next to each other and one person standing apart from them. From Dr. Brower's instruction, Britt realized that he had made the "correct" drawing. He divined that the "incorrect" drawing would have been a picture of two heads without bodies and another, separate, bodiless head. What abnormality such a drawing would have indicated, however, he had no idea.

The fourteen treatments, which Britt never lost his fear of, finally were over, and he was elated. Dr. Brower again summoned Britt to his office.

"How are you feeling now, Britt?" he asked.

"Well, I'm just relieved those shock treatments are over. I feel good.

"You seem to be doing well, Britt. However … ." The doctor hesitated.

Oh no, thought Britt, he's not going to tell me I need more treatments. Britt's heart began racing.

"I don't think you're quite ready to go out and deal with the problems and pressures of everyday life," the psychiatrist continued. Britt's heartbeat slowed a little. "We want you to get completely well before you go out on your own. But we've done all we can in a facility of this size. So we'd like to transfer you to the state Mental Health Institute in Mercyville. It has several large buildings, and there are a lot of patients—at least a thousand—with whom you can mingle in a relaxed atmosphere and learn to feel at ease in larger social settings. And you'll take part in group therapy sessions. What do you think?"

"Well … ." Britt paused, not sure what to think. "I … I mean, I guess it's okay. But just one thing: I won't have any more shock treatments, will I?"

"No, Britt, you won't. There is no need for you to have any more."

Britt sighed deeply.

"So," Dr. Brower said. "We're going to notify your parents and have them come and get you in a few days. They will take you home for a couple of days, and then they'll take you to Mercyville."

CHAPTER 22

A long, narrow driveway led to a cluster of buildings that comprised the state mental hospital on the outskirts of Mercyville. It was December, and patches of snow relieved the drabness of dead, brown-gray grass and barren trees permeating the broad grounds that fronted the buildings. Most of the edifices consisted of several stories and were of a classical brick architecture that harked back at least to the turn of the century. In the center of them was the main building, which housed the administration. Milton Rutgers drove the light-green 1958 Dodge, which he'd bought when the Plymouth's motor gave out, up to the entrance. He, Miriam, and Britt got out and walked slowly to the large, heavy door.

They entered and saw that the building was quite old, with flooring, doors, and molding of dark wood. On the right side of a wide hallway was an office door with a sign above that read, New Patient Processing. A middle-aged nurse greeted them pleasantly and asked that they follow her to a room with a desk and three lounge chairs. She handed Milton a couple of papers to fill out, and when he had finished, said, "Thank you, Mr. and Mrs. Rutgers. We're going to do our best to put your son on the road to recovery." The two said goodbye to Britt and told him they would be visiting in ten days, on a Sunday.

Britt waited while the nurse dialed the phone and said, "The new patient is here and needs to be taken to his room." In a few minutes, a man of about fifty arrived and coolly introduced himself to Britt as Jake. He wore dark-rimmed glasses and had a healthy head of hair that was neatly parted on the left side. "Grab your suitcase and follow me, young man," he said in a neutral tone, then led Britt to an intersection in the hallway and turned right. A door opened to a short sidewalk that led to an adjacent building facing the same direction. The sidewalk circled to the front of it, and Jake opened the door for Britt. "It's pretty cold today," Jake remarked. "Sorry to make you lug that suitcase around."

"Thanks," Britt said, and the attendant answered, "This is the dormitory where you'll be staying. You'll be in a room by yourself on the second floor. I'll lead you up the stairs and show you where it is." The hall on the second floor was dark. Britt's room was barren except for an antiqueish-looking chest-of-drawers, a wooden rocking chair and an iron bed. A small closet that obviously wasn't there originally had been built into the far right corner.

"The bathroom is down the hall on the left. You have an electric shaver, right? I'm sure your parents were told we don't allow razor blades."

"Yes," said Britt. "I had a Norelco, anyway."

"Good. There are some shelves on the wall above the two sinks, and you can put your Norelco on the empty one. You'll share the bathroom with three other men. You're to shower every morning and you'll get fresh towels daily. After you've put your things away and gotten settled, come to my station at the head of the hallway at six o'clock and I'll take you to where you're going to eat."

By the time Britt had arranged his clothes and toiletries, the sun was setting on the winter day, and he pulled a chain connected to a light fixture on the ceiling. It made the room barely light enough to read. He walked out of his room into an even darker hallway. Though high-ceilinged and about fifty feet long, it was lighted by a single ceiling bulb halfway from either end. The room light was a bulb enclosed in a glass shade, but the hall bulb, which appeared to be a sixty-watter, was exposed to allow maximum diffusion of light. Britt couldn't imagine anything looking drearier, and thought: Wow, if you weren't screwed up before coming here, you would get that way in a hurry. This place could make a cheerleader depressed. He remembered reading in a news magazine that criminals who went to prison often left with worse behavior problems.

Britt walked to the attendant's station a little early. The attendant told him the three other men on the floor would join them soon and they would all walk to the dining hall. Within a few minutes, the three—a fellow in his early thirties and two men about a dozen years older, all nondescript and uninteresting looking—sauntered up from their rooms, saying nothing.

"Okay gentlemen," said Jake, "let's go." He led them down the heavy oak stairway and out the front door, then down a winding sidewalk two hundred feet to a similar, old brick building. They walked up a stairway, which opened to a huge dining hall where, Britt estimated, about three hundred men and women already were seated. A stairway at the other end of the first floor led to the other end of the dining hall. Britt surveyed the crowd and thought, Oh my God, I don't belong in this place. It looked like a true lunatic asylum. He learned later that it opened during the Civil War as the Mercyville Lunatic Asylum, which evolved into the Mercyville Insane Asylum and finally the Mental Health Institute at Mercyville.

The patients looked disoriented and disheveled, wearing drab clothing, their hair unkempt, their faces gaunt. Their eyes were glazed, rolled back or buglike, mirroring a world behind them that they had gradually constructed to ward out a world in front of them which had become too painful to deal with. The meal consisted of comfort food—meatloaf, mashed potatoes, peas, and apple pie—and Britt thought it was fairly tasty.

Afterward, it was back to the dismal dormitory. There was nothing to do but sit in one's room and read, or pull a chair into the hallway and watch television on the twelve-inch screen with the attendant. Britt did both, then went to bed as required at ten p.m.

The bed was almost as hard as a board, and the pillow was like a slab of stone. He pulled the pillow jacket back and found that the pillow was wrapped in a nondetachable burlap casing. In the morning, he asked Jake if any softer pillows were available. The attendant said there were no others, and the beds and pillows were the original ones from when the hospital was built. He said it had been used for a short time to house prisoners from the Civil War. The bed and pillows were made of straw, which had hardened, he said.

Breakfast was in the same dining hall, and fewer patients showed up. Fear struck Britt as it occurred to him those who didn't come were having shock treatments, which might mean he would be getting them, too. Lunch was the same dreary affair, except the dining hall was full. Britt was taking a bite of his pork cutlet when he heard a commotion and, out of the corner of his eye, saw that something was happening two tables away. He turned quickly to look and beheld a man who appeared to be elderly, though he may have only looked old because of his deplorable mental state. The fellow was convulsing in his chair and about to fall to the floor. An attendant rushed up and helped him to a supine position, where a sickeningly gray, viscous fluid flowed from the corners of his mouth. The incident did not attract much attention from the surrounding patients, who gaped at the man for a few seconds and resumed eating. Britt, however, had lost his appetite, and walked to the entrance where Jake the attendant was waiting. They soon were joined by the other three men who shared the second floor in Britt's building.

In the mornings and afternoons, Jake accompanied the four men to a large recreation hall in another old building. There wasn't much in it except a book shelf with magazines and books, an eighteen-inch television, and tables with dominoes, checkers sets, and decks of cards. Britt never cared for cards and was not good at checkers, but he played the game with a couple of the patients who seemed to be mostly in possession of their faculties. One, a lean fellow in his early thirties who wore an intense look on a sharply featured face, defeated him soundly but said nothing during the match or afterward.

Milton and Miriam Rutgers drove to Mercyville to see their son on the Sunday ten days after he'd been admitted. Britt told them about the uncomfortable mattress and the rock-hard pillow, and the attendant's story that it was as old as the hospital, about one hundred years. Milton insisted that couldn't be true, and Britt said, "If you felt that pillow, you'd believe it. If you hit somebody in the head with that pillow, you'd kill him."

They chatted about the farm, and then Miriam said, "Do you want to hear something funny?"

"Yeah, this place is not exactly a barrel of laughs," Britt replied.

"You know that Kyra is a sophomore now at Colton High School."

"Yeah, of course. How is she coming with her lessons on clarinet and piano?"

"Oh, her teachers say she's learning fast," Miriam said. "Anyway, this boy named Roland has been interested in her, and he asked if he could take her to a movie in Mayfield last Saturday night. He's a senior and has been driving for at least two years. Kyra said that would be fine. So Roland pulls into the driveway, and of course, Sparks comes running out to his car. Milton had turned the yard light on, or otherwise Roland wouldn't have been able to see him because, you know, he's black. How many people has he bitten now, Milton?"

"Nine people," said Milton, "including Dale when he and Kevin were out in the field mowing hay and Sparks took a hunk out of his arm when he was petting him. Remember that, about five years ago? Oh, that's right, it happened just before you left the hospital in Iowa City the first time."

"Yeah, I remember Kevin and Dale telling me about it," said Britt.

"I've got to get rid of that dog," said Milton. "He's vicious. But every time I mention it, the others raise a conniption. I just don't understand why. Remember how you and Kevin and Dale would have to be so careful when you came home late from a night out, and listen for Sparks' low growling so you knew whether to enter the house through the garage or the back door?"

"Yeah, nobody can get near that dog," Britt agreed. "The only one who had any control over him was Kevin. Gosh, I'll never forget that time he stood in the driveway, about eight feet from Sparks, pointing his arm straight at him and ordering him to back away while Sparks just stayed in a crouch and growled low with his fangs bared. It's a wonder he never attacked Kevin."

"Well, anyway," Miriam resumed, "Milton grabbed a big long stick he keeps just inside the door and headed out to chase Sparks away so Roland could get out of the car. And all of a sudden … ." Miriam broke into uncontrollable laughter, then managed to blurt out in a high-pitched voice, "Roland backed up as fast as he could and raced off down the road. He saw Kyra's big dad coming out with a stick and thought he was after him." She laughed so hard that tears streamed down her face. Milton just sat with a look of sardonic amusement on his face while Miriam and Britt rollicked with glee.

After Britt's parents left, it was back to the dismal, daily routine. Two weeks passed, and he decided Dr. Brower probably had been truthful when he said Britt would not be receiving any more shock treatments. Then, at nine-thirty on a Monday morning, Jake appeared at Britt's room and said the superintendent of the institution, Dr. James Brown, wanted to see him at ten. Uh-oh, Britt thought, they're going to do it to me. He changed into a fresh shirt and combed his hair, and then Jake walked him to the administration building. At a door with a sign above that read, Conference Room, Jake escorted Britt inside and left. His heart was palpitating.

A large, oval table was in the middle of the room and eight persons were seated around it. The man at the head rose and walked up to Britt, extending his hand and smiling warmly. "Hi Britt. I'm Dr. Brown, the superintendent. Can you take this seat in the center on this side?" He was only about five feet eight and had a round face that showed him to be probably in his upper forties. He introduced Britt to the others: two psychiatrists, two psychologists, an internist, a nurse, and a social worker.

"Britt, you look a little apprehensive," said Dr. Brown. "Let me assure you that there is nothing at all to be afraid of. We just want to ask you some questions to get an understanding of your mental and emotional state. It's not a test. You're not going to be graded. I understand you've had several years of college, so you know what I'm talking about." He chuckled slightly and gave Britt that engaging smile. Britt felt an instant rapport.

Most of the questions were similar to those he'd been asked by the psychiatrists at the hospital in Iowa City on his two visits there, and the sole psychiatrist at the sanitarium in Des Moines. Then Dr. Brown asked if he could think of anything he'd done in the last few years that had made him ashamed.

Britt thought a moment, then: "Yeah, I had a dream. It was kind of hazy and disconnected. I was standing in front of a closet with women's clothing—you know, dresses and skirts—probably like my mother's closet at home. Mrs. Olson, who goes to our church and is friends with my parents, was standing just inside the closet, wearing a bra but no shirt or blouse, and she took one off a hanger and held it in front of her, smiling."

"Why do you feel ashamed of that?" Dr. Brown asked.

"Well … I would never want her or my parents to know about that dream, because I think they would think it was shameful."

Dr. Brown studied Britt with a slight, quizzical smile. "Did you date girls in high school and college, Britt?"

"I had one date when I was a junior in high school."

"Did you have any physical contact with her?"

"No. I drove her to a football game and she sat as far away from me as she could."

Britt scanned the professionals around the table and noticed looks of amusement on a few of them.

"How about college?" Dr. Brown wanted to know.

"Yes, I dated a girl in my freshman class. Candace Ten Horst."

"Did you do any necking, or petting, with her?"

"You mean, did I kiss and make out with her?"

"Yes."

"Not very much. I kissed her goodnight at the end of the dates if we thought the dorm mother wasn't checking. She and I stopped dating after the first year."

"Why did you break up with her?"

Britt hesitated. "She had too long a nose."

He heard chuckles and glanced around. The plump, late-middle-aged nurse at one end of the table wore an embarrassed grin and laughed quietly. Dr. Brown also was chuckling.

"Okay, Britt," he said. "Thank you for talking with us. That's all we need for now."

Britt had spoken without embarrassment, though he was surrounded by adults. The shock treatments had temporarily left him with little emotion.

Two days after his meeting with the staff, Britt was transferred to a building that appeared to have been added later—Britt guessed around the turn of the century, which would have meant it was about sixty years old, compared to the hundred-year-old building he was leaving. A dining hall was on the first floor, and patients were housed on the second floor, where there also was a large recreation room. It was obvious to Britt immediately that this was a "promotion," because these men seemed more aware of their surroundings and kept themselves tidier. Britt was greatly relieved that he wouldn't have to eat with the psychotic patients.

After a few days, the attendant escorted Britt to the office of a psychiatrist. The man was tall and lean, in his sixties, with a full head of straight gray hair framing an elongated face featuring a fairly prominent proboscis that was red, bulbous, and crusty, with large pores.

"Good to meet you, Mr. Rutgers," he said to Britt in a pronounced British accent. "I'm Dr. Jenkins. I just wanted to introduce myself, since I'll be your doctor. I'm afraid you won't be seeing a lot of me because I, like the other doctors, am assigned to approximately one hundred patients. But I am here for anything you need." He shook Britt's hand and bid him on his way.

The most colorful patient here was a fiftyish man known to everyone as John the Baptist, an appellation he earned from his one-time occupation as a Baptist minister and his continuing propensity to preach. The Baptist's ebullient spirit infused a ward of quiet, uninteresting patients with vibrancy. Never downcast, he wore an omnipresent expression of cheer, a hint of a smile that connoted goodwill and optimism. A thick lower lip protruded from a mouth that was ever open, even when he wasn't talking, which was not very often. His jaw jutted forth and there were gaps in his teeth. He continually spewed verses from the Bible or, in a perpetual regurgitation of the past, repeated passages from sermons he'd delivered.

"Repent ye of your sins or be forever condemned to the fires of hell," he would pontificate to no one in particular. "Salvation comes only to those who confess their transgressions and beg the mercy of the Lord."

A patient told Britt that the Baptist had undergone ninety-five shock treatments. And he still was spouting Scripture. The treatments had not erased his memory of Bible passages, of which he exhibited such a vast knowledge that he seldom repeated any. He had two favorites, however, both dealing with darkness. His eyes would close and a look of peace would spread over his face as he recited in dramatic style, "The people that walked in darkness have seen a great light: They that dwell in the land of the shadow of death, upon them hath the light shined." Then he would open his eyes and say matter-of-factly, "Isaiah 9, verse 2."

Another in which he seemed to find comfort was, "I am come a light into the world, that whosoever believeth on me should not abide in darkness. John 12, verse 46."

Britt found it interesting that despite the Baptist's garrulousness, he never interacted with patients—much like a politician who is known to everybody but personally knows hardly anyone. The Baptist didn't look at people; he looked through them or past them.

One afternoon, Britt was ambling aimlessly down a second floor corridor when, on one side of the hallway, he noticed a commotion in a room that had perhaps ten beds. Attendants were carrying a man out on a stretcher. Britt recognized him as a slim fellow with a somewhat small head, black hair, about thirty years old, whom he'd seen a couple of times before. An attendant was holding an oxygen mask to his face. Dr. Jenkins accompanied the stretcher, looking grim. Britt shuddered at the thought that the person on the stretcher could have been him. In the dining hall that evening, he heard a couple of patients discussing the incident and gathered that the man had suffered broken bones during a shock treatment and had stopped breathing. Britt never saw the man again, nor ever heard what happened to him.

Patients who were in possession of their faculties, and were deemed by doctors to pose little risk of fleeing, were allowed to walk around on the hospital grounds. With little to occupy his time, Britt donned his winter coat on several afternoons and strolled down the sidewalks that meandered among the hospital facilities. On one such excursion, he encountered a man and a woman in a gazebo where two sidewalks intersected, embracing with their winter coats unbuttoned and kissing passionately. When they spotted Britt, they separated, probably apprehensive that he might report them to hospital officials. He wouldn't have even if they'd been stark naked and copulating. Nonetheless, he heard it rumored later that the couple had been prevented from seeing each other further. What Britt witnessed probably hadn't been their first sexual liaison, and someone in authority must have seen or heard of their trysts.

After six weeks, Britt was transferred again, this time to a modern wing that had been added to another building, where the least-disturbed patients were housed. Wow, he thought amusedly, I've reached the top echelon. I'm now one of the elite. His room was the last one on the left side toward the end of the hallway from the attendant's station, and had two beds. But his roommate was released from the hospital a week later, and no one replaced him.

After Britt had put his clothes and toiletries away, a nurse summoned him to take a bath in a room on the right side where the hallway extended away from the patient rooms. An old-fashioned tub on legs, wholly out of character for a facility that was only about ten years old, sat in the middle of the fairly large room.

The nurse was a woman in her upper thirties, fairly full-figured but somewhat shapely, and pretty in a plain way. She put the plug in the tub drain and turned the faucets on, then said quietly, "Okay Britt, take your clothes off."

Britt, totally naïve, was taken aback. He saw no reason why this woman had to remain while he undressed, and felt exceedingly uncomfortable.

"Uh ... could you leave?" he asked.

"Oh, well, if you're shy about having a woman see you naked, then I guess I could do that," she said in a tone that was at once mildly deprecating and teasing. She left without closing the door. Britt bathed, and as he was drying off, she walked by and looked in, and Britt reflexively placed the towel in front of him. He dressed and returned to his room.

It was afternoon, and a short while later, the attendant, Clyde, came to Britt's room and told him the time for dinner and location of the dining hall. It was a part of the wing, and the modern ambience was a big improvement over the dining halls in the other two buildings where he'd stayed. After dinner, Clyde showed Britt the recreation room down the hall past the attendant's station. Two televisions were available to patients on opposite sides of the room, and chairs and sofas were fronted by oval coffee tables with magazines.

After a week in his new digs, Britt was interviewed by a social worker. She decided he was well enough and competent enough to work in the canteen, located in a small, single-story, newish building in the center of the hospital grounds. Patients who were allowed onto the grounds were permitted to buy snacks, sodas, milk shakes, cigarettes, and the like at the canteen. It was a busy place for socializing, as well. There were tables with chairs and an ice cream bar. Britt was assigned to work at the bar Monday, Wednesday, and Friday afternoons, making shakes, malts, sundaes, and banana splits, and ringing up the receipts on the cash register. He welcomed it as a diversion to occupy his mind and his time.

Another diversion for the patients was a weekly show in the auditorium. Those whose backgrounds indicated talent were invited to perform if they were of sound enough mind to get on stage in front of an audience. Several musicians performed regularly, most of them pianists playing in the popular, classical, and jazz genres. Britt found it entertaining.

Then, one week, a middle-aged, overweight woman walked onto the stage and announced that she would sing, a cappella, the achingly beautiful *Mon coeur s'ouvre à ta voix* aria from Saint-Saëns' *Samson and Dalila*. Singing with abundant power, she displayed the most glorious voice Britt had ever heard. He was spellbound. She surely must have been, he decided, an opera singer on the international stage.

In the middle of one afternoon, the manager of the canteen told Britt he was wanted in the superintendent's office. Here we go again, Britt thought. I'll bet they've finally decided to give me shock treatments. He determined on the spot that he wasn't going to let that happen, and felt a brief impulse to take off running from the institution. But he controlled his feeling of panic, and realized that he would have sufficient opportunities to flee later if the superintendent told him he was to receive ECTs. So, with pulse racing, he walked from the canteen to the administration building, where Dr. Brown asked him to sit down.

"I've reviewed your background, Britt, and see that you worked in a drug store while you were in high school. Is that right?"

Whew! Didn't sound like the subject was ECTs.

"Yes, I worked for two years at Noll's Drug Store in Mayfield. I opened the shipments of merchandise and marked the prices on the items, and then I stocked some of the shelves. I also filled the drawers in the pharmacy with bottles for prescriptions, swept the floors, and so forth."

"Did you make many mistakes?"

"No, not that I remember. My boss, Mrs. Noll, seemed to think I did a good job."

"Did you take any courses in chemistry in high school or college, Britt?"

"Not in college, but I took chemistry in my last semester of high school, which I finished after I had dropped out of school and was hospitalized.

"Did you get a good grade in it?"

"No. I think I only got a C."

"Nonetheless, you are an intelligent young man, and we think it would be good for you to help out in the hospital pharmacy, since you have had some experience doing that. We'd like to transfer you there from the canteen."

"Okay, sure, that's good."

"We'll have you continue working at the canteen on Wednesdays, and you'll work in the pharmacy on Mondays, Tuesdays, and Thursdays, two hours in the morning and two hours in the afternoon."

The next day, the ward attendant escorted him to the same building that had the huge, second-floor dining hall where he'd first had his meals. The pharmacy was on the first floor and was manned by a single pharmacist named Manny.

"Hi," Manny said, smiling faintly. "You can hang your coat on that rack in the corner." If one had to guess what Manny did for a living just by his appearance, pharmacist probably would be among the first few choices. Wire-rimmed glasses balanced on a round nose that complemented a round face. His thin hair was combed to the side and back, and he was a little stooped.

"I'm going to hand you the bottles of pills and you fill the patients' vials with the number of pills listed on them," he told Britt. "Think you can handle that?"

"Oh sure, that's pretty easy."

"Just be very careful that you put the right pills in the right vials. Okay?"

"Yeah, I can understand why that's real important," Britt said.

After he became accustomed to counting pills, Manny had him stock newly shipped bottles on the shelves in alphabetical order. Britt's nimbleness with the alphabet made it a task that he enjoyed. In his idle moments, which were plentiful, he sat on a chair and read *The Rise and Fall of the Third Reich*, by Willam L. Shirer. It was a thick volume that his parents had given him for Christmas because he was majoring in German in college. A history of Germany under the Nazis, it was replete with detail, and Britt found it less than interesting but kept plodding through it out of a sense of obligation. He did, however, become absorbed in the accounts of the sadistic medical experiments, the failed attempt by Count Claus von Stauffenberg to assassinate Hitler, and the torture and grisly hangings of him and collaborators.

Now and then a doctor would drop by to chat with Manny. Almost every conversation centered on the alleged folly of the nation's leaders in government, or on the greed of companies that made exaggerated claims about their products in television advertisements. Manny's face would screw up in frustration and he would shake his head in dismay at what he perceived to be grave ills that had befallen society. The subject of false sales claims on TV, especially, caused him endless consternation. In the absence of visitors to the pharmacy, he frequently used Britt as a sounding board for his low-key rants.

During his idle hours on the ward, Britt mingled with a few of the patients. One who attracted a lot of attention was Floyd, a skinny teenager, about five feet eight inches, with a high forehead and a Cyrano de Bergerac nose. He talked incessantly about the tritest matters, prompting most of the patients around him to flee from boredom. His obnoxiousness led two other teenagers to shove him around and threaten to beat him up. Britt figured the two surly boys were delinquents. On one occasion, they had Floyd on the floor in the hallway, up against the wall, when Britt happened by. They were holding Floyd by the top of his shirt with their fists raised, talking low and menacingly.

"Hey, cut it out," Britt said. The boys were younger, one was smaller than Britt, and he didn't fear them. "Just forget about it and leave him alone." The two glared at him but took their hands off Floyd, who decided not to push his luck as he scrambled to his feet and sauntered off down the hallway.

The same nurse who seemed to have a sexual attraction to Britt showed a similar interest in a patient named Larry, who shared a room with another fellow across the hall and over one from Britt's room. One night, shortly before the ten p.m. curfew, Britt saw her standing in the doorway and talking with Larry, who lay uncovered on the bed, wearing only his white underpants.

"You want to join me?" Larry asked, smiling broadly. He was quite tall and lanky, fairly good-looking, thirty-five or so years old.

"You're not supposed to ask me that," the nurse said, but remained in the doorway. It was now bedtime, and Britt closed his door.

He learned from other patients that Larry had spent time in prison for a conviction on check forgery. Another patient, Joe, only eighteen though he looked five years older, and Larry were friends. Joe was about six-feet-two inches, big-boned and muscular, with thick, jet-black hair and a rosy complexion that highlighted his sharp cheekbones. The hospital had a modern gymnasium that Britt occasionally visited, though it usually was empty and he would walk through it and leave. Twice, though, Larry and Joe were on a mat on the stage, wrestling. Britt watched from a distance. They never became angry and used their fists, but were extremely aggressive and competitive, twisting and turning mightily in an impressive display of power. They also were evenly matched, and neither seemed able to outdo the other.

A different doctor was assigned to Britt's case after he moved to the modern building. Dr. Rosalind Stover was a handsome, fairly large woman of about fifty. After a brief introduction, however, he never saw her until about six weeks later, when she prescribed a medication for him. She had hardly spoken with him, so her diagnosis and treatment were based almost entirely on his records.

Before Britt was transferred from the second building, he had begun playing ping pong with an internist, Dr. David Lerner. They met after lunch every day in the recreation room on the second floor above the dining room. They arranged to continue their sessions after Britt had been moved to the newer building. Britt had been the champion at Thessalonika College in his junior year. He always won over Dr. Lerner, though the internist was a capable player and the matches were spirited.

A week after Britt had started taking the medication prescribed by Dr. Stover, he began having problems with his ping pong game. He played an aggressively offensive game, slamming a lot—though only with the forehand, because the backhand felt unnatural to him. His coordination was off. He was tensing and hitting the ball too soon, so that it soared off the table to the left or the end. Dr. Lerner was beating him, though by small margins. He told the doctor what was happening.

"Well, I'm going to have to tell Dr. Stover to cut down on your medication," he said.

After learning of the effect it was having on her patient, Dr. Stover stopped the medication completely. Immediately, Britt's game was back to normal, and he was defeating Dr. Lerner again.

"You should have let her keep medicating me," he joked, and Dr. Lerner replied with a broad grin, "What was I thinking?"

CHAPTER 23

After about ten weeks, Britt was assigned twice a week to group therapy sessions with fifteen other patients. They gathered late Monday and Friday afternoons in a spacious room, forming an oval. The therapist, Dr. George Caster, sat in the middle on one side. The psychologist was broad-shouldered but quite short and thin, with a narrow face and a full head of brown-gray hair. He had a high forehead, which made his extremely thick glasses all the more noticeable.

Dr. Caster did not take a gentle approach with patients. He continually prodded, trying to cut through their facades to make them face up to their real feelings. He had a reputation for making many of his patients angry. Britt listened to what everyone had to say but never engaged in exchanges with the other patients. He thought that most of what they were saying was banal and didn't apply to him. And he felt little sympathy for them.

Caster got a woman patient to admit that she had a problem with other women who flirted with her handsome husband. So the psychologist told a story about a party where he flirted with a woman and his wife was upset with him afterward.

"I told her, look, I came home with you, didn't I?" he said.

Then he looked straight at Kim, a pretty woman, about thirty, who never said anything and wore an impassive expression that was etched onto her face.

"Do you think Britt is good-looking?" he asked her. She looked away from both Britt and Caster, and didn't answer.

"Why do you think Kim isn't interested in Britt?" he asked the group. "She's an attractive woman, he's a good-looking guy. Wouldn't you think they'd be interested in each other?" No one answered.

"Do you find her attractive?" Britt.

"Yeah," Britt answered. He had been interested in her from the first day of group therapy, frequently looking at her but never able to get her to return the looks.

"Why don't you tell her so?"

Britt hesitated, then said, uncomfortably, "I think you're attractive, Kim."

Kim looked away from Britt and said nothing. It was a hopeless exercise. Caster could not awaken her feelings. So he went to work on Britt.

"Britt, you don't say much. You must have opinions about some of the people here. I'd like to know them. What about Jack. What do you think of Jack?" Jack, sitting on one end of the oval, was handsome, about forty, with dark hair and the rugged, weather-beaten face of a man who worked outdoors. His mien was always intense, mirroring a mixture of one part repressed anger and three parts hurt. It was the expression of a man who had suffered a lot of unfair treatment. But Britt felt no sympathy for him, though he didn't know why.

"Well ..." Britt hesitated, "I think he's a simple farmer."

Jack was muscular, and the intensity and hurt on his face deepened, and then the anger dominated. Caster was shrewd enough to know that diplomacy was in order here.

"Do you mean that you think he's a *plain* farmer?" he asked. "There's a difference between simple and plain. Do you mean that he's a man who works hard with his hands and doesn't have the time and money to enjoy some of the things that city folks do?"

"Yes, I guess that's what I meant," Britt answered.

Caster obviously thought a shift in the subject was the best way out of this tense situation.

"I used to work with my hands, too," he said. "Not full-time, but I earned some money at it. I was a boxer. Bantamweight. I did it to earn money for college after my high school IQ and aptitude tests showed I was pretty smart. Teachers had always thought I was dumb, but the problem was I couldn't see the blackboard."

"Why?" a patient asked.

"I was blind. I was borderline legally blind. That's why I wear these super-thick glasses. The boxing has come in handy for me as a therapist. A huge, hulking patient once got furious with me at a group therapy session and charged headfirst at me like a bull at a matador. I reacted with split-second timing, just like I did in dodging right crosses, and dropped from my chair to the floor. The guy catapulted into the chair and over the back onto the floor. Almost killed himself. We had to take him to the emergency room."

"I misjudged that guy," Caster continued. "But I have pretty keen insights into most of my patients. Britt, for example. I know what his problem is." He paused while patients who had been sitting listlessly looked up at the psychologist.

"He was rejected by his parents."

To Britt, it was a sudden awakening of his subconscious. The thought had never occurred to him. Now that it was expressed, it didn't strike him as a revelation. It was something he knew all the time but had repressed. He sat quietly, looking downward at nothing, as heads turned toward him. Silence ensued for several seconds.

Aborting the dramatic pause, Caster finally said, "Well, that's it for today. See you all Monday."

In the first three or four weeks of Britt's stay at Mercyville, Milton and Miriam Rutgers had driven the one-hundred-forty miles from the farm to visit him every other Sunday. After that, they began coming every third week as the therapists told them Britt's condition was improving. After about fourteen weeks, they suggested that he make a weekend visit home a couple of times as a way of adjusting to society on the outside prior to his eventual release.

On a Monday afternoon before the first visit, Britt responded to a request from Caster that patients bring up problems they were having at the hospital. Britt said he was very annoyed by two guys in a room down the hall who woke him and the rest of the ward early every morning by playing records at high volume on a phonograph player they were allowed to have in their room.

"What have you done about it?" Caster asked.

"Nothing," said Britt.

"Why not?"

"I don't want to get them mad."

"So you're just going to let these guys run the ward and not do a damned thing about it."

"Well, what do you think I ought to do?"

"I think you ought to tell them to stop playing their damned records and waking everybody up early."

"And what if they refuse?"

"Then I think you should walk into their room and grab their record."

Caster dropped the subject, and entertained woes from other patients.

The next morning, the music was blaring from down the hall, as usual. Britt got out of bed, angry. Still in his pajamas, he marched to the source of the high-decibel noise and strutted into the room. One of the two occupants was sitting on the edge of his bed, staring at the floor. The other, whom Britt knew as Gary, was snapping his fingers to the music while casually going about making his bed. Without hesitating or saying anything, Britt walked straight to the phonograph player, grabbed the record from the turntable, and smashed it over his knee. He flung the remnants to the floor.

Gary stared for a second, his mouth open in disbelief, then followed Britt out the door and grabbed him from behind. Britt whirled, and Gary started swinging his fists. Britt swung back and connected with a top tooth, chipping it, whereupon Gary moved in to wrestle Britt in order to avoid getting hit again. Gary and Britt were of almost identical height, weight and build, but Britt was wiry and wrestled him to the floor, with Gary on the bottom. At that point, the ward attendant moved in and stopped the fight.

Gary and Britt saw each other only from a distance in the dining room a couple of times that week. One of those times, Britt chatted briefly with Elise, a young blond patient who had acted friendly toward him. But he didn't linger with her because he knew that Joe was interested in her. Joe, Gary, and Larry the ex-con were friends who wielded power on the ward.

At group therapy on Friday, Caster asked Britt if the music were still bothering him, and he narrated the incident. The psychologist didn't say anything for a moment, then, in a neutral tone, "So you broke his record." Britt thought Caster seemed surprised that Britt had gone even beyond what the therapist had suggested by breaking the record instead of just temporarily removing it.

"Do you feel better that you did this?" he asked.

"Well, yeah. At least he stopped waking me up with his music."

"Good," said Caster. But he then moved on to another patient, and Britt got the idea that he wasn't entirely approving of Britt's action.

After the session, a hospital attendant drove Britt, carrying a small bag with a few items, down the long driveway to the road. He boarded a Trailways bus that regularly stopped if any passengers were waiting. Milton picked him up at the bus station in Colton at nine p.m., and he chatted with his parents. Dale and Kyra were out for the evening. The next day, Britt related the fight over the record to his dad.

"How old was the other guy?" he asked, beaming. Milton shunned confrontations with others, but liked a willingness of his sons to fight.

"Oh, I'd say about thirty-two."

"You bested a man that much older than you, huh?" he asked with obvious admiration.

The visit was pleasant. Milton and Miriam decided against taking the family to church Sunday morning. Britt surmised the reason. What would they say to other church members? He imagined the scene.

"You remember Britt. He's on furlough from the institution."

"Oh, uh, yes, yes. Well, uh, hello Britt. How's everything at the, uh, the hospital?"

"Well, thank God they're not frying my brains at this place like they were at the other ones. I just had a fight with a patient, but other than that, I can't complain."

Best to stay away.

After Sunday dinner—for a change, the pot roast wasn't full of that slimy fat, which would almost gag him—it was time to head back. Britt told his parents they needn't drive him; he could hitchhike. He'd hitchhiked home after finishing his newspaper route a few times, and occasionally thumbed his way home on weekend visits from college. Milton and Miriam protested mildly, but Britt insisted it would be all right. So they drove him to the outskirts of Mayfield and dropped him off by the side of the highway. In ten minutes, he caught a ride with a farmer type who said he was going only as far as Okasawa, which actually was a good part of the way. The man was quiet most of the time, talking a little about the weather but asking no questions.

It was twenty minutes before another car stopped to pick him up on this lightly traveled highway. The occupants, a late-middle-aged couple, said they were headed for Danford, a little beyond Mercyville, if that were okay with Britt.

"That's great," he said.

The couple were outgoing and friendly, and wanted to engage in conversation with their guest, about whom they were curious.

"Are you a college student?" the man asked, turning his head a hundred degrees from the steering wheel to be more personal, while his wife smiled pleasantly.

"Not at the moment," said Britt. "I'm taking some time off from college."

"Oh," the woman chimed in. "We thought you might be heading for the university at Iowa City."

"Actually, I'm getting off at Mercyville."

The man and woman looked at each other quizzically.

"I'm returning from a weekend visit home from the mental hospital."

Britt didn't feel particularly uncomfortable making this confession. It was an indication that the shock treatments had temporarily dulled the part of his brain which normally would have made him sensitive to the stigma associated with mental illness.

The couple looked at each other again, this time with looks of mild shock. They'd picked up a mental patient. Britt calmly explained that he'd twice had to drop out of school, first high school and college four years later, when he simply couldn't cope with life anymore. Now he was involved in group therapy and felt much better about himself.

The slight alarm that was mirrored in the couple's faces faded as Britt talked on, and now they seemed merely uncomfortable.

"Well," said the man, a nervous smile playing on his lips, "I hope things work out for you."

"Yes, yes, I'm sure you'll be fine," his wife agreed.

"Thanks."

For the rest of the trip, the couple talked about their son and daughter, both grown and raising families. Britt kept up the conversation, and when they dropped him off in front of the hospital, they smiled warmly and wished him luck.

Group therapy the next day was proceeding uneventfully, with Britt remaining mum as usual. His mention of the problem with the guy playing the loud music had been the only time he'd volunteered anything, and those remarks were brief. He just couldn't feel sympathy or empathy with the other patients, most of whom bored him with their chattiness about problems Britt couldn't relate to. Late in the session, Caster zeroed in on him, asking pointedly, "Britt, why don't you want to take part in these conversations and get involved with the other people here?"

Caster had a reputation for getting patients to open up by making them angry, and if that was his modus operandi here, he succeeded beyond what his expectations likely were. Britt seethed inside, and then he exploded.

"What the heck do you want me to say?" he shouted, throwing his arms up. "I sit here for hours twice a week and listen to these millions of complaints and everybody wringing their hands, and I don't know what in blazes I'm supposed to tell them. I don't know what in the heck to do about their problems."

The other patients were rocked back in their chairs, stunned. Even the hard-headed Caster looked a little shaken. He sat silently for a few seconds, then said, "Okay, let's meet again Friday."

Walking out with the patients, the psychologist turned halfway toward Britt, who strode along near him, and said to no one in particular, "Whew! My God, I'd hate to be *his* wife."

Two days later, in late morning, Britt was walking down the hall toward the recreation room when Joe confronted him.

"Hey, Bob," he said in his low, measured voice, his face mean and surly. "I don't like you messing around with my girl. I saw you gittin' real friendly with Elise."

"Huh?" said Britt. "I didn't … ." In one motion, Joe shoved Britt and ended his verbal protestation with a right-hand blow to the mouth. Britt suddenly found himself lying on his back on the floor. He rolled onto his stomach and saw drops of blood fall to the tile. He wiped his mouth and rose.

"Look, Joe, I didn't flirt with Elise," he resumed. "She spoke to me and I … ."

"Shut up or you'll get more of the same," Joe warned.

Britt walked away, convinced that Joe had made a mistake.

Two more days passed, and it slowly dawned on Britt that Joe had used Elise's flirtation with Britt as an excuse to exact revenge for what he had done to Gary. Joe knew Britt had not returned Elise's overture, he realized. The strapping fellow had twisted the incident to justify his aim.

At group therapy on Friday, Britt needed to speak about the incident. So when Caster asked him if he still felt as angry as he was at the previous session, Britt answered, "No. But I'm upset about something."

"Want to tell us about it?" Caster asked, and Britt related the confrontation with Joe.

Caster, the ex-boxer, peered at him through his super-thick glasses, his head cocked, and said, "Well, if you're going to let a guy get by with punching you in the mouth and not do anything about it, you might as well go to bed and pull the covers over your head, 'cause you're never going to amount to anything."

"You think I should hit him?" Britt asked. "He's big, and really strong. I'm sure he could beat me up pretty bad."

Caster stared at Britt for a couple of seconds, then: "Why don't you go and see Jack Carter, the recreation director? He's a former boxer and he could give you lessons so you could handle this bully."

"Hmmm," Britt mused, rubbing his lips with the index finger of his right hand. "Okay, I will."

When the session was over, he located Carter in his office. He was a somewhat stocky fellow in his late forties.

"Mr. Carter, I want to take boxing lessons." Britt immediately sensed gentleness in the man's face.

He frowned and asked, "Why do you want to learn to box?"

Britt explained that he'd been punched by a patient and needed to retaliate. Caster had sent him to seek the lessons.

"No, no," Carter said slowly and thoughtfully. "I don't think that's a good idea. I don't want you getting into a fight with someone."

"But I can't just let this guy get by with what he did," Britt protested.

"Well, sometimes it's best just to let something like that pass," said Carter. "You know, you can get very seriously hurt in a bare-knuckle fight—or you can hurt the other guy more than you intended to."

Britt shrugged. "Well, okay then."

At group therapy the following Monday, he told Caster of his meeting with Carter. Caster said, "I disagree," and turned his attention to another patient.

The next few days passed uneventfully, with Britt never seeing Joe except at a distance once in the dining room. Britt was due to take a long weekend at home, leaving Friday and returning Sunday afternoon. Again, he caught the Trailways bus outside the hospital.

At the farm, Britt told his parents about the incident with Joe.

"How old is he?" Milton asked. When Britt said eighteen, Milton fell silent, then, "You let a kid four years younger than you get the best of you?"

"He's not a kid, Dad," Britt protested. "He's a big, strong guy about twenty-five pounds heavier than me, and all of it muscle. And he's a street fighter who knows how to handle himself, which I'm not."

Miriam changed the subject to Kevin, who had been home the weekend before from Cedar Rapids, where he was interning at a hospital to become a medical technologist. He'd been in a car accident, Miriam said, but was only slightly injured. He'd also met a gal who worked in his department and they were going steady.

After dinner on Sunday, Milton and Miriam drove Britt to the same spot where they'd dropped him off before. He waited on the side of the road about fifteen minutes, when a car with a lone, middle-aged man stopped. He was headed to Burlington to visit his daughter, and Britt said, "Perfect. I'm going to Mercyville." The man never asked Britt about his purpose there, apparently interested only in having a companion to talk with as a way of passing the time. He kept up a steady litany of his life on a farm near Ames, lamenting the prices he was paid for hogs, cattle, chickens, and what-not. He expressed amazement that he was able to make ends meet. Britt just nodded in agreement, interspersed with "Uh huh"s and "Yep"s, and an occasional, "You got *that* right," though he had no idea whether the guy knew what he was talking about. Finally, they arrived at the hospital, and Britt told the man he was getting off there. The fellow looked nonplussed. Britt thanked him for the ride and wished him good luck while walking up the drive to the institution, the man staring after him in bewilderment.

On Monday, group therapy was uneventful as Britt sat quietly listening, and Caster never engaged him in conversation. But Britt was still feeling the humiliation of the bullying he'd received from Joe, and was hatching a plan to confront him. He kept an eye out for his adversary the next day and noted that he worked out in the gym in the afternoon. On Thursday, Britt watched Joe from afar as he lifted weights. When he was finished, Britt walked to the locker room. He waited five minutes and entered the room. A few minutes later, Joe emerged from the bathroom.

"Hey, Joe," Britt called out. "I wanna talk to you." Britt's heart was pounding and he was trembling.

Joe sauntered casually toward Britt, who said through clenched teeth, his fists at the ready, "I'm gonna get you for punching me in the face. You knew I never flirted with Elise. You were just using it as an excuse because you didn't like what I did to Gary."

"Aw, Britt. Hey, I'm sorry, guy," Joe said, stretching an open hand toward Britt.

Britt hadn't figured on this and was unsure what to do. He stood motionless, ready to duck and hit Joe in the face with his right fist, wary that the big-boned punk was tricking him and about to throw a sucker punch. But Joe just stood there with his hand outstretched, and Britt finally, cautiously, extended his hand.

"You're lucky, buddy," said Britt. "I was ready to knock you to the floor."

Britt walked away, not satisfied that he had let Joe off so easily. At group therapy two days later, he told Caster what had happened. The psychologist replied, "Well, at least you stood up to him and got an apology. That's good." Caster engaged several other patients, skillfully facilitating dialogue among them. But it was a lackluster session, and toward the close, he captured everyone's attention.

"You all are going to be released from this hospital eventually. I've been eighty percent accurate in my predictions of which patients would be back, and which wouldn't." Glancing around the circle of patients, he said, "Ann won't be back, and neither will John. I don't think Howard will be back. Britt won't be back."

CHAPTER 24

Ten days later, after four more, uneventful group therapy sessions, Caster summoned Britt to his office.

"Sit down," the psychologist said. "I think you're ready to get the hell out of this place. What do you think?"

"Uh … yeah, yeah, that sounds great to me," Britt stammered when he'd recovered from the surprise.

"That doesn't mean you don't still have problems," Caster said. "What do you see as the main thing you struggle with?"

"I'm so awfully self-conscious," said Britt. "I really have trouble walking in front of a crowd, or even telling a joke with several people watching me."

"Yet I'll bet you're pretty good at it, because you're quite expressive and have a flair for drama."

"You think so?"

"Yeah. Is your problem that you don't have much self-confidence? Do you think other people are better than you are?"

Britt pondered the question. "I don't know." Then he was struck by a sudden, searing clarity—an epiphany. "You know what I think it is?" he asked rhetorically.

"What, Britt?"

"Well, why do you think I learned to walk on my hands as a kid, and bought a barbell so I would build muscles? I really had to work at those things. And why did I always act up in the fourth and sixth grades?"

"Why do *you* think."

"I think I was trying to get attention."

"Did you stop trying to get attention?" Caster asked, looking quizzically as Britt.

"Yes. And do you know why?"

"No. Tell me."

"My parents always criticized people for showing off. That was a no-no. And they were down on people who belonged to a lot of organizations and were well-known. They said those people were trying to make everybody think they were important. Another thing: My mother used to tell me that I was self-centered—that's the word she used. So I thought I was not a very good kid for trying to do things that I enjoyed."

"And what effect do you think all this had on you?" Caster asked, peering out of his thick-lensed glasses.

"Well, I think that without even knowing why, I felt ashamed of my desire for attention. So when I would walk in front of a crowd, like at a basketball game, I really wanted to be seen, but down deep was ashamed of that."

"So you've been living with these irrational feelings of guilt and shame, and think that people can see right through you and know what you're feeling," Caster said.

He stared at Britt for several seconds, saying nothing. Then, "You really want to be liked, don't you."

Britt hesitated, then said softly, "Yeah, I guess so."

"Loved?"

A longer pause, and Britt's lips began to quiver. He put his head down and said nothing for some seconds. A tear slid down his cheek, and he said, even softer, "Yeah."

More tears flowed, and neither one said anything. Finally, Caster, who had been leaning forward in his chair, straightened and said, "You're going to do all right, Britt."

Britt wiped his wet face with the sleeve of his shirt and stared into space.

"Your parents have already been told to come and get you this weekend," Caster continued. "You don't have to attend group therapy Friday."

"Good luck, Britt." Britt looked at the psychologist as they shook hands and perceived emotion behind the mask of hardness.

Back in his room, he sat on the bed, his back propped against two pillows and his legs stretched in front of him. Only a couple of patients were wandering the ward halls, and it was quiet. Reflecting on the conversation he'd had with Caster, his mind went back to those grade school and junior high years when he was garrulous and often played the comic. But that behavior, it occurred to him now, masked a desire to be taken seriously. He'd often been unruly in his formative years, expressing feelings of hurt and anger. To his parents, his behavior then seemed, no doubt, irrational. They didn't comprehend that it was a manifestation of an unmet need for gentleness, kindness—love—from parents who had little ability to show it. As he grew older, his sharp mind led him to the more rewarding way of waxing witty and comedic to gain attention.

Was that what these emotional breakdowns had been about—pleas for attention? Was he trying to get his parents to take him seriously, as they did their oldest son? Did he want them to recognize that their second son also mattered, and that he was bright, talented, good-looking, and loaded with personality? Did he want them to care what he did with his life?

He wasn't sure of the answers to these questions. But he wondered if maybe, just maybe, entertaining them might be a sign of incipient healing.

Milton and Miriam arrived early Saturday afternoon. Britt carried his belongings to the car and climbed in the back seat. His parents began chattering about how Kevin and Dale and Kyra were doing. It was early May, and Milton said he'd planted the corn, and the first cutting of alfalfa was only weeks away. Life was beginning anew.

Britt replied perfunctorily, wishing for solitude as the green Dodge carried him down the long, winding road away from his past and into the future.

EPILOGUE

"The initials of this former Los Angeles Lakers star are the same as those of the Chicago Bulls legend who played opposite him in the 1991 NBA finals." A short pause followed the question by Alex Trebek, host of television's *Jeopardy*.

"Oh, for crying out loud, I know that," Britt muttered to himself as he sliced red peppers on a tarnished wood cutting board that had little of its original enamel. The peppers would go in a salad, the same salad that he made for himself virtually every evening. It was a big, colorful, inviting-looking preparation of romaine and leaf lettuces, cucumber, red (usually) or yellow peppers, and a whole tomato. He had made the cutting board in kindergarten fifty-five years earlier and given it to his mother. She was too old to cook these days, and had returned it to him a few years earlier.

"MJ … Michael, uh … Oh, come on."

"Who is Magic Johnson," retorted the contestant, a forty-ish Naval officer who stood ramrod-straight, his shoulders back. "You got it," Trebek shot back.

"Why the hell couldn't I think of that?" Britt said with loud impatience to his empty apartment in Miami, where he worked for a tabloid newspaper. "I knew that almost like I know my own name." He knew the answer to his own question. It was always the same when he couldn't remember something familiar to him. His memory had been impaired many years before by shock treatments. He had revealed that problem to the psychologist guiding a group therapy session he'd attended for a few weeks in the waning months of his second marriage. Britt had agreed to join the group after yelling profanities and obscenities at his wife, Lassie, and kicking an antique chair (breaking it). He knew he had a low frustration tolerance level, and tried his damnedest to have a calm, rational discussion of some disagreement they'd had. Lassie once again obfuscated and circumvented and skirted the issue, managing to drive him up the wall. That was another experience he remembered with clarity, and his slicing speeded up. The paring knife nicked the index finger of his left hand as the scene played out in his mind.

Lassie was a mistress of histrionics. She dialed 911 as Britt's right foot, clad only in a soft deck shoe, connected with the chair, which merely toppled over, one of its legs broken. It wasn't as if he'd sent the thing flying, which could have had negative consequences for his foot (he wasn't *that* angry). He stared at it for a moment and said, "Hell, I probably saved you from sitting on the flimsy piece of junk and falling on your ass."

He headed for the closet to change clothes, intending to leave and stop at some bar, where he would cry in his beer. Striding across the room, he slapped the phone out of his wife's hand as she lay in bed. After dressing, he picked it off the floor and returned it to its cradle on the bedside table. No sooner had he done so than it rang. My God, he thought, was I yelling so loud the neighbors heard? He answered and said hello in a calm voice. It was the 911 dispatcher. The call had gone through, and she'd heard him cursing mightily. The O.J. Simpson massacre had happened only a few months before and, typical of police dispatchers using extra caution with domestic disputes, she'd insisted on sending a squad car. His wife had said—half-heartedly—that it wasn't necessary, but he could tell she really didn't mind at all if the cops came. It would get her more of the attention she craved.

Britt went downstairs, and waited on the couch for the sheriff's deputies to arrive. When he heard the squad car pull up, he opened the front door to meet the officers so they wouldn't fear a violent reception. After all, he had no hankering to get shot. As Britt stood in the doorway, the two lawmen walked warily from the squad car and stopped, hands on their holsters.

"Hello, gentlemen," Britt called. "Come on in." He'd drunk three or four glasses of wine that evening, as he did most evenings. The psychologist he saw later in the group sessions told him he shouldn't be drinking. He told the psychologist that, yeah, he probably drank more than he should. But he asked the shrink if his adamant opposition to alcohol weren't a byproduct of his own alcoholism, since reformed alcoholics and smokers so often turned into reformers. The guy was taken aback a bit but denied that was where he was coming from. Of course—a psychologist in denial. But at least he had enough sense to realize what was going on in the marriage of Britt and Lassie. When they broke up, he told Britt over the phone, "You were not the problem in this marriage"—consoling words that Britt welcomed, even if they were a little late.

The wine made Britt a little cocky and probably had something to do with the flare-up he'd had with his wife, though drinking didn't make him mean, as it did some persons he had known. Alcohol made him amorous—with other women, not with his wife, with whom he felt little warmth whether stone sober or under the influence.

Yeah, he had a temper—always did, from early childhood, when he chased Gary the neighbor kid after the sneaky brat had snatched a paper from his hand walking home from kindergarten. Fifty-five years later, he vividly remembered the incident. Thank God, his long-term memory wasn't harmed. Britt pursued Gary from the alley behind the two boys' homes into his schoolmate's fenced-in backyard, even though it was forbidden territory, and all the way into the house. He finally stopped, daring to go no farther for fear of encountering Gary's enormous mother. On another less than auspicious occasion, he'd flung a portable potty out the car window as the family drove down some highway (the contents splashed on the car behind, he later was told). This deed, however, may have been simply an expression of his innate ebullience.

But he had rarely become physical with anyone. Oh, yeah—that time with his first wife, when they were arguing in the bedroom of their Florida condominium and he pushed her onto the bed. She bounced back to her feet and swung her bra at him, the metal clasp raising a welt above his right eye—whereupon he decided to cease and desist. And once he'd retaliated against Sarah, his girlfriend of five years, instinctively lashing out with his right arm, the back of his fist hitting her in the chest. She'd suddenly punched him in the face as they were driving back in angry, stony silence from dinner while vacationing in Lake Tahoe. It happened on a two-lane road and he had to grab the steering wheel to avoid hitting an oncoming car. His reaction to Sarah's eruption had frightened him, because the blow to her chest could have caused serious injury, or worse. He shuddered whenever he thought about it.

The cops approached slowly, obviously mistrustful. Hadn't Britt read that domestic violence calls were the most dangerous of all situations for the police?

"What's the problem here?" demanded the youngest cop, probably in his mid-thirties. Lassie came down the stairs now, and the other officer took her into the kitchen. "You stay there in the living room," the younger cop ordered.

"Yeah, I'm a pretty dangerous guy," Britt retorted sarcastically.

"Now listen, you just keep quiet," the cop said.

"You better keep an eye on me, 'cause you never know what an evil-lookin' guy like me might do," Britt said, taunting the officer.

Now the cop was mad, his fair complexion turning red beneath close-cropped, reddish-blond hair. "One more word and I'm gonna haul you off to jail and have you locked up for the night," he threatened in a raised voice, stabbing a finger at Britt.

Britt could tell he meant it and turned his head away, his arms folded, and sat silent and sullen. The cop watched him, then said more softly, "I know this isn't easy. Marriage is tough. My wife and I argue, too."

"No problem," Britt said, quietly. His confrontational mood had dissolved and he felt sadly resigned. "You're just doing your job. It's just that I'm not a violent person, and she knows that. I've never hit her or any other woman—hell, I've hardly ever hit anybody, period. And this is really embarrassing. All the neighbors can hear your police radio blaring out there on the road, and of course they're all thinking that I beat up on my wife or something."

"Not necessarily," said the cop. "Hey Al, is everything okay in there?" he called to his partner, who had been interviewing Lassie in the kitchen. Britt could hear the two laughing. Lassie, an attractive woman, was a charmer.

"Sure, everything's under control," said Al, a disarming sort of fellow in his mid-forties. "You 'bout ready to wrap this up, Joe?"

"Yeah," said Joe. "I don't think this guy's gonna cause any problem." Then to Britt, "Maybe you oughtta go to a motel for the night, don'tcha think?"

"Yeah," said Britt, "that's what I had in mind."

The officers left, with Britt close behind. He drove to a bar, had a beer, then got a motel room for the night.

Britt went to the bathroom of his modest condo, retrieved a band-aid out of the medicine cabinet and wrapped it around the finger that he'd cut. *Jeopardy* was ending, and he finished making his salad, then broiled a chicken breast and steamed some broccoli. He sat down at the dining room table, and the only sounds were those of his dinnerware and the mastication of his food. The recollection of the chair-kicking incident with his wife (now ex-wife) Lassie opened the floodgates of other memories. Lost in reverie, he ruminated on his life in the forty-odd years since he'd left the hospital for the last time.

The first eight years after his release probably were the happiest of his life, he decided. He'd soon found a job in Des Moines in the shipping department of Berchtold & Sons, publisher of health newsletters. After a few months, he left home to rent an apartment with two other young acquaintances in Mayfield, the other direction from Des Moines. He declined his parents' request that he remain with them, choosing to drive the extra ten miles, thirty-five total, to work. He began dating a woman his age who lived with her Dutch parents and worked at Noll's drugstore. She was a kind, easy-going person with a ready smile, less than attractive but shapely, and they progressed from necking to petting. One night, while parked in Britt's Ford, she unzipped his pants and masturbated him until he had a mighty orgasm in his underpants. It was the first he'd experienced, as he fell with indescribable ecstasy into her arms. She continued this one-way pleasure service until, parked on a country road one night, they nearly had intercourse, Britt pulling away just as he was about to penetrate. During this time, Britt occasionally met with Professor Bregman of Thessalonika, who advised him to have a condom in his wallet when he went on a date.

After a year, he moved to Des Moines with the intention of finishing his last year in college at Drake University. He said goodbye to his girlfriend, feeling little of the emotion he would feel in breakups of later relationships. The emotionally numbing effect of the shock treatments wore off only gradually. She had been upset, but only a couple of weeks after their split, told him that she realized it was for the best.

Living in a six-room basement apartment with five Drake students, he thoroughly enjoyed the camaraderie, experimenting with alcohol and even doing some mild partying. His grades improved in this environment, which was free of his parents' stultifying influence. He attended a liberally oriented Presbyterian church by himself, and his fear of questioning the tenets of Christianity gradually diminished. He even had a few dates with an attractive divorcee who rented an apartment next door and attended Drake as an art student while caring for her child. On New Year's Eve, after they'd necked on the couch for a while following dinner at a restaurant, she asked him into the bedroom to show him the lingerie she had bought that day. As naïve as Walter in the 1950s TV sitcom *Our Miss Brooks*,

Britt didn't divine her intentions. But it didn't matter: The fear of eternal damnation for having sex outside of marriage still had a grip on him.

After a few months, he switched to Berchtold's addressograph department, working evenings, and enrolled at Drake. The classes in German and English were, for the most part, easier than those at Thessalonika. Britt, while still less than relaxed, nonetheless could concentrate better.

Even though he was afraid to have intercourse, he desired women. One weekend night he went to a country bar on the lower-class east side of Des Moines and slow-danced with an attractive woman twelve years his senior. She caressed the back of his neck and he asked her to meet him away from the bar. She said she'd have to take her mother home first, but she returned and they parked by a popular lake. They both were naked in the back seat and Britt was on the verge of entering her, but didn't, though she begged him to.

After two years, Britt graduated from Drake. He planned to work and save money for graduate school in German at the University of Iowa. Meanwhile, he decided to audit a course in philosophy at Drake because he'd never studied the philosophers beyond the earliest on record—Socrates, Plato, and Aristotle. Professor Bregman had inspired him to learn more. Fascinated by the ideas of Voltaire, Descartes, Berkeley, Rousseau, and others, he forgot about himself. From his seat in the back of the room, he frequently raised his hand in eager response to questions posed by the professor, whom Britt liked for his practicality. Posing the question of whether plants, such as blades of grass, felt pain when they were cut down, he supplied his own answer: "Of course not. That's just common sense."

The professor formed pairs of students to argue against or in support of ideas propounded by famous philosophers. Britt was teamed with a very bright sophomore, Martha Kane. They were to defend Blaise Pascal's Wager, or "leap of faith" proposal—the idea that we have nothing to lose and everything to gain by having faith in God. In working on their paper, for which they received an A, she advised Britt to visit Germany, as she had done as a high school exchange student. Five weeks later, Britt had a passport and a ticket for a trans-Atlantic crossing aboard the USS United States.

In Hamburg, he bought a used motorcycle, though he'd never ridden one. He allowed a nineteen-year-old Dutch fellow he met at the youth hostel to pilot the bike to his home in The Hague. Britt commanded the two-wheeler the next day, and soon felt confident enough to ride it on the express highway to Amsterdam.

After six weeks of touring, he heard about Germany's Goethe Institutes for teaching the language to foreigners. He wrote to his parents requesting a loan of two-hundred-sixty-seven dollars for the tuition to cover an eight-week course in a village south of Ulm. They protested that he should find work to earn the money, but then relented. Eighty persons from all over the world attended. They were university professors, business men and women, and students, ranging in age from nineteen to fifty. It was the richest, most enjoyable two months Britt had ever experienced. He helped a quiet, pretty young Iranian woman with her German. She wanted to go with him to the United States, where her sister, who'd married a government official with ties to the Shah of Iran, lived. They came close to having sex, but were interrupted by the licentious landlord of the room where she stayed as she hastily put her blouse back on. Britt likely would not have gone all the way, anyway.

A week after the course in German was finished, Britt flew home, a more confident person after having proved that he could, with little planning, travel on his own through France, Germany, Holland, and Belgium, living for three months on only three-hundred-eight-five dollars in traveler's checks. It had been a vacation from his inner self as he was forced to deal, on a day-by-day basis, with the practical issues of survival among strangers whose languages he didn't speak.

The publishing company allowed him to work for two months. He needed to earn money, combine it with unspent money from his trip, and use it to get through one semester at the U of Iowa by living frugally. And he did, eating pancakes at least one meal each day and getting by with two pairs of corduroy pants. But he found that the students in his graduate classes had spent much more time in Germany than he had and were far more advanced in the language. He disliked the Dutch professor for his German literature class, who bore an uncanny resemblance to the thin, stern-visaged figure in Grant Wood's *American Gothic* painting. Britt dropped the course at mid-term and coasted to the end of the semester, deciding that life as a German teacher wasn't for him.

He contacted Martha Kane, then met her father, who managed a railway freight depot and needed another clerk. Britt was hired, and saw Martha for several months until she finished college early and returned to Germany to study philosophy. Meanwhile, they became increasingly physical with each other. One evening while her parents were out, Britt was on top of her on the couch, his hand under her loose summer dress, when they suddenly returned. Alan Kane did not want her daughter having sex, especially with a man six years her senior. They hastily sat upright and, though disheveled, managed a modicum of embarrassed composure as the elder Kanes walked through the door.

Britt drove to Pliny and met with Professor Bregman, as he'd done several times since his release from the hospital. They had discussed his delusionary episode that night at Thessalonika, and Bregman said he understood the logic in Britt's thinking and hadn't been alarmed by it. On this visit, the professor said he'd noticed a flair for writing in Britt's class essays and his letters, and suggested he might be suited for a career in journalism. One aspect of his personality was deep sensitivity and introspection, Bregman said. But there was another, somewhat extroverted and competitive side that was manifested in such activities as sports. Journalism, he pointed out, dealt with these external affairs of mankind.

Britt wrote a short story about his experiences in Germany, many of which were unpleasant due to German hostility to Americans. He asked Bregman, himself the author of published poems and an unpublished novel, to read it. The professor made important suggestions on how to expand and improve it. The revised version met with Bregman's approval.

Though he didn't know how to dance, Britt began attending the Wednesday night ballroom dances at the Bel-Aire Ballroom on the west side of Des Moines. Most of the women were older than he was, but he liked that. They dressed sexily, and some made seductive overtures to Britt. He had a couple of dates with an attractive, voluptuous Italian divorcee, and they were almost naked on her living room floor, about to make love, when Britt pulled away. He still wasn't ready. When he stopped calling her, she deliberately got off the bus, which she rode home from her job, a block beyond her street to walk past the apartment house where he stayed. He sat on the porch but did not call out to her.

Without intending to, he was driving women crazy by being so hard to get.

One night, a fairly attractive woman a few years older than himself accompanied him to his car after the dance, and they began necking, then petting. She told him she was married to a teacher in nearby Ames, and he and she were dating others because he thought they should be "open to life's experiences." They moved to the back seat of Britt's car and stripped naked. Britt entered her and had an orgasm that was not very satisfying. Britt's mother was right: He always went to extremes. He hadn't just had intercourse: His first time was with a married woman.

He told her that he felt awfully guilty, and she suggested they have a bite to eat at a nearby motel restaurant. She kept saying that she didn't want to drive the twenty-five miles home that night, hinting they should get a room. But Britt was in no mood for further sex, and certainly didn't want to pay for a room.

A divorcee who came to the ballroom, Sally Cantrell, only a couple of years older than Britt, taught him a few dance steps. She was about five-feet-four, pretty with medium-length dark hair, and worked as a hairdresser. She was taking courses at Drake, intending to become a teacher. Britt accompanied her home one night, and they had sex on her living room couch. Britt's guilty feeling had finally evaporated. He saw her a few more times, and she showed him a term paper she'd written for a class. Britt was impressed with her writing. While she opened a bottle of wine one night in the kitchen, Britt kissed the back of her neck and her shoulders. For the first time, he felt a wave of warmth for a woman. They continued making love, and after graduating, she decided to look into attending graduate school at the U of Iowa. Britt drove her to Iowa City for the application, and they stopped at a motel on the way and made love. She had bought a newfangled bra, a push-up, because she was dissatisfied with the size of her breasts. Britt thought they were fine. He liked her a lot.

But selling her home and moving from the city where she'd grown up held no appeal for her, and she decided against graduate school in favor of seeking a teaching job. Britt, however, was off to the U of Iowa again. He wrote her a few letters in the first months and saw her a couple of times during occasional weekend visits to his parents, but contact gradually ended. Over the years, he often wished he'd stayed in touch with Sally.

Britt did well in his journalism classes, especially the reporting class that had him writing for *The Daily Iowan*. Kurt Vonnegut was the writer-in-residence at the university's famed writing school. Britt was assigned to do a story about the author's receipt of a Guggenheim Fellowship to do research in Germany for a planned novel (later published as *Slaughterhouse Five*). In the telephone interview, Britt asked if he would critique the short story. Vonnegut willingly complied, returning it with a note describing it as a "reasonably good piece of personal journalism" but not really a fiction piece. Britt was elated.

Britt still was uncomfortable in front of a group of people, and received only an average grade for an oral report he presented in a class in mass communications because, the instructor said, he'd spoken too softly. For the next report, which he again feared, he decided to bolster his courage with alcohol and drank five beers at a pub on the edge of the campus beforehand. He received a good grade, which would have been better had he not spoken so loudly, the instructor admonished.

He was nervous, but less so because the class was small, delivering two oral reports in a course on international communications taught by his faculty adviser. The adviser was much impressed with Britt's writing and research skills, and even his speaking ability.

The end of the school year was approaching, and Britt decided not to return in the fall and complete work for a master's degree because bills were piling up and he needed expensive dental work. The adviser pleaded with him to finish, but Britt reasoned that he was getting older—he now was twenty-nine—and advanced degrees mattered little in the newspaper business. So he applied for a job as reporter at a small but highly touted paper in Illinois. In the interview with the editor, he confessed to his breakdowns. A week later, the man gently told him that he probably wasn't ready for that newspaper.

In his next interview, with another Illinois paper, Britt decided to keep his mouth shut about his recent history and merely say he'd been doing assorted menial jobs while earning money for school and deciding on a career. He was hired.

Britt embarked on a career that would take him to newspapers and a wire service in several major cities. He had to learn fast, and struggled during the first few years while also having some noteworthy reporting and writing successes. The work was stressful, with the pressure of meeting deadlines ever present. But, while he sometimes felt as though he were going to sweat blood, he also found the demands of the work exhilarating. Gradually, he also became more relaxed at it.

Milton and Miriam visited him once in the small city where he held his first newspaper job. He'd reported on a meeting of a college board the night before and had a byline with the front-page story, which he proudly showed to his parents. Miriam looked at it and asked sourly, "Is that all you did all day?"

While his professional life had mostly ups, interspersed with a few downs, Britt was less successful in his romantic life. Once he'd broken free from the constraints of his religious upbringing, he found the attraction of women irresistible. He became ever more sexually active, to the point of promiscuity. Downing his dinner in the quiet of his apartment, he revisited a hypothesis he'd formed in recent years: He was constantly longing for the feminine warmth and touching that he'd missed since birth.

Although he'd gravitated toward older women because of their greater interest in him, he had two marriages, both lasting less than ten years, to women up to a decade younger. The two women had opposite personalities, the first quite introverted and the second, Lassie, the center of attention in every social situation. In cities several states apart, both had lived quite near him, and the relationships developed out of convenience. The first did not want children, and Lassie already had one. She and Britt considered having one, but thought better of it, and he had a vasectomy instead.

Near the end of his marriage to Lassie, the psychologist with whom Britt counseled individually and in a couple of joint sessions with Lassie told him he'd been misdiagnosed. He never should have undergone shock treatments—which were ten times more powerful at that time—the therapist said. A few years later, Britt learned in a telephone conversation with Kevin's wife, a medical technologist, that Kevin had said Britt's diagnosis was schizophrenia. She couldn't understand that, she said, because that was a lifelong illness. Britt mentioned the conversation to his sister, Kyra, who confirmed the diagnosis. Britt had always assumed it was acute depression.

Britt had begun playing tennis in college, and continued with that pastime. Gradually, it became more difficult for him to toss the ball straight over his head for the serve. His hand would jerk with the release. It was decades before he realized that the shock treatments had weakened something in his central nervous system. That also was the cause, he reasoned, of his gradually deteriorating handwriting, which now was so jerky that even signing his name was labored. Always over the years, he had problems with scattered memory. At times, he would recall an obscure name from the distant past, yet went blank with familiar names. In social situations, he would forget names of acquaintances—even friends—when trying to introduce them. That had consequences beyond embarrassment when he couldn't remember the name of his date.

In the 1980s, when his newspaper job and a long-term romantic relationship both became highly stressful, he began biting his tongue inadvertently when he ate, drawing blood. Not the side of the tongue, but the center. It became such a problem that he sought help from a doctor, to whom he related his background and his opinion that the shock treatments were the cause. The doctor was reticent about discussing the matter, attributing the neurological disorder to stress in his life, and offered to prescribe a tranquilizer. But Britt shunned drugs, and decided to wait and see if the problem would resolve itself. Gradually, it did, but not before a long, prominent scar had formed in the center of his tongue.

In recent years, a new affliction emerged. Britt's voice began trembling and wobbling. He related his background to his doctor, a young Chinese American with abundant empathy, and said he thought the vocal difficulty was a result of a weakened neurological system. The doctor said he thought the diagnosis of schizophrenia had been wrong. He didn't know, however, whether the shock treatments were the culprit in his affliction and referred him to a neurologist. The specialist in turn expressed bewilderment at the diagnosis. But Britt declined medication.

The vocal difficulty worsened, however, and he saw another neurologist, who agreed the shock treatments may have caused the condition. He diagnosed it as benign essential tremor. He prescribed a medication, which reduced the symptoms. But it still was an embarrassment in social situations, and Britt, single again, was actively pursuing women. He found that alcohol alleviated the symptoms.

All of these problems, especially the ones that appeared during Britt's middle-aged years, obviously were the result of damage incurred in the shock treatments. Decades earlier, Britt had read that persons who'd had far fewer treatments than himself had difficulty performing certain functions, such as playing the piano. Yet, he'd read recently that psychiatrists denied ECTs caused damage, even though they still were unsure of what happened when these electrical charges entered the brain. In fact, a resurgence in the use of ECTs had occurred in the last twenty years, though its application had been altered, with less electricity and shorter duration.

Britt had recently done some Internet research and found that critics of electroshock therapy said it did indeed damage the brain. It caused memory loss and disorientation, which created a temporary illusion that problems were gone. ECT's leading opponent, psychiatrist and author Peter Breggin, likened the procedure to hitting the patient over the head with a two-by-four, leaving him or her in a stupefied state.

Indeed, in looking back at his behavior in the early years after his treatments, Britt realized that he had become somewhat desensitized. He found it easy—too easy for his own good—to tell people about what had happened to him. An apartment mate in Des Moines had expressed concern that Britt might suddenly turn violent. And he strongly suspected a co-worker at the publishing company, who also was a Drake student, of telling others about Britt's past. His psychology professor, without looking at him, had told the class for no apparent reason that one needed to be careful about revealing personal information to those prone to gossiping. It was a wake-up call: He decided to keep the matter to himself from then on.

On reflection, he regretted the opinion of Jack as "a simple farmer" that he'd offered in response to prodding by the psychologist in the group therapy class. It was a cruel thing to say, and he could have been more tactful, but hadn't felt any sympathy. His emotions sharply contrasted with the irrational, supersensitivity that had made life miserable for him before his collapse. Just after his release from the hospital, while he was parked in his car prior to entering Mayberry Construction to apply for a job, he heard a radio news report about Jack: "A patient at the Mental Health Institute in Mercyville was found dead yesterday, the victim of an apparent drowning. Hospital officials said a groundskeeper spotted Jack Varner about four p.m., floating face-down in a lake on the property. Police said Varner committed suicide." Britt wondered if his remark had contributed to Jack's death.

In the first couple of years after his release, Britt was able to stymie fear out of shame for what he perceived as cowardice in himself. Even his dad told him to be more careful when he walked on the roof of the house on the farm to remove debris. Britt had ventured without hesitation to the edge, which was fifteen feet above the concrete garage entrance. Britt calculated that if he fell, he would only be injured, not killed. Walking around the fields with Dale one day, Britt tested his courage by touching, seven times, the electric fence that kept the cows from an acreage of corn. And when a tall, strapping young man at a service station tried to up the price of a tire repair from three dollars to four dollars after he'd finished, Britt stood inches from his face and yelled that he was paying only the agreed-upon three dollars. The guy had better accept it if he knew what was good for him, Britt threatened. The poor fellow was visibly shaken, and summoned his dad, the station owner, who accepted the three dollars and told Britt to be off.

But such behavior was not natural for Britt. It was as if a tourniquet had been applied to the storehouse of emotions in his brain. Breggin's opinion made sense to him. The treatments relieved the immediate pain that pushed Britt over the brink, but did not remove the underlying cause of the extreme unhappiness.

Britt finally did receive psychological therapy as his marriages were coming apart. He ended up seeing a skilled practitioner of the gestalt school for more than a year before and after his first marriage, and resolved some of the feelings of shame and anxiety that he'd continued to harbor. Shortly before his marriage to Lassie disintegrated, he'd been railroaded into group therapy by the female member (whom Britt intensely disliked) of a pair of psychologists who worked together. Those sessions did nothing for him, and the person who should have been having them was his wife, he felt.

The therapeutic sessions with Professor Bregman had steered Britt to a new understanding of himself. He was not the light-hearted, easy-going person whom he'd come to view through his own lens. Rather, he was a repository of strong emotions and creativity, with perhaps a high adrenaline level. This natural temperament, he'd grown to understand, surely made him acutely vulnerable to rejection and an exaggerated perception of the opprobrium of society.

Britt looked outside himself at that person who existed decades before. He became convinced that, when he no longer could cope with his environment while a senior in high school, he should not have been sent to the sanitarium and treated with electroshock. Perhaps that was and remained the best treatment for the most acutely ill, he surmised. But in his case, a far wiser, more effective course of action would have been therapy sessions with a psychologist in Des Moines to help relieve his anxiety and plumb the depths of his despair. He was not, after all, psychotic, though the sanitarium psychiatrist misdiagnosed him as such. Simultaneously, he likely would have benefited from social activities with peers, which should have been encouraged. These measures would have been less expensive as well as more salutary, he reasoned. In fact, the balm of time gradually made Britt more relaxed and less aware of himself, though he still felt considerable discomfort in certain circumstances. But, like aging pop singers such as Sinatra and Bennett, who adjusted their phrasing to compensate for a weakened voice, Britt managed to cope with the discomfort at best and pain at worst.

Pondering these imponderables as he polished off his dinner, it occurred to Britt that one never could fully resolve the issues that drove him or her to the crisis stage. One only learned to live with them and keep from going over the edge again while enjoying some measure of happiness. The certificate handed him upon his release from the hospital at Mercyville read "Cured." While he appreciated the vote of confidence by the doctors, he realized that it was a specious assertion.

Britt decided that, despite his problems, he'd led a meaningful existence. He was capable of much empathy, and was deeply moved by the profound beauties inherent in the world's great music, literature, and drama. Though he'd never been blessed with abundant material possessions, he had found fulfillment in many good relationships with friends and co-workers. He even was on good terms with the women in his life, possibly excepting his second wife (though he harbored little ill will toward her), after their romantic involvements had ended. Britt had kept up a good relationship with Milton and Miriam throughout his adult years, as he did with his siblings. Kevin had suffered a severe stroke in recent years. His handicap transformed him into a saintly person who had only kind words for everyone and nothing but praise for the brother with whom he so often was at odds growing up. Martin Brant managed to locate Britt, and he attended a Mayfield High reunion, joyfully—though somewhat shyly—reconnecting with his compatriots, who were full of goodwill.

But at this late stage in his life, he was far from ready to retire to a rocking chair and watch the world pass him by. His issues had gradually receded, at about the same pace as the hair on his head. He was keeping abundantly active, eagerly pursuing several projects while continuing to maintain the healthy lifestyle he'd always embraced.

The recently departed Frank McCourt, after the enormous success of *Angela's Ashes* late in his life, quoted F. Scott Fitzgerald from *The Last Tycoon*: "'There are no second acts in American lives.' I think I've proven him wrong … because I refused to settle for a one-act existence … ."

Ditto Britt—and the play wasn't over. The first act was tragedy. The second was recovery and resolution.

The third was under way. Triumph.

###